FOX

A Jessica James Mystery

By

KELLY OLIVER

Praise for The Jessica James Mysteries

"Jessica [is] the standout creation here, a refreshing blend of grad school smarts and dude ranch grit. The author portrays Jessica's fish-out-of-water position in grad school with infectious humor…A witty and engaging whodunit, with a "cowgirl philosopher" who's part V.I. Warshawski and part John Wayne."

Kirkus Reviews

"Jessica James is a welcome addition to the world of amateur sleuths. She's a unique combination of smart and witty and she can quote Nietzsche."

Charles Salzberg, author of *Swann's Lake of Despair*

"Kelly Oliver has created an intriguing, authentic, and genuinely amusing suspense yarn with a unique female lead in the titular character that will appeal to a broad range of readers."

Samuel Marquis, author of *The Coalition*

"Kelly Oliver is skilled at creating the kind of people we want to get to know better, a cast of characters who charm us from beginning to end.… a fun romp of a read through mystery and mayhem…"

Mystery Book World Live

"*Fans of Sophie Littlefield, Deborah Coonts, and Nevada Barr have something to celebrate. Jessica James is a new American original.*"

Jason Miller, author of *Down Don't Bother Me*

"*An entertaining, fast, and refreshing mix of murder, greed, philosophy, mystery, and woman power... very funny yet profoundly dark* "

Foreward Reviews

"*Refreshingly authentic...the author's penchant for perfectly timed punch lines is on full display throughout...A fast-paced and thoroughly engaging whodunit...* "

Kirkus Reviews

"*Simultaneously heartwarming, irreverent, clever, suspenseful, and humorous, this novel moves quickly and keeps the reader glued to the page. Oliver's characters—particularly the women—are fierce, unique, and largely unpredictable.*"

Killer Nashville

"*Kelly Oliver's FOX has it all: keep-you-up-at-night pacing, Crichton-worthy plot packed with interesting insight and info, and a heckuva heroine, Jessica James, a cowboy boot wearing doctoral student transplanted from the plains of Montana to the streets of Chicago... I cannot wait to read more from this superb author!*"

Catherine Finger, author of The Jo Oliver Thrillers

Popular medicine and popular morality belong together...
Both are the most dangerous pseudo-sciences.

— Friedrich Nietzsche, *Daybreak*

PART I

CHAPTER ONE

JESSICA JAMES CAME-TO on a jagged bed of gravel. She scraped her freezing body off the hard ground and grasped at cold steel to haul herself upright, then staggered to her feet. Leaning against the dumpster, she doubled over and braced herself for another cramp. Squinting into the disorienting darkness, she spat out a mouthful of dirt.

When the pain subsided, she exhaled a cloud of breath and gripped the frigid metal until her stinging fingers forced her to unhand it. Teetering and dizzy, eyes darting back and forth, she urgently tried to fix her whereabouts. She recognized the glowing Chicago skyline behind her, saw an empty construction site in front of her, and realized the dumpster must be in a vacant lot downtown.

She picked at the dried crust on her parched lips then wiped her swollen tongue on the back of her flannel shirt-sleeve. Cat-box mouth might be an occupational hazard for grad students living on straight bourbon and Snickers bars, but the sharp clawing in the back of her throat told her something was terribly wrong.

Her thighs were burning but rubbing them sent her into a panic. *What the hell?* No jeans, just skin. Instinctively, she crouched down next to the dumpster, covered her bare knees with her hands then stared into the icy breath escaping her mouth.

Squatting and hugging her knees to her chest, like a cornered animal, her eyes searched for an escape route. She surveyed the trash strewn across the frosted dirt in front of her, a grease-stained burger box, a length of rebar, strands of fiberglass insulation, and a blue latex glove. The damp outline in the frost where her warm body had lain next to the dumpster filled her with terror.

Fighting back her tears, Jessica wiped her eyes with the backs of both hands, balanced on numb toes, and forced herself to concentrate. The brutal wind slapping her face roused her brain. When she focused her eyes, she spotted a pair of familiar silhouettes standing at the foot of the dumpster. She scurried on hands and knees towards the well-worn cowboy boots standing next to a pile of neatly folded clothes: her suede jacket, long johns, faded jeans, and one wool sock draped gracefully over the mound. She rifled through the pile searching for her underwear and found her Trapper's hat stuffed inside a jeans' leg. She jammed it onto her head and tugged the furry flaps down over her ears, a shower of grit and one latex glove fell to the ground.

Grabbing the edge of the dumpster for balance, she righted herself again. When she wrenched her damp hand away this time, the icy steel tore off a hunk of flesh. Paralyzed with pain, she held her wrist and stood staring down at the bloody gash.

Heart galloping, Jessica wriggled into her long underwear and jeans then shoved her feet into her frozen boots. She jammed her arms into her jacket sleeves, stuffed the one wool sock into a pocket, and then stumbled out from behind the dumpster.

As she peered across the construction site, the bare earth of the vacant lot sunk beneath the Chicago skyline, a dark socket in a mouth full of gleaming teeth. Scanning the area, she recognized the Medical School campus on the other side of the street. Two long blocks away, she saw a beacon in the blackness: the hospital.

As she made her way across the empty lot and out into the street, a razor-sharp squall cut through her shirt. With stiff fingers, she buttoned her jacket to the neck, flipped up its collar, and leaned all of her 120 pounds headfirst into the wind. Disconnected from the rest of her body, her feet slipped along the icy sidewalk. As she picked up speed, a piercing pain ripped through her gut and she fell to her knees. Crouched on all fours panting, she squeezed her eyes tight, clenched her teeth, and waited for the stabbing in her womb to let up. Gasping for air, she hoped Jack would find her. *Where was he?* The last thing she remembered was waiting for Jack at O'Toole's. As she kneeled on the sidewalk massaging her aching temples, the evening's events came flooding back to her.

She'd been waiting for her friend Jack at the bar, minding her own business, drinking a beer and eating some cheese fries, when a cute guy in blue scrubs sat down on the stool next to hers and bought her a "Fiery Mule Slammer." Then he turned on the charm and got her motor running with a feisty debate about whether the mind could be reduced to the brain. He argued that someday neuroscientists would know a person's desires, fears, and dreams simply by opening their cranium. A sucker for a pretty face and a heated debate, she drank the wicked Slammer and the next thing she knew, she woke up face down behind the dumpster. The image of the hot young intern with soft black hair and keen blue eyes seared her brain like a branding iron.

Jessica took a deep frosty breath, stood up, and headed towards the glowing hospital. Her stuttering walk turned into an awkward jog, and the ache in her lower left side became a roar. At least the howling pain in her abdomen distracted her from desperate speculations on how she'd ended up behind a construction dumpster in downtown Chicago. *Where the hell was Jack?*

Arms still wrapped tightly around her torso, she picked up her pace again. Strands of frosty blonde hair whipped her in the face from under her hat, and now even her teeth hurt. If only the Ivy League dickheads in her class didn't find out about the dumpster, she promised the heavens she'd never drink again. She'd never live it down. They already thought she was a stupid hick who didn't belong in grad school. *Please God, don't let them find out.* Another cramp bit into her womb. "Please God," she pleaded under her icy breath. Religion may be the opiate of the masses, but the drilling pain in her pelvis suggested it wasn't working for her.

As the revolving doors sucked her inside the emergency room, Jessica decided that whatever had happened to her tonight, she couldn't let anyone at the university find out. The glass doors spit her out into the harsh fluorescent lights and glaring industrial flooring of the hospital foyer. Halfway to the reception desk, a wave of humiliation came crashing down on her, and she turned around and headed back towards the exit. Cringing, she imagined her mother's reaction to this latest disaster. She'd never hear the end of it.

Maybe her mom was right. She should move back to Montana, play house with a "nice boy," grow a garden, can some peaches, and procreate.

"Can I help you?" A voice from behind the desk startled her.

Flushing, Jessica turned around to face her accuser. "Ah, I wonder if I could use your telephone," she said, staring down at her wet boots.

"There's a phone in the waiting room. Local calls only. Dial nine to get out." The receptionist raised her finely plucked eyebrows then pointed around the corner.

Jessica nodded in response. Shivering and holding her side, she tiptoed into the crowded waiting room. Her stomach turned at the sound of retching. Across the room, a thin scraggly woman was barfing into a blue plastic sock.

Hot air blasted from a huge overhead vent onto the mangy herd, and Jessica immediately regretted coming to an emergency room. She put on mental blinders and hoofed it toward the beige pushbutton phone sitting on an end table in the far corner.

She collapsed into a wide plastic chair next to the table and stared down at the phone, trying not to look at the suffering around her. Out of the corner of her eye, she glimpsed a redhead doubled over in the chair next to her. Elbows on knees, head in hands, the girl's loose curls cascaded halfway to the floor.

The redhead looked tiny in an oversized chair especially designed for "bariatric guests" according to a small plaque attached to its arm. Jessica turned her back to the pallid girl and picked up the old-fashioned receiver. Listening to the dial tone, her hand hovered over the keypad. She'd always called her friend Lolita on her cellphone. *What in the hell was her number?* She took a deep yogic breath and let her mind go blank as she punched the buttons.

"Hallo." She recognized the sultry voice.

"Lolita?" she asked. "I remembered your number."

"This better be good *milyi* darling. I've got a penthouse full of rich marks, and they're tipping like canoes in the Katun rapids."

"Can you come get me?" Jessica whispered.

"Sorry, hold on for just a minute." Jessica heard laughter and poker chips clacking in the background, then a boisterous, "I need another buy in!" She white-knuckled the receiver, her lifeline, and averted her eyes from the other battered souls awaiting salvation in the bedeviled hours of the night.

"Sorry about that, darling, but when the highest batting average in Chicago asks for another buy in, I give him one. Now, what's going on? Where are you?" Lolita asked.

"I woke up naked behind a dumpster. I have frostbite in my fingers." Hot tears rolled down her cheeks. Her hands were shaking so violently that she pressed the receiver between her ear and shoulder then interlaced her stiff fingers in a frantic prayer for warmth. In shock, she'd forgotten her hand was bleeding from a gaping hole. She pulled the wool sock from her pocket and wrapped it around the throbbing wound.

"A dumpster? Frostbite? Where are you?"

"Prentice Hospital Emergency Room, downtown near the Med School." Jessica heard a click and then the dial tone. She wiped her nose on her sleeve, tucked her injured hand into her armpit, then leaned back in the wide chair and closed her eyes. Like a kidnap victim occupying his mind while waiting to be rescued, she counted the spider veins on the inside of her eyelids, trying to construct a beautiful fortress. When she opened her eyes again, she saw an orange monarch butterfly tattooed on her neighbor's neck and recognized the redhead as one of Jack's old flames. He had so many, it was hard to keep track. His smooth hypnotic voice and sleepy brown eyes mesmerized most women and turned them into rabbits swooning to a rattlesnake's charm. So far, Jessica had been immune to his charisma. In fact, the fierce and fearless way he swallowed life whole scared her.

What was the redhead's name—Ashley? Brittany? Courtney? Jack's ex-of-the-month-y looked like she was about to barf.

"Are you okay?" Jessica asked the pale girl.

"Not really," the redhead answered. "Aaaggg," she groaned and rubbed her stomach.

"What's wrong?"

"Let's just say I have complications from my complications." She sat up and shook the springy curls out of her red-rimmed rabbity eyes. "What about you?" she turned to ask.

"I'm just waiting for someone to pick me up."

The redhead stared at her for a second then asked, "Do I know you?"

"We've met. I'm Jessica, a friend of Jack's, Jack Grove."

"Jack Grove?" She narrowed her eyes. "Oh, I remember you, that *cowgirl* philosopher he gushed about all the time." Jessica doubted it. Jackass wasn't the gushing type.

"I'm Ashley Horton, *one* of his ex-girlfriends. How is

Jack?" she asked, rolling her eyes. "I haven't seen him since he got back from Oxford. Still having commitment issues?"

"If you mean Jackass should be committed, then yes." She did her best to smile, as she pressed the woolen sock into her aching hand.

"If it weren't for Mr. Jack Grove, I wouldn't be in the emergency room now," the girl said as she flipped a twist of curls over her shoulder.

"What do you mean?" Jessica asked, stifling a pained gasp.

"If Jack hadn't shown me that 'Hey, college girls, get rich quick' ad in *The Daily Northwestern*...." The redhead groaned and sunk her curly head between her knees. "I wish they'd hurry..."

She knew just how Ashley felt. She wished Lolita would hurry. Cramps still stabbing at her pelvis, Jessica considered checking herself into the hospital. But if she did, they'd call the cops and the cat would be out of the bag. She winced imagining telling her mom. After her first calamitous year in the Ph.D. program, her mom had said, "Jesse, you're like a cockroach at a square dance for all the conceited creeps trying to stomp on you. You'd better just come back home, settle down, and forget that snobby outfit back East."

The familiar rumble of Lolita's Harley Superlow drowned out another muffled, "I wish they'd hurry," from her seatmate. Jessica jumped up and peered through the thick glass and saw Lolita shake her sleek black hair out of her helmet and dismount her bike. Dressed in black from head to toe, a leather clad avenger to the rescue, her friend strode into the hospital, rounded the corner, and marched across the waiting room. Jessica stood up, frozen in her humiliation, her friend's steely gaze penetrating her shame.

"What the hell's going on? You look awful." At six feet tall, her no nonsense friend towered over her.

"I'm okay." Jessica grimaced. The pain in her side forced her to sit down again. "Sorry to take you away from your big game. Didn't Detective Cormier warn you about those illegal games?" Jessica picked at some black crusty stuff on the thigh of her jeans.

"I've got to pay my tuition somehow." Lolita sat down on the end table and put her arm around Jessica's shoulders. "Are you hurt? Let me see your hand." When her friend reached for her wounded hand, Jessica clamped it into her armpit.

"You're a mess." Lolita reached over and picked at one of the earflaps on Jessica's hat, detaching a twig, a fleck of pink insulation, and a corner of blue crepe paper, flipping them one by one onto the floor.

Jessica had forgotten she was wearing her Trapper. She took it off, shook more debris onto the floor then dropped the hat into her lap. A little corner of sticky green paper caught her eye and she tore it off her hat. Holding it between her thumb and forefinger, she sniffed it and detected the faint smell of rubbing alcohol. She peeled it off her finger, rolled it into a ball, and flicked it onto the floor.

"What's that?" Lolita asked.

"I don't know. Some kind of sticker. Smells like disinfectant."

"Tell me what happened, *milyi* darling." Lolita took her uninjured hand and rubbed it. "Jesus, your hand is freezing! What happened to you?" The warmth of her friend's hands made her whole body relax and she leaned her head on Lolita's shoulder.

"I was waiting at O'Toole's for Jack. I had a couple of fireball Slammers with a super cute intern. Then I woke up naked, frozen to the asphalt behind a dumpster."

"Behind a dumpster? Where?"

"At the demolition site of the old Prentice Hospital." She pointed toward the window. "You know, the one with oval windows that looked like a lunar colony." Her vision was blurry, and her friend's beautiful face dissolved into the sweaty mass of suffering in the background.

"You're delirious." Lolita frowned. "Sounds like sexual assault. We need to ask them to do a rape kit right away."

"No, I don't want to… Let's find Jack." The redhead glared over at her, and Jessica blushed.

"Come on, Sweetie. We're going to get you checked out." Lolita stood up.

"I shouldn't have…" She let the tears run down her face and drip onto the hat in her lap.

"Don't blame yourself. It's not your fault." Lolita held out her hand. "Come on, *milyi*, I'll take care of you."

When Lolita bent down, put her hands under Jessica's armpits, and hauled her to her feet, she felt her knees go weak. A Hawaii-Five-O sized wave of nausea crashed down on her. Everything went black and Jessica followed her Trapper to the floor.

CHAPTER TWO

LEANING AGAINST O'TOOLE'S leprechaun green storefront, Jack Grove plucked a joint from his jacket pocket and clamped one end between his teeth. Huddling in an alcove, he turned to face the brick wall, but the Windy City was outdoing itself tonight. After striking his lighter a dozen times, Jack flung it into Ontario Street. "Bloody hell," he said under his breath and put the joint back into his pocket. He zipped up his bomber jacket, yanked his black stocking cap over his ears, slid his hands into his leather gloves, and headed for his car.

The towering skyscrapers behind him emitted a dim glow that transformed the frosty air into a haunting fog. Usually downtown was still bustling after midnight, but with a blizzard on the horizon, Chicago was a ghost town.

Jack shook his head, sighed, and blew out an icy cloud. He should get in his car and drive straight home. But he'd promised Jesse. She'd been so distraught after Junior's death, you'd think the furry little fucker had been her friend, not his. Now he was risking four years of busting his ass in college and two hard-earned years of Medical School to go through with the crazy plan for her sake. And after she'd stood him up, too. Where the hell was that cowgirl, and why didn't she show up? It was her idea.

Jacked up on adrenaline, shoulders hunched around his ears, and hands stuffed into his pockets, he jogged at a brisk pace toward the Medical School. As he turned the corner onto a deserted side street, Jack dug his keys out of his jeans and headed for his trusty old Chevy Malibu.

He glanced around the deserted street, then popped the trunk, hauled out the duffle bag, and dropped it on the ground with a thud. He slammed the trunk shut, dragged the bag with both hands to open the driver's door, lifted the bag across onto the passenger seat then hopped inside.

Steeling himself to commit a felony, he took the joint from his jacket pocket, pushed in the vintage cigarette lighter then waited for the fiery glow. He touched the joint's tip to the orange coil and inhaled a calming resolve. The spicy smoke was a tonic for his frayed nerves. He sucked in one last lingering toke before crushing it out in the ashtray. He grabbed his bag of tricks again and headed back out into the cold dead of night.

Fighting the wind, he shifted the unwieldy bag from hand to hand as he crossed East Chicago Street and mentally rehearsed Amber's instructions on how to bypass the Med School's security system. Instead of entering through the arched wooden doors in front, Jack darted around the side of the old stone building and slid toward the backstairs.

Even after midnight on a holiday, a few of the ornate paned windows were illuminated—procrastinating researchers whipping out grant applications at the eleventh hour and overachievers pounding out journal articles until their finger joints ached. Poor bastards.

As he bolted down the stairs toward the basement entrance grasping the bag in one hand, he drew his stocking cap down over his face with the other then adjusted it to align the three holes he'd cut. Breathing hard through the bottom hole, he peered down through the other two, careful not to slip on the icy stairs as he descended.

He heard voices from above, froze in mid-step, and then stared up through the wrought-iron fence at two pairs of furry snow boots passing by. He held his breath until they were out of sight then continued down the stairs. At the bottom of the dark stairwell, he dropped the duffle, retrieved a magnetic ID card and unlocked the door. He'd just "borrowed" it at O'Toole's from an annoyingly arrogant classmate, Max White, a sadistic slacker cheating his way through Med School.

When Jack opened the basement door, an eerie red glow flooded the corridor with imminent danger. Adrenaline pulsing through his veins and stocking cap over his face, he pressed his back up against the wall and slid along the bricks trying to avoid the security cameras. Clasping the duffle bag to his chest with both arms, he skated one desert boot and then the other along the polished linoleum until he reached the end of the corridor.

When he rounded the last corner, he stood in front of two thick steel doors inset with red glass. At lab orientation, Professor Granowski had explained how scarlet panes blocked fluorescent light, thus allowing the rodents to maintain their normal sleep cycles and the lab techs to monitor their freaky rat dreams.

Reaching into his bag, Jack retrieved a paper envelope and gingerly removed a spoof fingerprint. He exhaled to moisten it then pressed it onto the scanner with his index finger. Nothing. He glided the spoof slightly to the right and waited. Still nothing. He slid it down and waited again.

His hacker ex-girlfriend, the Magnificent Amber Bush, had warned him it might take a few tries. After the news of the dehydration death of "Jack Junior," made headlines a week ago, she'd called with her condolences. At Jesse's insistence, Amber devised a plan to lift Granowski's fingerprint. She'd used wax paper to lift it, printed it out onto a transparency, applied some wood glue, and voilà, thirty minutes later, a spoof fingerprint.

Jack breathed hard onto the spoof again then placed it back onto the scanner. The red light turned green and the doors clicked open. Sliding inside, he dropped the duffel behind the door, removed a towel, and threw it up over the surveillance camera. Skin tingling with adventure, he tiptoed to the first row of incarcerated mice. He couldn't wait to see Jesse's face when she found out he'd rescued Jack Junior's chimp cousins, freed his doggy companions, and liberated his rodent friends. If only she were here, it would be the perfect caper.

Jesse. He couldn't stop thinking of that boney cowgirl. He had no shortage of girlfriends, and he even liked some of them. But perverse as it was, he loved the one girl who wanted a "Platonic relationship." Ahhh… unrequited love, perfect love, never sullied by commitment or infidelities. At least he could console himself that if he got caught, a federal prison would be the perfect place for purely spiritual love. Wasting away on jail rations, he could yearn for his ideal of Jesse uninterrupted by the real thing.

As Jack approached the cages, the listless rodents

stirred, aroused by the smell of a human predator. Sadistic researchers had purposefully diseased, bloated, and blinded the poor little bastards. As he was scanning the first cage door with White's ID, he heard a tapping noise approaching from the hallway.

He dashed across the room and ducked behind a biohazard bin in the corner of the lab. *Merde!* He'd left his gym bag under the mouse cage. Jack held his breath and listened to heels clicking on tile.

He cocked his head and focused his senses on the intruder. He peeked around the bin just in time to see the towel fall off the camera onto the floor behind a thin black woman wearing a long white coat and a blue surgical mask. She stopped, looked back over her shoulder, then continued across the room toward the dog pens.

Her straight thick black hair was pulled into a ponytail that poked out from under a blue paper cap perched on her head. Her plastic safety goggles reflected the lab's sickly red glow, reminding him of a sci-fi femme fatale with laser beams for eyes.

Jack watched as the creature glided by his hiding spot and gracefully crouched down beside the cage of a sleeping beagle. The dog squeaked with excitement as the woman stuck her hand through the bars to scratch its ears.

Jack almost tumbled from behind the bin when the interloper opened the cage and freed the pup. Afraid the beagle might bust him, he retracted his head, hugged his knees to his chest, and folded himself up like a tripod. Arms wrapped around his knees, he sat motionless for five long minutes waiting for her to leave. When he heard a soft melodic lullaby, he poked his head out again and saw the shape-shifting creature had transformed into a young pretty woman sitting cross-legged on the floor, gently stroking the floppy ears of the bandaged beagle in her lap. She'd removed her mask and goggles, and Jack could make out an elegant ebony profile in the dim light.

She looked too young to be a doctor or professor. Maybe she was a postdoc or med student, or maybe even an undergrad, a freshman biology student. Whoever she was, she wasn't following procedure. Not wearing shoe coverings or a mask, handling animals without gloves, caressing and singing, definitely against lab policies.

If Professor Granowski found out, she'd get her ass kicked out of Med School toot suite. A girl after his own heart. He wished she'd get the hell out of the lab so he could complete Jesse's "Operation Avenge Junior," before he got his own ass kicked out of Med School *and* thrown in prison.

The rule breaker put the squeaking beagle back in its cage then headed in his direction. Hopefully she was leaving. He held his breath and didn't exhale until he heard the door close behind her. She'd practically tripped over the damned towel on her way out the door but hadn't noticed it. Jack darted out from behind the bio-bin and opened one rodent cage after another until dozens of deaf, blind, and deformed mice were scurrying all around the lab.

He dug in his duffle for collars and leashes for the dogs and was headed for the sad beagle's cage when new noises from the hallway interrupted him. He stopped in his tracks and listened. The noises were definitely getting closer. He stuffed the dog paraphernalia back into his bag, snatched the towel from the floor, and lunged for the walk-in freezer just to his right.

Standing in front of the freezer door, hand on the massive latch, he could make out men's voices, and they were getting louder. The squawk of a walkie-talkie echoed through the hallway, and he considered his options. If he hid in the freezer, he might have hypothermia by the time the coast was clear. At minus 28 degrees it wouldn't take long. But if he stayed out in the lab, he'd get caught in the felonious act of "Operation Avenge Junior." Either way, his medical career was about to end thanks to his hopeless devotion to a smart-mouthed but damned pretty Montana cowgirl. Better his career than his life, he unhanded the freezer latch and raced toward the exit door.

CHAPTER THREE

A ZAPPING SOUND FOLLOWED by the flicker of fluorescent lights awoke her, and Jessica found herself staring up at a plump motherly face beaming down at her. *Where in the hell was she, and why was her arm strapped down?* The cramping in her pelvis refreshed her memory. She glanced around the antiseptic room then down at the rails on the hospital bed. "Beep, beep, beep." An evil machine was squawking all too close to her throbbing head. The plastic pillowcase stuck to her moist cheek as she turned to face the accusing mechanical green eyes blinking at her.

"We've sutured the wound on your hand. Keep the area dry and in a week we'll remove the stitches. I'm going to give you IV fluids and an antibiotic," the chubby nurse said, jabbing a sharp needle into the crook of her arm. Jessica instinctively tried to yank her arm back, and the sadistic nurse just smiled pleasantly and stabbed harder.

"Please, hold still like a good girl, and then it won't hurt. Just a quick drip to prevent infection in those nasty cuts on your hand, legs, and buttocks. Poor dear. We'll get you fixed up in time for pumpkin pie."

The nurse's lilting sing-song voice reminded Jessica of her mother's after a few drinks: saccharine and superficial.

When she closed her eyes, she could almost see the faded posters hanging on the mildewed walls of her mom's dilapidated trailer. A rainbow zooming down from a silver cloud to chase a unicorn, a smiley-faced mushroom growing out of a pile of poop insisting "everything happens for a reason," a dew-cheeked cherub splashing in a mud puddle taunting, "there has to be a morning after."

Yeah, there has to be a morning after alright, but it ain't always pretty. Sometimes it has mascara running down its face, holes in its panty hose, and puke crusted on its little black dress. Besides, that poster bullcrap wasn't true; there hadn't been a morning after for her dad. Even after he was impaled on the gearshift of his truck, her mom feebly continued to spout Hallmark card optimism as she looked for her silver lining in the bottom of a Vodka Collins.

"There. All done. Rest now. That's a good girl." The nurse's maternal cooing snapped her out of her reveries.

Jessica opened her eyes and saw Lolita's hazy silhouette across the room.

"What happened?" She forced the words out of her mouth. Her palms were sweating and a film had formed on her tongue making it difficult to speak.

"You fainted in the waiting room, my dear," the annoyingly chipper nurse replied. "Your friend insisted we do a rape kit. The DNA results should be back in about three weeks, the STD in a few days."

"Kit?" Jessica asked, hands shaking. She reached for the plastic cup of water sitting on the side table and took it in both hands. Slowly sipping, she pleaded with her eyes for Lolita to intervene.

The nurse smiled and patted her arm. "Rape kit. Your friend explained your situation. Poor dear." The nurse turned her lips down in a fake frown.

Jessica winced. Her *situation*. The night's grim sequence of events came flooding back to her: Super cute intern and spicy vodka drink, and then rocks in flesh, pain in side, and the stench of death. Yes, her *situation* was grim. Jessica was staring down at the bleached bedcovers and watched as a single tear hit the thin hospital blanket.

"Have you had an ovarian cyst removed recently or another kind of hysteroscopic surgery?" the nurse asked as if she were offering Jessica a lollypop.

"What?" Jessica asked, peeking up over the edge of the cup, tears stinging her eyes, and then answered, "Not that I know of."

"You don't know if you've had surgery?" the nurse asked sharply.

Lolita stepped out of the shadows and to her bedside. "She hasn't had surgery. Why do you ask?" When Lolita stroked her hair, a floodgate opened; a stream of hot tears flowed down Jessica's cheeks, rolled along her jaw, and pooled, cold and clammy, above her collarbone.

"The physical exam revealed signs of a fresh incision on the vaginal wall." The nurse gave her a questioning smile. "And no sign of forced..."

"Explain." Lolita interrupted.

"Your friend has had surgery recently, my dear." The nurse raised her eyebrows and tilted her head. "A tubal could make that kind of incision, but you're awfully young for a hysteroscopic tubal." She stared down at Jessica.

"A what?" Jessica asked, rubbing the rough hospital blanket between her thumb and forefinger.

"A tubal ligation. To prevent pregnancy." The nurse shook her head.

"Oh. Pregnancy." Jessica hadn't even thought about the possibility of pregnancy. Her mind reeled. She allowed her head to fall back onto the sweaty, plastic-covered pillow then took several deep yogic breaths, but they weren't working. Panic set in as she thought about pregnancy. She glanced up at Lolita, again pleading for help with her eyes.

"Sweetie, you've been through a lot." Lolita stroked her hair again then turned back to the nurse. "What about Plan B?"

"Plan B?" the nurse repeated.

"The morning after pill," Lolita answered.

"The exam didn't show any signs of rape…"

Lolita interrupted again. "The pill, please."

"Okay. I'll ask the doctor on call." When the nurse waddled out of the room, Jessica sighed with relief. All that sugary cheerfulness was making her head hurt worse.

She must have dozed off for a few minutes because the nurse woke her up when she whisked into the room with a small white paper cup.

"The doctor approved a dose of ulipristal acetate." The motherly nurse smiled with her eyes and presented the paper cup on the palm of her outstretched hand, pointing to the water pitcher with her double chin.

"Here, swallow it now with some water like a good girl," she sang. Jessica just closed her eyes and opened her mouth, a baby bird awaiting maternal sustenance. There had to be a morning after, and sometimes it came in the form of a pill.

The nurse dropped the pill into her mouth. "There, there, dear. Swallow it now like a good girl." Jessica did as she was told.

"Our social worker, Miss Sally, will be by to visit you soon." The nurse patted her head with a chubby hand. "The police kept your jeans and T-shirt to examine under a poly-light for physical evidence. Maybe your friend can bring you some clothes so you can go home in a few hours? Or, if you like, Miss Sally can provide you with some clothes."

"The police?" Jessica's breath caught. Now everyone at the university would find out. Her friggin' frat boy students already called her "rape bait" behind her back. Now, they'd be right.

"They had to call the police in the case of a possible assault," Lolita said, caressing her arm.

"Law enforcement requires us to use their kits and their personnel. They don't trust us not to mess it up." The nurse stared down at her again with another fake mother-knows-best smile.

"But they'll keep it confidential, right? I mean no one needs to know." Jessica gripped the edge of the blanket with both hands and pulled it up over her chin.

"Yes, of course. Don't worry." The nurse reached for the blanket. "Let me have your arm. The medicine is done and I need to remove your IV so you can go home, dear."

"Ouch!" Jessica said when the nurse ripped the tape off her inner arm.

The nurse gave her a fake apologetic smile and stuffed a cotton ball into the crook of her arm then covered it with more tape. "After you get some clothes and visit with the social worker, you'll be able to go home." On her way out of the room, she turned back and said, "Be a good girl and be careful."

Jessica closed her eyes and sighed. If she lost fifty pounds and took up drinking, smoking, and gambling, that nurse could have been her mom. Except her mom always said, "if you can't be good, be careful," and didn't sugar coat anything.

Lolita sat down next to her on the bed. "We're going to find the creep who did this to you and kick his ass." The steely glint in her eye told Jessica she meant business.

"But what about clothes? I can't leave until I get some pants and a shirt. A coat and gloves would be nice, too. Those cops didn't confiscate my Trapper, did they?" A tear sprouted in her right eye and she brushed at it with the back of her hand. "That was my favorite Star Trek T-Shirt."

"No, Sweetie, your furry friend is right here." Lolita held up the hat and using it as a hand puppet, said in a Cookie Monster voice, "Gonna kick bad guy ass." Then she threw the hat onto the bed and stood up. "I'll be back with some clothes."

"Don't leave me alone." Jessica pleaded.

"Sweetie, I'll be back in a minute." Lolita stroked her hair again. "I promise."

Jessica watched the hands of the wall clock ticking off the seconds as she waited for her friend to return. Tears ran down her cheeks, but she didn't bother to wipe them away. Staring straight ahead, she looked without seeing, the whole world drowning in a river of disgrace.

Maybe it was a good thing her dad wasn't alive to

witness her humiliation. Her mom was more judge than witness. Her mom was clueless about the perils of graduate school; she knew nothing of lecherous professors, Ivy League dickheads, or qualifying exams from hell, but that didn't stop her from criticizing her. If she had a wooden nickel for every time her mom asked, "What are you gonna do with a doctor in psychology?" she could build a bonfire. Psychology, philosophy, it was all the same to her, and neither produced those requisite grandchildren.

A shard of light from the hallway sliced through the room, announcing Lolita's return.

"Here. Pants, a shirt, and some undies." Lolita handed her a bag from the gift shop. "They only had kid sizes, but you're tiny." Jessica took it, peeked inside, and saw matching purple sweatpants and sweatshirt dotted with little cartoon characters holding tiny rainbows between their yellow hands. She looked up at her friend and rolled her eyes.

"SpongeBob Squarepants? Couldn't you find anything else? Hello Kitty, maybe?" Jessica shook her head.

"Better than SpongeBob Bare Ass. Put them on *like a good girl*." She imitated the nurse's cloying voice. "Hospitals give me the creeps."

Jessica did as she was told and wriggled into the silly child-sized outfit, her wrists and ankles exposed. The thick slip-proof hospital socks made it tricky to get her cowboy boots on, and once she'd jammed her feet inside, they were too tight. She tugged her Trapper over her ears then hobbled to the closet and grabbed her suede fringe jacket.

"Shouldn't we wait for the social worker?" Jessica asked.

Lolita removed a red woolen scarf from around her own neck and wrapped it around Jessica's.

"We'll do our own social work. Let's go."

Lolita led the way out of the hospital to the exit. Outside, at the corner emergency entrance, Jessica recognized her friend's red motorcycle sparkling under the humming fluorescent lights, parked illegally on the sidewalk.

Tugging the flaps of her hat down over her ears, holding her jacket shut with both hands, and ignoring the pain in her pelvis, Jessica shuffled to keep up with her friend. Winded, she stopped, put her hands on her knees, and tried to catch her breath. Lolita unlocked a compartment on the Harley, took out two helmets, and handed one to her.

"Are you okay?" Lolita asked.

"I think so," she said, taking the helmet.

She managed to fasten the mixing bowl over her Trapper, and then gingerly lifted her leg over the bike behind Lolita, and let out a frosty cloud of breath.

"Point me to the dumpster," Lolita commanded.

"It's a couple of blocks away. Where the old Prentice Hospital used to be, across from the Searle Research Building." Jessica pointed in the direction of the Medical School. Her friend revved the engine and took off. Jessica held on for dear life.

Daggers in the night, the wind cut through her sweatpants, and she clamped her thighs around the motorcycle as much for warmth as security. Lolita swerved around the corner, oblivious to the snow that had accumulated in the last couple of hours.

"That's it. Over there," Jessica yelled above the roar of the bike, pointing to her right.

The Harley skidded to a stop on an icy patch on Superior Street at the curb near the dumpster. Lolita got off and jammed the kickstand in place, and Jessica swung her leg over the bike and dismounted. "This is the place," she said, pointing at the dumpster just beyond a stretch of snow covered earth where a sidewalk had once been. "Over there."

Lolita stared at her for a few seconds, and then said, "Are you okay? You're so pale. Are you up for this?"

"I'll be okay. The painkillers that treacly nurse gave me are kicking in," she answered, shivering. "We've got to find my backpack with my phone, computer, and a year's worth of dissertation research."

Following close behind her black-belt friend, she waited for Lolita to go first. The snow whirling across the empty lot made it look haunted, as if spirits of avenging souls had been dredged up along with the concrete and clay. The construction site was almost creepier at the break of dawn than it had been in the middle of the night.

Seeing daybreak after a sleepless night always made her melancholy. Facing the awakening world in a state of utter exhaustion overwhelmed her.

Yet, from so many all-nighters working on her dissertation, the uncanny condition was as familiar as an unwelcome old friend. Nietzsche's *Daybreak* popped into her mind: "How much cleverer she would have become if she were not beautiful." He was referring to his beloved Lou Andres Salome, unrequited love as bittersweet muse, but so full of resentment. She thought of Jack.

Not concentrating on where she was going, Jessica slammed smack into the back of Lolita, standing still as a statue, frozen in mid-step in front of the dumpster.

"I woke up behind it," she said, pointing to the other side.

But Lolita didn't budge. When she stepped around her frozen friend, she saw why. Next to a neatly folded pile of clothes, a half-naked girl was lying face down in the snow, her strawberry blonde hair pooling out of her mouth like bloody saliva. Lolita knelt down beside the rigid girl and rolled her over. Backlit by the first harsh light of day, the girl's face came into gruesome focus, its blotchy blue skin and staring blind eyes a ghastly mask of dread and anguish. *There but for the grace of God*, thought Jessica. She grabbed a pink paisley scarf from the pile to cover the girl's horrid grimace then dashed around the side of the dumpster to barf.

CHAPTER FOUR

J ACK STRAINED TO hear the walkie-talkie as it
receded down the hallway. He switched the duffle
from his now numb right hand to his left then rushed
across the lab. He skidded to a stop in front of the thick
steel entrance. Pressing his face to one of the red panels,
he shielded his eyes with his free hand and peered into the
hallway. Nothing but the menacing scarlet glow reflecting
off the shiny polished floor.

He listened for the voices but heard only the whirring
of ventilation units and the rumbling of snoring dogs. He
slipped White's ID badge out of his back pocket and glided
it across the security screen. The door clicked open, and he
peered through the crack out into the empty hallway. Still
wearing the ski mask over his face, he crept down the hall,
trying to skirt the cameras again.

When Jack turned the corner and spotted Beagle Girl
with two security guards, he stopped fast in his tracks. A
blast from the walkie-talkies sent him plunging into the
nearest alcove. The cops had their backs to him, and he
hoped they hadn't heard him. From his hiding place, he

eavesdropped as one of the cops confronted Beagle Girl. He peeked around the corner to see what was happening.

"Whatcha doin' here, Lassy?" the bigger of the two cops asked in a thick brogue. Beagle Girl pointed to an ID badge clipped onto the lapel of her lab coat, but the cop just folded his hairy arms atop his immense beer belly, using it as a shelf.

"I'm a post-doctoral student. My name is Samantha Brewer. I work in Professor Granowski's lab," Beagle Girl said, pointing back towards the lab. She unclipped her badge and handed it to the ruddy-faced guard. "See."

He smiled as he scanned her body up and down then stared down at the ID badge.

"Tink we outta haul her in, Vanya?" he turned to the wiry tattooed cop standing behind him. Skinny legs spread wide, big black boots spic-n-span, his sidekick continued chewing on a toothpick.

"Call Professor Granowski. Janet will confirm that I work here," Beagle Girl said. She went to remove something from her lab coat pocket and the abusive cop grabbed her arm.

"Watcha doin' there, Lass?"

"My phone. I was going to call Janet, Professor Granowski."

These two yahoo dickheads would never have stopped her if she were white. The fat wanker flipped the ID card back at her, and it hit her on the chin. Beagle Girl's mouth dropped open, but when the barrel shaped cop touched his sidearm, she tightened her lips and glanced around looking for help. Jack ducked back into the alcove. He'd watched enough Facebook videos of racist cops gunning down innocent black men to worry. He removed his phone from his back pocket and turned on the camera to record then stuck his head and the phone around the corner of the alcove.

"We're takin' ya in, Dolly." The bastard grabbed her by one arm. "Take 'er other arm, Vanya," he shouted over at his partner. When the skinny dude didn't budge, the red-faced wanker yelled, "Grab her, dammit," his spittle misting the terrified woman's face. His ink-stained partner watched from the sidelines as the bully yanked the girl down the hallway. Then, his partner spit his toothpick onto the floor, took a pack of cigarettes from his shirt pocket, tapped one out, put it between his lips, and crossed his arms over his sunken chest. The unlit cigarette dangled from his mouth.

"Sir, please. I assure you," Beagle Girl pleaded. "I *am* a post-doc. I got my Ph.D. in biology from Harvard, my undergraduate degree from Penn, and I have been a researcher in this lab for two months now. You have my ID, what more do you need?"

When she looked over in his direction, Jack whipped his head and phone back into the alcove. Beagle Girl had quite the pedigree. When he peeked out again, Jack saw the fat bastard's partner, unlit cigarette still dangling from the crooked mouth and both tattooed arms slack. *Why is he just watching this bloody brutality?* Jack realized he was doing the same and took several quick breaths and then counted to three.

"Ouch, you're hurting me!" Beagle Girl tried to jerk away from the Irish cop, but he grabbed her by the shoulders with both hands and slammed her against the wall. This joker was seriously threatening an innocent woman with at least two Ivy League degrees. Jack balled his hands into fists.

"Let me go or I'll have your badge, Sir." Beagle Girl stiffened and stood up to what must have been a full five feet three inches and glared at the bastard cop.

"Are ya threatenin' me then, Lass?" The cop laughed. He shook the frightened girl, and her heel slipped, sending her to the floor where she landed in a crumpled heap. Still laughing, the nasty copper kicked her shoe across the hall with his big ass boot. She scooted backwards, pressing herself up against the wall and clutching at her lab coat to protect her legs.

Jack swallowed hard, counted to three again, and sprang out of the alcove into the hallway just behind the wiry partner. "Leave her alone!" He shouted.

"Who the hell 're you?" the brutal cop asked as he spun around. "And what's with the mask? This a hold up?"

"I'm with her. I'm a medical student. We work in the lab together." Both cops stared at him. He'd forgotten he was still wearing his knit cap over his face but he didn't move to take it off.

When the click of a gun being cocked echoed through the hallway, Jack dropped his phone. As it slid across the polished floor, he glimpsed Beagle Girl covering her dark eyes with her tiny hands. He lunged for his phone and landed hard on the cold linoleum, face first. He lay on the floor wheezing, staring up at an armed face-off between two bloody cops. He turned his phone camera on record again.

"Thatz enough, Fergus. Let her up," the wiry one belted out in a thick Russian accent, his gun pointed straight at his associate's beer gut.

"Move away from her." The skinny guard spit his unlit

cigarette onto the floor then waved his pistol, motioning toward the far side of the hallway.

"Come on, Vanya, Buddy." The Irish wanker chuckled but took a step away from his prey.

Motionless on the floor, through the holes in his ski mask, Jack watched the altercation between the Irish bully and the stoic Russian. He hoped the two pigs would blow each other to kingdom come.

"I didn't sign up for this shit, beating up girls." The Russian gestured toward the opposite wall with his head. "Move it, *Buddy*." Beagle Girl's lips relaxed into a tiny smile.

"You'll lose your job. Is this piece of chocolate worth it?" When the burly bastard took another step away from her, Beagle Girl scrambled to her feet, pressing her back up against the wall, her ashen face a mask of terror.

"Shut your rot, *súka*, or I'll blow it off." The skinny cop raised his gun and pointed it at his partner's ugly gob. Jack made out a rose tattoo carved into the back of his boney hand and blocky Russian letters going up his arm.

"Toss your gun belt over here, Fergus."

"Vanya, Vanya, Vanya, buddy…"

"Don't test me, *múdak* asshole," the Russian dude interrupted, waving his pistol in the other cop's face. The boar slowly unfastened his gun belt and laughing, shook his head then lobbed the belt at the Russian's feet and took a few steps backwards. Still on the floor, Jack scrambled on hands and knees towards the pistol and dove on top of it.

The copper's ugly face contorted into a grimace as he glared at his partner. "You've gone off your nut, buddy."

"Quit shooting off your *blyad* mouth, or I'll shoot if off your frickin' face." The Russian spat out each word.

Facing each other from opposite sides of the hall, the two cops were having a stare down. The Russian dude held the gun in his right hand and with the left, in one fluid movement removed the pack of cigarettes from his shirt pocket, tapped out another smoke, and lifted it to his lips. The Irish bastard just stood there with his smug smile. Steadying herself against the wall, Beagle Girl slowly stood up then, glancing from cop to cop, scurried across the hall to retrieve her shoe.

Jack balanced on his toes and picked up the gun. It was heavier than he expected. Without taking his eyes off the ugly cop, he stood up and walked toward Beagle Girl then held out his hand. She just stared at him, mouth open, fear in her eyes. "The mask," she whispered.

"I'm on your side," he said, ripping the stocking cap off his head. "Take my hand."

The Russian looked in Jack's direction and gestured towards the elevator. "Come on. Let's blow this bitch."

A bewildered look on her face, the girl took Jack's hand, and he dragged her toward the elevator. Still laughing, sweat running down his craggy face, the big Irish wanker stood stock still twenty feet away just shaking his head. Jack pushed the girl into the elevator, and the Russian jumped in after her, knocking Jack down on his way. Overhead, he heard Beagle Girl yell, "I'm reporting *you*. And you're the one who won't get away with this, Officer Fergus Doyle, badge number 57321."

Without a second thought, Jack jumped up and dove into the elevator just before the doors closed behind him.

"I quit." The Russian had unpinned his name badge from his uniform and tossed it out onto the linoleum. It bounced and dropped through the crack between the elevator and floor. Once the doors closed, the Russian stuffed his gun back into its holster and flashed a golden grilled grin.

"My name's Ivanov, but everyone calls me Vanya. Who are you, and what's with the ski mask?" he asked in his thick accent, pointing at Jack. His 100-watt smile broadened.

Jack looked up at him from the elevator floor. "Depends," he said as he leapt to his feet. "Are you a cop or not?"

"Not anymore. One week was enough to be on wrong side of law." He lit his cigarette with a fancy titanium lighter then glanced from the girl back to Jack. "So, you two Bonnie and Clyde?" he asked, sucking in more smoke.

"I'm Samantha Brewer." The girl almost smiled. "But my friends call me Sam." When she shook the Russian's hand, Jack noticed inky cat fangs poking out from under a short uniform sleeve.

"Glad to meet ya, Sam. And what about Clyde here? A friend of yours?"

"I've never seen him before in my life." She turned to Jack. "What were you doing in the lab?" she asked raising her eyebrows.

"I could ask you the same question, but I already know the answer." He ran his fingers through his dense hair, pushing it back out of his eyes. *Damn.* He'd left his duffle bag in the alcove. He mentally scanned its contents: bolt cutter, dog collars and leashes, portable dolly, spray paint, and a tire iron… just in case. Now that fat bastard would have hard evidence to connect him to the break-in. *Merde.*

Goodbye Medical School, hello federal prison. He had to go back inside and fetch his stuff before Officer Doyle found it, or his ass was grass. But first, he had to get Beagle Girl out of here.

"Let's go!" With the girl in tow, Jack burst out of the elevator and ran full bore towards the front entrance and out the heavy wooden doors. Sliding to a stop under a lamppost, Beagle Girl slammed into him, and he caught her before she slipped on the ice. Squinting to see through the brewing blizzard, he saw the Russian skate past, yelling, "This way!"

He grabbed Beagle Girl's hand and followed Vanya out into the snowstorm, across the street, and into the parking garage.

"Follow me," the wiry Russian said as he sprinted up the steep ramp. Jack trailed the Russian up the ramp, with Beagle Girl on his heels. Vanya stopped in front of a black Cadillac Escalade, and its lights flashed in response to a push of a button on his keychain. Jack doubled over out of breath. He really should stop smoking so much weed and get back to the gym, especially if he was going to chase tattooed cops through downtown Chicago.

"Hop in!" Vanya pressed a button on his keys and the Caddy's headlights flashed again.

Jack opened the passenger side door and waited for Beagle Girl to climb in. He heard the scratchy sounds of a walkie-talkie approaching from the bottom of the ramp. The Irish cop was shouting from the garage entrance, "Feckers. You're not gettin' away." Jack pushed Beagle Girl into the front seat and then dove into the back. When he turned to look out the back window, he saw another uniformed cop running up the ramp, pistol drawn. The bastard must have called for backup.

"Step on it, Vanya!" he yelled as his face grazed the carpet. "Beagle Girl and I have a lot to lose if we get caught. Two brilliant medical careers ruined."

"Beagle Girl?" Vanya asked, laughing.

"She knows what I mean."

Jack slid into the fancy leather seat. When he brushed the snow off the shoulders of his leather jacket, he remembered the gun in his pocket, the one he'd taken from that Irish pig. Removing the pistol from his pocket, he examined it, turning it over in both hands. He'd never handled a gun before, let alone shot someone, and he didn't fancy a shoot-out. "Do no harm," the Hippocratic Oath, first thing they taught in Medical School. The shouting was getting closer. Outside the tinted back window of the Caddy, Jack could see the armed cop approaching fast, with the Irish bastard close behind them.

"Stop or we'll shoot." A shot echoed through the parking garage.

CHAPTER FIVE

BALANCING THE PISTOL on the seat back, Jack gripped its handle, cocked its hammer, and aimed it towards the back window.

"*Chuvak*, don't shoot my ride," Vanya said, eyeing him from the rearview window. "This baby can outrun those suckers."

"Mr. Vanya," Beagle Girl said, her voice quivering. "Could you please take me home?"

"Not right now. I just pulled my pistol on a cop and that's a big no-no," Vanya said, tapping out another cigarette. "I knows a place we can hide out until the air clears. Stick with me, Bonnie and Clyde." Hopped up on nicotine, Vanya swerved around the two cops running up the ramp then sped out of the garage. He skidded around a corner and slid to a stop in an alley behind one of the research buildings

Hands shaking, Jack put the gun on the floor then took a joint from his jacket pocket, lit it, and took a long drag. From the frying pan into the fire. He offered the joint to Beagle Girl, but she turned up her nose and shook her head like he'd offered her a turd sandwich.

"Suit yourself." He took another long drag. "How about

you, Vanya?" A rose covered hand appeared between the front seats and Jack handed him the joint. The crazy Russian poked the end into his lips next to the cigarette already there and inhaled.

"So what's up with the mask? What you two up to back there?" Vanya passed the joint back to Jack.

"I told you. I've never met Mr... Mr..."

Jack interrupted her stuttering and extended his hand between the seats. "The name's Max, Max White." When she didn't take his hand, he reached into his jacket, retrieved the stolen ID badge and flashed it in her direction. "I'm a third-year med student." He stuffed White's badge back into his pocket.

"In whose lab?" the girl asked incredulously. "Why the mask?"

"I saw those cops roughing you up and got scared," Jack said, leaning forward between the seats.

"Hey, I wasn't roughing her up," Vanya said. "I was trying to stop him. As we say in Russian, CTONXAM, Stop a douchebag."

"Do you work in the animal research lab?" Beagle Girl glared over her shoulder at him from the front seat with her laser beam eyes.

"I do research on reproductive technologies and genetic engineering with Dr. Dude."

"Dr. Dude?" Vanya asked.

"That's what we call Dr. Manly."

"The one who cloned glow-in-the-dark cats?" Beagle Girl's eyes widened.

"Fluorescent Felines, that's him."

"Feline flashlights?" Vanya blew out a series of smoke rings, filling the Caddy with a white haze. "What for?"

Stifling a cough, Beagle Girl said, "Actually, it's ingenious. Engineering with fluorescent proteins enables us to track human genetic diseases in animals. We can label a specific gene with fluorescent dye and when that gene is activated, the brain lights up and sometimes the whole animal, depending on what we're testing. This technology can show us the way to curing a whole host of genetic diseases, from cancer to Down's Syndrome."

"Maybe," Jack said, taking another hit. "And it makes for a heck of a party in the lab after dark."

"Mutant neon cats. Sounds like a horror movie." Vanya said, a multicolored arm crushing out another cigarette on top of the pile of its dead comrades.

"Coast is clear. Let's blow this bitch." Despite the blizzard broiling into a full-blown white out, Vanya punched the accelerator and the Caddy screamed out of the alley and onto the deserted icy streets of downtown Chicago toward Lake Shore Drive.

"Stop!" Jack yelled. Vanya slammed on the breaks and the Caddy spun a one-eighty on the ice.

Jack stared out the window of the Escalade in disbelief. Lolita's red Harley was parked on the street next to an empty lot, and the outline of one of the two figures kneeling next to a dumpster was distinctly Jesse's. No one else could get away with wearing that silly Elmer Fudd hat. What in the bloody hell were they doing in a vacant lot in the middle of a blizzard on their knees next to a dumpster?

"Pull over. I know them." Jack pointed toward the dumpster.

"*Bozhe Moy!* That's my cousin." Vanya cranked the steering wheel and the Caddy slid into the curb, barely missing Lolita's motorcycle.

"Lolita Durchenko is your cousin?" Jack asked.

"My very beautiful cousin." Vanya flashed a smile. "Come on, *chuvak*, let's see why they're praying to that garbage bin."

"Please, Mr. Vanya. Can you take me home first?" Beagle Girl asked. "I've got a grant application due on Monday."

"Here, this will calm you down." Jack offered her the joint. "You're as whiny as your little beagle friend back in the lab."

"No, thank you." She shook her head indicating a decided negative. Jack didn't trust people who didn't smoke dope. She was definitely one uptight puppy.

"Are yous coming or not?" the Russian asked impatiently.

"I prefer to wait here, Mr. Vanya. If it isn't too much trouble, would you mind raising the heat?" Beagle Girl tightened her lab coat around her thin torso and slipped her hands under her thighs.

"No problems." Vanya ground out his cigarette in the overflowing ashtray and punched a button on the dash. "There's a butt warmer if you push that button on your seat," he said proudly, pointing a boney finger in her direction. "We'll be back in a giffy."

"You mean jiffy," she corrected.

"That's what I said. Be right back." When Vanya hopped out of the Caddy, a frosty blast coated the driver's seat with a dusting of snow.

Jack licked his thumb and forefinger, pinched out the end of his joint then put the dead roach back in his pocket.

He pulled his stocking cap down over his ears, zipped his jacket up around his neck, jumped out, and then trailed after Vanya towards the dumpster.

Lolita stood up and turned in their direction, and Jesse crawled around on hands and knees near a snow-covered mound of clothes. The howling wind spun snow cyclones across the empty lot. Snow stuck to the frozen ground spreading over every surface, suffocating the earth. The blizzard was amplifying the dawn's violet light, and he had to squint to follow the Russian's dark uniform through the snow to the dumpster.

As he came up behind Jesse, he had a sinking feeling. He stood behind her, and his heart leapt into his throat as he stared down over her shoulder. He recognized the lovely body, its face covered with a blotchy cloth and pants draped sideways over its groin. Sliding between the girls, he knelt down and removed the scarf.

Within the bloated purple face, he knew the dead eyes staring back at him as those of Sara Shaner, a fellow medical student and his most recent lover. He was stunned. Just hours earlier, he'd caressed that now rigid body and kissed those now blue lips. Maybe the cold had slowed her heart rate enough to just mimic death.

He pressed both palms firmly into the middle of her chest and pumped briskly, knowing in his gut it was too late. After several thrusts, he pinched her cold nose shut, tipped her head back, and blew into her cold mouth. The lips so pliant and responsive earlier were hard as steel. His stomach turned as he forced himself to continue pumping and locked lips with the cold girl in another death kiss.

"It's no use," Lolita said. "We already tried."

"Jesus," he whispered then dropped to his knees, put his head in his hands, and wept.

"Do you know her?" Jesse asked. She bent down and put her hands on his shoulders then slipped her arms over his chest, resting her head on his back. Through cloudy eyes, he stared at the body once so alive and so receptive to his touch. Jack choked back tears but couldn't respond. He'd seen plenty of corpses before, even dissected them, but never someone he'd known, or kissed, or cared about.

"Was she a friend of yours?" Lolita asked, kneeling on the other side of the body.

Jack wiped his eyes on his sleeves. Tears freezing on his face, he just stared over at Lolita, unable to speak.

Vanya blew out a cloud of smoke then grinned at Lolita. "Good to see you again, coz." He was pacing back and forth behind his cousin, puffing on a cigarette, hands in his pockets.

"Aren't you supposed to add, only I wish it were under different circumstances?" Lolita said, shaking her cousin's hand. "What are you doing here, Vanya?" She looked him up and down. "And what's with the cop outfit? Are you a mole for Bratva now?"

"Who's the stiff?" Vanya asked, shifting from foot to foot.

"Her name is Sara Shaner," Jack said, wiping his eyes with the palms of both hands. He stood up and yanked the phone out of his back pocket. "We need to call 911."

"Already did," Lolita said. "The dispatcher ordered us to wait here even if we freeze to death."

Screaming sirens accompanied flashing red and blue lights bouncing around like a Grateful Dead lightshow in the snow cloud. Jack turned in time to see two police cars squeal to a stop behind Vanya's Caddy. One was a cruiser, the other an unmarked black Lincoln. A tall black man got out of the Lincoln and two white uniformed officers jumped out of the squad car. Grim faced, the trio marched towards him. For the first time since he'd arrived at the grisly scene, he looked into Jesse's eyes. She'd been crying and was wearing some ridiculous outfit, but even surrounded by tragedy, she radiated a *je ne sais quoi* that made him ache inside.

"Are you okay?" he asked her.

"I'm glad you're here." She moved closer to him and put her small hand on his arm. Sideways snow stinging his face, his duffle bag left behind at the lab, on the lam with a gun crazy Russian, finding his lover frozen stiff, he wondered what he had to be thankful for on this terrible Thanksgiving morning. He dropped into Jesse's waiting arms. He held her tight, grateful for her friendship.

The homicide detective approached first. "We need to question you all. But no reason to keep you out in this blizzard. We'll take two vehicles." He turned to the officer behind him, "Sargent Prescott, take these two gentlemen to the station and make them comfortable until I get back. O'Brien, we'll examine the crime scene, and you'll wait for the evidence team, while I take Ms. James and Ms. Durchenko in my car." He gestured toward the cars, flashing lights still bleeding into the frosty clouds.

"What about my vehicle?" Vanya asked nervously. "I'm an innocent bystander. I don't know nothing about this situation, so hows about I just leave yous to it?"

"I'm afraid that's not possible, Sir," O'Brien, said. "You'll have to come with us. Don't worry, we'll bring you back to get your vehicle when we're done at the station."

KELLY OLIVER

"Yeah, an' it'll be buried under two feet of snow by then," Vanya said under his breath.

"More likely towed by the city," Sargent Prescott said. "Are you university police?" She nodded at his uniform and gun belt. "Mind if we take your sidearm for safe keeping?"

Vanya unbuckled his belt and handed the weapon to the Sargent. "I'm, or was, a security guard at the Med School." He flashed her a golden grin.

She smirked. "You two men come with me." Sargent Prescott pointed to the Caddy. "Who's that in the vehicle?"

"A brainy post-doctor into kinky glow-in-the-dark stuff." Vanya smiled.

The cop scowled and said, "Okay. Let's bring her along to the station." The officer led Jack and Vanya to the waiting squad car and then went to fetch Beagle Girl from the Caddy.

Sitting in the back seat of the cop car between his two accomplices from the lab escape, Jack rode in silence, staring straight ahead into the whiteness of daybreak for the ten-minute eternity it took to get to the precinct. Once inside the police station, Jack excused himself, went to the men's room, and flushed his dead roach down the toilet. Police made him nervous.

Studying forensic psychiatry, he'd worked with the cops before. They turned crime into pathology and turned desperate people just trying to survive into hardened criminals. His palms were sweating as he exited the bathroom and headed back into the cop shop waiting room.

He sat down on a plastic chair next to a woman wearing

44

a lot of makeup but not a lot of clothes, bottle blonde hair, big fake boobs, and tiny hot pants. A magician, she removed a cigarette from a secret compartment in her bustier, smiled sweetly at Jack, and asked, "Got a light, Hon?"

Jack extracted a lighter from his jacket pocket.

"No smoking in here," a clerk said as she came out from behind her desk and handed Jack a clipboard. "Please fill out these forms. Someone will be here shortly to take you to Detective Cormier's office. Would you like a cup of coffee while you wait?"

"That'd be nice." Jack smiled up at the full-figured receptionist.

"Tania, get this gentleman some coffee," she said to a younger, thinner, African-American girl sitting at a desk behind her.

When Jack had filled out the form, he sipped the tepid brown liquid wishing he had a real cup of coffee instead of this piss water. A large man with a pockmarked face approached from the back offices and stopped in front of him. Jack wiped his palms on his jeans and inhaled deeply. He looked up at the bull's crooked nose, probably a football player who didn't make the big leagues so he became a cop instead. The officer led him through an oppressive hallway to an office in a remote corner of the building.

"Have a seat, Mr. Grove. Detective Cormier is on his way. He'll want to ask you some questions." He waited for Jack to sit down, then left and shut the door behind him. Unlike the receptionist's desk, Cormier's was neat and orderly. Compared to the rest of the dingy police station, the detective's office with its panoramic view of downtown might as well have been a penthouse in the Sear's Tower.

Right knee bouncing, Jack troubled the corner of his leather jacket, eager to get this interrogation over with. Good thing he was a practiced liar.

CHAPTER SIX

STILL SHIVERING, JESSICA watched through the tinted windows of the Lincoln Towncar as Detective Cormier and Officer O'Brien searched around the dumpster, occasionally putting bits and pieces into paper envelopes. She'd been relieved to see the handsome detective in his brown overcoat and leather gloves, snowflakes sticking to his short-cropped hair, and even more relieved when he told her to wait in his toasty warm car.

"What are you doing here Mzzz. James?" he'd asked in a buzzing baritone. "You'll freeze out here without a proper coat." When he glanced down at her SpongeBobs, Jessica thought she saw a faint smile grace his somber face.

Another police car whined to a stop behind the Towncar, and two more uniformed officers got out. Tucking her hand into her sleeve, she used it to rub the fog off the inside of the car window so she could look outside again. Spreading out in concentric circles from the body, the officers combed the area. One of them even climbed inside the dumpster. She hoped he'd find her backpack so she could retrieve her computer and a solid year's worth of dissertation research.

As her body thawed, she realized she was exhausted, and

more than anything in the world, just wanted to sleep. She closed her eyes and her mind drifted off into the snowy nights, back to sleigh rides and hot chocolate on the ranch, before her dad died and her world turned upside down.

Lolita's voice in her ear startled her. "Cousin Vanya's right. My bike will be buried or stolen by the time these idiots get through with us. You know you're going to have to tell them what happened to you, right?" Lolita's sage-green eyes drilled into her very soul, and she realized her friend was right.

Reliving the night's indiscretions in front of strangers was going to be gutting. Signing up to be a "victim," when she really needed peace and healing, was going to be brutal. Anyway, she knew the statistics: one in four college girls got sexually assaulted; the cops never believed them or blamed them for wearing short shirts and flirting; then even if they could catch the attacker, DAs rarely prosecuted and juries almost never convicted. It would be easier just to keep her mouth shut and find the creep herself.

Only now it wasn't just assault but murder. The dead girl's ghoulish grimace came back to haunt her. Cold comfort knowing she wasn't alone, but she'd lived and the other girl hadn't. Whether it was survivor's guilt or victim's shame, deep in her throbbing pelvis she was desperate to keep the whole nightmare a secret. But a girl was dead, and maybe she had information that would help the cops catch the pervert who raped, killed, and left folded clothes in neat piles next to his victims. She rested her head against the seat and wondered what exactly she had survived. She thought of Nietzsche: "To live is to suffer. To survive is to find some meaning in the suffering." She leaned her head on Lolita's shoulder, and her friend put her arm around her. As if reading her mind, Lolita said, "We'll get through this, Sweetie. Just tell the cops what happened."

Comforted by Lolita's familiar Jasmine perfume, she closed her eyes again. She inhaled deeply through her nose and exhaled slowly through her mouth trying to calm herself. She was exhausted and wired at the same time, like she'd drunk a gallon of coffee and then been hit by a train. The sound of the car door opening startled her. She sat bolt upright, opening her eyes in time to see Detective Cormier brushing snow off the sleeves of his cashmere coat before getting into the driver's seat.

"We'll wait for the ambulance to arrive for the body then head to the station." The detective turned around to face the back seat. "Shouldn't be long now." His faint smile didn't reassure her. "What were you girls doing out here?"

"Tell him, Jessica." Lolita nudged her with her elbow.

"Tell me what?" the detective asked.

Jessica blushed. "Well, last night I had a couple of drinks with a guy in blue scrubs, and then…." She couldn't get the words out.

"And then?" the detective asked.

Suffering from hysterical muteness, she moved her lips but no sound emerged.

"Go on," the detective encouraged. "You had a couple of drinks."

Jessica took a deep breath then blurted out, "And I woke up behind that dumpster." She pointed toward the construction site.

"When?" the detective asked.

"A few hours ago."

"Where were you drinking?"

"O'Toole's, just down the street. It's a hangout for med students."

"And who was the guy?"

"I don't know. He was wearing scrubs, black curly hair, about six feet tall, well built."

"White?"

"Yes." Jessica hadn't thought to add that detail.

"Had you seen him before?"

Jessica's cheeks were on fire now. "No, I just met him tonight… last night."

Detective Cormier looked stoic. "What else can you tell me about him?"

"He was talking about genetics, how death was life's greatest invention."

"What do you mean?" the detective asked, his amber eyes flashing.

"Evolution, change, progress," Jessica sat forward, meeting his gaze.

Approaching sirens interrupted her explanation, and a cold blast hit her in the face as Detective Cormier reopened the car door.

"I'll be right back. Then we can go someplace and start over at the beginning," he said as he got out of the car.

"As long as it's someplace warm with caffeine," Lolita called after him.

Jessica watched as the paramedics struggled in the snow to lift the corpse into a body bag, zip it up, and carry it to the ambulance. She couldn't imagine facing the things nurses and doctors saw every day. The sight of blood turned her stomach. That's why she'd taken geology to meet her science requirement so she wouldn't have to dissect frogs.

The intrusive indelible image of the dead girl's sorrowful visage made her gag. She felt lightheaded and hoped she wasn't about to faint again. She wondered if cop cars had barf bags. She looked around just in case then decided she'd better get out of the car. When she did, she noticed the other squad cars were gone. Maybe the police were already questioning Jack and Lolita's crazy cousin Vanya.

Wait, what was Jack doing in Vanya's rig? Maybe he had come looking for her after all. But with Vanya? She was confused and too tired to even try to figure it out. She got back in the backseat of the cruiser and cuddled up next to her friend.

"What'd you see out there?" Lolita asked.

"Nothing," she whispered and leaned her head back onto Lolita's muscular shoulder and closed her eyes. She'd worry about Jack later, after a good twelve-hour snooze.

When Detective Cormier opened the car door again, a blast of frigid air slapped her face, and she woke up and wiped a drop of drool from her lips. She'd finally warmed up and was coming down off the adrenaline high.

"Are you okay, Ms. James?" the detective asked, settling back into the driver's seat. "Would you like some breakfast? There's an all-night dim sum place in Chinatown near the station. Some warm food and we can start over from the beginning. Sound good?"

"I could use some tea," Jessica said, glancing over at Lolita, wondering why he wasn't taking them to the police station.

"Chi Café?" Lolita asked. "That's cool with me." She just shrugged in response to Jessica's questioning eyes.

"That's the place. The only one open all night." The detective put the car into gear and pulled out into the storm. The blizzard was letting up, but snow devils still whirled along the city streets giving Chicago a ghostly aura, the fog shrouding the skyscrapers like a burial cloth. The snowplow up ahead was hurling snow into great plumes along the street, and Detective Cormier followed at a prudent distance.

"Usually, it takes only ten minutes," the detective apologized.

Lake Shore Drive was reduced to one lane each way. Out the window, Jessica watched Lake Michigan churn, an angry caldron about to boil over. As they passed Navy Pier, the Towncar shook from the wind whipping off the raging lake. When the car skidded sideways on the ice, still shaken from the girl's gruesome death mask, Jessica grabbed her friend's hand and didn't let go until they reached Chinatown. By the time they pulled up in front of Chi Café, Jessica was queasy, but at least the cramps were easing. Hopefully some hot tea and warm food would help.

On the outside, Chi Café was a hip little glass storefront with brightly illuminated hot pink neon panels embossed with wavy black Chinese characters. Inside, it looked like an aquarium with red lanterns swimming around the ceiling, splashes of turquoise on the walls, and ebbs and flows of colorful light encircling cozy booths. In the back, chunky white leather stools surrounded long, shiny white tables boasting trays of different sauces in rectangular dishes sitting at jaunty angles. Just walking into the multicolored all-night hangout made Jessica feel better.

She chose a corner booth next to the bar, waved Lolita in first then wriggled in next to her friend, across from the detective. An Asian waiter appeared and the detective said, "*San bei chá.*"

"You speak Chinese?" Jessica asked.

"Just a little Mandarin. Tell me more about this guy at O'Toole's. Do you remember anything else about him?" The detective glanced up as the waiter delivered a steaming pot of tea and three tiny cups. As he sat them on the table, the waiter looked at Jessica and smiled. "Nice PJs." She glanced down at her pants and blushed. She'd forgotten about SpongeBob. As Lolita poured the tea, Detective Cormier ordered dim sum in Chinese.

Jessica sipped her strong oolong tea, sighed, and closed her eyes. If only morning tea could wash away the sins of the night before.

"Tell me more about what happened at O'Toole's. Start again at the beginning," the detective said. "How long were you at the bar?"

"I don't usually drink with strange men." Jessica flipped the collar of her jacket up around her neck to cover her embarrassment. "But I was there waiting for my friend Jack to get out of class and I was by myself, and he was wearing blue scrubs, so I figured he worked at the hospital. He started talking to me about genetics and was obviously well educated. I mean, he didn't seem suspicious in any way. So, to be polite, I took the drink."

Detective Cormier gave her a kindly smile and said,

"I'm not here to judge you, Ms. James. You don't need to explain…"

She interrupted, "But I want to explain. I don't want you to think I'm a… that I'm… that I go around with strange men."

"It doesn't matter what I think, Ms. James. What's important is that we find the perpetrator, and any information you can provide will help. Most likely, whoever assaulted you, also assaulted Ms. Shaner."

The waiter returned with a tray full of bamboo baskets and sat dish after dish on the table, announcing each as he went. "Chinese broccoli in oyster sauce, shrimp dumplings, snow pea dumplings, vegetable dumplings, wood-ear mushroom dumplings, and congee."

Jessica ladled the syrupy white slime into a bowl and drank it straight from the bowl. The warm simple porridge revived her and lifted her spirits. When she let out an audible sigh, her dining companions both laughed. She'd been so focused on the congee, she'd almost forgotten about the interrogation.

"Please start at the beginning, and tell me about your friend, Jack," the detective said, deftly using chopsticks to pick up dumplings and drop them onto his plate.

"What about Jack? He's a friend."

"Tell me more about your relationship with Jack," the detective said. "What's his full name?"

"Jack Grove." She glanced at Lolita, wondering where the detective was going with these questions. "He is a med student in criminal psychiatry. I met him a couple of years ago when I was a teaching assistant for the late Professor Wolfgang Schmutzig, and we've been friends ever since."

She added, "*Just* friends, nothing more." She stopped mid-sentence, wondering why she'd added that tidbit. "I'm not sure how he knew to find me at the construction site."

"Okay, so you're waiting for this friend and then what happened?" the detective asked.

"I told you, an intern with black curly hair, blue eyes, and an obsession with unlocking the secrets of human DNA bought me a couple of Fiery Mule Slammers." Fiddling with her chopsticks, Jessica managed to flick a dumpling onto the floor. She reached her foot out and kicked it under the table then picked up a fork. She stabbed one of each veggie dumpling from its steaming basket and placed them on her small plate. She popped a soft doughy bundle into her mouth and, cheeks bulging, enjoyed the savory chewy contrast to the syrupy congee.

"He seemed harmless at the time," Jessica said through a mouth full of dumpling.

"They always do," Lolita added.

"But this guy's an intern at Northwestern."

"Or so he said." Lolita refilled the teacups. "Anyone can put on scrubs and claim to be a brain surgeon, and even neurosurgeons commit felonies."

"But not everyone can have a compelling argument about whether or not the mind is reducible to the brain," Jessica responded.

"No need to get defensive, Ms. James," Detective Cormier said. "As you know, smart people commit crimes, too. Just ask your friend Jack Grove, the forensic psychiatrist. Serial killers and serial rapists who evade law enforcement are intelligent. That's why they're so hard to catch."

"You have to think like a criminal to catch a criminal," Lolita said.

"That's where you could help out," Jessica said, poking her friend in the arm. "Or, better yet, Jack."

"Is your friend, Jack, a criminal?" the detective asked.

Eyes wide, Jessica looked at Lolita and almost spit out her dumpling. "Do victimless crimes count?" Jessica asked.

The detective scowled. "Do you think he had anything to do with Ms. Shaner's death?"

"No way." Jessica raised her voice.

"And what about you, Ms. Durchenko? What do you think? I hope you aren't still running those illegal poker games," the detective said, stabbing a dumpling with one chopstick. "Messing with those kind of people could get you into a lot of trouble. And you've already been warned once."

"Yes, Detective Cormier," Lolita purred, giving him a winning smile.

"Now, Ms. Durchenko, why don't you tell me everything you know about what happened. Why were you at the dumpster this morning? How did you come to find the body? Please start at the beginning."

"My best friend was raped and dropped behind a dumpster. She survived, and the other girl died. What else is there to say?" Lolita put both elbows on the table and stared across at the detective. "Girls are sexually assaulted every day and no one knows or even cares. A girl is dead and someone better start paying attention."

In awe of her badass friend, Jessica's eyes widened and stared across the table, swallowed a gulp of hot tea, and absently picked at the bandage on her hand.

CHAPTER SEVEN

ALMOST TWO HOURS had passed and Jack was still waiting in the detective's fastidious office. Fidgeting in the uncomfortable chair, he stared down at the coffee grounds in the bottom of the empty Styrofoam cup and wondered if the cops had Jesse holed up in another room. *What was she doing kneeling next to Sara's body?* He'd kept his relationship with Sara a secret, as if Jesse would care. He wished he could spend the day curled in her arms instead of in the cop shop. He hoped the cops hadn't been interrogating her all this time.

The squeaking door took him by surprise. He jerked around and saw the plain clothed cop from the dumpster enter the room. The clean-cut detective sat behind his desk then took out a tape recorder and a notepad. No introduction, he got right down to business.

"Do you mind if I record our interview, Mr. Grove?" he asked.

When Jack didn't answer, the detective asked again. "I'd like to record our interview, if that is okay with you."

"Sorry, I thought it was a rhetorical question," Jack answered.

"So, it's okay?"

"Do I have a choice?"

"Technically, yes, but if you give your permission, it makes things easier."

"If you insist, I'll submit myself to your interrogation as long as you keep the waterboarding to a minimum." He knew he shouldn't mess with the cops, but he couldn't help it. He was just too fucking shattered to care.

The detective narrowed his brows. "This isn't a joke, Mr. Grove. A girl is dead and you may have information that could help us catch the perpetrator. In this case…"

Jack heard his voice but wasn't listening. *A girl is dead.* The words echoed in his skull. *Perpetrator,* in this case it meant murderer, killer, rapist, psychopath. The criminal mind was his specialty. *To Perpetrate, bring into existence, from the Latin,* pater, *father.* From father to criminal, the telling etymology of words. His own father was an abusive alcoholic. And *in this case,* the perpetrator had taken out of existence a beautiful woman. Jack tightened his lips.

"Why were you at the dumpster, Mr. Grove? What was your relationship with the victim?" the detective asked, plucking a pen from his Chicago Bears penholder. The level of organization and neatness of both his person and his desk suggested obsession, an anal retentive personality, probably OCD. Obviously, Detective Cormier didn't like chaos, and he probably imagined himself bringing order to a disorderly world.

"Yes, I knew her," Jack answered.

"How well did you know her, Mr. Grove?"

"Depends." Jack sat back in the chair and stretched his legs out in front of him. "I was just learning my way around the contours of her body, but I'd hardly begun to navigate the maze of her mind."

"What is that supposed to mean?" the detective asked irritably.

"She shared her lovely body with me but kept her keen mind to herself."

"What do you mean by that, Mr. Grove?" Detective Cormier stared across the desk at him.

"Two weeks ago, I met Sara Shaner at O'Toole's. That's where medical students go to unwind after a rough day dissecting cadavers and curing diseases. She bought me a drink and invited me to her place afterwards. We hooked up a few times since. She'd text and I'd come." Jack's chest tightened. He hoped his body wouldn't betray him. He crossed his arms over his racing heart. "A dog on a leash," he mumbled to himself.

"Was Sara Shaner also a medical student?"

"Yes, she was an ace fellowship student in Gene Ontology."

"Gene Ontology?"

"She was a computer wizard developing bioinformatics to standardize gene attributes across species and databases to make cross-referencing easier. Just the kind of thing the criminal justice system will hijack and use to hurt rather than heal."

The detective looked nonplussed. "When did you last see Sara Shaner?"

"We had dinner together last night and then went back to her place for dessert." Jack forced a smile to hide his nausea.

"You may be the last person to have seen Sara Shaner alive. What time did you leave her after dessert?" the detective asked, square jaw set, staring straight at him with his penetrating brown eyes.

Jack slid his feet back under the chair and sat upright. His knee started bouncing again and he sat on his shaking hands. *The last person to see Sara alive.* His hands summoned the warmth of her thighs, and his mouth, the taste of her lips.

"Do you remember what time you left her, Mr. Grove?" The detective's deep voice shook him from his melancholy memories.

"I guess it must have been around seven-thirty. My class starts at eight, and we stayed in bed too long, so I got there late."

"And how long were you in class?"

"The class ends at ten."

"What did you do after class?"

"After class, I went to O'Toole's to meet Jesse."

"Jessica James?"

"Yes, Jessica."

"When did you and Jessica leave O'Toole's?"

"She didn't show up." If Cormier had interrogated Jesse, he'd know this already; he might even know why. "I waited for her until closing." It was almost the truth.

"So Jessica wasn't with you at O'Toole's?"

"No, she wasn't. When she didn't show up, I went back to the Med School to look for her. I thought maybe we'd gotten our wires crossed, and I was supposed to meet her there. I was trying to find Jesse when I encountered one of your species brutally harassing an innocent post-doc outside her lab. That ink-stained Russian specimen, the one you found with me, helped us escape. We were fleeing bullets from your brethren when we saw Jesse and Lolita kneeling over Sara's…. body." Jack wiped his palms on his jeans.

"What do you mean fleeing bullets?"

"As I said, we were escaping the research lab with fat Fergus hot on our heels."

"Fat Fergus?"

"Officer Fergus Doyle, the racist arshole badgering Samantha. Ask her. She got his badge number. Or are you one of those blue-lives-matter cops who protect their own no matter what?" Both knees were bouncing and Jack could barely sit still. Sweat dripped off his brows and stung his eyes.

"Can you at least open a window?" Jack asked, pointing toward the glass. He was losing his shit.

"Picture windows. They don't open."

"Figures. Nothing is what it seems when it comes to so-called criminal justice. Can I go now? I need my beauty sleep."

"What do you have against law enforcement, Mr. Grove?" the detective asked calmly.

"Do you want a dissertation?" Jack snapped in response. The windows weren't enough to compensate for the small, dark, stuffy room; its walls were closing in on him. "Claustrophobia," he muttered to himself. Claustrum, *lock, plus phobia, fear.* He wanted to scream, *Let me out of here*! But instead he sat on his hands. *Keep it together, Jacko.*

"The criminal justice system is just an excuse to lock up poor people and the mentally ill. Lock-ups make people sick; they don't cure them, they've *perpetrated.*"

"Please calm down, Mr. Grove. Just a couple more questions and you can go, I promise." From the other side of the desk, the detective scrutinized him then asked, "Do you know how your girlfriend ended up behind the dumpster?"

"How the fuck would I know?" Jack blurted out. He needed this interrogation to end before he reached across the desk and strangled that smug cop.

"No need to get aggressive, Mr. Grove. Just one last question and then you're free to go." Pen hovering over his legal pad, his countenance inscrutable, the detective just stared at him for a few seconds and then asked, "What do Sara Shaner and Jessica James have in common?"

Jack leaned forward in the chair.

"Can you think of a reason why someone would target those two women?"

"Target? What do you mean?" Jack ran his sweaty fingers through his hair. "What's this got to do with Jesse?"

"We're speculating that the same person dropped them both behind the dumpster around midnight." The detective looked up from his legal pad.

"Someone dropped Jesse behind that dumpster, too!" Rocking back and forth in his chair, Jack prepared to bolt. "Is she here? Is she okay? Can I see her?" He couldn't breathe. He felt like he was about to toss his cookies. He had to escape. He had to see her. "Where is she?" He tightened his fists, barely able to stay seated.

"I took her home," the detective said. "What's your relationship to Jessica James?"

"She's my best friend." Jack stood up. "Look, I really need to go now."

"You can go for now, but don't leave town. We may need to ask you more questions. If you think of anyone or anything that might connect Sara Shaner and Jessica James, contact me immediately."

Jack collapsed back into the chair and squeezed his eyes

shut. His head hurt, and he wished he hadn't flushed all his pot down the toilet. He needed something to calm his nerves. He saw Sara winking at him over her veggie stir-fry, suggesting they go back to her place for "dessert." Her winsome blue eyes, wild blonde hair, and wacked out brain had reminded him of Jesse.

"They're both blonde and smart as hell," Jack blurted out, and then added as an afterthought, "and they're both vegetarians." Breathless, he jumped up and headed for the door. He flung open the office door then turned back to the detective. "They could both smell you coming from a mile away."

He bolted from the suffocating room, raced down the hall, flew past the receptionist, and threw himself into the revolving door. Tears froze on his eyelashes as he pushed headlong into the wind toward the closest red line "L" stop, Chinatown. He had to make sure Jesse was okay.

As he approached 18th Street, he saw a familiar form on the sidewalk, huddled under a scrawny tree, shifting from foot to foot, and smoking a cigarette. Jack started to cross the street then thought better of it, turned around, and came up behind the thin man in uniform. The rough rose tattoo on his smoking hand confirmed it was Vanya, the campus cop.

"Vanya, fancy meeting you here," he said.

The Russian swiveled around with a start. "Sneaking up like that could be bad for your health, *chuvak.*"

"Apologies, man." Jack extended his hand, and Vanya hesitantly shook it. "How was your interrogation with the big boy police?"

"I hate cops," Vanya said, dropping his cigarette and

stamping it out in the snow with his black boot. "How about you, Clyde? Where's Bonnie? Cops rough her up some more?"

"Wait, aren't you a cop?" Jack asked. "Self-loathing, interesting. Explains a lot about police behavior."

"I don't know nothin' about self-loafing, but cops is bad news. When I was a kid in *Moskva*, one time me and my cousin Dmitry stole the gun off a *politsiya*." When Vanya laughed, his grill reflected sunlight ricocheting off the snow. "Where ya headed? Need a lift? My cousin Dmitry should be here any minute. We're going back to the lab for the video tape."

"Video tape? You mean the surveillance video?" Jack asked. "Not a bad idea." He was starting to like this wiry Russian cop-hater.

"Right. Got to get it before Fergus does. Like Bratva, cops always protect their own."

"Bratva?" Jack asked.

"The Brotherhood. My former employer." Vanya flashed his golden smile. "The Russian mob, *chuvak*."

"You're part of the Russian mafia?"

Still smiling, Vanya removed a pack of cigarettes from his shirt pocket, tapped out two, lit one, took a puff then touched its red glowing tip of the other, and offered it to Jack.

"Are you really Lolita's cousin?" Jack asked, taking the cigarette.

Vanya's smile broadened. "Drop dead gorgeous, isn't she?"

A silver Toyota minivan pulled up and honked.

"Get in." Vanya pointed to the back door then hopped into the passenger seat. Vanya rolled down his window and yelled, "Come on, get in, *chuvak*." Jack tossed the cigarette into the street, tugged the handle on the van, and climbed into the back seat.

"I'm Jack Grove," he said, nodding to the driver.

"You said your name was Max White. What ya trying to pull?"

"Right. I did, but my friends call me Jack."

"Well, I calls ya, Clyde." Vanya pointed to the driver. "This is my cousin Dmitry, the lovely Lolita Durchenko's papa."

"Mr. Durchenko," Jack said, examining the handsome driver for any resemblance to his daughter. He had the same jet-black hair, only his was wavy and hers was slick and straight. When Mr. Durchenko turned around, he saw the familiar piercing sage-green eyes.

"That's right. Now what trouble have you gotten into this time, Vanya?" Mr. Durchenko asked, turning back to his cousin. "I thought you were going straight since I got you the job at Northwestern."

"Well, coz, I was, but..."

"Never mind your excuses, where to?"

"To steal a video tape from the Medical School," Vanya said, lighting another cigarette.

"What? You want me to be an accessory to theft? Open your window and use the ashtray." Dmitry Durchenko shook his head.

"It's for a good cause, coz. Trust me. Anyway, I've sat in that video room every night for the last week, and it's a piece of pie."

"Cake. Piece of cake," Dmitry said. He stepped on

the accelerator, pulled out onto State Street, and headed towards the Medical School.

"I'll leave you to sort out dessert," Jack said. "Would you mind dropping me at my car? It's near the Medical School and I need to check on Jesse. She was assaulted..." His voice trailed off and he put his head in his hands.

CHAPTER EIGHT

J ESSICA PUT HER pillow over her head, but the buzzing wouldn't stop. Still wearing her SpongeBobs, she crawled out of bed, padded over to the window, and peeked through the blinds. Jackass was bouncing from foot to foot, hands jammed in his jeans' pockets and a Greek fisherman's cap on his head. She buzzed him in then went into the closet to ask the microwave what time it was; her phone was in her missing backpack. The microwave just flashed 12:00, refusing to tell her what time it really was.

She wriggled out of the kiddie outfit then dug through the top dresser drawer for her last pair of clean undies, and scooped up some semi-clean jeans and a crumpled long-sleeved Henley off the floor. The jeans had thick wool socks conveniently stuck in their legs, so she put those on too. She'd just tugged her pants on when she heard one tap and then three short raps on her door, Jack's signature knock.

Moving quickly had reawakened the pelvic pain, but unlike last night's whip cracking agony, now it was just a tiny tweaking pinch. When she opened the door, Jack wrapped her in a freezing embrace. Cold emanated from his entire body. She shivered and twisted free.

"Brrr. You're an iceberg. I'll make some coffee."

"Are you okay, Jesse?"

"I guess so. What about you, Jackass? You look like something the cat dragged in." Jack just shrugged and blinked his red eyes, his five-o'clock shadow almost a full eclipse.

"Caffeine. That's what we need," she said, jabbing the air with her index finger for emphasis.

She skated across the hardwood floor of her efficiency apartment and into the "kitchenette," otherwise known as a clothes closet where she kept the microwave on top of a miniature refrigerator, along with a hot plate, and her great-grandmother's vintage dresses.

Skirting a box of unpacked books, a pile of dirty clothes, and the bass guitar she swore she'd learn to play someday, she scooted into her closet, opened the pint-sized refrigerator then stared inside. The light bulb was burnt out, but that didn't matter since there was nothing to see except a moldy head of lettuce, half a cheese sandwich, and a bottle of chocolate milk. She grabbed the milk and hesitantly twisted off the cap.

"Yuck!" She carried it at arms length across the apartment to the bathroom and poured it down the drain of her tiny sink. She ignored the tub full of dirty dishes, went back to the fridge, and opened the tiny freezer compartment in search of coffee. All she found was a pint of Ben and Jerry's Cherry Garcia surrounded by an igloo of freezer frost.

"Heartland?" Jack asked. "Your treat. Or if you don't feel up to going out, we can order on Grubhub."

"Heartland sounds good. But you drive," Jessica said, tugging on her cowboy boots.

"I left my car downtown after 'Operation Avenge Junior' went south." Jack made air quotes and sat down on a bar stool, the only seat in the fourth-floor walk-up besides the futon bed that doubled as her desk, but it was strewn with more clothes, books, a computer, and pillows.

"You went without me?" Jessica tucked a lock of hair up into her Trapper then kicked at the pile of dirty clothes until she uncovered a buried cardigan and put it on. She grabbed her fringe jacket off the chair and stuck her arms into it then dug around the floor of her closet until she found her spare gloves (only one small hole). She topped off the ensemble with Lolita's red wool scarf. "Let's go get some coffee and you can tell me about Operation Avenge Junior," she said, heading out the door. She gestured for Jack to follow and locked up.

Heartland Café was only two blocks away, near Morse "L" stop and another reason she'd moved to Roger's Park the week before classes started. Her little hovel may have seen better days fifty years ago, but it was better than living near campus in snooty Evanston. She was living in the city and it suited her. After leaving Whitefish, Montana, a year ago, she swore she'd never again live where skunks outnumbered people. Although she did insist, "Skunks are people, too."

Jessica loved the groovy vibe at Heartland Café and Buffalo Bar, a combo diner, bar, and hippy knick-knack store. She ordered a stack of vegan pancakes with a side of seitan bacon and a double cappuccino with a ginger shot.

"How can you eat that Satan shit?" Jack asked, wolfing down his burger and fries.

"Tastes like chicken," she said, performing the Heimlich maneuver on the honey bear over her coffee cup.

"Rubber chicken. Is that what you ate on the farm?"

"How many times do I have to tell you, dumbass? It's a ranch."

"I thought you grew up in a trailer park."

"Okay, but a trailer park with a horse barn and two horses constitutes a ranch, at least by Chicago standards."

"I'm surprised any self-respecting Montanan would eat that fake bacon crap with all those tasty pigs out there on the farm."

"I'll have you know, I grew up eating wild game my dad shot." Her mouth watered thinking about venison steak. "As a kid, I'd smack my lips whenever I saw Bambi." She doused her pancakes in maple syrup, giving the fake bacon an extra dose. "Eating animals is childish. I don't want to eat my animal friends now that I know better. Speaking of which, tell me what happened with Operation Avenge Jack Junior."

"Let's just say it didn't go as planned. But I did manage to liberate a bunch of sorry-assed rodents," Jack said, his mouth full of cow. "Apologies, I mean to your animal friends. Yours and Snow White's."

"Why didn't you show up at O'Toole's?" Jack's face turned pale and botchy. "That cop friend of yours said you'd been... you were found behind the...."

"I don't want to talk about it." Jessica's cheeks were burning, and she took a drink of ice water. "Do you know an attractive intern, tall and muscular, with black hair and blue eyes? Super cute?"

"Northwestern Memorial is a big place, Jesse." Jack scarfed his last ketchup-drenched fry. "Super cute, eh?" He winked.

"Just wondering. I met him last night at O'Toole's, and he might be the one."

"The one?" Jack asked, a strange, almost scared, look on his face.

"Never mind. Let's go get your car and look for my stuff."

The snow was so deep it packed into her cowboy boots as she climbed across a snowdrift to get to the "L." Jack tried to help her, but she shook him off. She'd been climbing snow berms since she was a kid. Chicago winters may be brutal, but Whitefish's were no pansies. Power outages had interrupted service, and the red line from north Chicago to downtown was delayed. She watched as a guy in a padded orange jumpsuit with an industrial facemask and professional earmuffs used a loud machine to blow snow off the elevated train platform and clear a path to the train.

Snow devils whirled across the platform as the train pulled up. Jack waved his arm toward the sliding door in an exaggerated gesture. "After you, *ma chérie*."

Minding the gap, she stepped onto the train, headed for the back of the car then slid into a plastic seat and waited for Jack to join her. Huddling close to him for warmth, she whispered, "Why didn't you come find me last night instead of going to the research lab by yourself?"

"I thought you'd stood me up." He poked her arm with a gloved finger.

"Try the other way around." Jessica jerked her head back and glared at him.

When they arrived at the pub, O'Toole's was surprisingly busy for a holiday, a sea of blue scrubs fresh from the trenches. Obviously more than a few people were celebrating Thanksgiving with burgers and cheese fries, at least the ones who worked at the hospital. Jessica made a beeline for the near side of the circular wooden bar. She crawled around on the floor under the stools, but couldn't find any sign of her stuff.

"Did you find a parka and backpack in here last night?" she asked the bartender.

"Sure did." He bent down under the bar then held up a battered black ski jacket and an army surplus pack with a Bass Beer sticker on it. "This it?"

"Thanks." The bartender looked familiar. "Were you here last night?"

"Sure was."

"Did you see me with someone, a tall man with black hair in scrubs?" she asked, reaching across the bar for her stuff.

"Super cute," Jack said in a snarky voice.

"Sure did. You were sitting here," the bartender answered, polishing the bar into a shining mirror.

"Do you by any chance know his name?" Jessica munched on some peanuts.

"Sure don't. So many scrubs come in here after their shifts. That one always leaves with a different pretty girl on his arm."

"Bastard," Jack said.

Jessica dug in her backpack for paper and pen then tore a page from her Moleskin and scrawled her phone number on it. "Would you do me a favor? If you see that guy in scrubs in here again, would you find out his name?"

"Sure thing," the bartender said and went back to polishing the wooden bar to a flawless sheen.

"And if you find out, would you call me?" Jessica wiped her salt covered fingers onto her jeans then put her parka on over her suede jacket.

"Let's go get the Batmobile," she said to Jack.

"First my duffle bag." Jack added. "I left it at the Med School last night."

Jessica rolled her eyes. "You're hopeless without me."

"*C'est vrai.*" Jack flashed her a wicked smile.

"*Oooo lá lá.*" Jessica put on her parka, slung the pack over her shoulder then turned back to the bartender. "Did you see me leave with that guy last night?" Jessica asked blushing.

The bartender stared at Jack and then looked back at her with a quizzical look. "No, you left with him." He pointed at Jack.

"Me?" Jack's mouth fell open.

"What? Are you sure?" she asked.

"Sure am. See you two in here together a lot."

She gave Jack a questioning look, but he only shook his head. "Let's go get my duffle bag." He led her up the stairs and back out into the frigid air.

Crunching through the snow, trying to step in Jack's footprints, Jessica followed him the two blocks to the Medical School. He ducked around the corner of the building, and she had to jog to catch up. She held onto the wrought-iron railing as she sailed down the stairwell and landed right on his heels.

"Ouch!" She doubled over and held her pelvis. "Damned period. Cramps."

"You okay?" Jack helped her up, and she brushed the snow from her pants. Her pride was hurt worse than anything else. She snatched up her Trapper from the bottom step and shook the snow off of it.

"I didn't leave with you last night, right?" she asked.

"I told you. I waited for an hour, but you didn't show. Sounds like you'd already left with the super cute rapist."

"Not funny, Jackass." She kicked him in the shin with her pointy-toed boot.

"Ouch!" He danced away from her. "Sorry, you're right," he said. He retrieved an ID badge from his back pocket and inserted it into the scanner; the door clicked open. She scooted in behind him, and then followed him down the hall. Her snow-covered boots were more like ice skates, and she slipped along the polished floor, waving her arms in the air to keep her balance.

Jack bolted down the hall, disappeared into an alcove, and when she got there, he was rifling through his duffle bag.

"I can't believe the fat bastard didn't find this," he said laughing. "Hey, no one's around. I still have Amber's spoof. Let's go, cowgirl." Jack glanced around the hallway then danced around the corner. Slipping and sliding in her wet boots, Jessica skated to keep up.

Jack plucked an envelope out of his jacket pocket and held it up. "Voilá. Behold the genius of The Magnificent Amber Bush. One of her many talents."

Jessica put her hand on his sleeve. "Wait, are you nuts? It's broad daylight."

"You wanted to avenge Junior. Now's your chance. Anyway, it's Thanksgiving. Maybe we'll even pardon a turkey." Jack pressed the rubber fingerprint onto the screen and the second door clicked open.

"Why do I follow you?" she muttered as she slipped inside behind him.

Rabbits sprouting tubes and eye patches, dogs shaved and scarred with bandages, and worst of all the cats, wires coming out of their lopsided heads, tethering them to mechanical beasts with glowing green eyes. Overwhelmed by the amount of innocent suffering, Jessica burst into tears.

"What are we going to do, Jack?" she asked through her sobs. "This is terrible. Opening cages isn't enough. These poor creatures."

Wiping her nose on her sleeve, she dropped to the floor next to a cage with a miniature monkey curled up in the corner and stuck her finger through the bars, but the little guy didn't budge. One eye bandaged, he stared at the wall of his cage in a sad stupor.

"I'm sorry, Jesse. Medical science may be brutal, but these experiments save lives." Jack unzipped his bag and took out a can of spray paint. He started spraying fuzzy black letters onto a cabinet above the sink.

"Whose lives? Human lives?"

"Like every animal, we have a survival instinct, but ours is the cruelest." Jack took a step back and admired his handwork. He'd sprayed "SCIENCE NOT SADISM," in dripping bold letters across the cupboard. He came to her side, knelt down, and put his arm around her. "Come on, cowgirl, I want you to meet Sam's beagle."

"Who is Sam?" Jessica asked as she took his hand and let him lift her to her feet. When he led her to the beagle's cage, the dog squeaked with excitement, and she couldn't help but smile. She bent down to pet the little wet black nose poking through the bars.

Her breath caught, and she stood erect, body rigid. "Someone's coming. I hear footsteps." She scanned the lab then bolted towards a giant metal door. "In here!" She pushed down on the latch with both hands and wrenched the heavy door open.

"We'll be lucky not to freeze to death," Jack said, following close behind her. He pushed her inside and shut the thick door. A blast of frigid air stung her eyes, and she realized what he meant. Maybe a deep freeze wasn't the best place to hide. She ran smack into Jack as she headed back towards the door to escape the cold.

Terror in his eyes, Jack grabbed her by the shoulders. "Holy shit! Don't move! Don't turn around." Her heart leapt into her throat and she panicked.

CHAPTER NINE

JESSICA TRIED TO turn her head to see what Jack was staring at over her shoulder, but he'd dropped his duffle bag at her feet and put a gloved hand over her eyes before she could get a look.

"What's wrong?" she asked, slapping at his hand and struggled to free herself from his claws digging into her arm.

"Never mind. Just don't turn around," he ordered, his face pale.

"It's so cold in here, my nose hairs are frozen," she said. She turned her head slightly to peek over his shoulder at the back of the freezer, but Jack caught her head in both hands.

"Tell me what's going on. What is it, Jack?"

"You don't want to know. Trust me," he said. "I wish I hadn't seen it."

"What?" she demanded.

Jack clasped his hand over her mouth and whispered, "Be quiet. Wanna spend the next decade in a federal prison?" Outside the freezer, someone was banging around in the research lab. By now, they must have seen Jack's graffiti and called the police. As usual, tagging along with Jackass meant risking her career, if not her life.

"I thought you said it would be deserted," Jessica accused in a whisper. "Who'd be here on Thanksgiving?" When she tried to turn around toward the back of the freezer again, Jack grabbed her shoulders, pivoted her on her heels toward the freezer door, and held her there.

"You'd be surprised at how many dedicated tossers come in to check on their experiments everyday and at all hours." Jack put his arms around her and held her close. He smelled like fried onions, and she closed her eyes, absorbing his warmth.

"How long can we survive in here?" she asked, pulling out of his embrace and looking up into his stubbly face.

"An hour, tops." Jack tugged on the earflaps of her hat. "Just don't turn around. Actually closing your eyes will keep you warmer. Studies have shown it keeps your eyeballs from freezing." Jack was rummaging around in the freezer looking for something. She did as she was told and closed her eyes.

"Maybe we should just fess up to whoever's out there and throw ourselves at their mercy." Jessica opened one eye.

"Vandalizing an animal lab is a felony. Wanna write your dissertation in prison?" Jack picked up a large bone, examined it, and put it back on the shelf then glanced back at her.

"Keep your damn eyes shut." Jack scowled at her, and she closed both eyes again.

"It would be better than freezing to death." Shifting from foot to foot, she wrapped Lolita's scarf around her face and hugged herself. Moving just made her colder, so she crossed her legs and pressed her thighs together. She couldn't feel her fingers or toes.

"I'm not sure about that. Have you ever been in a federal prison?" he asked.

"Have you?" she asked, opening one eye again.

"I'm studying forensic psychiatry, remember?" Jack put his finger to his lips. "Shhhhh… close your mouth. Studies have shown it helps prevent frostbite."

She fake punched his arm. "Studies have shown you're making that up!"

"You pack quite a punch," he whispered.

"But I didn't even swing."

"If you had, I could've ducked," he said, giving her a strange sad smile that sent a shiver up her spine.

Jack had ordered her not to look at the back of the freezer, so for the next ten eternal minutes, while he paced back and forth in front of her, she stood stock-still listening to the sounds outside in the lab: cupboards shutting, water running, heels tapping on the floor, a dog squeaking and then barking.

Fighting the urge to turn around, she counted specimen bags on the shelf in front of her until the stacks of baggies filled with animal pieces made her queasy. At least she'd stopped shivering and was warming up. In fact, she was overheated, and her skin was burning. She took off her jacket and rolled it into a ball for a pillow. She needed a nap.

"What are you doing?" Jack whispered. "Put your coat back on or you'll freeze to death." He took the jacket from her hands, put it around her shoulders then wrapped his arms around her back and held her tight. She was too tired to resist, so she slumped against his shoulder.

"I'm sleepy," she said, surprised at how hard it was to speak. "I was going to lie down."

"*Merde*! We've got to get you out of here." He pressed her to his chest. "You're showing signs of hypothermia."

"Hypothermia," she slurred.

The clicking and banging noises in the lab disappeared and were replaced by Brahms's lullaby. She must be delirious. A voice as clear and melodious as a mountain stream was singing:

Lullaby, and good night, you are
Samantha's delight.

I'll protect you from harm, and you'll wake in
my arms.

Sleepyhead, close your eyes, for I'm right
beside you.

Guardian angels are near, so sleep without fear.

I'll protect you from harm, and you'll wake in
my arms.

Go to sleep, little one, think of puppies
and kittens.

Go to sleep, little one, think of butterflies
in spring.

Go to sleep, little one, think of sunny
bright mornings.

Hush, darling Snoopy, sleep through the night.

She was drifting off to the sweet strains of the lullaby when Jack pushed her away. She opened her eyes and scowled at him. "Why'd you do that? I was just getting comfy."

"Listen!" he said. "I know that songstress. Come on. We've got to risk it. We're getting out of here."

"You hear it, too?" she asked. "Who is it?"

"Let's go." He took her hand and led her staggering to the freezer door. Slowly, he pushed down on the latch. It didn't budge. He dropped her hand and she teetered, almost falling backwards. He put both of his on the door latch then, throwing his body weight into it, he shoved on it again.

"Bugger!" he said under his breath.

"What's wrong?"

"The door's jammed." Jack slammed his fist into a big red button next to the door. Nothing happened. He pounded on it then stepped back, and kicked it with the heel of his shoe.

"*Merde*. The emergency exit is broken. That explains Granowski." He pounded on the door with both fists. "Help! Get us out of here!"

"Why won't the door open?" she asked. "What's Granowski?" She was too tired to wait for an answer. She slumped to the floor and laid her head on a cardboard box labeled "fluorescent dye." She needed sleep more than any-thing. Curling up, she turned on her side and found herself face-to-face with another sleeping form, a wan thirty-some-thing woman with sharp features accented by red lipstick, white lab coat, blotchy blue skin, and frosty black hair.

"Hi, sleepyhead," she said to the other woman. "You wanna use my coat for a pillow? We can share." She moved closer to the woman but stopped short when she saw the dark unblinking eyes staring back at her, and the tiny blood-filled blisters on her face. "You don't look so good, girlfriend."

For some reason she couldn't comprehend, Jack was still yelling and pounding on the door. She wished he'd shut up so she could sleep. She pushed her coat up against a shelf, laid her head on it, closed her eyes and drifted off into a lush meadow on a sunny day riding up to the peak of Gunsight Mountain with her dad. The sun bore down and her skin started burning. She screamed as she watched her dad catch on fire and burn to black ashes, the horse along with him. She was alone and heard a voice in the distance, a man's voice, a single-malt voice...it sounded familiar. Jack. *Why was he shouting at her?* Someone touched her arm and she flinched. Her body was shaking, and as she opened her eyes, a blurry face came into soft focus.

"Darling Jack," she whispered. "What are you doing here? Are you going to Sperry Lake, too?"

"Wake up, dammit." He was shaking her.

"Stop shaking me! What are you doing?" she slurred. "I'm sleepy."

"You've got hypothermia. We've got to get you out of here now."

"I'm burning up," she screamed. "Help me, Jack." She was desperately ripping at her clothes. She felt his body on top of hers, pinning her to the floor, his warm breath in her ear. "Hold on, Jesse. I'm going to get us out of here."

CHAPTER TEN

JACK BELLOWED AS loud as he could and pounded the freezer door with both fists. If Beagle Girl had already left, they were gonners for sure. He had to get Jesse out soon or she would die of hypothermia. She already had severe symptoms. He glanced over his shoulder and saw her curled up sweetly on the floor, frost forming on her long eyelashes.

In another five minutes, she'd be as rigid as the poor stiff lying next to her. He cringed. Professor Granowski must have gotten locked in, too. Maybe she had been dying in the freezer last night and he'd almost joined her. He was not going to become another specimen in this fucking deep freeze horror show. *Bloody nightmare.* Jesse probably only had a few more minutes.

Loud music started blaring in the lab, a symphony. Good news, Beagle Girl was still out there: bad news, she probably couldn't hear him over Beethoven's Ninth.

"Come on Samantha, I know you're out there. Can you hear me? Open this door," he yelled at the top of his lungs, pounding again. He had to find a way to get the door open on his own.

He frantically searched the freezer for a tool to pry the door open. He saw a large femur bone lying on a shelf, plastic drawers filled with lizard specimens, vials of medicines, bottles of white and pink powders, a clothed dead body, and another one on its way. No tools. Pacing the length of the freezer, he stumbled on his duffle bag still lying in the middle of the floor.

He remembered the tire iron he'd been lugging across downtown all last night. He unzipped the duffle and seized the steel bar in both hands. Feet apart for balance he slammed the tire iron into the metal latch and then tried prying at the door's lip. Even if he didn't break the door open, he'd definitely make enough noise to get Beagle Girl's attention.

"Come on, Samantha. Open the goddammed door!" He shouted and swung the steel bar against the door again. A clanking sound stopped him mid-swing, and he lowered the iron to his side and listened. A second later, the door burst open, hitting him in the arm.

"Max, what are you doing in there?" Samantha asked, eyes wide. "Were you locked in? Isn't the latch working?"

"I've got to get Jesse out and raise her body temperature. You call 911." Jack dragged Jesse out of the freezer then dashed to get warm blankets from the heater. He'd seen them used on the animals when they'd come out of surgery.

"I'll get some heat packs in the back." Samantha was standing outside the freezer, staring down at Jesse's unconscious form. "Your girlfriend has hypothermia. If her body temperature falls below 80 degrees, she could die."

"She's not my girlfriend. Call 911."

"We have to be careful raising her body temperature. We can't raise it too fast; it could cause cardiac arrest." Samantha disappeared around the corner and reappeared with a box of disposable heat packs.

She tore open the box and snapped the center of the metal discs one by one to activate them then passed them to him by the handfuls. "Nazi doctors at Dachau used cold-water immersion baths and calculated death at 77 degrees Fahrenheit," she said.

"Not exactly reassuring." Jack wrapped warm blankets around Jesse's head and torso, and then arranged a patch-work of heat packs on top of the blankets. He removed his gloves, then hers, and rubbed her little frozen hand between his palms.

"Come on, Jesse," he begged.

"At 87 degrees the heart goes into arrhythmia."

"Tell me something I don't know."

"Okay. Did you know many hypothermia victims die from rewarming shock when the constricted capillaries reopen all at once, causing a sudden drop in blood pressure? A decade ago, twenty Danish fishermen shipwrecked in the North Sea were rescued, taken below deck, given hot drinks, then dropped dead, all twenty of them."

"That's bullshit," he said, but he put two fingers on Jesse's wrist and checked her pulse anyway. "Come on, wake up, Jesse." He gently rubbed her pale cheeks. "Please wake up."

"Do you know hypothermia victims feel a burning sensation before death and often rip off their clothes? Many are found half naked and presumed to be assault victims. Maybe that's what happened to the girl you found last night by the dumpster." Arms akimbo, Samantha was standing staring down at Jesse's unconscious form. When Jack looked up at her, he noticed some of the spray paint had been washed off the cupboard. He narrowed his eyes and asked, "What's your deal, Beagle Girl?"

"What do you mean? I told you last night, I work for Janet Granowski." She blinked her almond shaped eyes.

"Not anymore."

"Why do you say that? You're not going to report me for petting Snoopy, are you?" Samantha pouted. "Anyway, you're a fine one to talk. I've been scrubbing your stupid graffiti." She pointed to the cupboard. "What were you doing here last night with that stupid ski mask? Hey, were you the one who opened the mice cages? You ruined a year's worth of research. You're a criminal, and I should report you."

"I won't report you if you don't report me." Still piling heat packs on top of Jesse's chest and thighs, he nodded toward the steel door. "But you might want to look in the deep freeze. Someone's been up to much worse than paint and mice."

"Is this some kind of a trick, Max?" Samantha narrowed her dark eyes. "Why should I trust you not to lock me inside? You're a terrorist."

"Look, I saved your ass last night. You should show some gratitude," he said, still kneeling next to Jesse. Some of the heat packs had slipped off her stomach, and he was picking them up and replacing them.

"Mr. Vanya saved my posterior while you lurked in the shadows wearing that stupid ski mask like some amateur television burglar." She raised her eyebrows.

"What did you tell the cops about last night?" Jack asked, rubbing Jesse's other hand.

"I told them the truth, of course." She crossed her arms over her chest and stared down at him. "What did you tell them, Max?"

"Who's Max?" Jesse asked in a sleepy voice, as she opened her beautiful cerulean eyes.

"You're awake. How do you feel?" He smiled down at her. "Can you sit? We've got to get out of here." Placing his hand on her back, he helped her sit up. "Hey, Beagle Girl, get some hot water in one of those beakers."

"Beagle Girl?" Jesse asked, rubbing her eyes. Hot packs dropped off her limbs and plopped into piles around her recumbent body.

"Remember what I told you about those Danish fishermen." Samantha returned with a beaker of steaming water and handed it to him. "Make sure she drinks it very slowly. You don't want to cause ventricular fibrillation."

"I know." Jack held the beaker to Jesse's lips and she sipped the warm water. "There, feel better?"

"I feel prickly all over," she said softly.

"That's to be expected," Samantha said. "As your skin warms, you may experience a tingling sensation. It will pass."

"Here, have another sip," Jack said, holding the beaker to Jesse's lips. "I hate to rush you, but we've got to get out of here." He stood up and held his hand out.

"Can you stand?"

He almost cried when she gazed up at him, pale white skin, sleepy blue eyes, chattering teeth. "Come on, Cowgirl, let's get you home to bed."

She reached up and took his hand, and he lifted her upright then pulled her into an embrace. Holding her around the waist, he turned her around and guided her to the door.

"Wait here. Don't move." He propped Jesse against the wall. "Samantha, hold on to her. I'll be right back."

He jogged back into the freezer to retrieve his duffle bag. He stopped and stared at the corpse. He walked over to it, knelt beside it, and tried to close the lids on its dead eyes. Professor Granowski had been a fine scientist, even if, according to Jesse, she "tortured" animals; and, even if she'd kicked him out of her research group his first year in Medical School for being a smart mouthed twat.

He looked around for something to use to cover the contorted face for Samantha's sake. As he pulled the towel from his bag and gently placed it over her purple face, he thought of Sara Shaner. He shuddered and took a deep breath.

With his duffle in one hand, he jogged back out into the lab and slid to a stop by the door. Samantha was steadying Jesse as she swayed back and forth on unsteady feet. With his free hand, he grabbed Jesse's slack arm and dragged her staggering along.

When he kicked at the lab door to open it with his foot, a red light flashed from the security screen. He dropped the duffle, took White's ID badge from his pocket, and scanned it. Jesse was leaning against the door and fell forward when he kicked it open. He caught her by the arm then took her by the hand and led her out into the hallway. Using his foot, he shoved the duffle through the heavy door. Suddenly alert, Jessica grabbed the ID badge out of his hand and stared at it with wide eyes.

As he turned to pick up his bag, he called back, "Hey, Beagle Girl, did you call 911?"

"Aren't you taking her to the hospital?" she asked, standing near the freezer, arms still akimbo.

"Samantha, I'm serious. You have to call the police." Jack grabbed Jessica's elbow with his free hand then shouted over his shoulder, "Look in the freezer. Professor Granowski's dead."

Chapter Eleven

JESSICA YANKED HER elbow away from Jack's hand and zigzagged into the hallway on her own steam. When she recognized the sly smile on the ID badge, she grabbed it out of Jack's hands.

"Hey, that's him!" She stared at the photo. Wavy black hair, deep blue eyes, fine pale skin, and lush ruby lips upturned into a cunning smile. "This is the guy who fed me that fiery Slammer at O'Toole's last night. The dickhead intern who dumped me behind the dumpster."

"What? Max White? Are you sure?" Jack narrowed his eyes and shook his head. "He may be a dickhead, but he's not a rapist. More like an arrogant slacker with a deep dish sense of entitlement."

"You know him?" She threw the badge at him, and it bounced off his chest onto the floor.

Jack snatched the badge up and tucked it into his jacket pocket. "Come on. We've gotta get out of here before the cops show up. Unless you want a rap sheet instead of a Ph.D."

"I hope that creep's not a friend of yours." She stomped her boot on the tile floor for emphasis. She slipped and

Jack caught her. "What happened to me back in the freezer? Why was I on the floor in the lab? I feel kind of queasy."

"You're suffering from moderate hypothermia. You'll be okay if we get outta here and get you hydrated. That is, if we don't get caught and Beagle Girl doesn't spill the beans."

"Beagle girl?"

"That girl back in the lab. I met her last night. I'll tell you about it later. Come on. One foot in front of the other, Cowgirl." Jack tried to take her hand again, and she slapped it away.

She heard the telltale ding of an elevator, followed by walkie-talkie screeching, and scrambled through the nearest door, the men's bathroom. Jack was close on her heels as she burst inside the bathroom. Glaring at her partner in crime, she whispered, "Now what, Jackass?"

"Nature calls." Jack dropped his duffle next to a urinal, turned to face it, and unzipped his jeans. "I wonder what Beagle Girl will tell the cops."

Jessica turned around to face the stalls so she wouldn't have to watch him peeing. Her whole body was shaking, even her eyeballs. "I don't feel so good," she said.

"You're still in shock from the hypothermia. It should pass when your body temperature normalizes," he said, unzipping his bomber jacket. He came at her arms open wide. "I'll warm you up."

"I'm fine. Leave me alone. And wash your hands."

"We'd better get out of here before all hell breaks loose."

"What do you mean?"

"Well, about now, those walkie-talkies are going to be reporting a dead body." Jack shuddered. "Remember, Professor Granowski, your bunkmate from the freezer?"

"Holy crap!" Jessica's face was burning and her stomach was churning. "You mean that purple lady? Oh my God, she was dead. That's why she didn't want to… I remember now. I was dreaming I was in Montana." She fell back against the wall next to the urinals.

"Be quiet." Jack ordered. "Listen, do you hear anybody in the hall?" He crept over to the bathroom door, leaned his ear against it, and then opened it a crack before peeking out into the corridor. "The coast is clear. Let's get out of here before the shit storm hits."

Jessica skated down the hall after him, slid around the corner, and skidded to a stop in front of the elevators. Jack-ass was already inside holding the door open for her. As the doors shut, she heard a man shouting down the hall, "Hey you. Stop!"

She pushed all of the elevator buttons.

"Why'd you do that? It will just slow us down."

"Sorry, thought it would throw them off our scent."

As the door opened on every floor, like her mom in a slot machine tournament, Jessica jammed on the close door button. When the door opened on the third floor, Jack jumped out.

"We'll hide in my cubicle. Come on." He grabbed her hand and jerked her out of the dark elevator into an expansive blast of sunlight that penetrated the huge floor to ceiling windows. Blinded, she shielded her eyes with one hand, while Jack dragged her through a fancy reception area with the other.

"Quit pulling me," she said, jerking her hand away. She gawked around at the bamboo floors, leather chairs, and posh lamps neatly arranged into a sitting area. "Wow, fancy."

She followed Jack to the double glass doors at the end of a corridor and watched as he dug his wallet out of his back jeans pocket, fetched his own ID card, slid it into a slot on the door lock, and popped the door open. She'd never visited his cubicle in the Med School's sleek office suite and was surprised by its swanky mahogany furniture and ritzy glass interior.

"Figures," she said as he led her past rows of high-end modular desks separated by elegant white panels. Even on Thanksgiving, some of the cubicles were occupied by various sizes and shapes of bespectacled geeks staring at computer screens. "You scientists are living high on the hog while we poor humanists get your table scraps." She rolled her eyes. "Figures."

Gesturing her into a cubbyhole, Jack stopped in front of what had to be the messiest workspace in the entire suite.

"Wow, and I thought I was a slob," she said, surveying stacks of fat medical books, well-worn journals, paper scraps and note pads, not to mention crusty fast-food wrappers. "Look at this rat's nest!" She swiped her arm across the seat of his chair, sending a dirty sweatshirt, a couple of ballpoint pens, and a Styrofoam container to join the rest of the crap on the floor then she slumped into the seat.

"I'm still dizzy," she said, crossing her arms on top of the pile of books on his desk to cradle her head.

"I'll get you a cup of tea. Don't go anywhere. I'll be back in a flash." She peeked around the corner of the compartment and saw Jack hightailing to the back of the office and disappearing into what must be the kitchen. Curious to see the rest of his digs, she tiptoed after him. An arm reached out from one of the cubicles, grabbed her, and pulled her inside.

"I thought it was you." His deep whisper vibrated along her spine. "What are you doing here, Jessica James?"

She almost puked when she realized she was face to face with the rapist intern from last night. She tried to meet his fierce gaze, but ashamed, she glanced down at her boots. "What did you do to me?" she demanded, yanking her arm out of his grip.

"Do to you? Nothing," he said. "I tried to find you after you said you wanted to get some fresh air, but you disappeared."

"What do you mean?" When she looked up into his eyes, she noticed his pupils had dilated into black discs eclipsing his deep blue irises. She stared into his cubicle at the flat surface of his sparsely covered desk.

"Don't you remember?" He asked. She looked over at him as dimples framed his mouth.

"All I remember is you buying me a drink and then waking up behind a dumpster at the Old Prentice construction site." Tears welled in her eyes, but she fought the urge to cry.

"Dumpster?" He quit smiling and put his hands on her shoulders. "Whiskey, Tango, Foxtrot. What do you mean?"

"Get your paws off me and tell me what you did to me last night." She jerked her torso away.

"Okay, okay. Calm down." He troubled the thick gold ring on his pinky finger. "We were having a drink and talking about my research. Do you remember that?"

She shook her head.

"Well, you started feeling unwell and said you needed some fresh air. I asked you to wait until I got back from the bathroom, but when I came back, you were gone. I looked for you outside, then I waited with your stuff for another hour. Eventually, I just gave up and went home." He looked genuinely concerned. "The bartender said you left with some other guy."

She softened her stance and considered what he'd said. Truth was, she didn't remember anything after the Fireball Slammer or Hammer or whatever that stinger was called.

"Where did you go? Why did you leave the bar? I thought we were having a great conversation." He gazed down at her, blue eyes blazing, and stroked his chin.

"So, you didn't drug me, assault me, and drop me behind a dumpster?" Her mind was galloping faster than a quarter horse.

"Are you kidding me? That's a serious accusation. In fact, it's pretty darned offensive." His eyes narrowed into a piercing stare.

"Sorry. I just thought... Never mind." Embarrassed, Jessica turned on her heels.

"Wait. Don't go. Please." He stepped out of his cubicle and stood in her path. "I could show you my fluorescent mice," he said. Despite her fears, she turned around. When he smiled at her, his perfect white canines sparked a deep inarticulate desire in her belly.

"Your mice have taken a holiday." Jack's voice came from behind her. Startled, she turned back around again to see him standing there holding two steaming cups. "Smooth-talking Dr. White, chatting up pretty girls as usual?"

"Stoner Jack Grove to the rescue, eh? Why don't you

give it a rest Jackoff." The mercurial intern, med student, or whatever he was, had completely changed his tone from seductive snake luring her into his lair to aggressive ape pounding his chest at a rival.

"Where'd you two meet?" Jessica asked as she stepped out into to the corridor.

"Last quarter in Genetic Mutations, I watched White stick his nose so far up Dr. Dude's ass his head disappeared." Jack handed a warm mug to Jessica then reached into his jacket pocket. "Oh, by the way, Max, I found this on the floor at O'Toole's last night." He flicked the ID badge onto White's neat desk. "You should be more careful, my friend."

Max White scooped the badge up off of the desk and smiled.

"Thanks, man. I was wondering where that went." He clipped it onto the lapel of his white lab coat and looked at her. "Jackoff is just jealous because now I'm running Dr. Manly's clinic."

"Playing Frankenstein isn't my game, White. I prefer giving psychotropic drugs to criminals and releasing their creativity." Jack held out the other cup to Max White. "Would you like some tea, or do you prefer something with more of a bite? Like rat poison perhaps?"

White narrowed his eyebrows. "That's right, while Dr. Manly and I are trying to perfect the human race, you're unleashing the potential of the criminal mind. Someday, doctors like us will make forensic psychiatry a thing of the past. Then, you'll be out of a job, Jackoff."

"Yeah, right. You think with your Onco-mouse you can eliminate evil in the world? Just because you can engineer a knockout and give it cancer doesn't mean shit. You think you can control genetics? Hubris, sheer hubris." Jack's face reddened and he shook his head.

"What's a knockout?" Jessica asked.

"We can knock out target genes by modifying embryonic stem cells. Or we can create transgenetic mice by pronuclear injection…"

"Yeah, yeah," Jack interrupted. "He either gives the little bastards cancer using transgenetic injections or he knocks out tumor resistant cells. Either way, the mice are buggered. The irony is no matter what White takes out or puts into an embryo, it's going to have to be born and eventually die. That's the bottom line. There's no evading the maternal womb or the grim reaper."

"Objection, evasion, joyous distrust, and love of irony are signs of health; everything absolute belongs to pathology," Jessica said under her breath.

"*Beyond Good and Evil*," Jack responded, playing their game name-that-Nietzsche-quote. "Speaking of evil, what did you put in Jesse's drink last night, asshole?"

"Good and evil are merely a matter of genetics. Once we crack…"

"That day will never come, my friend." Jack pushed past his rival, sat down at White's desk, and slammed the steaming cup onto it, sending hot tea splashing onto the computer screen.

"You're a mess, Jackoff." Max White took a blue crepe towel out of his scrubs' pocket and threw it at Jack. "It's really none of your business, but I've already explained to Jessica what happened at O'Toole's last night. I'm not one of the bad guys, remember?" He smiled at Jessica.

"The noble soul reveres itself," Jack said, wiping at the computer screen.

"The noble soul is nothing more than good genes," Max White said smiling.

"Who's to say what's noble?" Jessica jumped in. "You get to decide what makes one person better than another? I wasn't convinced last night, and I'm still not convinced. You can't breed morality or goodness."

"I can breed mice who are docile and share their food," Max White said. "I can even breed mice who go without food to save others that need it more."

"Playing around with genetics is a dangerous business." Jack stood up. "You have no clue what you've bred in, or out, of those altruistic mice, no clue how it will affect them in the future."

"Why leave our fate to evolution when we can perfect ourselves. Why take a chance when we can be sure...."

"There's no such thing as a sure thing," Jessica interrupted. "Except maybe in poker, and even then you can be bluffed. Only a fool thinks he can master life."

"Your precious Nietzsche believed in a superman who would master himself. That's what we're doing in Dr. Manly's lab, mastering the human genome."

It made her teeth hurt when people used Nietzsche to justify a master race. "You're talking about eugenics, not self-overcoming, and we know where that leads." She pointed her finger at the computer screen as if it were to blame. "Jack's right. You're playing God."

"There is no God, only science," Max White said.

"That may be, but there's more to science than codes

and equations," Jack said, turning on his heels and stomping back toward his cubicle.

"Jack's right. The mind can't be reduced to the brain." She downed the rest of her cold tea, and when she slammed the cup on White's spotless desk, he scowled and reached over to slide a paper towel between the mug and the desk.

"Sorry," Jessica said, picking up her cup and standing to go.

"Come on, Jessica, don't leave in a huff. Stay." He gave her a weak smile. "Even Nietzsche said God is dead. So we're just taking up the slack."

"Nietzsche is right. God is dead, and we've killed him. Now when everything gets all screwed up, we'll have no one else to blame but ourselves." Jessica turned to go but stopped when White put his hand on her arm.

"Really, I hope you're not angry. There's no reason to take it personally. Can't we agree to disagree? Maybe over coffee?"

"I suppose in your sci-fi future, there won't be any disagreements once you knock out the right genes. For now, my disagreeable boot-cut jeans fit me just fine." She raised her eyebrows and tightened her lips.

"On that point, we agree," he said smiling.

Jessica's face burned. Flustered, she headed back toward Jack's fetid nest. When she reached his cubicle, she plopped into the chair, leaned her head back, and sighed. "How long before it's safe to leave the building?" she asked, peeking up at Jack.

"There's so much turmoil in the lab by now that probably no one will notice if we leave. Anyway, we should leave soon before they put the building on lock-down," Jack said, leaning against a partition.

She looked up at him, "If I didn't leave O'Toole's with you or with Max White, who did I leave with? And how are we going to find him?"

PART II

CHAPTER TWELVE

OLGA DAVIS SNEAKED a peek at her cellphone under the table and read the text: "We're ready for you at the clinic. Get here within the hour."

"Excuse me," she said to her Sunday luncheon guests. "Apologies, but I'm not feeling well, so…" Olga dabbed at her lips with her napkin then discreetly slipped her phone into her Armani jacket's hidden pocket. As she left the formal dining room, she avoided making eye contact with her husband seated at the head of the table. He'd be furious. Her hospitality and "charm" were supposed to be helping him close a million-dollar deal with the Coates brothers. John and Harris Coates had already devoured a tin of Olma Beluga Sturgeon caviar and their trophy wives had downed two bottles of Dom Perignon.

She hurried through the kitchen, heels tapping on the tile floor. Once out of earshot of the dining room, she retrieved the phone from its secret pocket and called her chauffeur.

"Pick me up behind the greenhouse in twenty minutes. Don't let anyone see you," Olga whispered into the phone.

"Understood," replied the deep voice. José would do anything for her.

She took the service elevator to the third floor, snuck through the servants' quarters and out onto the landing. Glancing down at the foyer two floors below, she tiptoed on the marble floor until she reached her dressing room.

She threw off her heels, rummaged through her closet, and changed into a black velour tracksuit, and leather platform sneakers, and wrapped a gray chiffon scarf over her blonde chignon.

She wriggled her fingers into gray leather gloves, and snatched a pair of oversized sunglasses from her dressing table for good measure. Olga opened her coat closet and petted her favorite mink, but thought better of it, and chose a long fur-lined black leather coat with a matching black leather purse instead.

Checking the hallway to make sure none of the servants were lurking about, Olga hurried to the end of the hall and the door to Ronald's study.

Looking around first, she slipped inside, and quietly closed the door behind her. She fingered the Visconti fountain pens in their gold case until she found the black and gold "forbidden city." She screwed off its cap and tapped a small key into her gloved hand. Holding the key between her thumb and forefinger, she turned it in the tiny lock to the top drawer of Ronald's desk. She slid the drawer open and felt around for a release latch to open the secret compartment.

One wooden slat on the drawer's side levered open to reveal a small plate, engraved with three numbers. She removed the plate, memorized the numbers, and then flipped it over to read the complicated instructions.

Olga froze when she heard noises from the hallway. She waited until the familiar sound of Maria's heels tapping on the marble floor had receded then walked across the study to a row of bookcases filled with boring books about business and tax laws.

She ran her hand along the inside edge of the center shelf until she heard a click. Gently, she drew the bookcase toward her. It popped out and slid in front of its neighbor to reveal a black steel door with a shiny silver tumbler in its center. She'd never broken into her husband's safe before. She'd never needed to. He'd given her everything she'd ever wanted... well almost everything. He showered her with expensive jewelry and designer clothes, but kept a tight grip on his cash.

Now with the family fortune in the balance, Ronald blamed her for not producing an heir. Her ogre father-in-law already had three granddaughters by Ronald's first and second wives but was demanding a grandson.

Olga followed the instructions on the plate, slowly turning the tumbler in one direction and then the other, two rotations to the left, stop, three rotations to the right, stop. She felt each number click into place. Carefully, she pressed down on the handle and opened the safe. As if a wasp from her garden had flown out at her, she jumped back when she saw it. Why did Ronald have a gun? Moving closer, she lifted the corners of manila envelopes, trying not to disturb the gun. Where did he keep the cash?

When she peered into the safe, she spied a metal box at the very back, and slid it out, careful not to move anything else. She tried the latch on the box, but it was locked. *Damn.* She thought she'd worked out everything, but she hadn't counted on yet another lock. If only Ronald wasn't so tight with his money.

She sat down on one of the high-backed leather chairs near the fireplace and stared down at the box on her lap. A four-letter combination lock stared back at her. *Double Damn.* Ronald would be looking for her soon.

Hopefully, he wouldn't think to look in here. His study was the one place in the house she wasn't allowed to enter, or so he said. The tiny cylinder had four rows of letters. She tried her name, OLGA. No luck. She tried it again just to make sure. What other four-letter word might he use? Although nobody called him Don, she tried DOND, and various other versions of the letters in his name. He didn't allow any pets in the house, and as far as she knew, he'd never had one. What else might he use as a combination?

A light bulb went off, and she dialed in INGE, his mistress, Miss Sweden. The box sprung open and inside she found a neat stack of bills wrapped in mustard colored $10,000 currency straps. She grabbed five straps, stuffed them into her purse, and closed the box.

She put the box back in the safe, returned the plate to the secret compartment in the desk drawer, dropped the tiny key back into the top of the pen, and tiptoed to the study door. She cracked it open and peeked into the hallway. When she saw it was empty, she exited the study, secured the door behind her, and then took the back stairs down to the kitchen.

Olga left the house through the back door. Heart pounding, she forced herself to walk at a normal pace across the garden to the greenhouse. She opened the glass door and stepped inside her own tropical paradise. She inhaled the scent of Madagascar Jasmine and Brugmansia Trumpet, picked a few dried petals off the Butterfly Ginger, and stopped to mist the Bamboo Orchid before exiting the glass conservatory through the back door. When her driver saw her, he jumped out of the car and opened the back door of the shiny black sedan.

"Where to, Mrs. D? The usual?" he asked as he settled back into the driver's seat.

"Yes. Thank you, José." Olga opened the bottle of water waiting for her in the cup holder, took a sip, and then settled back into the soft leather seat and closed her eyes for the short journey from Chicago's Gold Coast to the hospital. She'd have to make up some story to tell Ronald to explain why she ran out of his precious luncheon, even though she did it for him.

Ronald's father couldn't have made it any plainer. Whoever produced a male heir first would inherit the family fortune, along with the political dynasty. She'd already tried fertility teas brewed with Black Cohosh and Dong Quai, months of acupuncture with burning Moxa, and endured several rounds of Clomiphene and its nauseating side effects. She'd thought she had more time, but when Ronald's brother Daniel got married last summer, she knew the race was on.

Even if she had gotten pregnant the old fashioned way, there was a good chance she carried the Tye-Sachs gene, a death sentence for any baby. She thought of her sister. Poor little Anna, locked up in that institution in Kiev until her tiny broken body had given out at age five. She blocked the image of Anna from her mind. She couldn't afford to think about her sister; she had to get to the clinic and finally get through the ordeal.

By the time the limo pulled into the clinic's back entrance, Olga had worked herself into a full-blown panic attack. She tapped a little yellow tablet out of a pearl encrusted pillbox, popped it into her mouth, took a deep breath, and waited for José to open the car door. She held onto the handle of her Gucci purse, now bulging with cash, and scurried to the back entrance.

She recognized Doctor Manly's handsome young assistant waiting just inside the glass vestibule. His blue scrubs offset his vibrant eyes and reminded Olga of the first time she'd met her husband. She'd been modeling during Junior Fashion Week in New York and literally ran into Ronald on the stairs leading to the stage. He'd taken her hand and guided her up the steps. His piercing blue eyes and graceful practiced manners caught her in his web and now there was no escape.

"Where's Doctor Manly?" Olga asked, troubling the edge of her scarf between her thumb and forefinger. "I thought he would perform the procedure himself. I specifically asked for him."

"Not to worry, Mrs. Smith," the bright young doctor said. "I've performed this operation hundreds of times. It's very straightforward. Of course, Doctor Manly prepared the implants. But since it's time sensitive, and you insisted on discretion, and rightfully so…." He gestured for her to follow him.

"We'll use the back entrance. Don't worry, Mrs. Smith, discretion is our priority. Our clients' identities are sacred to us." He held the door open, and she stepped out into a brightly lit antiseptic foyer. She'd forgotten she'd used the name Smith. She couldn't let Ronald find out, or anyone else for that matter. It would ruin her reputation, destroy her husband's career, and insure that her sister-in-law would beat her to the pot of gold.

"Can I at least see Janet? Dr. Granowski?" Olga asked. "She's been overseeing my case along with Dr. Manly." She glanced around the deserted clinic, not another soul in sight. The doctors must go to extreme lengths to keep VIP clients' secrets, like when the President visited the Vatican and they cleared out the tourists, or Bergdorf Goodman closed down so Taylor Swift could buy a dress.

"I'm afraid Dr. Granowski is indisposed. And we don't want to miss our window of opportunity, do we? This way please."

"Can I at least talk with Dr. Granowski? I'm a little nervous, and I'd feel better if I could talk to her before the procedure." Olga had met Janet Granowski at a fundraiser for reproductive health. She'd convinced Ronald to donate by telling him it was a prolife organization.

Luckily, he didn't pay much attention to her charitable causes; as long as she had some to make him look more compassionate to his shareholders and his future constituency whenever his father handed his senate seat over to Ronald. Olga and Janet had gotten along right away, and through their friendship, she'd learned about Northwestern Memorial Hospital's fertility clinic.

"Don't be nervous, Mrs. Smith. I'm happy to answer any questions about the procedure." The attractive doctor led her down a hallway to a lounge. "Please make yourself comfortable. I'll be right back." The small immaculate waiting room was equipped with a Swiss Jura Impressa coffee maker, an illuminated glass refrigerator filled with sleek bottles of Voss Artesian water, and a basket of individually wrapped French chocolate truffles. The soft lighting and ivory divans put her in mind of a spa she'd visited last summer in Bali.

Olga removed her leather driving gloves one finger at a time, then took off her sunglasses and scarf and dropped them on a glass end table. She helped herself to a bottle of water and tried to relax on one of the sofas. Leaning her head back against the cool leather, she closed her eyes and sighed. It would be over soon. Ronald and his family would have their damned heir, and she would have done her duty. She just hoped it didn't hurt too much.

In twenty-seven years, she'd never had surgery or been in a hospital, except to visit her baby sister. Olga sipped her water and watched the door, waiting for someone to come back for her. After a few minutes, the young doctor appeared in the doorway wearing his blue scrubs, complete with a blue paper hat and blue booties over his shoes.

"Come with me," he said, gesturing into the hallway.

"Is it usual to do this on Sundays with the clinic deserted? What if something happens during the procedure?" Olga asked nervously.

"Don't worry, Mrs. Smith. I've done this hundreds of times. Why you could do it at home with a turkey baster." He smiled.

"Won't there even be a nurse?" Olga asked.

"Remember, Mrs. Smith, you're the one who requested absolute privacy. This way, we insure your privacy. In here please." He opened a door to an examination room. "Please undress and put on that gown on the table. It opens and ties in the front. I'll step out, scrub up, and be back in a few minutes."

Olga slipped out of her jacket, jeans, and blouse then removed her panties and bra. She stood barefoot, shivering as she put on the paper gown. She tied the gown in front, then spotted a towel dispenser over the sink and took a towel to wipe off her moist palms. She could feel the blood coursing through her veins, and it was getting difficult to breathe. She sat on the table and waited.

The doctor returned and backed through the door pulling a cart behind him. Olga's heart leapt. The first thing she saw was a giant needle sealed in plastic lying on the blue medical paper. The cart also held latex gloves sealed in plastic, various sized sealed pads, a gleaming metal speculum, and several vials filled with clear liquid.

"Please lay back on the table and put your feet in the stirrups, Mrs. Smith. This won't take long." The doctor's smile looked practiced and false.

Olga slid back on the exam table, tentatively lifted her legs, and placed a foot in each stirrup. She instinctively clenched her knees together and stared up into the blinding fluorescent lights.

"Would you like a tranquilizer, Mrs. Smith? I could give you a tiny injection of valium."

"That would be nice."

She watched as the doctor used a small syringe to suck fluid out of a glass vial. Thank God it wasn't the big one.

"Please scoot your bottom to the very end of the table," the doctor said. "You'll feel a tiny prick as I inject the medicine into your thigh." The alcohol pad was cool as he wiped her thigh, pinched her skin between his gloved fingers, and stuck the needle into her flesh. Within seconds, a golden warmth flowed over her entire body and some of her anxiety melted away. The doctor put a gloved hand on each of her knees to spread them apart. Olga took a deep breath then closed her eyes.

"I'm inserting the speculum now," the doctor said, prying open her privates with his latex fingers. "It may feel cool." She gritted her teeth as the doctor clamped the cold metal instrument into place. "Now, I'm inserting a tiny rod to begin to dilate your cervix. You may feel a slight cramping sensation, but it should pass. As your cervix muscle relaxes, I will insert a slightly larger rod until the opening is wide enough for the implantation."

Olga sucked in breath as a stabbing pain struck deep in her womb.

"That's right, breathe."

Each time he inserted a new rod, the cramping made her wince and whimper. After the third rod, she lifted herself up on her elbows and gave him a pleading look.

"Please lay back and try to relax. It's almost over. That was the worst part," he said, giving her a rehearsed reassuring smile. When he unsheathed the monster needle, inserted its sharp tip into one of the vials, and drew liquid into the syringe, she closed her eyes again, and wished she had the turkey baster option. Sucking in air, she concentrated on the sounds of the doctor's rustling gown, the buzzing fluorescent lights, and the clanking instruments.

"I'm inserting the implantation needle now. I've put all of the zygotes into one syringe, so we're almost done. There," he said. "All over. It wasn't that bad, was it?" The blood vessels throbbing in her ears drowned out the doctor's authoritative voice.

The doctor removed the speculum and draped a paper apron over her lap. "You did great. And, I have a surprise for you." Olga clamped her knees shut and sat up on her elbows again.

"What do you mean?" she asked. She didn't like surprises.

He held up two vials. One had a pink label with black letters FOX and the other had a blue label marked FOXY. "See, a boy for your husband, and a girl for you. And she will be a very special girl, we've made sure of that."

"What do you mean?" she asked again, confused.

He held one of the vials closer to her face. "F O X." He spelled out the letters. "Fertilized Ovua, with X chromosomes, female. A girl. And not just any girl, a brilliant feat of genetic engineering. Now let's hope your uterus welcomes her home."

"A girl." Olga whispered. She'd always wanted a little girl. Ronald would be furious.

CHAPTER THIRTEEN

JESSICA STARED AT her computer screen and sipped her Witches Brew tea from a chipped mug. It had been three weeks since the dumpster disaster, and it was time to pull herself together and get back to her research. The blinking cursor was mocking her, a tiny middle finger flashing against the expansive blank page of her dissertation. She took her phone from her jacket pocket and checked the time.

Lolita was ten minutes late. Usually her Russian friend had already slammed a couple of espressos by the time Jessica showed up.

She shut her computer, leaned back in the booth, and took in the lunch crowd, enjoying the low glow coming from the bakery case. Since she'd moved to the city, she'd missed coming to Blind Faith Café. Heartland was great, but nothing beat the desserts at Blind Faith. Jessica had already eaten two gluten-free Thumb Prints and had just ordered a piece of vegan carrot cake. She sipped her tea then closed her eyes and lost herself in the din of the diners, the savory smells from the kitchen, and the tang of the bitter brew washing away the sweetness of the cookie.

"Why if it isn't Jessica James." The baritone voice startled her. She bolted upright in time to see Max White scoot into the booth across from her.

"What are you doing here?" she asked.

"I was checking out some research the head of the biology department is doing on OR5A1, the olfactory gene." Max smiled and placed his smooth long-fingered hands on the table.

"Slumming it in Evanston? I thought you worked downtown." Jessica gathered up her computer and stuffed it into her backpack.

"What are you working on?" he asked, his eyes dancing, annoyingly charming.

"I'm supposed to be working on my dissertation." She took a bite of carrot cake then licked the vegan cream cheese frosting off her upper lip.

"I've told you about my research, now you tell me about yours." When he pushed a lock of black wavy hair out of his eyes, a shiver galloped up her spine. She didn't trust him as far as she could throw him, but he certainly was a very pretty boy.

She rolled her eyes. "If you insist. I'm writing on Nietzsche's influence on the Blue Riders, the Russian and German Expressionists just after the turn of the twentieth century."

"You mean Kandinsky and Franz Marc, that crowd?"

"You know about the Blue Riders?" *Who was this guy?* Jessica stared across the booth and marveled at the contrast between his pale skin, black hair, and blue eyes. "I thought you just dissected frogs and spliced genes, Jurassic Park kind of stuff."

"Well the Art Institute is just a couple of blocks away from our lab and the Clinic. So, when I need a break, I wander over there and check out an exhibit. In fact, there's a Paul Klee retrospective showing now. Have you seen it?" he asked.

She felt her face flush. This biologist dude was more up on the local art scene than she was. "Yes, I saw it when it opened last week." She hoped he didn't call her bluff.

"Did you have a favorite?" he asked.

"All of his work is so great. It's hard to say. I need to go back and spend more time…"

"My favorite Klee is *Flower Myth*," he interrupted. "It looks like he painted it with blood. In fact, in a way he did." He gave her a sly smile.

"What do you mean?"

"Like all great artists, Klee's talent and genius was in his genes."

"Okay, Dr. Frankenstein, is that what you do in your clinic?" Jessica asked, only half joking. "Breed geniuses?"

"What we do in the Clinic is top secret." Max winked at her. "Actually, it's a fertility clinic specializing in IVF using both ovum and sperm donations. But, most of our clients prefer anonymity."

"Like test tube babies?"

"Actually, we use a Petri dish. But, yes. Eggs are collected using follicular aspiration, then we inject sperm and when the fertilized eggs divide, we implant the embryos." He smiled.

"How much does that cost?"

"A lot."

"So, you cater to rich women who can afford designer

babies to match their designer outfits?" Jessica tipped up the teapot and drained the last drops of Witches Brew into her cup.

"Our clinic isn't just about our clients. It's about our genetic research. Anyway, the clients can afford it."

Jessica put her elbows on the table, leaned closer, and whispered, "Like who?"

Max wagged his finger at her. "Uh, uh. Doctor patient confidentiality."

"So do these rich ladies get to choose from a menu or how does it work?" she asked. "Why don't they just get pregnant the old fashioned way?" She blushed. "By having sex. Or they could adopt."

"We're offering new and improved pregnancy. Most of our clients need assisted reproduction to conceive. Usually one of the partners is infertile or both partners are of the same sex. And some people just want to control the outcome. We can engineer for hair and eye color and some other physical attributes with pretty good accuracy, obviously we can select for sex. We use negative eugenics to eliminate diseases and birth defects. But most clients also want high I.Q.s, attractive features, and agility."

"Positive eugenics?" Jessica rolled her eyes.

"Exactly." Max smiled.

Jessica's pulse quickened, and she geared up for another fun debate about genetics. "I'd bet my life you couldn't engineer someone who could paint like Paul Klee. Even if genetics is a mathematical equation, there are all sorts of variables you can't predict or control."

"But why leave to chance what we can control?"

"By control, you mean weeding out people with

disabilities." Jessica knew she had him now and thrust her mental dagger into the heart of his argument. "What would blind or deaf people think of your attempts to eliminate them from our evolutionary history? What makes a sighted or hearing person 'better'?" She made air quotes with her fingers. "Wouldn't it be better to change perceptions of disability?" She was working herself into a lather.

"If you could choose, would you choose to have a child with a disability?" Max asked.

"We all become disabled if we live long enough. You can't change that, or have you found a gene for immortality?"

"But don't you think parents have a moral obligation to select against disabilities if they can? We just give them the option, so they can make the right choice." Max smiled.

"I don't see how trying to control what can't be controlled has anything to do with morality. Sounds more like fantasy to me. Anyway, do you think Beethoven could have composed what he did if he hadn't been deaf?"

She slammed her empty mug on the table for emphasis. "And would Klee have become a great artist without drinking himself silly and screwing prostitutes? He was a wastrel living with his parents until he was almost thirty." She gloated. "Is that your idea of perfection? He died from a degenerative disease you would eliminate from his genetic code. But that part of the code might very well have held the key to his talent. Certainly, without the pain of his disease, he'd never have painted *Death and Fire…*"

"Yes," he interrupted, "but perhaps we'd have something even greater. If he'd lived, he could have painted even more masterworks." The twinkle was back in his deep blue eyes. "Hey, I have an idea. Since you're so keen on Klee, why don't we go see the exhibit again together? We can continue our discussion at the Art Institute while looking at the paintings. If you don't have any plans, we could even go this evening. The museum is open late on Fridays."

"Actually, I can't. I'm waiting for a friend." Luckily, she had an excuse; otherwise she might be tempted. She followed Max's gaze as it traveled across the room.

"Speak of the devil," she said. "There she is." She waved and Lolita sauntered over to the booth, turning heads as usual. Jessica scooted over and Lolita joined her in the booth, then kissed her on the cheek.

"Sorry I'm late. Cousin Vanya needed to talk," she said, glancing at Max. "I'll tell you about it later." She unwound a mink scarf from around her neck and let it drop onto the booth between them. Jessica picked it up and examined what she hoped was fake fur.

"This is Max White," Jessica said nodding. "The intern from O'Toole's."

Lolita narrowed her eyes and gave Jessica a questioning look. "*The* intern?"

Blushing, she shook her head then took another bite of cake.

"Let me get this straight." Lolita glared at Max. "You're having a tea party with the creep who drugged you, raped you, and dropped you behind a dumpster?"

Jessica choked on a bite of cake and grabbed her water to wash it down.

"Wait a second!" Max protested. "Not that again."

"You have thirty seconds to explain yourself, Mister, or I'll kick the shit out of you." Lolita's fierce sage eyes flashed rage.

"She's not joking," Jessica said, mouth full. "She's a black belt in karate."

"Look. This is crazy." Max played with his thick gold ring, twisting it around on his pinky finger. "I bought Jessica a drink. We talked. That's it. I admit that I find her very attractive and I thought the feeling was mutual." Jessica felt that tingling sensation running up her spine again and waited to hear more.

"I'm sorry about what happened to Jessica. It's terrible. If she would have just waited for me to come out of the men's room, it never would have happened. I was going to take her home. Scout's honor." He crossed his heart and held up two fingers.

"If you're lying, I'm going to kick your ass," Lolita said, flexing her fingers and balling her hands into fists.

"Dumpster Girls, that's what they're calling us," Jessica said.

Turns out two other Northwestern women woke up behind dumpsters near the hospital just days before she did. And in the weeks since Thanksgiving, three more girls reported similar attacks. All of them had been drinking in bars near the downtown campus, dumped behind dumpsters, their clothes neatly folded next to them. All of them were thin and blonde and pursuing advanced degrees, most of them medical students.

"Detective Cormier assumed it was a serial rapist until all the rape kits came back negative and physical exams showed no signs of force. Only those weird incisions…"

"Did you ever go to student health and have that checked out?" Lolita asked.

"Yeah, Mommy, I did," Jessica said. "They didn't know what to make of it either. All they saw was a tiny incision."

"If you ladies will excuse me," Max interrupted, "I've decided to get my sandwich to go." He swung his long legs out from under the table and stood up. "Jessica, if you want to see the Klee exhibit, I'll meet you at the entrance to the Art Institute tonight at 7:30. It was a pleasure to meet you, Lolita."

Jessica just nodded and continued eating her cake.

Max paused, then turned back to face the booth. "Lolita, are you a grad student at Northwestern, too?"

"She's an Honor's student." Jessica bragged.

"Brains, beauty, and a black-belt," Max said. "A geneticist's wet dream."

CHAPTER FOURTEEN

OLGA GARGLED TO get the sick taste out of her mouth. No doubt about it, she was pregnant.

She wiped her mouth on a monogramed bath towel, a wedding present from her mother-in-law. The IVF had worked. Ronald would be ecstatic. Hopefully her sister-in-law wouldn't beat her to the punch. She still had to carry the baby to term, and for all she knew, Sarah might be pregnant by now, too.

If her sister-in-law had a son before she did, then the old man's fortune, fame, and a political dynasty would go to him. Ronald had made it clear that if she couldn't deliver the goods, he'd find someone else who could. Of course, he never considered the possibility that he might be the deficit one.

As he constantly reminded her, his modeling agency had discovered her, a "poor street urchin" from the Ukraine, and he could "un-discover" her in a heartbeat. Within a month of bumping into him on the stairs at the Junior Fashion week, Ronald had divorced his super-model second wife and married Olga. Her life changed overnight. She went from wondering where she'd get her next meal to supervising formal dinners for Ronald's clients. He expected her to be a proper society wife and hired tutors in everything from English to cutlery. Luckily, she was a quick study. She had to be to survive.

Olga splashed her face with cool water and patted her hair back into place. Her driver would be there in fifteen minutes. She rushed to get out of her dressing gown and wriggled her skinny jeans over one leg at a time. Her favorite True Religion jeans weren't going to fit for much longer, so she might as well enjoy her flat tummy while she still could. She'd worked hard enough to keep it.

Riding through the slums of North Chicago reminded her of how far she'd come, and she didn't want to go back. For all his faults, thanks to Ronald, she'd never have to go back to selling her body in Kiev nightclubs. Her driver drove around to the back entrance to the Clinic.

The special entrance was shielded from view by brick walls, practically a fortress, designed to keep out paparazzi intent on stealing photographs of famous women with fertility problems then selling them to the highest bidder. What business was it of theirs? Those parasites were hard to shake, especially without Ronald's bodyguards along.

The sleepy clinic she had visited three weeks ago had since come to life. An attractive receptionist with collagen lips and a Botox forehead led her to the private waiting room. "Please make yourself comfortable, Mrs. Smith. Doctor Manly will be with you shortly. Help yourself to herbal tea and biscuits."

Olga made a cup of rose petal tea and wondered what exactly she *was* expecting. She hadn't thought about giving up her beloved cappuccinos every morning and her champagne flutes every night. She'd read that a little wine was actually good during pregnancy. But, of course, no more sneaking a cigarette in the green house with Maria. Maybe she should ask the doctor about tranquilizers. Ever since she'd learned about Ronald's affair, she'd been taking them whenever he was "working late," which was at least three times a week now.

The squeak of the door startled her, and she spilled tea down the front of her Escada blazer.

"Let me help you," the nurse said, rushing across the waiting room to get a cloth napkin from the counter. She opened the small refrigerator, took out a Perrier, twisted it open, and saturated the cloth over a tiny stainless steel sink. Hurrying back, she said, "We don't want any stains," then dabbed at Olga's jacket.

"Sorry to be so clumsy," Olga said. "Ever since I found out I'm finally pregnant, I haven't been myself."

"Pregnancy is a major change," the nurse said with a smile. "Please follow me, Mrs. Smith." She waved a long dark arm towards the hallway. "I'm Doctor Samantha Brewer. I'm a post-doc in Janet Granowski's lab. I'm taking over her clients. I'll be assisting Dr. Manly this afternoon." She extended her small hand and Olga shook it.

"Why you're so young, I thought you were a nurse." Olga laughed nervously and felt her cheeks get hot. Embarrassed, she wondered if the real reason she'd assumed the young lady was a nurse and not a doctor was because she was African American.

"I get that a lot," Dr. Brewer said.

Olga tiptoed down the hallway so her heels wouldn't tap on the wood floor. She followed Dr. Brewer past several closed doors with charts in racks on the walls next to them. The young doctor gestured her into the first open room. "Please have a seat in the chair, Mrs. Smith. The doctor should be with you soon. Do you need anything while you wait? Water, more tea?" Olga shook her head. The young doctor smiled and left, closing the door behind her.

Inside the exam room, a sterile hospital atmosphere replaced the ambiance of the pampering spa. Instead of wool carpet, soft lighting, and warm sconces, she was met with shiny linoleum, medicine cabinets, and of course, the dreaded stirrups.

Olga picked up a tattered copy of last month's *Vogue* and absent-mindedly flipped through the pages. She wondered if her child would grow up to look like one of these models. At least she wouldn't have to rely on her looks to save her from poverty. For all she knew, one of the attractive boys smoldering off the page could be her baby's father.

A rap on the door signaled Dr. Manly's arrival.

"Mrs. Smith," he said exuberantly. "Good to see you again." He shook her hand with a bit too much force for good manners.

"I told you I was a miracle worker." He smiled and with a grand sweep of his arm, gestured for her to move from the chair to the table. "Let's take a look at my handiwork, shall we?"

Olga climbed up onto the table and took a deep breath, hoping this exam would be over soon.

"Please remove your jacket," the doctor said. He took the stethoscope from around his neck and plugged it into his ears. "Take some deep breaths. Good. Now breathe normally." He slid the cold instrument down the front of her blouse. "Just a quick listen to your heart. Good." She noticed a thick gold bracelet around his wrist and the strong scent of musty cologne as he brushed his arm against her cheek.

"I'm going to do a sonogram to see how successful the implants were and how many took." He went to a drawer and retrieved a paper gown. "Please undress and put this on so it opens in the front. Dr. Brewer and I will be back in a few minutes." He handed her a large blue folded paper apron. "You can put this over your lap and have a seat on the table when you're ready." He patted her on the back. "I told you we'd fix you up."

"Dr. Brewer mentioned she's taking over Dr. Granowski's clients. Has Janet left the clinic?" Olga asked. "I haven't talked to her in weeks."

"Haven't you heard? Janet unexpectedly passed away. Terrible news. An accident in the lab." He took a neatly folded handkerchief from his jacket pocket and wiped his brow. "But don't worry. It won't affect you." He must have sensed the terror in her eyes because he patted her shoulder again adding, "It has been difficult on all of us. Janet and I were partners for five years. We moved here together from New York to open this clinic." He paused then gave her a bemused smile, but the twitching in his left eye made her uneasy. "Trust me, Mrs. Smith. You're in good hands. Mine to be exact. We'll be back to examine you." He left the room and closed the door.

Olga's mind was racing. She couldn't believe Janet was dead. An accident in the lab? What kind of accident? And how could Dr. Manly take it so lightly? After all, Janet was his wife, well, ex-wife. Maybe like most men, he was good at hiding his feelings. She tried to remember the last time she'd seen Janet Granowski. It was at the Hope Foundation benefit auction on Halloween weekend. That's when she told her about the affair and the divorce, and had said she'd be quitting the clinic within the year.

Now, Olga wondered. She looked around the exam room, the same one where Janet had performed the ultrasound confirming that her ovaries weren't producing in spite of the fertility drugs. That's when she told her about egg donation and IVF. She'd made it sound straight forward and simple. Now, it seemed strange and creepy. She had someone else's baby growing inside her. Whose baby was it really? Not hers or Ronald's.

Olga undressed down to her socks then slid the scratchy gown over her goose bumps. She knew gowns, and this flimsy swath of butcher paper was no gown. It was cold naked humiliation. She stepped up onto a metal stair, slid her bum up onto the waxy paper covering the exam table, unfolded the blue paper over her lap, and waited. The fine blonde hairs on her bare arms stood on end, and she rubbed one arm and then the other to warm up.

Her mind was as numb as her arms. Rattled, she slid down to fetch the magazine to take her mind off Janet and the stranger growing inside her womb. When she heard a rap on the door, she climbed back onto the table. The young African American doctor followed Doctor Manly into the room, and then shut the door behind her.

"This is Doctor Samantha Brewer," Doctor Manly said. "She's going to conduct the sonogram while I interpret. Please lay back on the table." The young doctor rolled a machine closer to the table and sat down on a chair next to it.

"I've warmed the gel, so hopefully it's not too cold." Olga looked into the pretty doctor's kindly brown eyes as she squirted gel in a figure eight onto Olga's abdomen. The gel was warm enough but the sensation of sticky wetness on her stomach was still unpleasant. Olga closed her eyes.

"I'll just be applying some pressure," Doctor Brewer said, then pushed the Doppler and rubbed it around above Olga's pelvis.

"Ah, there, see!" Doctor Manly exclaimed. Olga opened her eyes to see him pointing to some black and gray pulsating patterns on the screen. "One, two, three, four, five. Yes, looks like five zygotes have attached. That's fantastic. Am I good, or what?"

"What do you mean, five?" Olga asked in alarm. Eyes wide, she stared at the screen. But all she saw were wavy lines and a few black dots. "Five babies!" A wave of nausea swept over her and she squeezed her eyes tight. She couldn't have five babies. She wasn't an animal giving birth to a litter. It was unnatural.

"Yes, remember, Mrs. Smith, when I explained the procedure." the doctor said, putting a condescending hand on her shoulder. "We implant several zygotes because we want to ensure that at least one of them takes. And even better, in your case. We have five to choose from. All five are attached to the wall of your uterus: one girl and four boys. Now we can select the very best of the bunch to insure the healthiest, happiest baby."

"I can't have five babies!" Olga sat up on her elbows.

"You never told me there would be so many. Aren't there rules against that?"

"Unlike in Europe, assistive reproduction involving egg donation is unregulated here. We implant more embryos than we need, so selective reduction is a necessary evil…"

Dr. Manly scowled and interrupted his young assistant. "What Samantha, Dr. Brewer, is trying to say is now that there are five, we have a choice. Rather than leave your baby's health to nature or fate, we can choose the very best." He nodded his head in agreement with himself.

"What do you mean choose?" Olga asked, sitting up on her elbows.

"Selective reduction, Mrs. Smith," the doctor said, taking off his latex gloves and dropping them in the biohazard bin. "As I explained at our initial consultation, selective reduction is standard procedure with IVF. We choose the best zygote based on various factors, like lack of any obvious birth defects, for example. You can even choose to have twins if you like, one girl and one boy. A lot of women go that route. Two for the price of one!"

"And what about the other babies? The ones we don't choose," Olga asked.

"I've already told you, Mrs. Smith. Selective reduction." The doctor smiled down at her. "Nothing to it."

Her stomach churning, she asked, "You mean abortion?"

CHAPTER FIFTEEN

JESSICA CHECKED HER phone again. 6:35, ten minutes later than the last time she checked. She paced the length of her efficiency apartment, twelve steps to be exact. She'd tugged on her tight white jeans, her "trolling jeans," as her mom called them. Digging through a pile of clothes in a corner of the closet, she found her best Western shirt, azure with white piping and pearl snaps. It was Jack's favorite shirt. He said the color made her blue eyes pop. Underneath, she was wearing a nude thong and black pushup bra, not that he'd ever see them, of course. Purely for her own pleasure, she told herself.

She polished her ropers with a damp washcloth then put on her silver buckled belt and fringe jacket. She checked the mirror and combed her messy hair with her fingers to get some of the knots out. A brush would just make it worse. She licked her index finger and used it to smooth her eyebrows into place, and smiled at her reflection. Not perfect, but good as it was gonna get.

Her boots tapping on the hardwood floor, Jessica paced the length of her efficiency three more times, counting the steps as she went. She stopped in front of her closet. *Should she, or shouldn't she?* She looked at her phone: 6:45. If she was going, she'd better git.

It took ten minutes to walk to the station, a good half hour from Morse to Monroe on the red line, then another five or ten minute walk to the Art Institute. She grabbed her Trapper and parka and dashed out the door before she talked herself out of going.

As Jessica opened the heavy outside doors to the Sheridan Apartments, the wind barreled down the narrow courtyard and tore at her earflaps. Bracing herself, she pushed her way through the wind tunnel. She stepped out onto the sidewalk, then glanced up and down Sheridan Road.

To her left, Shiva Beauty Salon was lined with middle-aged ladies sitting under hairdryers, with foil hanging from their heads, magazines in their hands, and gossip on their lips. A sign on the door read, "3D Brow Micro-Blading, A Must." To her right, Sweet Magic's picture windows exhibited a radically different clientele, women sporting paisley yoga pants, crystal necklaces, and Starbuck's coffee cups. She chose direction "Micro-Blading" and hoofed it up Morse toward the "L" stop.

A full moon hung low in the evening sky and the brisk night air nipped at her cheeks. As she passed the Red Line Lounge, the strong smell of stale cigarettes and beer, accompanied by loud punk rock music, greeted her like an old friend. She climbed the stairs to the elevated platform and waited for the southbound train.

When the train arrived at the station, arms pinned to her sides, she squeezed into the bottleneck of folks boarding through the sliding door, hopped over the gap, and zigzagged through the winter coats, to the back of the train.

She stood holding onto a steel pole for support as the train pulled out of the station. Lights blurred by as it picked up speed. "Loyola," "Granville," "Thorndale," an automated voice announced the familiar names. When the Purple and Brown Line Express trains whizzed by on either side, Jessica felt queasy. She closed her eyes until they passed.

The lights of the city were getting closer. She marveled at the view of the skyline, dotted with monster cranes. Then after the stop for Wrigley Field, the train descended underground. *Whoosh.* The rattling and shaking of trains battling wind above ground subsided. Below ground the subway's even rhythm made her sleepy, and she leaned her head against the pole.

"Monroe," the voice announced. Jessica fought through the throng to get off the train before the doors closed and she was trapped. Stepping off the train, she moved to the center of the platform to get her bearings.

Bright red signs overhead contrasted with the deep blue of the tunnel walls. She reached inside her parka and took her phone from her jacket pocket and snapped a picture of the symmetrical pillars framed by the contrasting colors. A crusty old man scowled at her as he passed in front of her view.

Now that she had her land-legs back, she exited on State Street, and hiked towards Adams Street, a straight shot to the Art Institute. Clutching her phone in her gloved hand, she tapped it for the time. The black screen was unresponsive. Navigating the crowded sidewalk, she tugged at a finger of her glove with her teeth, holding tight to her phone with her other hand. Glove hanging from her mouth, she strode

down Adams, and maneuvered her thumb over the button
then glanced at her phone, 7:32. She was late.

She looked up just in time to avoid crashing into a
hotdog truck, stopped short, tucked her phone into her
pocket, skirted the wagon, and picked up her pace. Winded,
she bounded up the museum steps to the entrance, glancing
to admire the red-bowed evergreen wreaths forming ferny
manes around the necks of two verdigris lions on either side
of the entrance.

Outside the institutional stone building could have
been a bank, but inside was another world, sleek, modern,
and bright. Jessica glanced around the mob in the reception area. She removed her parka and tied its arms around
her waist, then got in line, pulled her wallet from her back
pocket, and removed her student ID. Shuffling her feet, she
inched along toward the ticket counter, one section of the
middle segment of a long centipede.

Staring at a giant banner of the institute's most famous
painting, Grant Wood's *American Gothic*, she wondered if
those were some of the people Max White would eliminate
from the human race if he could, the weather-worn staff of
life in America's bread basket, simple farmers armed with
pitch-forks and pretentious gothic architecture. She chuckled, remembering that the model for the mean-faced man
of the incestuous couple was the artist's dentist.

"You came!" the deep voice behind her caught her off
guard. "I didn't think you would."

She'd never seen Max White out of scrubs. No longer a
soap opera star playing a doctor on TV, now he was dressed
in black jeans, black shirt, and gray sharkskin jacket, ready
for a behind the scenes photo shoot.

"Neither did I," she said, her cheeks on fire.

"What a pleasant surprise," he said, gently taking her arm. "I'm a member. I got our tickets already." He attached a green sticker to the lapel of her fringe jacket. "Shall we go see the exhibit?"

Standing in front of Klee's *Cat and Bird*, staring into the patchwork cat's intense green eyes, Jessica thought of the poor animals suffering in the Feinberg basement. What was going on in their minds? Did those tortured cats dream of birds or biopsies? Mesmerized by the painting's little pink mouth and red heart nose, tears pooled in her eyes.

"What's wrong, Jessica?" Max asked, putting his hand on her shoulder. "Are you okay?"

"I'm just remembering the trauma of visiting the animal research lab," she said, stifling sobs.

"I was traumatized too when I realized someone ruined years' worth of our work. Research that could have helped eliminate genetic diseases. It's tragic."

"That's not what I mean," she said, pulling away from him. "I can't get the image out of my mind. The cats, especially."

"Not everyone can be saved, Jessica," he said.

"That's no excuse not to try." She took a tissue from her jacket pocket and blew her nose.

Liza's aria from Tchaikovsky's "The Queen of Spades" blasted from her pocket. *Damn.* All heads turned in her direction. She'd forgotten to silence her phone. She yanked the offending device from her pocket and answered Lolita's call.

"I can't talk now," she whispered, stepping into the corner of the crowded room.

"Where are you?" Lolita asked.

"Um. I'm at the library," she lied.

"On Friday night?" Lolita asked, incredulous. "Okay. I'll meet you out front in ten."

"The downtown library," Jessica said, hoping her friend wouldn't call her bluff.

"What? How soon can you get to my dorm?" Lolita asked.

"Why? What's up?"

"It's Emily."

"Emily? You mean your roommate, Emo?"

"Don't call her that. Just get your ass over here." The phone went dead.

Jessica turned around and found herself in the arms of Max White. "I've got to go," she said, averting his gaze.

"What's going on?" he asked.

"An emergency with my best friend's roommate, Emo." She unwrapped the parka from her waist.

"Emo?"

"Sorry," she said.

"Will I see you again?" he asked.

"Email me. Jessica dot James at Northwestern dot edu." She peeled off the museum sticker and stuck it to her index finger. She couldn't find a trash bin, so when Max moved in for a hug, she stuck the green sticker on the back of his blazer.

"Goodbye, Jessica," he whispered in her ear. Skin tingling, she pulled out of his embrace while she still could.

"Bye, Max." She slipped her arms into her coat, kissed him on the cheek, and took off.

Swimming upstream through the crowded museum, she fought her way outside then hightailed it to Adams Street Station in hopes that the purple line express would still be running. She kept looking over her shoulder as she jogged up the dark streets towards the "L." She had a strange feeling someone was following her. She looked over her shoulder and glimpsed the shadow of a man in a long black coat.

Crap. She was too late; the express train from the loop to Evanston had stopped an hour ago. Facing two trains and at least an hour, not to mention some creepy guy trailing her, Jessica bit the bullet and called an Uber. Thirty minutes later, she was knocking on Lolita's dorm room door. When she removed her hand from her glove, she noticed a little corner of the green museum sticker stuck to her index finger. As she flicked it onto the floor, she had an eerie feeling of déjà vu.

Lolita opened the door. "Wait until you hear what happened to Emily."

Emo was sitting on her twin bed, a blanket wrapped around her shoulders, even more depressed than usual. Lolita led her into the small space then went to sit next to her roommate.

"What's going on?" Jessica asked.

"I came back to see if Emily wanted to get dinner and found her in bed." Lolita put her arm around Emo then brushed a blonde lock out of her roommate's face. "I assumed she was sick, but when she told me some guy drugged her, I called you. Tell Jessica what happened to you this afternoon."

Emo looked up at her with sad eyes. "I was having coffee in Norris Center about two this afternoon and this guy comes up and starts flirting with me. Anyway, he was pretty hot, so I chatted him up. He was asking me about my studies and if I was an honor's student. I don't know how he knew. He bought me another latte and a cookie. I started to feel kind of weird, and he took me outside for some fresh air. Then three hours later, I woke up on a bench outside Hogan. I have no idea how I got there."

"What did this guy look like?" Jessica asked.

"He was tall, dark wavy hair," Emo stared at the carpet. "Cute."

"What was he wearing?"

"A winter coat. Cashmere, maybe." Emo put her head in her hands "I've been so groggy since I woke up I can hardly remember. I think maybe I was drugged or something. I'm still so tired."

"Did you wake up half naked?" Jessica asked, picking at the scar from the stitches.

"What? No. It was freezing outside." Emo pulled the blanket tighter around her torso.

"What did the guy say to you?" she asked.

"Like I said, he asked me about my major. And I told him I was pre-med. He asked where I was from and about my parents. I mean he seemed really interested in me. He even asked if my family were all in good health. It was kind of weird, but he was so nice and so cute." Tears sprouted from Emo's eyes.

"It's okay. Don't cry, Sweetie," Lolita said. When she put her arm around Emo again, her roommate laid her head against Lolita's shoulder.

"Do you remember anything else?" Jessica asked.

"Wait. I remember now," Emo said, sitting up, eyes flashing. "His name was Jack." She sniffled.

"Jack the Ripper," Lolita said, stroking Emo's hair.

"No, Jack Grove. He told me his name was Jack Grove."

"Jack Grove?" Jessica asked. "Are you sure?"

"Yes, I remember now. He introduced himself as Jack Grove. Why? Do you know him?" Emo tucked her legs up onto the bed and rearranged her blanket to cover them.

Jessica retrieved her phone from her jacket pocket and speed-dialed Jack's number. It went directly to voicemail. She hesitated, not knowing what to say. She gave Lolita a questioning look, then scrolled through the pictures on her phone, looking for one of Jack. He refused to have his picture taken, and the only one she found was of him dressed up as Hannibal Lector for Halloween.

"Let's go find Jack," Lolita said, jumping up from the bed. "We'll have to hurry though. I have a big game later tonight. A couple new whales I'm hoping to turn into regulars if they're good tippers. "

"Wait. Come on. You don't think Jack drugged Emo… Emily, do you?" Jessica narrowed her eyes and stared at her friend. "Jackass may be a womanizer, but no way he would do anything like that." She speed-dialed Jack's number again.

CHAPTER SIXTEEN

THIS WAS THE place. 333 East Ontario, McClurg Court Apartments. Jack entered the code from Samantha's text, then adjusted his fisherman's cap. Buzz, click, and the door opened. He entered the building and glanced around the fancy foyer. Its marble floors polished and gleaming, giant potted ferns overflowing mod white pedestals, and light cubes suspended from the ceiling made him think of Stanley Kubrick's *A Clockwork Orange*.

Samantha's apartment was on the seventh floor, pretty chichi for a post-doc. She answered the door wearing a skirt and pumps, and he wondered if she always dressed up at home, or if she had something business-formal in mind for their evening, hopefully not "milk-plus," aversion therapy, and Beethoven. Maybe he should have worn his cricket whites instead of his bomber jacket. He stepped inside the immaculate one bedroom and admired the stunning view of Lake Michigan.

"Nice place, Beagle Girl," Jack said, raising his eyebrows. "Post-docs must get paid pretty well."

"Please quit calling me that," she said, gesturing him into the living room.

The flawless white furniture was intimidating, and he was afraid of shedding a few skin cells or dropping a loose hair and contaminating Beagle Girl's sterile bubble. She pointed to one of the leather easy chairs sitting across a glass coffee table from a matching leather sofa, probably upholstered with antimicrobial fabric. He took off his cap and sat down, trying to keep his boots from touching the cream carpet; hopefully it was bacteriostatic and would repel the dirt from his desert boots.

"Priorities, *Mr. White*. I don't drink. I don't go out. I go to work and come home. Studies have shown that a relaxing home environment improves productivity."

"I don't know about relaxing, but you could probably perform surgery on this coffee table," he said, pointing to the sparkling table.

"Would you like tea or coffee, Mr. White?" she asked as she glided across the spotless carpet towards her impeccable kitchen. She probably used an autoclave instead of a coffeemaker.

"I'll take some coffee if it isn't too much trouble." He squirmed in his seat. "My friends call me Jack."

"*Chuvak!*" He heard a familiar voice, and Vanya appeared from the hallway wearing his campus cop uniform. "I knew you'd come help Sam outta this jam." The Russian pulled the pack of cigarettes from his shirt pocket, looked up at Samantha, lowered his eyes, and replaced it. "We gotta set this thing straight," he said, bright eyes set on Jack.

"What thing?" Jack asked, wiping his palms on his jeans.

"The animal lab," Vanya said. "They suspect Sam did that graffiti and freed them mice. But, we knows better, don't we?" He flashed his grill.

"Samantha's a suspect? Why?"

"I was there, that's why," Samantha said, carefully carrying a tray with a silver coffee pot and three porcelain cups teetering on matching saucers. "Doing science while black." She poured them each a cup then sat in one of the easy chairs and smiled over at the Russian. An uptight post-doc and a former mob rat seemed an unlikely pair, but who was he to question the laws of attraction.

"That racist cop?" Jack asked. "He didn't believe you when you told him I did it? What about the other cops?"

"I didn't tell them about you, *Mr. White*." Samantha sipped her coffee. "Remember, three weeks ago, back in the lab when your friend had hypothermia, you threatened to report me for petting Snoopy?"

"So what, you petted a dog?" Jack said. "That's not a crime."

"But it's against protocol and enough to get me suspended from the lab, perhaps even lose my post-doc."

"That's absurd." Jack blew on the steaming coffee and tried not to spill on the carpet. "It's all racist bullshit. And why has it taken them three weeks?"

"Perhaps because graffiti wasn't all they found in the lab."

"Don't forget the popsicle doctor." The unlit cigarette in Vanya's mouth bobbed up and down as he spoke.

"The police are investigating events in the lab that night, including, I suspect, the fact that Professor Granowski fired you from her lab last year. Why did you get dismissed from the lab, *Mr. White*?" she asked.

"Let's just say she didn't like my attitude." Jack held his cup in both hands and carefully took a sip.

"Bottom line, *chuvak*, you needs to confess to take the heat off Sam," Vanya said.

"Confess to what? I didn't kill Granowski if that's what you're intimating." Jack laughed. "You sound like some 1940's mobster threatening to put me in cement overshoes and drop me in the lake."

A cloud of hurt hung over Vanya's sunny countenance. "I learned English from watching old Hollywood gangster movies. Seemed 'propriate for the family business."

"Family business?" Jack asked.

"Bratva." Vanya's cheerful smile reappeared. "The brotherhood."

"The point is, *Mr. White*, you were in the lab the night Professor Granowski died," Samantha said, "the same night the rodents' cages were tampered with. Then, the next day, you were back in the lab with your friend when I found the graffiti and reported the corpse." Her pupils bled into her dark irises and her penetrating stare unnerved him.

"Wait. You two don't seriously think I killed Professor Granowski?" Jack's cup cracked when he dropped it on the glass table. "*Merde*. Sorry about that." He stopped the flow of black liquid with his sleeve before it reached the edge of the table. Samantha jumped up and headed for the kitchen then returned with a dishtowel.

"I know you're lying," she said, staring at him point blank. She dropped the towel into the lake forming on the other side of his arm. "I know you aren't Max White," she said. "I met him at the clinic three weeks ago just after Professor Granowski's death. Imagine my surprise when Dr. Manly's right hand man turned out to be none other than Max White."

When the white dishtowel had completely devoured the black liquid, she lifted the sopping mess onto the tray, picked up the muddle, and headed back toward the kitchen. "What a coincidence, I'd met another med student named Max White vandalizing the animal lab just a few weeks ago." She stopped halfway and turned around, fixing Jack in her hard gaze. "If you're not Max White, who are you?" she asked.

"Yeah, who the hell are you, *chuvak*?"

"It was a joke, that's all." Jack forced a smile. "Max White is a medical student in genetics and works in Manly's clinic. He's an arrogant wanker and completely full of shit. I borrowed his ID badge and freed his mice. It was a practical joke, that's all. Rivalry between classmates, a sophomoric stunt, avenging an old debt. Call it what you will, but I didn't kill anyone."

"Debt?" Vanya asked. The Russian wasn't smiling. He'd transformed from gangster wanna-be with slicked back hair, ink-stained arms, and goofy gold grill, into a Rottweiler off its leash, teeth bared, and ready to attack. "Answer Sam's question, *chuvak*." Vanya snapped his lighter open and shut. "Why you 'personating Max White?"

"Max White is a tosser who thinks he knows more than he does. He's a conniving con man who has everyone at Feinberg fooled into thinking he's some kind of genius." Jack sighed and shook his head.

"What basis do you have for those claims?" Samantha asked.

"Would you believe me if I told you he'd cheated off me all through first year of Human Behavior." Jack glanced over at the scary Russian to gauge if he was buying it. "He's scamming his way through Medical School."

"You're saying Max White is the liar, not you?" Samantha asked. "And he's a cheater, too?"

"He's a cunning asshole," Jack said. "but he doesn't even have the integrity of a cheater. Honor among thieves and all that. I bet you understand what I mean, right, Vanya?" He held his hand out palms up entreating the Russian.

"A raven doesn't peck out the eye of another raven," Vanya said with a wink. "Thieves Code." He lifted his right shirtsleeve revealing a tattoo of a fanged cat. "I was crowned a *Vor*, thief-in-law, in a *Moskva* prison. See this." He pulled the leg of his trousers up over his knee to show three eight pointed stars. "This mark means I kneel to no man. You don't tell me about honor among thieves," he said, then flashed a grin.

Merde! This dude was serious. Jack knew better than to mess with someone else's delusions of grandeur.

"Interesting." Samantha sipped her coffee from a million miles away. Her new boyfriend's body read like a rap sheet and that's all she had to say.

"*Chuvak*, you've got to clear Sam's name so they don't come after her," Vanya said. "We don't want them cops to charge her wit killing that lady professor, do we?"

"How do we know she didn't do it?" Jack asked. "Professor Granowski was already long dead when I found her in the deep freeze. And Samantha was in the lab the night before, which is probably when she was locked in there. It's a helluva lot more likely that Samantha killed her than I did."

"Sam couldn't hurt a flea," Vanya said. "She's as gentle

as a Baikal Seal and just as cute." He grinned at Beagle Girl and she smiled back. Jack marveled at their off kilter chemistry. He'd read that *la différence* makes relationships edgy, exciting, and even a little scary. Of course, there's a fine line between a little scary and down right frightening.

"Why would I do something like that?" Beagle Girl smoothed her straight shoulder length hair.

"I don't know," Jack said. "Maybe she left your name off a research paper or something."

"True. I should get credit for the research I did. But that's no reason to kill."

"Or maybe she found out you'd been stealing from the lab or her clinic or something," Jack said, making up shit as he went along.

Samantha's hands froze in midair, her face ashen. She averted his gaze, and slowly picked up her cup and sipped.

"She's a Robin Hoody," Vanya said. "Sam steals from the rich and gives to the poor, right *milashka*?"

"Is that true?" Jack asked. "You really did steal from Granowski's lab?"

"Not the lab, the clinic. I took medical supplies from Granowski's Evanston clinic, and I started a free women's health center on the South Side. I only took contraceptives, small instruments, supplies for routine operations, nothing big." Samantha gently sat her cup back on its saucer, and placed both on the coffee table. "But now they're watching my every move and my South Side clinic is suffering and so are the poor women who depend on us." She tugged at the hem of her skirt and sat forward on her chair. "I have a proposal for you, Mister, Mister... What is your real name?"

"Jack, Jack Grove."

"Well Mr. Grove, I have a proposal for you. I'll keep quiet about your vandalism, if you'll help Vanya get supplies. Doctor Manly has more than enough, more than he needs. Vanya doesn't know what to take or where to look, but you do. We need those supplies to help prevent teenage pregnancy and the vicious cycle of poverty. Doctor Manly and his high-end clients will never miss it."

"You want me to steal from Dr. Dude?" Jack unzipped his bomber jacket and wiped his forehead with the back of his hand. "Are you crazy?"

"Piece of pie," Vanya said, slurping his coffee.

"You look overwrought, Mr. Grove. Would you like a glass of water?"

"Yes, some water would be nice." He took off his coat and laid it over the arm of the sofa, wet side up. Samantha scooped up the dripping jacket, and continued toward the kitchen. "I'll wipe this off and hang it up. Be right back."

"She's quite a gal, isn't she?" Vanya asked.

"Yeah, a regular Robin Hoody." *What had he wandered into?* Beagle Girl wasn't as sentimental as she'd seemed with her lullabies. And the Russian dude was downright menacing.

"Here you are, Mr. Grove." Samantha laid a coaster on the table then sat the glass on top of it. "You say Max White is a cheater. Well, Doctor Richard Manly is a cheater, too. His clinic is not what it seems." She brushed the back of her skirt and sat down again.

"What do you mean?" Jack asked.

"Some of what he does at that clinic is unethical and probably illegal," she replied.

"Illegal? Like what?"

"Never mind. The first thing you can do, Mr. Grove, is help me restock my South Side clinic. If you don't, I may be forced to tell the police who you really are."

"Who I really am?" Jack asked. "I'd like to know the answer to that question myself."

"Maybe this video will refresh your memory, *chuvak*." Vanya held up a small black box in his open palm. "Smile, you're on candid camera." When Jack tried to grab the box, the slick Russian closed his palm and snatched his hand away. "No no." He sat back, smiled, and blew out an imaginary smoke ring.

"So, will you help us or not, Mr. Grove?" Samantha asked.

"Do I have a choice?" Jack clapped his fisherman's cap back onto his head, and then took his phone from his pocket to check the time. "I've got to go."

"Yes, you do," Vanya said, snapping his lighter. "You're coming with me to meet a guy, and then we'll get Sam's supplies. I'm not letting you out of my sight, partner. Not until everything is cleared up for Sam."

"Well, this will be interesting. Are you planning to come to class with me and chaperone my social life, too?" Jack narrowed his brows. Five messages from Jesse. Something must be up. He glanced up at Vanya, and then scrolled through her texts.

CHAPTER SEVENTEEN

JESSICA SLID HER phone back into her jacket pocket. "He's still not answering. Now what?"

"I have to get ready for my game and get to the Marriott downtown by eleven. Keep trying," Lolita said from the bathroom. "Maybe he's at O'Tooles. We could stop there on the way to the poker game."

"We?" Jessica asked.

"You might as well come to the game. I'll stake you if you want to play. You know you'll wipe the floor with those guys, and you could use the cash." Lolita emerged from the bathroom, long lashes darker, full lips redder, sage eyes brighter. "Are you going to be okay?" She tucked the covers up around Emo's shoulders. "Call if you need anything, Sweetie," she said. Emo nodded. "Let's go," Lolita ordered.

"Go where?" Jessica asked.

"To find Jack and drag him to the poker game if necessary." Lolita zipped up her thick black leather jacket, tugged on her heavy black boots, and slipped a beanie over her slick black hair.

"Okay, but no way Jack drugged Emo." Jessica followed her friend out of the dorm room, into the elevator, and outside towards the Harley Superlow parked in the first spot in the lot. Lolita handed her a bowl-shaped helmet, tucked her long hair up into one of her own, and mounted the bike. Jessica hopped on behind her.

She hugged the warm bike with her thighs and held tight around Lolita's waist, both to stay warm and to keep from falling off as her friend weaved in and out of Friday night traffic Lake Shore Drive. She buried her face in the back of Lolita's jacket, but the wind still stung her eyes, so she turned her head and stared out at the lake, a black hole sucking her gaze into infinity.

She closed her eyes to shut out the nothingness and Max appeared. Her spine tingled again remembering their hug at the museum. Lust had become her constant companion. Were the sparks between them just hormones or something more? The mischievous twinkle in his eyes, his sly smile, those extra white teeth set against his red lips, pale skin, and black hair, and then that intriguing brain of his.

Jessica abandoned herself to daydreams of playing doctor with Max White. Of course, she had despised him when she thought he'd drugged and left her for dead, now that he'd been cleared, she couldn't stop thinking of him.

By the time they reached O'Toole's, her nose hairs were frozen, her eyes were parched, and Max had been put back into his box in her imagination. She hopped off the back of the Harley.

"Aren't you coming in, Lolita?" she asked.

"I'll wait here. Go see if Jack's inside."

"And if he is?"

"Tell him to meet us at the Marriott in an hour."

Jessica descended into the cavernous bar, scanning the dark tavern for signs of Jackass. He'd probably corralled his latest girlfriend-of-the-month and was letting her buy him beer and dinner before they went back to her place for dessert. She walked the length of the bar and back. No Jack. She bounded back up the stairs and outside into the frigid night air.

She stopped short on the sidewalk when she spotted Max White leaning against a parking meter next to Lolita's bike. Her heart leapt into her throat, and she stuffed her hands into her parka pockets and sauntered over to him.

"Jessica. What a pleasant surprise. Twice in one evening," he said.

Lolita gave her a quizzical look, and Jessica averted her piercing gaze and stared down at the dirty snow on the curb.

"Did you take care of your friend in need?" he asked. "Would you two like to join me for a drink?"

"We have better things to do," Lolita said. "Jessica, get on. We're late."

Jessica scowled at her friend and pitched her leg over the back of the bike. "No need to be rude," she said as her friend revved the engine. "How about a rain check?" she called back into the plume of exhaust.

The expansive Marriott Penthouse suite had a spectacular view. "Nice joint," Jessica said, admiring the sparkling skyline through the wall of windows. Rubbing her hands together, she headed for the wet bar and helped herself to a Gentleman Jack, straight up. Just what the doctor ordered, some antifreeze.

Lolita had the penthouse stocked: top shelf booze, expensive snacks, clay poker chips, and felt topped card tables. Smooth Jazz oozed from tiny speakers embedded in the ceiling.

"What's your buy-in these days?" Jessica asked, sipping her Gentleman.

"Same. Ten grand." Lolita was busy filling ice buckets, setting glasses onto trays, and arranging chilled shrimp around a crystal bowl of cocktail sauce.

"Who's playing tonight? Anyone interesting?" Jessica asked.

"The usual. Rich thrill-seekers trying to outdo each other at cards, and, luckily for me, on tips. Vance the drama queen is still playing, of course. You'll know some of the others, too." Lolita placed small silver bowls of mixed nuts, and larger bowls of potato chips, on each end table.

"Not Nick Schilling, I hope." Jessica hadn't seen Nick since she'd met with the playboy art collector (and sometimes art history professor) to tell him she was taking him off her dissertation committee. After sleeping with him last spring, it was just too complicated keeping him on.

"He's quit coming since the shootout last year," Lolita said, glancing up with a smile.

"Don't remind me. I can still see Vladimir the Pope's dead eyes staring up at me. Gives me the creeps thinking about it. Isn't that when Detective Cormier told you to cool it on the poker games?"

"What the detective doesn't know won't hurt him." Lolita surveyed the suite with a pleased smiled.

"Yeah, well I hope it won't hurt us, either. No more mafia

bosses in the game?" Jessica asked, grabbing a hand full of nuts from a silver bowl and popping them into her mouth.

"Hey, don't touch those," Lolita slapped at her hand. "Eat from the bag in the kitchen."

Jessica did as she was told and headed back into the kitchen. Finally warm, she was ready for her usual Jack and Coke.

She dropped a couple of ice cubes into a tall crystal glass, added three fingers of whiskey then cracked the tab on a Coke can and enjoyed the sound of the fizzy sweetness filling her glass.

"Ahh." She took a sip, the perfect balance of sugar, caffeine, and alcohol. "So who else is playing?" she asked, reaching for the bag of mixed nuts. She was famished and wished she'd eaten before running off to the museum. She lifted the bag and dumped nuts directly into her mouth nosebag style.

"One new guy," Lolita said. "Ronald Davis. His old man, Ronald Senior, owns Davis Tower and half of Chicago. Supposedly, he's resigning his senate seat next year and hoping to pass it on to one of his sons, Daniel or Ronald."

Jessica rolled her eyes. "Anyone with enough money can buy a senate seat. Self-interest is only worth as much as the person who has it."

"These jokers are worth only as much as they tip," Lolita said.

Jessica raised her glass. "To jokers who tip well and hold the second-best hand."

An hour later, the game was in full swing. A dozen guys sat around two tables, smoking cigars, drinking fancy whiskey, and tossing high value chips like horse shoes—all except the bad-tempered actor Vance Hamm. He took the game very seriously, drank only fresh pressed vegetable juice, and snorted oxygen from a tank for fun.

Vance was the most aggressive player in the game, so Jessica sat to his left to avoid betting into his crazy raises and tripping over his nasal cannula tubing. When she won the latest pot, Vance joked, "You know you play too much poker when your wet dreams are of the nuts, come hands, and straddling tops and bottoms."

The new mark sat across from Jessica, smoking a fat cigar, laughing at the lewd joke, and counting his last stack of chips. Wall Street insider from old money, Ronald Davis exuded privilege with his beady gray eyes and slicked back hair. He had the nerve to insist they play stud in a hold 'em tournament.

Lolita ran interference and set up a side game during a break. Jessica peeked at her cards one at a time, a three, another three, a nine, and a third three. Her heart skipped a beat. So far, three treys and a possible full house. When she looked at the last card in her hand, she had to bite her tongue.

Ronald was beaming, not exactly a poker face. When she'd checked to his shit-eating grin, he bet two grand. She called the bet with Lolita's money. Ronald stood pat, and so did she. Vance took three cards, inhaled deeply from his oxygen tank, picked up his new cards, and with a hang-dog look promptly folded. That left Jessica and the big boy going head to head.

On the next round of betting, he pushed all of his chips into the center of the table. "I'll tap you," he said.

She glanced over at Lolita, since it was her stake. When

her friend just shrugged and winked, she pushed her stack of chips into the pot. "I'll call."

The next senator from Illinois laughed and turned over a full house, kings over sevens. She laid her cards down one at the time in the order they'd been dealt. After the third trey, Ronald Davis let out a whoop and reached to scoop up the chips.

"Not so fast, Mr. Davis," she said, turning over her last card, a fourth trey. "Four of a kind beats a full house no matter what kind of poker you're playing."

She was raking in the big pot when a knock turned all heads toward the hotel room door.

"Are you expecting someone else?" Vance asked. "I don't like papparatzi and that's why I always request the guest list in advance, and by my counts, we're all here, with the addition of the lovely Ms. James, of course." He nodded in her direction.

"No worries. I'll get rid of them," Lolita said on her way to the door. Jessica watched as her friend put her eye against the peephole then unlatched the chain, opened the door, and stepped out into the reception area.

"I'm expecting someone," Ronald Davis said, glancing around at the other players, finishing his high-ball.

"Excuse me, gentlemen," Jessica said as she stood up from the table. Curiosity got the best of her and she left her chips unattended, and headed toward the door to see who else had a special key to the Penthouse elevator. Before she was out the door, she recognized the familiar smell of caramelized onions and the sound of his smooth single-malt voice.

"Jack, what are you doing here?" she asked, opening the door and joining Lolita in the foyer.

"I could ask you the same thing," Jack said. "For better or worse, I'm with him." He nodded toward Vanya.

"Cousin, I'm afraid you'll have to wait here," Lolita said. "I can't let you into the suite."

"Why not? As your papa says, you can't spoil porridge with butter." Vanya smiled.

Lolita opened the door a crack and glanced back into the suite. "The fat cats are getting restless. I have to go. Jack, wait here. We need to talk to you. Jessica, you'd better get back to the game before the guys mutiny. Cousin Vanya…" She shook her head. "Cousin Vanya, just be sure to use the ashtray." She pointed at the cigarette receptacle near the elevator.

"Be back in a few minutes, guys. I'll jam on it and put those rich dudes out of their misery," Jessica said to Jack. "See you in twenty minutes. Don't go anywhere."

"Can't we at least get a drink?" Jack asked, pacing the foyer like a caged tiger.

"How'd you get up here?" Lolita asked. "You need a keycard."

Vanya held up a copy of the special card. "I have an appointment," he said, unleashing his glittering grin.

"Here?" Jessica and Lolita asked in unison.

CHAPTER EIGHTEEN

JACK PACED BACK and forth in the foyer outside the Marriott Penthouse Suite, tossing his cap from hand to hand, watching the smokestack Russian puffing away near the elevator. Friday night, he should be partying with a curvy post-doc instead of acting as an accomplice for some cartoonish gangster. He leaned his head against the glass window and looked down wondering what must go through someone's mind falling a thousand feet before hitting the pavement: regret or relief, exhilaration or sheer terror.

A light hand on his shoulder startled him, and he turned around to face another abyss, Jesse.

"You're still here," she said.

"You told me to wait, and your command is my wish," he said, tipping his cap.

"I cleaned their clocks." She waved a wad of hundreds under his nose.

"Well, Bob's your uncle. Now how about dinner? Your treat." He smiled. "As soon as I can lose this ink-stained chimney." He nodded towards Vanya.

"Sounds good," she said, boots tapping as she headed back to the suite door. "I need to talk to you about Emo."

"Watch out," Jack said as the door swung open and almost hit her. A heavyset fifty-something man in suit and tie stepped into the foyer. The mop of hair flopping over his skull was either fake or the worst comb-over in history; his orange complexion suggested he'd taken sulfur drugs and spent too much time in the tanning bed, and his swollen eyes and sagging jowls evoked a lifetime of debauchery.

"You must be Vanya," the bloated businessman said, crossing the foyer, and extending his puffy hand to the Russian.

"Mr. Davis?" Vanya asked, shaking his hand. "Good to finally meet you in the flesh."

"Likewise." The suit turned to Jack, thin lips puckered into a butthole shaped oval. "Do you mind? We have some business to discuss in private." The suit gave a cursory smile to Jesse and nodded towards the elevator.

"Of course, Mr. Davis. Just give me a minute," Jesse said. "Then I'll go back inside and help Lolita clean up and give you some privacy."

"I was wondering whether you'd seen Emo today?" she asked Jack.

"Who's Emo?" he asked.

"Lolita's roommate, Emily," she said, stuffing bills into her wallet.

"Can you kids take this inside? I have urgent business with Vanya." The businessman scowled.

"Yeah, Mr. Davis and me have an appointment," Vanya said.

"Come on, Jesse. Let's go help Lolita." Jack took her by the elbow, but she shook him off.

"Okay," she said, turning on her heels and heading back into the suite. "But I have to ask you something." Jack was about to follow her when Vanya held up his hand and said to the suit, "This here's my associate, Clyde. He's okay. I'll vouch for him."

"What I have to say is for your ears only," the suit said.

"For *our* ears or the deal's off. Clyde here's my partner." Vanya's penetrating stare was menacing.

"Your partner but not the girl. She took too much of my money already. Isn't that right, honey?"

"I didn't take it. I won it fair and square," she said. "I just have to ask Jack one question. Were you with Emo, Emily earlier?"

"Who's Emily?"

"Lolita's roommate."

"I've never met her. Why?" Jack answered.

"She said she was with you earlier." Jesse stared up at him accusingly.

"I couldn't pick her out of a lineup," he said.

"She had coffee with you, then she woke up behind Hogan Hall."

"Maybe there's another Jack Grove on campus. I don't know, but it wasn't me. I went to the gym, then to class, and then... I've been downtown alone all day and with Vanya all evening." He turned and pointed at the Russian smoke-stack leaning against the wall near the ashtray.

"Clyde's telling the truth," Vanya interjected, taking a drag on his cigarette. "He's been with me at Sam's place."

"Do you mind?" the businessman glanced at his Rolex. "This is time sensitive. Can you please just give us five minutes alone before the others come out?"

"Sure, Mr. Davis," she said. "Come on. We aren't wanted." She rolled her eyes at Jack.

"Clyde stays," Vanya said. "We're partners now. Right, *chuvak*?" He patted the pocket where he'd put the small black box.

"Whatever you say, Vanya." Jack tossed his cap from hand to hand and watched Jesse disappear into the suite.

"Well, if you're sure." The businessman thrust the puffy hand in Jack's direction. "Glad to meet you, Clyde. Now, step into my office." The suit called the elevator. When it arrived, he gestured them inside, stepped inside himself, and pushed the button for the lobby. "This won't take long. One trip down and back. I'll get right to it." The businessman pulled an envelope from his inside jacket pocket. "My wife is having an affair and I want you to tail her."

Vanya shrugged his shoulders. "No problem."

"My contacts tell me you have connections to the Ukraine," the suit said. "That's where she's from."

"Small world," Vanya said, snapping his lighter open and shut.

"Find out about her past. I don't want any nasty surprises when I run for Senate." The elevator door opened on the lobby level and the suit waved away the crowd waiting to get in then inserted his keycard for the penthouse and sent the lift back up.

"If necessary, reinvent a past for her," he said. "Something charming, Russian princess or something."

The businessman slapped Vanya on the back. "An associate told me this type of investigation is your forte. I trust you'll find out what the little minx is up to now."

"Sure thing, Boss," Vanya said grinning.

"I think she's messing around with some doctor. Find out, and get pictures. The more I know, the better.

Knowledge is power, as they say." He handed the envelope to Vanya. "Here are two pictures of my wife. Our wedding picture. And a baby picture with her parents. Find out everything you can about them."

When Vanya tapped out a cigarette, Jack shook his head and pointed to the elevator smoke detector. Vanya put the cigarette behind his ear, took the envelope, and eyed the businessman. He carefully opened the paper flap, removed one of the photographs and stared down at it with a curious look on his face. Jack peeked over the Russian's shoulder at a wedding picture of a sullenly beautiful teenage bride on the arm of the suit, same comb over, same beady eyes, but slightly less girth.

"Very pretty. This is your wife?" Vanya asked, looking up at the businessman. "You say her name is Olga? She looks familiar. What's her family name, before married?" Vanya slid the photo back into the envelope.

"Yudavik or Yukovitch, something Russian," the suit answered, then sent the elevator back down to the lobby level.

Vanya raised his eyebrows as he stared down at a baby picture. "Yudkovich?" Vanya asked, eyes blazing. "Very small world," he said under his breath.

"Do you know her?"

"Maybe yes, maybe no," Vanya said, stuffing the envelope into the pocket of his leather overcoat.

The suit took another envelope from his pocket and handed it to Vanya. "Half now and half when you get the information and the proof."

The Russian smiled, counted the bills, and stuck the envelope into his inside jacket pocket.

"My wife will be at the Holly Ball this Saturday night,"

the businessman said. "I have to work late and can't attend. I suspect she's meeting her doctor friend there, and I want you to watch her every move. I don't trust that little minx. She's got men buzzing around her like flies on shit." He handed Vanya a red and green embossed invitation with festive white script: *Children's Charities invites you to the Holly Ball, Saturday December 23rd, 8:00pm to Midnight, The Racket Club, 1365 North Dearborn Parkway, Black Tie.*

"Our business is concluded. Now, if you'll excuse me, gentlemen." The elevator door opened on the ground floor. "Remember, you've never seen me before. None of this can be traced back to me." He inserted his keycard again, then stepped out of the elevator. "Don't call me, I'll call you. Got it?" The lift doors whooshed closed behind him and he disappeared into the lobby.

"What was that all about?" Jack asked.

"Come on, *chuvak*. I'll show you." After a free ride back up to the Penthouse, Vanya pushed the lobby button.

"Can I just say goodbye to Jesse?"

Vanya patted his jacket pocket and pushed the button again.

"Where are we going?" Jack asked, flipping his cap back onto his head. "To rent tuxedos?"

"Wait until Cousin Dmitry sees this!" Vanya stepped out the elevator into the lobby. "Follow me."

Jack slid out of the elevator just as the doors were closing. "Do I have a choice?"

Taking a back route north out of the Loop, cigarette hanging from his lips, white-knuckling the steering wheel of his Escalade, Vanya sped through the midnight streets of downtown. Jack rolled down his window, releasing a cloud of smoke from the Caddy then inhaled the brisk December air blasting in from outside.

"Can I at least see the photos, partner?" Jack asked.

Vanya slid the envelope out of his pocket and without taking his eyes off the road, handed it to him.

"We're hired to tail Olga Davis. That was her husband Ronald back there. He owns half of Chicago," Vanya said, blowing out smoke rings.

Jack removed the photographs then pressed a small button to illuminate a mirror on the back of the visor and get a better look. In one, the girl looked like she was playing dress-up in her lacey bridal gown, heavy make-up, and flowers braided into her long blonde hair. Her melancholy expression and piercing green eyes reminded him of Jesse.

He put the photo back in the envelope and pulled out the other picture, a grainy black and white of a rail thin woman with haunting eyes holding a baby on her hip and standing next to her an angry man in a nice suit, holding his palm out in front of the camera. Captivated by those haunting eyes, Jack lost himself in the awkward familial scene that took place in front of some place called Skybar, a rundown nightclub by the looks of it.

Jack was thrown against the seatbelt as Vanya swerved in and out of traffic. "You're a menace on the roads. Slow down, dude." The Escalade tore up Dan Ryan Expressway, left rubber on the Skokie exit, and sped up a side street.

Vanya skidded to a stop in front of a modest saltbox house in the suburbs, threw the Caddy into park, yanked the keys out of the ignition, and jumped out. "Come on, *chuvak*."

A blurry-eyed "Cousin Dmitry" answered the front door, but didn't let them in. "It's one A.M. What do you want, Vanya?" Dmitry tugged his flannel robe shut, leaned against the doorframe, and glared at Jack. "Who's the Greek fisherman?" he asked.

"My new associate." Vanya turned to Jack. "Give me them pictures." He waved his hand frantically, gesturing for the envelope. When Jack obliged, Vanya grabbed the envelope and removed the wedding picture, and then thrust it at his cousin. "Look, coz. Who does this remind you of?" he asked.

"You didn't wake me up to look at pictures? What are you playing at, Vanya?" Vanya shoved the picture at his cousin again, and Dmitry reluctantly took it.

"Looks like a teenage bride. Maybe one of those mail order brides The Pope used to arrange," Dmitry said. "Her husband looks old enough to be her father."

"That's Olga Davis," Jack said. "Apparently, she's the wife of Ronald Davis. You've heard of Ronald Davis, owns half of Chicago."

"So why get me out of bed to look at Ronald and Olga's wedding picture?" Dmitry asked.

"Who does she look like?" Vanya asked again, bouncing from foot to foot.

"I don't know. That Russian long jumper, Darya Klishina?" Dmitry guessed, wearily.

"What? No. Look again."

"I give up. Quit playing games and let me go back to bed."

"Doesn't she look just like your brother? Look at her chin, those eyes. She's like a girl version of Sergei."

Dmitry straightened up and stared down at the photo.

"And it can't be a coincidence that she has your last name." Vanya was nodding his head yes, in agreement with himself.

"Her name is Durchenko?" Dmitry asked. "I'm not following."

"No, your *real* last name, *Yudkovich*," Vanya said, still nodding his head.

"Your last name isn't Durchenko?" Jack asked. *Who were these crazy Russians?*

"Look, Clyde, we could ask you the same thing. Mr. White, also known as Jack Grove." Vanya said.

"I told you, that was a joke." Jack laughed nervously. "So you guys know her?"

When the cousins started speaking in Russian, their body language made him even more anxious. He was in over his head with these fellows. Studying criminal psychology was one thing, committing crimes was quite another. Vanya must have sensed his anxiety. He fake punched Jack's shoulder, flashed his grill, and said, "Don't worry, Clyde. We never get caught."

"Unless caught stealing," Dmitry said absently, "one is not a thief."

"That may be, but I don't want to test my luck," Jack said.

Vanya patted his jacket pocket that held the little black box. "What about helping Sam? Or would you rather go to jail?"

"What's Beagle Girl have to do with Olga Davis?" Jack asked.

"Sam seen Olga Davis in that ladies clinic where she

works now. Seems Olga gets her picture on the internet a lot, being so rich and all."

"So what? Women go to health clinics all the time."

"Mind if I go back to bed while you two argue over women's health?" Dmitry closed the door behind him.

Vanya knocked and his cousin reopened the door a crack. "Please, Vanya, let me be. I'm tired. Unlike some people, I have a job and have to be at work tomorrow morning."

Jack stood behind him as Vanya pushed the second photograph through the gap. "Look at this, coz. Then tell me it's a coincidence. Maybe the rumors are true and Sergei didn't die at the hospital the night you escaped Russia." The cousins were speaking English again, maybe for Jack's benefit.

"Impossible. I heard the shots," Dmitry said, opening the door wide and exposing his bare feet. Behind him a German Shepherd wagged its tail. "I was there…"

"Yeah. But no one found the body," Vanya said, "remember."

"Hold on, guys. What body?" Jack asked. "Who's Sergei? What's this have to do with Olga Davis?" He felt like he'd walked onto the set of a B gangster flick. "Better yet, what's this have to do with me?"

"It's not like Bratva to catch flies while letting hornets go free," Dmitry said, gesturing for them to come inside the house.

"Hornets?" Jack asked, crossing the threshold into Chicago's underbelly.

CHAPTER NINETEEN

JESSICA STOOD ON the toilet lid in her tiny bathroom trying to see her dress in the medicine cabinet mirror. Teetering on the platform heels she'd borrowed from Lolita, she stuck out a leg to see if the designer shoes worked with the vintage dress. She was excited to be wearing her great grandmother's black evening gown for the first time.

Balancing on one leg on the toilet lid, she leaned in front of the mirror and steadied herself holding onto the shower rod a couple feet away, then admired the lace bodice, three-quarter length sleeves, and form fitting satin skirt that flared mermaid style just above her knees. Twisting to get a glimpse of her butt, she lost her balance, grabbed the shower curtain with both hands, and ripped it clean off the rod then crashed to the floor.

On her way, her cheek hit the side of the sink, and she could already feel it swelling. The dress was unharmed, but a shoe strap had busted and she wasn't so sure about her jaw. Jessica lay on the cold tile, pressing both hands into her stinging face.

When she got her wind back, she reached up, grasped

both sides of the sink, and hauled herself upright. *Crap!* She stared at her reflection in the mirror and saw a shiner blossoming on her right eye.

She threw open the medicine cabinet and rummaged around in the tangled mess of ointments, Band-Aids, and headache remedies for some makeup to cover the purple plum under her eye. Beneath tubes of cortisone gel, antifungal cream, and Neosporin, she fingered an ancient tube of tinted sunscreen she hadn't used in years. The cap was glued on, so she ran hot water over it until she could screw it off, and slathered the oily tanning lotion over her bruise. The sticky white zinc in the sunscreen transformed the deep purple plum into a violet cauliflower ready to drop off her face.

She remembered the old toiletries bag she kept tucked behind the toilet. She scrounged around in it until she snagged an old compact with a cracked mirror and disintegrating makeup pad. She used a cotton ball to pat on a layer of khaki powder, turning the vegetable into a mineral, a Montana igneous like she'd seen in her high school geology class. Taking another tack, she combed her bangs over the offending eye and used hand lotion to glue the fringe to the side of her forehead and over her eye, the split ends forming a sideburn at her right ear.

When the doorbell rang, she was fixing the strap on Lolita's shoe with duct tape. She limped to the buzzer, one heel on her foot, the other in her hand, and buzzed Jack up.

"I like your new hairdo. Very mod," Jack said, taking off his gloves and rubbing his hand together. "You clean up pretty good for a cowgirl." He smiled and winked. "Ready to go?"

"Holy Holly Ball, Batman, hob-knobbing here we come," Jessica said, ducking into her closet for her parka. She stretched her vintage opera gloves over her fingers, stopping midway to inspect her fading scar. "I hope there's a coat check."

Jack slipped his leather gloves back on. "After you, Cinderella." He gestured into the hallway. "Your coach awaits."

Resisting the urge to brush the bothersome hair out of her right eye, she stepped out into the hall after him and locked her apartment door. "All you have to offer is the Batmobile," she said. "I bet Max White has a carriage pulled by four genetically enhanced mice the size of Clydesdales."

"Why don't you shag him and get it over with?" Jack headed for the stairs and took them two at a time. She didn't catch up with him until he was through the courtyard and already on the street. Turned out Jack's chariot was the Red Line to Division Street, followed by a brutally cold walk to The Racket Club. By the time they reached the Gold Coast Historic District, Jessica's eyes were watering, her lashes were frozen, and her lungs ached.

"Cool old building," she panted as they approached the entrance.

"A 1920's revival," Jack responded, opening the door for her.

A butler met them at the door, looked down his nose at them, and asked for their invitations.

"Where's the coat check?" Jessica asked, reaching to brush the itchy hair from her right eye then remembered the lump on her cheek. A one-eyed pirate, she jostled her way through the trophy wives in their leather and furs to the coat check line.

After the woman in front of her handed over her dead animal to the coat check girl, Jessica dumped her parka then made a beeline for the bar. Jack had beaten her to it and was waiting for her inside the ballroom with a drink in each hand. He offered her an amber whiskey in a stout crystal glass. She took it in both hands. *Note to self, quit messing with bangs covering ugly bruise.* With her one exposed eye, she stared at Jack.

"Where'd you get that fabulous tux?" she asked. "You look amazing. Rockin' the penguin suit."

"Thanks." His face lit up. "Courtesy of Vanya."

Jessica downed her whiskey and gazed around at the ballroom. Its wood paneling, high ceilings, and ornate moldings exuded decades of wealth and privilege, a throwback to the time when rich white men gathered in the boys-only club to blow off steam, cut meaty deals, and rule the world. *Ah, the good old days of patriarchy.* The country club set waltzed and jived in tails and gowns to an orchestra playing in the balcony.

"Quit gawking," Jack said. "You look like a tourist. Remember, this isn't anthropological research on how the other half lives; we're on a mission."

"Hey, over there." Jessica pointed to the lavish buffet. "It's Vanya and Beagle Girl."

"Let's go see if they've found the target," Jack said. "Rich bitch, Olga Davis."

"Explain. Why are we tailing her, again? What are we supposed to be looking for?"

"Her husband, mover and shaker Ronald Davis, thinks

she's having an affair with some doctor. Vanya's being paid to follow her. And Sam's seen her at Dr. Dude's fertility clinic."

A tuxedo clad waiter offered to take her empty glass. "Shall I bring you another, Miss?" he asked, one white gloved hand holding a tray and the other behind his back.

"Sure, how about a Jack and Coke?" she asked.

"You can take the cowgirl out of the country…" Jack shook his head and sipped his single malt.

Jessica rolled her eyes. "So, fill me in on Olga Davis. I still don't understand. Who cares if she's getting fertility treatments?"

"Obviously, her husband," Jack said. "He's a controller. Women with low self-esteem who see themselves as victims are often attracted to controlling men. Her husband wants to dictate her life down to the last detail, including her feelings. It's classic control freak behavior."

"He sounds like a total dickhead." She stomped her strappy platform shoe. "I hate him already. Rich or poor, no woman deserves to be treated like a blowup doll."

"According to Vanya, Olga Davis wasn't always rich. He recognized her father in a photograph of Olga as a baby. Her mom was so young and desperate, eyes pleading with the camera for help. Her dad obviously didn't want his picture taken, threatening the photographer. They're in front of some place with a big sign called the SkyBar, but the flash makes it look like they're dissolving into a cloud. It's eerie. A tense moment frozen in time." Jack stared down into his glass. "I wonder who took that picture." He tipped the glass to finish the last drops of his scotch.

"Speak of the devil." Jessica nodded toward Vanya whose

golden smile parted the crowd like the hand of Moses over the Red Sea. She watched as Vanya led his beautiful date straight up the middle of the ballroom. Whether it was the stunning black woman in a green satin dress or the slick gangster sporting plenty of bling, or the surprising combination, heads turned and suits stepped out of the way.

"Those two don't blend in," Jack said.

"No more than we do," Jessica replied. "Although you're looking pretty smart in that tux."

"Have you tried these meatballs?" Vanya asked, sidling up to her. He popped a pile of them into his mouth from a napkin he was palming. "Delicious," he said, cheeks bulging.

"Jesse's a vegetarian," Jack said. "She only eats seitan's balls."

"Too bad. These are made in heaven." He pulled another napkin full from his pocket and rolled more meatballs into his mouth.

Jessica grimaced.

"We haven't been properly introduced." The pretty black woman extended her hand. "I'm Samantha Brewer. Last time I saw you, your body temperature was dangerously low, so you probably don't remember me."

"*Beagle Girl* from the animal lab," Jessica made air quotes and smiled. "I'm Jessica."

"Snoopy is being retired if you're looking for a pet. I'd take him myself, but I have all white carpets, and..."

"And you're into saving people, not animals," Jessica interrupted.

"Let's just say I have my priorities straight," Samantha said, raising her eyebrows.

"Girls!" Vanya said. "Heads up. There's Olga Davis.

Red dress, three o'clock." He signaled her location with his eyes.

Olga Davis was gorgeous in a scarlet sleeveless evening gown, her long wavy platinum hair cascading over her narrow pale shoulders. Standing alone, back against a pillar, she was a million miles away, staring up at the chandelier.

"Wow!" Jessica said. "She looks like a movie star." She couldn't take her eyes off Olga. She watched as the beauty took a hankie out of her heart-shaped velvet bag and dabbed at her forehead. Jessica squeaked and pointed when she saw a man in black leathers wearing a motorcycle helmet approach Olga from behind and hand her something. Olga looked startled and gasped open-mouthed as the man retreated through the crowd and slipped out of the ballroom. Clutching something to her lovely cleavage, Olga Davis darted around the pillar and disappeared.

CHAPTER TWENTY

JESSICA SET HER empty glass on the tray as a waiter passed by. "What just happened?" she asked. "Who was that guy? What did he give her? And why did she run away?"

"We'd better find out," Vanya said. "Let's go." The Russian led the charge through the throng towards the pillar where Olga had been standing.

Hot on the Russian's heels, from over his shoulder, Jessica spotted a flash of scarlet ducking into the women's bathroom. Sliding across the ballroom on platform heels, straining against her tight dress, Jessica scooted past her companions and hightailed it for the can.

The ladies restroom at The Racket Club was bigger than her entire apartment, and better equipped. Olga Davis was seated on a short cushioned stool at a vanity in front of a large framed mirror. Her head down, she was reading a letter. When Jessica plopped down on the stool next to her, Olga stuffed the letter into her purse, and took out a lipstick, then applied it to her perfect lips. Tears pooled in her green eyes and she let out a little whimper.

"Are you okay?" Jessica asked.

"I'm pregnant," Olga Davis replied.

"Oh. Hormones?"

"I guess so." Shoulders shaking, Olga started sobbing.

"Gosh," Jessica said, moving her stool closer and putting her arm around Olga's bare shoulders. "Don't you want to have a baby?"

"It's complicated." Olga pulled back, gazed straight into her eyes, and then gave her a quizzical look.

Jessica's face was on fire, and she glanced down to avert Olga's penetrating gaze. When she did, she saw the velvet heart open wide to reveal the corner of an envelope. She drew the other woman close again. With Olga weeping into the collar of her great-grandmother's vintage dress, Jessica reached around and slowly slid the envelope out of the purse, gently dropped it onto the floor, then kicked it under the vanity.

"I'm so embarrassed, but you're so sweet. I should probably be going," Olga said, picking up her handbag from the vanity. "Perhaps I'll see you again," she said, standing and adjusting her gown. "I'm fairly active on the charity circuit."

"Yeah, me, too," Jessica bluffed.

"I'm surprised I haven't seen you before." Olga extended her hand. "I'm Olga Davis." Even through her retro opera gloves, the touch of Olga's small warm hand caused a pang of guilt. She glanced down at the floor and saw the corner of the letter peeking out from under the vanity and kicked at it with her platform heel.

"Are you okay?" Olga asked.

"You know how it is," she said. "These heels are killing me."

Olga smiled. "The things we do for beauty."

"Vanity keeps a beautiful woman warm," she said, realizing that she'd just quoted Nietzsche to a perfect stranger.

"I suppose so. Thanks again for being so sweet." Olga adjusted her dress again, patted her platinum bun, and swished towards the door. Mesmerized, Jessica watched the socialite exit the lounge. As soon as the door clicked shut behind her, Jessica lunged for the letter, folded it into a small square, and tucked it into her opera glove. She burst out of the bathroom, flushed and beaming with excitement.

"What's going on?" Jack was waiting for her outside the bathroom.

"I've got something. The letter that guy gave Olga Davis. I have it up my sleeve." She could hardly contain her exhilaration.

"Mrs. Davis is leaving and Vanya's gone after her," Sam said. "I'm going home."

"Come on," Jack said. "We can still catch Vanya." He grabbed Jessica's hand, pulled her through the crowd, and back out the front entrance. The cold night air punched her in the face, and she remembered her parka back inside. Eyes watering, she searched the sidewalk for Vanya's distinctive skinny hunched form and slicked-back hair.

"Look, over there." Jack pointed to a black sedan pulling up to the curb. A chauffer jumped out, ran around to the back, and helped Olga Davis inside.

As the car sped away, Jessica saw the ember of a cigarette glowing in the darkness against the corner of the building.

"Come on. It's Vanya," she said. Jack tried to take her hand again, but she pulled out of his grip and took off toward the glowing ember. She didn't get very far before she tripped on the hem of her dress and stumbled forward. Jack arrived just in time to catch her.

"Whoa. Slow down there, Cowgirl." He offered his arm and this time she took it. Obviously Vanya wasn't going anywhere, so no reason for her to break her fool neck.

When they reached Vanya, he'd stamped out his smoke under his Italian lace-up, then in one graceful move, he pulled a pack from his tux pocket, tapped out another, flipped it into his lips, and lit it. Vanya blew out a cloud of smoke, and Jessica's frosty breath came out in a matching cloud. Jessica shivered and Jack pulled her closer.

"Aren't you going to follow her?" Jack asked.

"Why bother? She's just going home." Vanya answered. "Olga Davis may be in the soup, but she ain't having no affair."

"No, she's having a baby," Jessica said, squinting to keep her eyeballs from freezing.

"What?" Jack asked.

"In the bathroom. She told me she was pregnant." Jessica plucked a crumbled envelope from inside her opera glove. "Look. I got the letter that motorcycle guy gave her."

Jack took the envelope out of her hand and unfolded it. As he carefully removed the typed letter, two small photos floated to the concrete. Vanya snatched them up.

"Pictures," Vanya said. He stared down at one of them, then looked up and asked, "What's this?" He held it out.

Jack took it and examined it. Jessica looked over his shoulder at the glossy photo of five gray dots in a black cloud.

"Looks like an ultrasound," Jack said.

"What does it mean?" Jessica asked.

"You said she was pregnant. Maybe it's an ultrasound

of the fetus, except I don't see a fetus, only tiny dots." Jack retrieved his cellphone from his tux pocket, turned on its flashlight, and continued examining the strange ultrasound picture.

"Let me see the other one," Jack said. Vanya handed it over. "It's Olga Davis wearing oversized sunglasses and a scarf, entering Dr. Dude's upscale fertility clinic. Looks to me like someone is blackmailing her," Jack said.

"What do you mean?" Jessica asked.

"Listen to this." Jack turned his flashlight on the letter and read aloud, "$100,000 cash or these pictures and your IVF story go to press. Wait for instructions. Follow them exactly, or these pictures will be in next week's society pages."

"Why would someone blackmail Olga Davis for using a fertility clinic?" Jessica asked.

"Because," Samantha's voice came from behind them. "She's a celebrity in this town. IVF, especially with egg donation, is still seen as unnatural and fodder for gossip columns. And as you've seen from her ultrasound, she's not having one baby, but five."

"No shit." Jessica gasped.

"Holy litter of puppies, Batman," Jack said. "Quintuplets? Like Octomom, only Quintomom."

"I wouldn't have told you, but you've already seen for yourself," Samantha said.

"We didn't know what we were seeing. Looked like five dots to me. Seems too early for a fetal ultrasound." Jack handed the picture to Samantha.

"With in vitro fertilization, we always check after one month to see how many embryos attach. Usually, we perform selective reduction if more than one is viable. It was a shock for Mrs. Davis to learn she was carrying five viable embryos." Sam put her hand into the crook of Vanya's arm. "Funny, these upper-class women come into the clinic wanting desperately to get pregnant, resorting to donor eggs, donor sperm, flooding their own bodies with chemicals. When they get more than they bargained for, they balk. They can't accept that selective reduction comes with the territory."

Sad eyes reflecting the streetlights, she said mournfully, "Why they can't just adopt, I don't know. There are plenty of babies out there without parents. Vanity and narcissism are the only explanations. They want to reproduce themselves for all to see." Samantha raised the collar on her wool coat and wrapped a fleece scarf around her slender neck. "You all should get your coats before we have another bout of hypothermia on our hands."

Teeth chattering, Jessica asked, "I take it selective reduction is the same thing as abortion? These rich ladies do anything to reproduce but can't accept the consequences of their choice. Selective reduction. Sounds right up Max White's alley," Jessica said, shaking from the cold. "He'd like to reduce the whole human race to perfect specimens. Nietzsche's Übermench on steroids."

"Here," Vanya removed his tuxedo jacket. "Take this, Miss Jessica. Your lips are turning blue."

"Thanks. I guess we'd better go fetch our coats. How about some hot toddies at my place? I have a hot plate, running water, a plastic bear full of honey, and a bottle of whiskey. What more do we need? We can put our heads together and figure out what's going on with this letter and those pictures."

"Yous can help me 'vent a story for Mr. D.," Vanya said smiling.

"I bet there's not a clean cup in that rat's nest of yours." Jack winked. "The whiskey may kill the bacteria growing on those cups in your bathtub, but your tea service won't be up to Samantha's standards. We'll have to use that ransom note as a coaster."

"Are you making fun of me, Mr. Grove?" Samantha asked, her hand still resting in the crook of Vanya's arm.

"I've got plenty of overdue library books we can use as coasters," Jessica said. "Anyway, we've got more important things to worry about than etiquette. Someone's blackmailing poor, pregnant Olga Davis."

CHAPTER TWENTY-ONE

OLGA WAS STILL shaking when she arrived home from the Holly Ball. She asked Maria for a cup of chamomile tea and went straight up to her bedroom. Ronald was "working late" again. Just as well. She couldn't face him now. She had to plan what to do about the letter.

She slipped off her heels and hose, and her ladies maid had just unzipped her dress, when she heard Ronald's voice in the hallway. Trembling, she stepped out of her dress, unclipped her bra, threw on her dressing gown, and climbed into bed. She motioned for Maria to leave then pulled the duvet over her head.

As Ronald entered the bedroom, she peeked out from under the blanket. He approached the bed, and she closed her eyes, pretending to be asleep. After he moved away, she opened one eye and saw him standing over her dressing table, fingering her velvet handbag. He glanced over at her, and she held her breath. She watched from under the covers as he went through her purse. Her heart was racing. He'd find the letter and then all hell would break loose. He dropped her bag back onto her vanity then went into his

closet. She listened to the sound of his trouser rack whirring. She rolled over to face the closet and saw him emerge
in his silk pajamas.

"Are you awake?" he asked. "How was the charity thing?"
She just stared at him as he climbed into bed next to her.

"Sorry I couldn't make it. Damn report due tomorrow."
When he kissed her on the forehead, she smelled Inge's perfume. "Sweet dreams," he said, slipping under the sheets,
then hitting the button next to the bed to turn off the lights.

Why wasn't he saying anything about the letter? Olga's
entire body stiffened as she listened and waited. A few minutes later, Ronald's steady snoring reassured her he was fast
asleep. She pulled the bedcovers back as slowly as possible,
slid her legs over the edge of the bed, and sat up.

The snoring stopped, and she held her breath; she
glanced over at Ronald. He shifted position but didn't open
his eyes. She waited for his regular sleep rhythm to return
before setting her feet on the carpet.

In slow motion, she stood up, tiptoed across the room,
and lifted her purse from the vanity. She'd left her robe
draped over an easy chair, and she picked it up on her way
to the bedroom door. She slipped into the robe, fastened it
around her already expanding waist, and a centimeter at a
time turned the doorknob. She opened the door a crack and
inched it open just enough to sneak through. She stopped
short when it creaked then looked back at her sleeping husband. Olga slid through the opening and gently closed the
door behind her.

Light from a full moon poured in from the windows,
illuminating the wide corridor. Barefoot, Olga tiptoed
along the cool marble floor until she reached the end of the

hall. She glanced around the hallway then opened the door to Ronald's study and snuck inside.

Her heart was pounding so hard she thought her ribs would burst. The babies' hearts must be pounding too, all five of them. Her swollen belly quivered and she put her hand on her abdomen. "Calm down in there," she said softly. "You'll wake up your father, and then we'll all be in trouble."

Olga crept to her husband's desk and found "the forbidden city" fountain pen, screwed off its top, retrieved the key, and opened the top drawer. Panting, she released the secret compartment, recovered the combination plate, and studied the instructions, committing the numbers to memory.

She repeated the combination over and over again under her breath. But her brain felt so foggy and a wave of nausea hit her just as she was about to replace the plate. It was impossible, as hard as she tried, she couldn't keep the numbers in her head.

She grasped the plate in her right hand and steadied herself on a sofa as she made her way across the room to the bookcase. She held the plate to catch the moonbeams streaming in through the picture windows, and studied the instructions again, memorizing the next step then slowly turned the tumbler twice to the left until it clicked on the next number.

When the overhead lights flickered on, Olga caught her scream in her hand and jumped back from the safe. Ronald was standing in the doorway wearing his silk robe and slippers, his hair was sticking straight out to one side of his head like a shaggy Ukrainian mountain goat.

"I figured it was you," he said, closing the door behind

him, then turning the key in the door lock, locking her in. "How long have you been stealing from me, my dear?"

She froze and stared at him in terror. The metal plate slipped out of her hand and landed on her bare foot. She grimaced but stood stone still in spite of the throbbing in her toes.

"I don't like thieves," Ronald said. "Haven't I given you everything you ever wanted? Why do you need to steal?"

Tears streamed down her face, and she just stood there, a mute statue unable to say a word. She couldn't tell him about the IVF... and she didn't dare mention the ransom note.

"Answer me, Olga." He raised his voice. "Why would you rob your own husband?" When he was angry, his face turned as red as the scarlet cockscomb in her green house.

"Calm down, Ronald," she whispered. "You'll wake the servants."

"It's my house, I'll shout if I want to," he said even louder. "What are you doing breaking into my safe, goddammit."

"Okay. Please calm down. I'll tell you, but you have to promise not to yell." Light-headed, she braced herself against the bookcase, and he stomped across the room to his desk.

"I'm not making any promises until I hear the truth." He sat down on the chair behind his desk, and commanded, "And give me my combination plate, now." He held out his hand, wiggling his fingers impatiently.

When she bent over to pick it up, her head started spinning, and she thought she might pass out. She grasped the plate and stood up slowly, using her knees for support. She steadied herself on the back of each high-backed chair she passed on her way across the room to the desk. A naughty schoolgirl visiting the principal's office, she stood next to his desk, hands folded in front of her clasping the plate, staring at her bare feet.

"Hand it over," he bellowed. She shuttered and dropped the plate onto his desk. He tucked it back into the compartment, scowled at her, then took the little key off the desk, locked the drawer, and made a show of dropping the key into the pocket of his pajamas.

"I take you off the streets of Kiev and this is how you show your gratitude? I'm surprised at you, my dear. I truly am." Ronald pressed his blonde comb-over back into place. "Now sit down and tell me what you're doing with my money. By last count, I'm missing about fifty thousand in cash. Does that sound about right, sweetheart?"

Olga sat on the edge of the chair closest to the desk, and folded her arms around herself, rocking back and forth to steady her nerves. "I've been meaning to tell you...."

"Please do."

"I wanted to be sure, and now I am." She closed her eyes and took a deep breath. "Ronald, I'm pregnant."

"What? Seriously? Why, honey, that's wonderful news." Ronald came to her side and put his arm around her shoulders. She leaned into his fleshy warmth. "Is it a boy? My father insists on a boy. If it's a boy then we've beaten Daniel." He laughed. "He'll be so pissed." He pumped his fist in the air. When he kissed her on the forehead with his dry lizard lips, whiskey breath, and Miss Sweden's perfume lingering in his comb-over, she fought the urge to jump up and run away. All he cared about was getting his father's fortune and the Senate seat.

"And what if it's a girl?" she asked.

"It won't be." He smiled. "I have a good feeling about you, my dear. My first two wives only produced girls, but you're finally going to give the old man an heir." He put his hand on her stomach and she flinched. Then he put both arms around her, held her tight, and whispered in her ear, "But you still haven't told me why you're stealing my money." He held her by the shoulders and stared down into her face. "You don't look so good. Maybe I should call Maria," he said.

"I'm exhausted. I need to lie down. Can we talk about this in the morning?" She twisted free and tightened her robe around her waist.

"Whatever is best for the baby." Ronald took her by the elbow and led her back to the bedroom. "Ronald Junior," he said, beaming. "The old man will have to hand over those Swiss bank accounts now." He was giddy. "I'm going to invite dad and Danny to lunch next week. I can't wait to see their faces. I bet Dan's been screwing his new bride morning noon and night trying to knock her up." He chuckled. "I knew my soldiers would penetrate that fortress of yours eventually." When he put his arm around her waist and pulled her closer to him, this time she smelled more than just Inge's perfume in his hair.

"I'm so proud of you. You'll be such a good mother to my son, and we'll get him the best nannies and tutors. Finally, an heir to carry on the Davies' dynasty." He lead her down the corridor and back into the bedroom, then shut the door and turned the key in the lock.

"I'm going to have to take better care of you. I'm not going to let you and Junior out of my sight. Don't worry. I'll arrange everything. Tomorrow, I'll get you the best doctors, a live-in nurse, and a new cook. That's right. We have to change your diet. And no more alcohol or caffeine, no more sneaking cigarettes, isn't that right? You can't just think of yourself anymore, my dear. You have to think of our son."

"Yes, Ronald. May I go back to bed now?" Olga climbed up onto the mammoth king-sized bed, slid her legs under the covers, and clung to her pillow.

She couldn't tell Ronald why she needed the money. He wouldn't accept that his sperm had been defective, or that she'd used someone else's eggs to get pregnant. If her assisted reproduction made the papers, it would tarnish his precious reputation; people might think he was impotent in his old age. And once his father found out the baby wasn't Ronald's biological son, no doubt the deal would be off.

She buried her face in her pillow so Ronald couldn't see her tears. She almost wished she were back in Kiev. There, she sold her body in a nightclub, but at least she was her own boss. Here, she sold it in a penthouse and Ronald controlled her every move. Choking back tears, she realized she'd left her purse in Ronald's study. He was sure to find the ransom note now.

CHAPTER TWENTY-TWO

FIVE DAYS HAD passed since the Holly Ball, and Jack had completely forgotten about the disposable cellphone Vanya gave him until it started jingling from his backpack. Heart pounding, he reached into his bag and pulled it out, holding it between his thumb and forefinger like a mouse by its tail he was about to throw out of the house.

He stared at the caller ID, even though he knew it had to be Vanya. His classmates glared at him, a few snickered, and the lecturer at the forensic psychiatry workshop stopped midsentence. Glancing around the room, Jack picked up his pack and tiptoed towards the door.

"Where are you?" Vanya asked.

"I'm in a workshop and can't talk now," Jack whispered, averting the stares of his classmates on his way out of the seminar room.

"Where?"

"Feinberg."

"Okay. I'll be there in half hour. Meet me out front." The line went dead. Jack returned to the seminar room. Instead of listening to the lecture on fitness to plead, distracted, Jack watched the clock. When he got up and left the workshop early, the lecturer stopped again, scowling at him as he skipped out. He took the stairs two at a time to the lobby and braced himself for the blast of cold air as he exited through the front double doors.

Sure enough, the smoke-filled black Escalade was parked illegally in front of the building. Jack skated on the icy sidewalk until he reached the Caddy then tapped on the window. He heard the locks click and opened the passenger door.

"Get in. Sam says Mrs. Smith, A.j.a, Olga Davis, has an appointment at the clinic this afternoon. Let's find out what's up."

"A.k.a.," Jack said.

"Whatever. Don't just stand there with the door open. Get in, *chuvak*."

Jack hopped into the passenger seat and slammed the door. Vanya had been smoking so much that all the oxygen in the Caddy had been replaced by carbon monoxide. Jack rolled down the window.

"Hey, put that back up. My balls are freezing over here," Vanya said, cigarette dangling from his lips.

Jack rolled the window back up and shook his head. He took a joint from his backpack, lit it, took a big hit, and blew the smoke towards Vanya. Oblivious, Vanya drove three blocks to Manly's clinic and parked next to a dumpster in the back parking lot. Every time the Russian lit another cigarette, Jack relit his joint. Fighting fire with fire, they were having a smoke-off when a familiar black sedan pulled up. Wearing her sunglasses and head scarf, Olga Davis got out of the backseat, glanced around, then ducked into the back door of the clinic.

"Now what?" Jack asked. "We can't just follow her in."

"You're a doctor, right?" Vanya asked, tapping more ash onto the overflowing pile of snouts and butts already in the ashtray. "So you can go in and find out what she's up to."

"What? I can't do that. First, I'm not a doctor yet. Second, even if I were, I'm studying psychiatry not obstetrics." Jack's knee was bouncing up and down, and his palms were sweating. "I need to get back to my workshop. I paid good money for it." He wiped his hands on his jeans.

"Look, man, if you don't help out, it's gonna cost you way more than your shop. I'm tryin' to be nice here. Sam's countin' on ya. And I got the video tape, remember, *chuvak*?"

"So what. I was wearing a mask."

"You took it off in the hall. Anyway, Sam and me are witnesses. You wrecked the lab and that could get you prison time. Believe me, prison's no picnic. You wouldn't like it. Bad food and worse attitudes. So, get in there. Scram. Sam's waiting inside."

"If Sam's inside, why does she need me?" Jack asked.

"You axe a lot of questions, *chuvak*." Vanya played with his titanium lighter. Click, click, click. "If you knows what's good for you, you'll get your ass out of my ride and into that clinic."

Jack laughed. "Are you for real?"

"Don't test me, punk."

The reflection off his golden grill made Jack blink. "Why is Sam helping you spy on Olga Davis? I really don't get what's going on between you two crazy mixed up kids."

Jack sighed and ran his fingers through his tangled hair. Hanging around Vanya was exhausting.

"Sam's got class. And she's smart. And she's helping them poor kids. She's got heart."

"Yeah, I know, a real Robin Hoody." Jack rolled his eyes. "Okay, I'll go inside. But then what?"

"Just bring Mrs. Davis out here to me."

"Why?"

"I want to introduce her to someone. Just get her out here."

"And how am I supposed to do that?" Jack asked, shaking his head. "I don't have superpowers. I can't make us invisible. Her driver will see us."

"Let me worry about him. You get Mrs. Davis into my ride, and I'll take over from there." Vanya stretched black driving gloves over his broken knuckles.

"You're not going to hurt her or her driver, are you?"

"Depends."

"Wait a minute. I'm not going along with any more violence. I've had enough gunplay. Count me out." Not sure where he was going, Jack opened the passenger door and hopped out.

"Okay, okay. *Chuvak*, buddy, come back," Vanya said. "I swear on my granny's grave, no violence… not unless absolutely necessary."

Jack leaned against the door wondering whether to get back in. *How in the hell did he get into this mess?* It was all Jesse's fault. The more she pushed him away, the more he wanted her. It was perverse, but that's how desire worked. Maybe he was actually in love with desire itself, and Jesse was only a means to fuel the fire.

Jack looked up when he heard the clinic door open. An elegant woman appeared in the doorway. If he hadn't known it was Olga Davis, he wouldn't have recognized her in her sunglasses, scarf, and overcoat.

"Get her," Vanya said. "Hurry, she'll get away."

"Okay, okay. Don't have a psychotic break." Jack shut the car door and headed to intercept Olga Davis.

"Excuse me," he said as he approached. "Mrs. Davis?"

She stopped and stared at him. "You must have me confused with someone else," she said, turning on her heels. She gave him her back and walked briskly towards the black sedan parked across the lot.

Jack caught up with her and took hold of her arm. "Mrs. Davis, don't be alarmed. I'm a doctor, a medical student, really…a friend of Dr. Samantha Brewer. She's your doctor, isn't she?"

She took off her sunglasses and looked him straight in the eyes.

"You're not from the media?" she asked.

"No. No, not the media. Another friend of Samantha's, that is, Dr. Brewer's, would very much like to meet you."

She narrowed her brows. "Why would Dr. Brewer's friend want to meet me?"

"He knows your family back in Russia." Jack knew better than to mention Samantha or the Russian family connection, but it seemed the only way to get her into the Caddy. "He recognized your father from a photograph taken outside SkyBar in Kiev."

Her mouth dropped open and he saw fear in her eyes.

"Is this blackmail?" she asked.

"No, no," Jack said. "At least, I don't think so." Over

her shoulder, he saw her chauffer come charging out of the black sedan. "Can we discuss this in private?"

She gave him a questioning look. She jerked her head around when her driver put his hand on her back. "Everything okay, Mrs. D.?"

"I'm not sure, José."

"Is this man bothering you?" the chauffer asked, stepping in front of her, nose to nose with Jack.

Jack heard the Escalade door slam shut and turned to see Vanya rushing towards them. He was speaking Russian and waving a photograph. The strong current of words streaming from Vanya's mouth wrapped around Olga Davis like invisible threads binding her to some unspeakable past. She dropped her glasses and her handbag onto the asphalt and broke into sobs. Bewildered, Jack stepped aside, away from the storm breaking on one side and the tsunami approaching on the other.

"Leave her alone," the chauffer yelled, puffing himself up like a blowfish.

"Stay out of this, *súka*," Vanya said, pulling a switchblade from his jacket pocket and flipping it open.

"Come on, Vanya," Jack said. "You promised, no violence."

"Unless absolutely necessary," Vanya said. "Well, *súka*, is it necessary?" he asked the driver.

"Please," Olga Davis said through her tears. "Put that away. There's no need for violence. I'll meet your cousin. We can go right now. Where can we find Mr. Yudkovich?" She bent down, picked up her glasses and handbag, then pulled a handkerchief from inside her handbag and dabbed at her eyes.

"*Klassno!*" Vanya said, snapping his blade shut and

shoving it back into his pocket. He removed his phone from his jacket. "I'll call Dmitry." His grill beamed in the sunlight.

Another torrent of Russian words, then Vanya repeated, "*Klassno*," and put his phone away. "Pavlov's Banquet in an hour. Best *Selyodka pod Shouboy* outside *Moskva*. You'll love it. Promise." He smiled and lit a cigarette.

"What's *Selyodka pod Shouboy*?" Jack asked.

"Herring…" Olga Davis answered. "Literally translated, it means Herring under a coat." She tucked her hankie into her purse, replaced her sunglasses, and said, "I'll have my driver follow you."

"You're not just trying to give us the slip, are you, Mrs. Davis?" Vanya asked.

"No. I give you my word," she said, "I'll follow you to Pavlov's Banquet.

Jack had never been to Pavlov's Banquet, although he'd heard Jesse rave about the Blinis and frozen vodka shots and spout warnings about the Russian mobsters who owned the joint. From the outside, the brick building looked more like a warehouse than a restaurant. In front of the tired structure, a life-sized wooden horse-drawn carriage complete with wooden horse, punctuated the uncanny scene. Directly across the street, a sprawling green cemetery opened onto heaven, making the suburban scene even more eerie.

"Eat at Pavlov's and you can die happy," Vanya said as they pulled into the parking lot. Jack tried not to think about the connection between Pavlov's Banquet and death. He'd heard enough about the Russian mafia to worry. Olga's black sedan swung into the parking lot behind them. Puffing away as usual, Vanya waited in his Caddy until Dmitry arrived in his minivan, then he hopped out and dropped his cigarette and ground it into the asphalt under his shoe. Trailing behind the Russian entourage, Jack brought up the rear, right behind Olga, as they entered the restaurant.

"Holler if you need me, Mrs. D," the chauffer called from the sedan. Without turning back, "Mrs. D" just nodded and followed Vanya inside.

The smell of grilled meat reminded Jack he hadn't eaten all day. He'd only had time to grab a Starbucks on his way to the forensics workshop. Pavlov's Banquet was a Russian funhouse.

Crazy contrasting pastel colors, blue, pink, and orange, bows and ribbons, sashes and drapery, every corner a study in kitsch, from Jesus icons to Russian nesting dolls. A feast for all of the senses: a buffet table loaded with meats, cheeses, and vegetables, all artfully arranged on crystal trays and strewn with edible flowers, a band playing Russian folk dances, and delicious rich aromas wafting into the dining room from the kitchen.

The wait staff recognized Vanya and a portly waiter led them to a secluded table in the back. Vanya rattled off something in Russian and the waiter disappeared. Sitting across the table, Dmitry Durchenko gazed at the elegant stranger with sad eyes, eyes that had seen too much.

Unlike his strident daughter, Dmitry was a broken man, sullen and reflective, a quiet rage hiding deep beneath his brooding exterior. Jack had seen Dmitry many times on campus at Brentano Hall polishing the wooden banister or dusting the antique chandelier.

In his undergraduate years, Jack had been a regular

at the musty old philosophy department. Back then, he couldn't get enough existential angst and melancholic nihilism. He ate it by the handful, especially if it came from the beautiful lips of Jessica James. Deep in thought, the whispered conversation in Russian washed over him and lulled him further into reminiscence.

He remembered the very first time he'd seen Jesse pound her little fists on the lectern, giving a sermon on Kierkegaard's leap of faith. "It's easy to leap," she sang. "Landing gracefully is the hard part." When she'd stomped her red cowboy boot against the wooden floor for emphasis, the skirt of her vintage dress danced around her slender hips and that's when it hit him. He was smitten with the cowgirl philosopher.

When the waiter sat a shot glass in front of him and filled it from a frozen bottle, Jack shook off his reveries and saw the table laid out with platters of caviar-filled eggs, smoked salmon on brown bread, sliced beets with lemon wedges, and rose-shaped salamis. The cold vodka shot enlivened his taste buds, and he filled his plate with Russian delicacies.

"Sorry to interrupt," Jack said, popping half a boiled egg into his mouth. "But could someone please tell me what's happening here in a language I understand, English, French, or even German, perhaps?"

Vanya was on his second helping and had already downed several vodkas. Dmitry drank only strong Russian tea and looked dour. Tears in her eyes, Olga sipped from a champagne flute. Jack loaded his plate and paused, glancing around the table.

"Is something wrong?" he asked.

"Family reunion," Vanya said, his mouth full. He pulled

a small photograph from his shirt pocket and sat it on the table in front of Olga.

"Where did you get that?" she asked, picking up the picture and examining it, her green eyes ablaze.

"From your husband," Vanya said. "Mr. Davis hire me to follow you. Thinks you're having an affair with a doc, and want to know about your parents."

She gave him a sharp look and tightened her lips then slid the photograph into her purse.

"We know you're faithful. But your husband don't know who he's dealing wit." Vanya smiled and poured himself another vodka from the bottle chilling in a stand next to the table. "Blood runs thicker than wine."

"Water," Jack said.

Vanya poured him a glass of water from the pitcher in the center of the table. Jack just shook his head.

"What's this about family?" Jack asked.

"My family is from the Ukraine." Jack was surprised when Dmitry finally spoke. "They emigrated to Russia decades ago."

"His father was the Oxford Don," Vanya said proudly.

"Anton Yudkovich was a very dangerous man, the head of Bratva, the Russian Brotherhood, very powerful, very dangerous," Dmitry said, staring down at the napkin on his lap.

"Tell them about the hospital, coz," Vanya said. "When your old man asked you to…"

"When I was only nineteen," Dmitry looked up and continued, "my father asked me to kill my own brother. Sergei had been stealing from him and he didn't allow disloyalty. I tried, but I couldn't do it. I went out to the hospital—an abandoned hospital where Bratva disposed of moles and stool pigeons. I held a pistol in my own brother's face." He troubled the corner of his napkin. "But I couldn't pull the trigger. I couldn't do it. I couldn't kill my own brother." Dmitry put his face in his hands, and said softly, "I heard two shots...." His voice trailed off.

"What does that have to do with Mrs. Davis?" Jack asked.

"Sergei Yudkovich is my father," Olga said. "And he's very much alive."

PART III

CHAPTER TWENTY-THREE

NEW YEAR'S EVE at O'Toole's was always crazy. The bar was packed, and Jessica was ready to put the last dismal year behind her. Her dissertation director's murder, the tragedy that killed her cousin, her mom's trailer burnt to the ground, and now the dumpster assault she was trying so hard to forget. Jessica looked across the booth at her two best friends and raised her glass.

"A toast: May the best days of our past be the worst days of our future, and the worst days of our past gone for good." She downed the rest of her Jack and Coke.

"I'm hosting my annual New Year's Eve game tonight," Lolita said. "Wanna start the year flush? I'll stake you. What about you, Jack? You could spell Raul as dealer."

"I don't want to ring in the new year flipping cards for a bunch of rich tossers," Jack said. "I'll stay here and take my chances." He glanced around the bar.

"Chances with what?" Jessica asked, looking around at his options.

"That I might be lucky enough to start the New Year off with you." A loud jingling coming from Jack's backpack interrupted his flirtation. "What the bloody hell?"

"Did you change your ringtone?" Jessica asked.

Jack pulled a cheap cellphone from his pack, holding it like it might bite him. "*Merde*. It's Vanya. He gave me this phone and said he'd call me when it was time."

"My cousin Vanya?" Lolita asked. "Time for what? Why is he calling you?"

"Hello," Jack said tentatively. "O'Tooles with Jesse and Lolita."

Jessica watched and listened, wondering what was going on.

"What?" Jack asked. "Okay, okay. I'll be outside in twenty minutes. No need to threaten." He rolled his eyes and shook his head. "Yes, Vanya, I've got it," he said into the phone. He shifted in his seat, shook his head, and stuffed the phone into the bottom of his pack.

"Bloody hell," he said. "What have I gotten myself into? This is your fault, Cowgirl."

"What do you mean? What's going on? Why is it my fault?"

"You insisted on avenging Junior and now that Russian bloke has me on video tape vandalizing the lab, and his uptight girlfriend is extorting me. Robin Hoody, my ass."

"Vanya has a girlfriend?" Lolita asked.

"Dr. Samantha Brewer. They've been thick as thieves since your cousin, Prince Charming, rescued her from that fat-faced racist cop."

"Vanya, Prince Charming? Going out with a doctor?" Lolita burst out laughing.

"Yes, I know, it's hilarious. Beauty and the beast, or in this case, brains and the beast. They're forcing me to help get supplies for a clinic on the South Side. Samantha is on a humanitarian mission to give free contraceptives and antibiotics to poor black women." Jack sighed. "Vanya's picking me up to help him break into Dr. Dude's clinic. As if I'm not in enough trouble already."

"You're not going, are you?" Jessica asked.

"What choice do I have? Anyway, why not steal from the rich and give to the poor. Might be fun."

"Are you crazy?" Jessica reached across the table and put her hand on his arm.

"Your concern is touching. Providing I'm not in jail, how about a nightcap later?"

"Well, as my mom always says, If you can't be good, be careful," Jessica said. "Call me when you're done."

"Careful is my middle name." He smiled and raised his eyebrows.

"Seriously, Jack. Don't do anything too stupid."

"Like get caught stealing pregnancy tests, birth control pills, and antibiotics? I'll make you a deal," he said with a wink.

"What deal?" Jessica asked.

"If I'm a good boy and don't get caught then I get a reward, a midnight kiss."

"And if you're a bad boy and get caught, then what?"

"You bake me a cake with a file in it."

"Don't worry," Lolita said. "Vanya won't get caught."

"How can you be so sure?" Jessica asked.

"He's a professional. You don't become a ranking member of Bratva by getting caught."

"The ink on his body says otherwise," Jack said. "I did a little research and some of his tattoos are from Russian prisons. His body reads like a rap sheet. I'm guessing that's why he left Russia. Probably wanted."

"He's been around." Lolita chuckled.

"What's so funny?" Jessica asked.

"My gangster cousin trying to go straight as a campus cop. Bet my dad got him that job." Her long red nails wrapped around the flute, Lolita sipped her champagne.

"Well, believe it or not, he's still working as a campus cop." Jack snorted. "I guess that makes our mission tonight an inside job." Jack finished his martini and scooted out of the booth dragging his backpack along after him. "I'll call you later, Cowgirl. Let's hope it's not my one phone call from the cop shop."

Jessica watched as Jack made his way through the crowd of revelers and fought his way up the stairs of the subterranean pub. Her heart skipped a beat when a minute later she saw Max White descending the stairs. She'd hoped she might run into him tonight. She smoothed her bangs and took a deep breath.

"How do I look?"

"Like always," Lolita replied. "Why? Who do you have your sights set on now, *milyi*?"

Jessica pinched her lips shut and gestured with her eyes to signal Max White's approach. He'd spotted them and was on his way to their booth.

Lolita's slick black hair flew around her shoulder as she twisted in the direction Jessica had indicated.

"Oh. The rapist." Lolita looked nonplused. "I hate to leave you alone with him, but I've got to go."

"Don't say that. He's not a rapist. Stay for just one more drink," Jessica pleaded. "Please, just one more. For me?"

Lolita sighed. "Okay, one more then I'm off. But I'm taking you with me, to save you from yourself."

Max White sauntered over to the table, one curly lock draped over his forehead, his dimples lighting up the bar. "Can I buy you ladies a drink?"

"No thanks," Lolita said.

Jessica scowled at her friend and kicked her under the table. "Sure. Thanks. Wanna join us?" She smiled up at Max.

"Ouch." She turned to Lolita, who had kicked her back.

"I'll get us some drinks," Max said. "Looks like champagne and a whiskey and Coke, right?" He maneuvered through the throng to the bar.

"Something about that guy I don't like," Lolita said.

"You never like anyone I'm interested in."

"Well, none of those losers are ever good enough for you."

Max returned carrying a champagne flute in one hand and a highball glass in the other, and sat the drinks down on the table.

"Where's yours?" Jessica asked.

Smiling, Max pulled a bottle of beer out of his back pocket then scooted into the booth next to Jessica. The corner of his cashmere coat caressed the thigh of her jeans and he radiated heat.

"Neat trick," Lolita said, dipping her fingernail into the champagne. "I bet you're full of tricks." She glared at him.

"Looks like you are, too," he said, pointing to her fingernail; it had turned from red to blue.

"Will you excuse us a minute," Lolita said, grabbing Jessica's hand. "We have to go to the little girls' room." She stood up and gestured to Jessica.

"I don't…"

"Yes, you do," Lolita interrupted in her commando voice, glaring at her with those soul piercing sage eyes. "Please accompany me."

"Sorry." Jessica sighed. "We'll be right back." She gave Max an apologetic look and he let her out of the booth.

"Don't go anywhere," she said.

"I'll be here." When he took off his winter coat and scooted back into the booth, she noticed the sticker.

"Did you come from the museum?" she asked, reaching down to peel off the sticker.

"Oh, yes. I always forget to take off those stickers." He smiled.

"Come on," Lolita said, grabbing her elbow. She dragged Jessica into the bathroom, shoved her into a stall, stepped behind her, and slammed the door.

Jessica rolled the sticker between her fingers, trying to flick it to the floor.

"Look." Lolita held up her blue tipped index finger. "He drugged those drinks."

"What? No way." Jessica said, her mouth hanging open.

"Under Cover Color. A brand new nail polish that detects rape drugs in drinks. My red polish changed to blue. No doubts about it. Max White just slipped us a roofie."

"What? Why would he do that?" She narrowed her brows and stared down at the little wad stuck to her index finger. "Oh my God. Maybe he *is* the serial rapist." She held up her finger to show her friend.

"Let me see that." Lolita peeled the wad off her fingertip and examined it. "When I came to Prentice Hospital Thanksgiving Eve, you had a piece of a sticker stuck to your hat. A sticker just like this one." Lolita pushed the sticker back into place on the front of Jessica's shirt.

"Max goes to the museum all the time," Jessica said. "It's him."

"You think?" Lolita took her by the shoulders. "We're going to find out."

"How? Not by drinking that poison?"

"Don't be stupid." Lolita pinned her to the side of the stall with her gaze. "Here's the plan. We play along. Dump your drink and act drunk. If he is a serial rapist, I want to know what he's up to and how he's been getting away with it for so long."

"You think Max is responsible for the 'dumpster girls.'" She made air quotes with her fingers. "But none of us showed any signs of being raped."

"All the more reason to find out what White does with the girls he drugs. Act drunk, but keep on your toes. Let's beat that fox at his own game." Lolita opened the stall and let her out then held the bathroom door open. "Ready?"

"Ready." Jessica followed her friend back to the booth. Max White smiled up at her as she slid in next to him.

"Happy New Year!" He raised his beer bottle. "May all your genes be dominant."

Jessica clinked her glass against his bottle and pretended to take a sip. Glancing around for a potted plant or spittoon, she settled on the bumpy red bowl of burnt down candle wax in the center of the table. When the clattering of a tray dropping distracted Max, she dumped most of her drink into the candle. Lolita took the opportunity to pour her champagne into her empty coffee cup.

Jessica raised her half empty glass. "May we always stay

positive and always test negative." Max laughed, and she clinked his beer bottle with her glass again.

Lolita raised her champagne flute. "Strength to all of the survivors who've been sexually assaulted, and castration with rusty scissors to all of the men who've assaulted them."

"Indeed," Max said. "Another reason for filtering out violence and criminality from the human gene pool." He raised his beer bottle. "Perhaps the human race would be better off if we did away with men altogether and relied entirely on genetic engineering with frozen sperm from the best specimens. We could evolve females for autogenesis."

"I'll drink to that!" Lolita raised her empty champagne flute.

"Looks like I'd better get us another round," Max said. "I'll be right back." He scooted out of the booth and smiled.

"Actually, I'm feeling a little light-headed," Lolita said. "Maybe we should get out of here and get some air."

"I concur," Jessica said. "I'm kinda dizzy, too."

"I'd be happy to escort you ladies upstairs for some air," Max said. He helped Jessica out of the booth, and she took his arm. He extended his hand to Lolita. Her eyes twitched, but she took it. He led them through the crowded bar, up the stairs, and out onto the sidewalk. The night air was a slap in the face that brought tears to Jessica's eyes.

"Are you alright?" Max asked.

"I'm not feeling well." She staggered and bounced off the brick building for effect.

"My van is parked in a garage across the street. I could take you home, if you're not well."

"Yes, take me home," Jessica said.

"Good idea," Lolita said, swaying back and forth. "Can you drive us, Max?"

"Wait here. I'll get my van and pick you up. I'll be right back." Max jogged across the street and disappeared into a parking garage.

"Now what?" Jessica asked.

"We go with him and see what he's up to."

"Shouldn't we call the police or something?"

"What would we tell them? My fingernail turned blue, we dumped our drinks, and now we're catching a ride with a Doctor Jeckel who may really be Mr. Hyde?"

"What if he is the serial assaulter?"

"Then I'll kick his ass. Don't worry, I've got him outnumbered."

A black van with tinted windows pulled up to the curb. Max White rolled down the passenger window. "Get in," he said. "I'll drive you home."

"After you." Lolita gestured toward the passenger door. Jessica gave her a skeptical look but opened the door and climbed in next to a potential sexual predator. Lolita got in the back and sat on the one seat. The rest of the full-sized delivery van had been converted into a mobile research lab with a built-in miniature refrigerator and sample cases stacked with petri dishes.

"Do you feel up to a party?" Max asked. "How much have you girls had to drink tonight? Have you eaten anything? Maybe you just need some food."

Lolita lay down on the floor between the seats. "I'm so queasy," she moaned. Following her lead, Jessica slumped over the dashboard and groaned.

"There, there, girls," Max said. "Dr. White will take

good care of you. Are you comfortable, Lolita? There's a pillow in the back. I'll get it for you." Her forehead against the dash, Jessica heard rustling and felt his arm brush past her as he reached between the seats.

When a sharp unforgiving odor hit her in the face, her eyes flew open, and she saw Max struggling to hold a cloth over Lolita's nose. Her friend got in one good punch to his face before her body jolted and then went limp.

Terrified, Jessica held her breath and squeezed her eyes tight. *Please don't let him kill us, Please don't let him kill us.*

A gloved hand pressed a damp cloth over her mouth and its bitter vapors zapped her brain into oblivion.

CHAPTER TWENTY-FOUR

WHEN JESSICA TRIED to move her arms, she realized she was fastened to the table. She tugged at the restraints, kicking her naked legs against cold steel. Queasy and disoriented, her head rolled from side to side and her eyes struggled to keep up. *Where had Max taken her?*

The dimly lit room was awash in a bitter blue glow and smelled of bleach and desperation. To her right, a long-necked square-headed lamp was shining a spotlight at her groin. Overhead, monstrous mechanical creatures with arms going in every direction sprouted circular faces, boxy torsos, and flat tongues sticking out to mock her. To her left, an ultrasound machine became a robot standing at attention with its computer face flickering ominously.

"Who's there? Where am I?" she asked, grogginess dragging her towards unconsciousness. She struggled against the restraints again, jerking her head from side to side, forcing the room into focus. She was strapped on to an operating table in a surgery bay.

"If you resist, I'll administer a shot of Propofol," a deep voice warned her. "True, your friend over there is a geneticist's dream: perfect specimen, brains, beauty and physical strength. But you, Jessica, you are a rare jewel, one for the record books."

She gazed up at the blurry face, trying to concentrate on what he was saying. When she saw Max White standing over her with a scalpel in his hand, terror struck with the razor edge of a skinning knife to the gut.

"First there's your golden blood, Rh-null…then those beautiful eyes, both distichiasis and heterochromia iridum, lush lashes framing sparkling flecks in your sky-blue eyes. I've never seen anything so beautiful, speaking as a geneticist, of course."

"Max?" she asked. "What's going on? What are you doing to me?"

"I've been studying your DNA for weeks now. And your true genetic jackpot is at OR5A1, the olfactory gene. You know Jessica, your enhanced olfactory sense could outmatch a bloodhound. With training, you could use your gift in so many ways."

"Gift," she repeated, barely able to keep her eyes open.

"Gifts, plural," Max said.

She pried her eyes open and tried to comprehend what he was saying.

"You're a genetic wonder, Jessica James. Everyone is unique, but you're special. I'd love to meet your parents. Both of them must have some of these same genetic mutations that make you such a rare bird."

"Why are you doing this, Max?" she asked. Her mouth felt disconnected from her brain, but she finally managed to speak. She was out of her body, watching herself from above, looking down at her half-naked body strapped to the operating table.

"Because I don't believe in luck and I don't believe in gambling, especially not with the human race. We can't leave our future up to chance. We can control our destiny by controlling our genes. We can make better people and finish what evolution started. You, my beautiful Jessica, can help me create another brilliant little girl, a perfect little girl, one without your variations on chromosomes 4q27 and 16."

"Variations," she repeated. "You're cloning me?"

"No, my love." He laughed. "I'm improving you."

Jessica heard groaning coming from across the room.

"Excuse me, dear one. I need to attend to your friend. I'll be right back. Don't go anywhere." His sly smile turned her stomach. She followed him with her eyes and barely made out the silhouette of Lolita strapped to a bed on the other side of the room.

"F-you, asshole!" Lolita's shout startled her. Jessica jerked her head around and saw her friend land a kick to Max White's dimpled chin. Max stumbled backwards and knocked over a steel tray, sending instruments crashing to the floor; speculums, syringes, scalpels, and scissors clattered across the tile. Max wiped blood from the corner of his mouth and laughed.

"I can't wait to get into your genes and poke around. I bet your DNA is as feisty as you are."

"No one is getting into my jeans," Lolita growled. "Just try it, creep."

"It will be my pleasure. You couldn't be as genetically interesting as Jessica, but you'll make a fantastic egg donor for some privileged woman and at the same time allow me to improve the human genome."

"Yeah, well take one step closer, asshole, and I'll improve the human race by taking you out." Leveraging her legs against the table, Lolita reared up and strained against her arm restraints.

"In a minute," Max said. He slinked across the medical bay to a cabinet and removed a small syringe. Then he opened a refrigerator and took out a small vial. He wiped its top with an alcohol pad, pulled back the plunger on the syringe, inserted the needle into the vial, pushed the plunger, then he turned the vial upside down and slowly pulled the plunger back again. He tapped the syringe with his finger then removed the needle from the vial. Everything was happening in slow motion.

"Coming, dear," Max said in a singsong voice. He walked around the head of the table to avoid Lolita's feet.

"Watch out!" Jessica shouted, trying to free herself. "He's got a needle." She tried to move her legs, but Max had strapped her feet into the stirrups.

"Yes, this injection will make you more cooperative." Max wiped Lolita's upper arm with an alcohol pad. She was lying so still Jessica wondered if she'd passed out again. When Max came at her with the needle, Lolita jack-knifed both feet up over her head, and kicked him back against the wall. As he bounced off the wall, the syringe dropped from his hand.

"We may have to do something about that aggressiveness. I'll definitely be checking for MAOA variants in your DNA. It's a delicate balance to get physical strength without violence." White picked himself off the floor and retrieved the syringe. "Don't want to risk infection," he said, wiping the needle with an alcohol pad.

"Leave her alone." Jessica shouted feebly. Desperate to get free and help her friend, she fought with all her strength. "Lolita," she gasped.

"I dare you to try that again, creep," Lolita slurred. "I'll crush your skull with my bare feet."

"Yes, let's try it again, Miss Durchenko. Just relax." Needle in hand, Max made a wide berth around the bed and came at Lolita from the side. As she bent her knee to slam him with another kick, he grabbed a foot, smashed it down on the metal table, and sat on her shin. "You may feel a prick in your thigh," he said through gritted teeth, as he stabbed the needle into Lolita's right thigh.

She swung her left leg up and hooked him around the neck. The syringe clattered to the floor, and both of Max's hands flew to his neck. Lolita squeezed his neck in the crook of her knee, like a nutcracker cracking a brazil nut. Max's face was crimson, and he was gasping for air. Lolita's leg went limp against the table, and Max slumped to the floor. They must have both lost consciousness at the same time.

No matter how much she flailed and wriggled, Jessica couldn't break free of the straps digging into her stinging wrists. In her drug-induced haze, the terror of captivity took her back to third grade recess when Tommy Dalton hogtied her with a jump rope, then yelled, "squeal little piggy," as he dragged her around the playground until her wrists were bleeding, the other kids laughing at her. Now, with all her might, she pulled at the ropes, but in response they only dug deeper into her wrists and ankles until they broke her skin, and she fell back against the table, spent and desperate.

With no escape from violence all around her, life had her hogtied. Like struggling against the straps binding her to the table, sometimes fighting back just made the pain worse.

She'd always wished she could be more like Lolita, karate kick first and ask questions later. No remorse.

Her wrists and ankles may be bleeding, but her heart hurt most. She never thought she'd see the day when Lolita couldn't get the upper hand. Her best badass girlfriend lying unconscious on a metal slab was gutting and there wasn't a damned thing she could do about it.

Lolita had saved her butt so many times, and now all she could do was lay there waiting to see who came to first, her stalwart friend or the insane geneticist.

She didn't have to wait long. Max White gasped and raised himself to his hands and knees. He shook his head, then reached up, grasped the edge of the table, and pulled himself upright. He glanced over at Jessica, rubbed his neck, and smiled. "Can't say I wasn't warned. You told me she was a black-belt in karate." He strolled to a stainless steel sink the size of a trough in the corner of the room, turned on one its three faucets, and splashed water on his face. He pumped out strong smelling disinfectant soap and scrubbed his hands up to the elbows.

"Let's start over, shall we?" He went to the refrigerator, drew up another syringe, then sauntered back to the table where Lolita was still lying unconscious.

"Lolita, wake up!" Jessica shouted.

Max White sat the needle on a tray next to the table.

"For good measure. And if I don't use it on her, it's your turn next, my lovely." He rolled an oxygen tank closer, and attached a plastic mask to Lolita's nose and mouth then adjusted a nob. "She won't wake up until the harvest is over."

"Harvest?" Jessica panicked.

"That's right. I'm harvesting her eggs."

"What?"

"Attractive college girls can earn upwards of twenty thousand dollars for quality egg donations. My donors do it for free. I may not get the yield I could if they were properly prepared with fertility drugs, but my overhead is much less. In fact, the barren wealthy women of Chicago have given me quite a nice nest egg, pardon the pun." Max chuckled.

"You're stealing our eggs?" Jessica burst out.

"A regular fox in a hen house as they might say in your redneck of the woods."

"Why?"

"I need money for my research." Max tightened the mask around Lolita's face. "Shall we begin, Ms. Durchenko?" he asked the motionless form. He strapped Lolita's feet into the stirrups, opened her knees, and attached long bands hanging from steel arms overhead to her thighs to hold them in place then draped a blue paper apron over her lap. He sat on a stool at the end of the table and rolled the tray of instruments closer.

When he pulled apart the ends of a paper envelope, ripping it open, dusty latex gloves fell out onto the tray. He snapped them onto his hands one by one, and surveyed the row of shiny tools, fingers fluttering as he chose his weapon.

"I'm going to insert the speculum now. It may feel a little cold. I apologize," he said to Lolita's limp body, as he picked up an instrument. "It's a simple procedure, really. Ten minutes tops. So, you won't have to wait long for your turn, Jessica, my dear."

"Does Dr. Manly know that you're drugging girls and stealing their eggs?" Her stomach turned just thinking about it.

"Manly is an egotistical ass. He doesn't care how I get the eggs as long as he can continue his own research on Klinefelter syndrome. He has KS and he's obsessed with it. Whatever he lacks in genitalia, Manly makes up for in arrogance." Max White moved the bigheaded light closer to Lolita's open legs and then inserted a plastic wand. Looking up at a screen on the ultrasound machine, he guided the rod.

Jessica couldn't watch. Tears pooled in her eyes, and she wanted to scream.

"Now that Granowski's out of the way, I have free reign at the clinic. As long as I bring in the best eggs, Manly doesn't care how I get them," Max said distractedly as he maneuvered the wand inside Lolita.

"What do you mean out of the way? Did you kill Professor Granowski?"

"I'm not a murderer."

"But you killed that other dumpster girl? You did, didn't you?" Blood raced through her veins and hammered at her brain.

"That was an accident."

She regretted glancing across the room just in time to see Max White insert a giant needle into Lolita. "No!" she shouted. "Not Lolita."

"Don't worry. Your friend will be fine. Complications are

very rare. Internal bleeding is a possibility, but highly improbable. I suspect that the poor girl who died suffered from internal bleeding; possibly she had a reaction to the anesthesia and froze to death before she woke up. It wasn't supposed to go that way. Believe me, Jessica, I feel terrible remorse. But, she's the only one. All the rest of you have been just fine."

"Are you insane? Do you think if you woke up half-naked behind a dumpster you'd ever be the same again? Would you be just fine?" she yelled. When she fought against the restraints again, it felt like someone was taking a hacksaw to her wrists.

"You want to know the best part?" Max White smiled over at her. "I don't need to pay sperm donors either. In cases where both sperm and egg donors are required, I supply the sperm. Just think, Jessica, we will be the biological parents of a race of superior human beings, the new and improved Adam and Eve."

"Yeah, and look what happened to them. You're bat-shit crazy, Doctor Frankenstein." The monster had already harvested her eggs, inseminated them, and implanted them in some rich woman's womb. He'd violated her and used part of her body to make a child. Chills ran down her spine, her lips moving in a silent prayer, *please let this be a nightmare, please let this be a nightmare.*

CHAPTER TWENTY-FIVE

SAMANTHA'S APARTMENT WAS as tidy and spotless as it had been on Jack's last visit. This time, she led him into an alcove with a mahogany desk and matching bookcases full of thick medical tomes. Scanning the bookcase, Jack noticed the bottom shelf overflowed with paperback romance novels, their tattered covers sporting scantily clad women and bare chested men. Obviously, Beagle Girl's fantasy life was more interesting than her real one, at least until she'd hooked up with the tattooed Russian. She must go in for classic Harlequin romance fantasies of bespeckled librarians wooed by beefcake bikers.

He imagined the Russian passionately ripping off Beagle Girl's lab coat and then at her insistence hanging it neatly in her closet before igniting the secret flame burning in her loins. He bent down and picked up one of the trashy novels.

"Put that back," Samantha commanded. "Please, don't touch anything." She grabbed the book from his hands and slid it back onto its shelf. "Now, pay attention, Mr. Grove. You have work to do."

Jack couldn't believe he was spending New Year's Eve with a crazy Russian gangster and his harlequin-reading

girlfriend plotting to steal contraceptives and medical supplies from a fertility clinic. Beagle Girl was clearly calling
the shots. Using a felt-tipped pen, she drew the clinic layout
on a legal pad.

After she finished her scale model of the place, she
picked up a red pen and wrote tiny numbers on three cabinets and closets, then she selected a third pen from a holder
on her desk and made a key to the numbers in blue ink
at the bottom of the page. Jack watched over her shoulder thinking maybe she should have been an architect with
such exact drawing skills.

"You're in the clinic twice a week." Jack said, eying her
drawing. "Why you can't just take the stuff you need a bit
at a time? Why a heist?"

"I told you before. They're watching me constantly. Dr.
Manly is already suspicious of me, so he's watching me. It's
like he's been out to get me ever since Dr. Granowski died,
constantly criticizing me and second-guessing my every
move. And now, thanks to you, the administration suspects
I had something to do with the vandalism at the animal
research lab. Maybe Dr. Manly blames me for Janet's death.
After all, I'm the one who reported it to the police, again
thanks to you."

"How well did you know Janet Granowski?" Jack asked.
The police had labeled the case an accident, but he didn't
believe it. He knew someone had rigged the door and the
emergency unlocking mechanism. It was too much of a
coincidence that both were broken. If Samantha hadn't
come back to the lab that afternoon, he and Jesse would
have died in the freezer, too.

"Well, I worked for her for two years," Samantha said.

"I know she moved to Northwestern from New York with Dr. Manly to set up the fertility clinic. Last October, she divorced Dr. Manly and was looking for another job. She wanted to leave Northwestern." Samantha continued to draw the clinic's floor plan, shading in the furniture and fixtures.

"Maybe she quit 'fore she got fired." Vanya was leaning up against the wall drinking a beer. Other than his fancy brown shoes, he was wearing his navy campus cop uniform: gun belt, walkie-talkie, badge, and even a brand new nametag.

"I guess Manly couldn't fire his wife and partner. If only he'd just fired her instead of killed her," Jack said. "Why didn't he just wait for her to leave?"

"You think Dr. Manly killed his ex-wife?" Samantha asked.

"Maybe he didn't want a divorce," Vanya said.

"She did. Dr. Manly was having an affair with his new nurse," Samantha answered. "He's a real womanizer. Always hitting on interns and nurses."

"Did he hit on you, Sam?" Vanya asked, then tightened his lips, biting into his unlit cigarette. "If he did, I'll turn *him* into a popsicle."

"Most murders are crimes of passion," Jack said.

"How do you know it wasn't an accident?" Samantha asked.

"You saw the locks in the freezer. You know as well as I do someone tampered with those locks. That freezer has more safeties than an AK47. And it's as deadly a weapon if you lock someone inside," Jack said. "Whoever broke those locks almost killed me and Jesse, too." He shuddered as he remembered Jesse's blue lips and frosty eyelashes. "What about his new girlfriend, the nurse?" Jack asked. "Why would she want the ex-wife out of the way?"

"I've heard they're getting married next summer. He's old enough to be her father. Disgusting," Samantha said, putting her pens away and rubbing her palms together. "Here's your treasure map," she said, handing Jack the legal pad. "Vanya will get you in, and you get the supplies we need. The impoverished South Side women depend on them."

"Piece of pie!" Vanya said grinning, playing with his titanium lighter, an unlit cigarette still hanging from his lips. "Well, *chuvak*, let's go." He slapped Jack on the back and headed for the door. On his way out, he turned back to Samantha, "We'll get your stuff, Sam. Don't worry." He removed the cigarette from his lips and gave her a gushy kiss then continued into the hallway.

Jack followed him out, and as soon as they were in the elevator, Vanya lit his cigarette. Jack just rolled his eyes.

"Sam don't want me to smoke in her place," Vanya said, staring down at his Italian lace-ups.

Fifteen minutes later, Vanya pulled into the parking lot of Dr. Dude's downtown clinic. The clinic was dark. Jack surveyed the area around the back entrance and was curious about the black van parked in the handicapped spot. Maybe an employee had left the van there to party downtown. It was choice real estate. Vanya got out of the Caddy and sauntered to the entrance. Jack followed then watched over the Russian's shoulder as he unlocked the door with a key.

"Won't it look suspicious if you use Samantha's key?" Jack asked. "They'll know whoever stole the stuff had a key."

"We'll break up the place on the way out after we get the stuff."

"And who's going to believe burglars broke in to steal birth control pills? This is ridiculous. Why doesn't Sam just pay for what she needs?" Jack asked.

"Maybe you weren't listening, *chuvak*." Vanya turned around and stared in his face. "Sam wants more than pills. She wants redistribution of wealth." He spat out his cigarette butt and slipped inside the entrance. Jack followed on his heels.

"Where's that map?" Vanya pulled a pen light from his back pants pocket and shone it on the drawing. "Sam said there's boxes in the storage room. Let's fill 'em and get outta here. Look." He pointed at Samantha's floor plan. "Go for these closets with the red numbers."

"Did you hear that?" Jack asked.

"Hear what?" Vanya replied.

Jack put his finger to his lips. "Shhhhh...." He strained to listen in the darkness. He heard the sounds of heavy equipment scraping across tile coming from a room down the hall. Something metal clattered to the floor. He tiptoed down the hallway towards the sounds.

"I hear voices," he whispered. "Someone's here. Let's go." Heart racing, Jack turned back toward the entrance. He stopped short, then tugged on Vanya's sleeve, and moved his face closer to the Russian's tattooed neck. "That's Jesse. I recognize her voice. What the hell?" Ears on high alert, Jack listened again. He recognized the other voice, too. That wanker Max White.

"Come on. Jesse must be in trouble." Jack removed his shoes and padded down the hallway toward the voices.

Vanya followed him, heels clicking on the tile floor. Jack stopped and pointed at Vanya's shoes, gesturing for him to take them off. Vanya just shrugged, pulled his pistol out of its holster, and continued clicking down the hallway, gun first.

Light was coming from under one of the closed doors along the hallway. Jack gestured and pointed to the light pooling on the tile in front of him. Vanya held up three fingers and pointed at the doorknob. Jack grasped it.

He recognized Max White's voice talking to Jesse. Jack looked from the doorknob to Vanya. Two fingers. When Jack turned the knob, he heard running water. One finger. Jack pulled the door open, and Vanya rushed in waving his gun.

"What the hell is going on in here?" Vanya asked, horror in his voice.

Bathed in icy blue light, Jack saw Lolita's limp body tied to an operating table in a surgery bay. His eyes traveled across the dim room, and his heart leapt into his throat when he saw Jesse strapped to another table across the operating room.

"Help!" Jesse yelled. "He's getting away. He's over there, by the sink."

Vanya swung around, waving his pistol in all directions. "Stop, or I'll shoot, *súka*." He swung around again. "*Ty che, blyad*. Where the hell is he?"

Jack saw a shadow moving along side Jesse's operating table. "He's over there." He pointed towards Jesse, but the form had disappeared behind the ultrasound machine. "Behind that machine." Jack gestured as he sprinted to Jesse's side and started unstrapping her from the table.

Gun first, Vanya slid between the operating table and the ultrasound machine, a hound dog on a scent. He ducked as he came around behind the equipment, but it was too late. Max White lunged at him with a hypodermic needle and pierced his left shoulder.

Vanya fired his pistol, and the bullet ricocheted off the ultrasound and boomeranged into his own thigh. Vanya let out a string of Russian curses as he leapt on Max White and landed one good punch before Max stabbed him with another syringe. This one must have been loaded with anesthesia. Just before he passed out, Vanya mumbled, "*schas po ebalu poluchish, súka, blyad.*"

Max bolted out the door of the operating theater.

"Don't let him get away!" Jesse yelled, sitting up on her elbows.

"I can't leave you," Jack said, gently pushing the matted hair out of her eyes.

"Go after him," she yelled.

"I don't want to leave you."

"Stop him." She pushed at his arm. "Just hold him here. I'll call the police. Go!"

Jack sprinted through the door and down the hall, slipping and sliding in his socks. He scrambled through the glass entrance and out into the parking lot in time to see Max White putting a sample case into the back of his black van.

Jack ran around and dove inside, but Max slipped out of his grasp and climbed up into the driver's seat. He turned the key in the ignition and threw the van into reverse then jammed on the accelerator.

The van jolted backwards, and Jack felt himself being

sucked out the back door. He clawed at the carpet, then grabbed a handhold, and using all the strength of his core muscles, pulled his feet inside the van. On hands and knees, he crawled towards the front seat then threw himself up onto the center console and seized Max by the right arm.

Reaching over from the driver's seat, Max put both hands around Jack's neck and squeezed. The van pitched, shook, then stopped when it hit a brick wall, throwing Jack against the dash and sending Max's head into the windshield. The geneticist's heavy body lay limp on top of Jack's chest.

Still lying across the center console, Jack reached across and grabbed the steering wheel with his right hand then elbowed Max in the face with his left. But the blow only woke him up. Locked in an urgent embrace, Jack struggled to get the upper hand. Max leaned his muscular torso across Jack's chest and stretched his arm out towards a medical bag sitting in the passenger's seat.

When Jack tried to wriggle out from under the crazy geneticist, he felt the prick of a needle break the skin of his neck and immediately tasted the metallic tang of whatever Max had just injected into his bloodstream.

"Jesse," he whispered, and his world dissolved into bitter blackness.

CHAPTER TWENTY-SIX

AFTER THE LAST hour's hair-raising ruckus in the operating theater, the silence soured to a curdle as Jessica gazed down at her beautiful best friend lying unconscious on a metal slab, drool glistening on the edge of her sweet lips. Jessica's world had turned upside down, and she'd give anything to trade places with Lolita to save her the humiliation.

At least her friend wouldn't wake up half-naked behind a dumpster. She shuddered to think of Lolita as one of the dumpster girls. She untied her friend's arms and held her hand. "Wake up, Lolita," she pleaded.

It had been a low blow seeing Lolita-The-Invincible incapacitated by the insane geneticist. She'd always imagined her friend as a Harley driving Russian version of Wonder Woman complete with a lasso of truth, Amazon bracelets, and killer moves, fighting sexual predators wherever she found them. She gathered Lolita's panties and leather pants from the neat stack on the counter where Max had left them. She put her friend's clothes back on her limp body the best she could, then wiped off her lips, combed her hair, and waited.

The syringe must have been empty because it had no effect on Vanya. The Russian was sitting on the other operating table, muttering to himself. With a curse or two, he'd pulled the sword-like needle from his shoulder then tore his pants where the bullet had entered, and applied a tourniquet.

Oblivious to the blood running down his shin and pooling on the floor, he tapped out a cigarette and lit it. He swung his legs up onto the bed then laid back and took a deep drag, blowing out smoke rings. He lifted his good leg into the air. Sitting up on his elbow, he exclaimed, "*Blyad!* My shoes are stained." He lay back again and continued puffing on his cigarette. "Sam is on her way," he said. "She's a doctor. She'll get us squared up. Poor cuz. What'd that *súka* do to her?"

"Max White stole her eggs," Jessica said.

"Stole her eggs?" Vanya asked. "What kinda freaky stuff is that?"

"He surgically removed eggs from her ovaries. She got in a few good kicks to his fat head, but he stabbed her with a needle full of anesthesia. Poor Lolita."

"That's some messed up shit," Vanya said, sucking on his cigarette.

"We thought Max was a sexual predator. But he's a thief. He's stealing the life right out of our bodies. Who knows how many babies he's made with eggs he's stolen. I could be the bio-mom to fetuses growing inside rich women all over town. And mad Max is the father of all of them. It's creepy."

"I knew them glow in the dark cats would lead to some horror show." Vanya flinched when he dropped his legs over the side of the table and sat up. "She is going to wake up, isn't she?"

Jessica heard a storm of activity entering from outside the clinic. Samantha Brewer burst into the operating room and let out a gasp when she saw Vanya smoking and bleeding. He smiled at her and took a comb from his back pocket and ran it through his slicked back hair. She flew over to him, grabbed the cigarette out of his mouth, threw it in the sink, then pushed him back down onto the table and examined his leg.

"Just a flesh wound," she pronounced. "I'll clean it up, then we need to get you to the hospital." She efficiently washed and bandaged his leg and shoulder.

"See. No biggie," Vanya said.

Jessica continued to wipe off Lolita's face, hoping she'd wake up soon.

"What anesthesia did he use?" Samantha asked, blowing across the room.

"I don't know. The bottle is on that tray. And he used some gas." Jessica pointed at the tank and mask next to the bed.

Samantha picked up the vial and examined it. "Propofol," she said. "Mother's milk as Michael Jackson called it. It's deadly in high doses. Where's the syringe that he used? I need to see how much he gave her. It should wear off fairly quickly unless she's allergic to it or had some kind of reaction." She took Lolita's wrist and felt her pulse. "Her heart rate is dangerously low."

"Is she going to be okay?" Jessica asked.

"I'll do my best," Samantha answered.

Jessica felt the blood drain from her face. "You mean...."

"She's slipping into a coma. We have to act fast. Attach that mask to the oxygen port on the wall." Samantha pointed at a nozzle poking out of a recessed box in the nearest wall. "Turn the dial to 5 and put the mask over her nose and mouth then attach the straps around her head."

Samantha whooshed to the sink, washed her hands, then opened the drug refrigerator and scanned the different color capped vials. She snatched one, swirled to Lolita's bedside, and hovered near the same tray Max had used. Examining the tools on the tray, she quickly opened an envelope containing latex gloves, snapped them onto her fingers, and tore open a fresh syringe.

"Adrenaline," she said, sticking the needle into a vial and drawing out the amber liquid. "Does she have an IV port?"

"What?"

"Standard procedure. Didn't Max White put in an IV before the retrieval?"

"I don't think he was following standard procedure."

Samantha ripped open an alcohol swap, rubbed it on Lolita's upper arm, then stuck the needle into her muscle and pressed the plunger.

"Where is that ambulance?" Samantha asked under her breath.

"The hospital is only two blocks away," Jessica said. "What's taking so long?"

"Bureaucracy. They have to fill out a sheaf of forms to dispatch."

Another unlit cigarette hanging from his lips, Vanya slid off the table and flinched. He'd only limped a couple of steps when Samantha said in a commanding tone, "Sit back down and wait for the ambulance. You're in no shape to help anyone." He sat on the edge of the table, lit his cigarette, took a drag, and blew out smoke rings. Samantha scowled and continued attending to her unconscious patient.

Jessica stood up but her head was spinning so much she collapsed back into her chair. She was relieved to hear a siren approaching.

"Vanya, go out and show the EMTs where to find us," Samantha said, then added, "and please finish that cigarette outside."

Vanya flashed a golden grin and limped towards the door, the right leg of his blood-stained pants torn completely off, his thigh wrapped in a blood soaked bandage, a hole in his white undershirt peeked through blossoming red to match the epaulette tattooed on his shoulder.

"Find Jack," Jessica said. "Make sure he's okay."

"Sure thing, Miss Jesse," Vanya said. Holding onto the casement, he pulled himself out the door and disappeared into the hall. The cadence of his gait made a regular tap-scrape, tap-scrape, tap-scrape, until he was outside.

"Is Lolita going to be okay?" Jessica asked.

"I think so. But I'm glad the EMTs are here," Samantha replied. "Her breathing is better and her heart rate is up. How about you? Are you okay? Can you walk or do you need a wheelchair?"

"I think I can walk," Jessica said. "I'll try."

Two burly EMTs stormed into the room with a stretcher. "What's the situation?" the taller one asked.

"Possible allergic reaction to Propofol from forced egg retrieval under anesthesia," Samantha said to the EMTs. "Both girls were rendered unconscious with inhalational trichloromethane, chloroform. This one was then injected with 40 mg Propofol, combined with inhalational isoflurane. I administered subdermal Epinephrine, and she is responding well."

"We'll take it from here," the tall EMT said. He put both hands under Lolita's shoulders and his partner took her feet. No sooner had he touched her than her left foot flew to his face and sent him to his knees.

"Don't touch me," Lolita slurred. She shook her head and glanced around the room. "What's going on?"

"Lolita!" Jessica exclaimed. "You're alive."

"Where's that asshole, White?" she slurred. "And where are my boots? They'd like to have a chat with him."

Jessica retrieved the black motorcycle boots from the closet where Max White had neatly stored them along with Lolita's leather jacket and red scarf.

"Here." Jessica handed her friend the boots and jacket. "I put your pants on as best as I could."

The EMTs retreated as Lolita stood up, tugged her leather pants into place, then sat back on the edge of the table to put on her boots and jacket. "So, where is White? He's not going to get away with this. No one touches my *kiska* without an invitation and lives to tell about it."

"Miss Durchenko, please calm down. You're coming out of anesthesia and need to be careful. Please accompany the EMTs to the ambulance. We need to get you to the hospital," Samantha said. "You seem to have had a reaction to the Propofol or perhaps to the isoflurane."

"The only thing I'm reacting to is that bitch stabbing me with a needle and violating me. And he's about to pay.

Where is he?" Lolita walked slowly but steadily towards the door. "Come on, Jessica. Let's find that creep."

"Jack's holding him outside," Jessica said. "The cops should be here by now."

Leaning on each other, Jessica and her friend inched towards the exit and the ambulance waiting outside. The sun was coming up and streaks of orange blazed through the glass doors. Panicked, she looked around the parking lot. The steely cold daybreak had nothing on her dawning awareness that the black van was gone and Jack with it.

Chapter Twenty-Seven

WHOSE BABIES WAS *she carrying?* Lying on a yoga mat in the exercise room, Olga was doing leg lifts. Her new trainer's soft voice was lulling her into a meditative state, her body doing whatever the trainer said, leaving her mind free to wander.

No matter how many laps she swam in the new pool, or how many warrior poses she did, or how many times she bounced on the exercise ball, she kept coming back to the same questions: *Whose babies were these? Who were their real mother and father?*

"Arms in front, like you're holding a platter. Good. Now bring the platter towards you, then push it away. Beautiful. Bring it towards you, push it away. Three more," the trainer said in soothing tones.

As Olga's arms moved back and forth holding their imaginary platter, she saw the platter piled with stacks of hundred-dollar bills, the blackmail money she still needed to steal from Ronald's safe. He'd had the new pool built and hired a new cook and a prenatal trainer so she wouldn't turn into "a fat cow." He'd given her a five thousand dollar gift certificate to Séraphine's "Fashionably Pregnant," but he wouldn't give her even fifty dollars in cash.

After he'd found her in his study, Ronald had tightened security around her and had his henchmen watching her like hawks. He insisted on monitoring her every move. He'd even changed the combination to the safe, had another plate made with the new numbers, and kept it in his wallet, which never left his person. Like a cowboy in an old Western sleeping with his gun in his hand under the covers, Ronald slept with his wallet tucked into his pajama pocket. She was going to have to find some way to pry his billfold out of his sleeping hands and get the ransom money by midnight.

After the Holly Ball she'd been both relieved and terrified to discover that Ronald didn't have the threatening ransom letter. But the scary man who claimed to be her long lost cousin did. Vanya had promised her, "Blood is thicker than wine," still she couldn't take any chances.

She was being squeezed from both sides, Vanya and the blackmailer on one side, and Ronald and his demanding father on the other. She hadn't told him about the fertility clinic or the five babies already making their appearance in her protruding belly, and she wasn't going to either. She knew angry men could be dangerous.

That was the only lesson her mother had taught her before abandoning her. That rainy Kiev morning clawed at her heart. She was seven and her sister was four and already very sick from her disease. Sobbing, her mother bent down and gave Olga a final hug, tucked a picture in her tiny pocket, and whispered in her ear, "I love you, little butterfly, but this is for your own good. Your father is dangerous. We have to hide you." Her mother handed her sister over to a dour woman dressed in gray, smelling of vinegar, and then the stern woman took Olga by the hand and led her inside Orphanage #12, a state-run institution for "mentally retarded" children, a nightmare of illness, neglect, and sorrow.

After her sister died, Olga ran away to live on the streets, the tattered baby picture her only memento from a broken childhood, her round baby face already full of longing for a savior. When she was seventeen, she thought Ronald was that savoir. Now, she was putting her hopes on the baby.

She'd decided to give Ronald and the Davis dynasty their heir. They could have their precious baby boy. But the girl would be hers, and no matter what happened, she'd never abandon her baby girl. She'd love her and care for her with enough passion to make up for all the love and care lacking in her own life. The doctor said her daughter was special, and she would be the most cherished girl in the whole world.

"Mrs. Davis, your left leg, not your right." Her trainer gently adjusted her pose. "Here, use the blocks for support."

"Sorry," Olga said. "I was lost in thought."

"Imagine your thoughts as clouds in the sky. Watch them pass through your mind. Breathe. Fill your lungs with nourishing breath, and remember your body is the earth, the foundation. Your emotions are only the clouds over-head. They change, but the sky stays the same."

Olga tried to see her stormy emotions as passing clouds and her baby-filled body as her foundation, but instead she remembered a fairytale told by the principal at the orphan-age about the dangers of reaching for heaven and trusting in charlatans who promise the sky. The principal was a harsh disciplinarian and never spared the whip to "dispel day-dreams beyond your station in life."

Every Saturday afternoon, he gathered the children around him on the floor as he sat above on a wooden chair and dispensed morality tales. One of them had stuck with her. It was the Saturday before she ran away, the very morning her sister had died. She refused to get out of bed and got the whip. Her entire being had gone numb, and she sat at his feet while he told the story of an old man and a cabbage.

An old man planted a cabbage in his cellar. It grew so big, he had to cut a hole in his floor and another in his roof. When it reached to the sky and into the clouds, he climbed it and found cake with kasha on top. He ate his fill and then slid back down to tell his wife to climb up and see the wondrous cake. She was skeptical, so he climbed up behind her, pushing her along until, with his final shove, she dropped back to the earth and shattered into pieces. Heartsick, the old man flooded his house with tears.

A fox heard his lament and promised to cure the woman with oatmeal, butter, and privacy. The old man brought the requested provisions to the kitchen and waited outside. When he asked how his wife was recovering, the fox answered, "She's starting to stir," as he put her bones in a pot with the oatmeal. A few minutes later, he asked, "Now how's she getting along?" Gobbling up his homemade pudding, the fox replied, "You're a lucky man. Your wife makes a lovely porridge."

"Mrs. Davis, are you okay?" the trainer asked, putting her hand on Olga's shoulder.

"Oh, I'm sorry," Olga said. "I guess I'm distracted."

"Why don't we stop for today and I'll be back tomorrow." Her trainer patted her shoulder. "Remember to breathe."

Olga took a deep breath and adjusting to her changing pregnant center of gravity, staggered a bit, then stood up. After her trainer left, she locked the door and headed into the bathroom for a hot shower to clear her head if not cleanse her soul. She had an appointment at the clinic in an hour to undergo the dreaded selective reduction. *How could she so easily dispose of three babies she'd worked so hard to get?*

She thought of three little boys, lives dashed before they began. These babies weren't livestock—cows or sheep bred only to be killed. She stood in the shower, her tears mixing with the hot water streaming down her face. Why hadn't she understood from the beginning? Why had she allowed them to plant five babies? Now she had to decide how many to kill. Selective reduction was another name for murder. It wasn't right. And she was the murderer.

She opened her mouth and let the hot water pulse against her teeth. She couldn't have five babies. It wasn't natural. Nothing about this situation was normal. And on top of everything else, she was being blackmailed.

Olga stepped out of the shower, removed her shower cap, towel dried her expanding body, then stepped into her underwear, tugged on the faux leather panel maternity leggings, "as worn by Anne Hathaway," and slid the black turtleneck maternity dress, "as worn by The Duchess of Cambridge," over her head. She brushed her cheeks with blush, coated her lips with gloss, and applied mascara to her thick lashes. She stared at her reflection in the mirror. The stranger staring back at her looked vaguely familiar from another lifetime.

She had to figure out how to get the ransom money in time to stop the blackmailer from going to the press with the story of her unnatural pregnancy. She could see the headlines now, "Naughty or Nice? Santa Brings Society Girl a Bundle of Babies" or "Business Mogul's Wife Expecting a Litter," or "Octomom's got nothing on Olga Davis." She felt nauseous again. Dr. Manly was right, and she'd have to submit to the "selective reduction" planned for today. Still undecided about the four boys, her mind was made up, she was keeping the girl.

Olga slipped into her fur lined dress boots and called José to pick her up in ten minutes. Surrounded by servants, bodyguards, personal chefs, private trainers, and handlers, Maria and José were the only ones she could trust. They may take Ronald's money, but they'd always have her back. From the coat closet off the foyer, she selected the baby blue cashmere coat, "as worn by Kate Middleton," added the matching hat and gloves, and was out the door.

"To the clinic, Mrs. D?" José asked, opening the door for her.

She nodded and climbed in the backseat. She closed her eyes and rested her head against the seatback as the car pulled out into traffic. Her hands were sweating, soaking her gloves, and she felt like she might have to ask José to pull over so she could vomit. She tried to imagine her soul as the blue sky overhead and her stormy emotions just passing clouds, but all she saw behind her closed eyes was a giant cabbage and the old woman falling to her death.

As soon as José pulled into the parking lot, an even darker cloud fell over her mood. The moment of truth. She had to decide how many babies to keep and how many to "reduce." "Reduction" sounded like making a sauce, not a baby. Her whole pregnancy had been the result of an unnatural stirring in the pot of life. She hoped that in her case, too many cooks wouldn't spoil the broth.

"Wait for me here, José," she said, stepping out of the car. She took a deep yogic breath, and repeated, *Imagine your emotions as passing clouds in an eternal sky.* She grabbed her handbag from the backseat, shut the car door, and headed for the entrance.

A nurse was waiting just inside the glass doors. "Good to see you again, Mrs. Smith. Please follow me to the waiting room. May I say, you're looking radiant. May I take your coat?"

Olga removed her hat, gloves, and coat, handed them to the nurse, then followed her to the familiar waiting room where she helped herself to an apple and a bottle of water. Sitting on the edge of a divan, thumbing through the latest issue of *Vogue*, she almost wished for the freedom of her teenage modeling days. She may have lived hand to mouth, but at least she was her own boss.

She looked up when she heard tapping heels approaching from the hallway. Dr. Brewer appeared at the door to the waiting room. "Mrs. Smith, how are you feeling?" she asked. "Please follow me to the examination room." Olga's heart skipped a beat. She would have to decide once and for all. The finality of her decision hit her like the frigid slap in the face of a Kiev winter gale.

"This way, please," Dr. Brewer said with a fake smile. "We're in the large room today for the procedure."

The *procedure, selective reduction,* euphemisms for the most heart-wrenching day of her adult life. Of course she couldn't have five babies. The idea was absurd. But who was she to decide which lived and which… She couldn't think about it anymore. "Beautiful day, isn't it?" she asked.

Dr. Brewer seemed stumped by the rhetorical question and looked at her quizzically. "Did Dr. Manly do your implantation?"

"No. His assistant did. You know the young handsome doctor?"

"You mean Max White, the medical student?"

"Is that his name?" Olga asked. "I can never remember."

"Were you…. happy with the procedure?" Dr. Brewer asked, stopping in front of the exam room door and turning to face Olga.

"Was I happy?"

"Was everything satisfactory?" Dr. Brewer asked, her face blank.

"Actually, the whole thing seemed unreal and strange."

"Strange in what way?"

"First, I got the call on a Sunday. I remember because I was hosting an important luncheon. It seemed odd that the clinic was open on Sunday."

"Yes, that is very odd. Go on."

"Then, there was no one else here. That seemed strange, too."

"No one? No other clients?" Dr. Brewer asked, alarm in her voice.

"No one. No other clients, no nurses, no other doctors. Only Dr. Manly's assistant, the young…Dr. White, and me. That's not typical is it?" Olga asked. This line of questioning was only making her more anxious.

"Nothing about Max White is typical I'm afraid, Mrs.

Smith." Dr. Brewer motioned her into the exam room. "Max White no longer works at the clinic." Dr. Brewer stepped into the room after her and closed the door. "Please sit down, Mrs. Smith. I have some bad news."

Olga's heart leapt into her throat and she sat in the nearest chair. "The babies?" she asked.

"The outcome is perfect, but the procedure was unorthodox, even illegal. Max White, the assistant who implanted your zygotes, is wanted by the police."

"What? Why?" Olga was stunned. "He always seemed so nice, so professional."

"Did you ever pay Mr. White directly for services at the clinic?"

"Yes. He asked for fifty thousand dollars in cash up front to perform the implantation," Olga said, eyes widening.

"You paid him fifty thousand dollars in cash? Didn't you think that was odd?" Dr. Brewer's dark eyes drilled into her brain.

Blushing, Olga picked at her pearly fingernail polish. "I guess it did seem a little strange." She felt tears welling in her eyes. Until now, she never questioned the young doctor's behavior. She should have seen how strange it was. "I was desperate..."

"No need to explain, *Mrs. Smith*." Dr. Brewer emphasized "Mrs. Smith" in a way that suggested she knew Olga's true identity.

Olga hadn't chewed her fingernails since she was a kid, but she fought the urge to gnaw on one now. "I *am* pregnant. And I am going to have five babies, right?" she asked.

"You are pregnant. And today we will select the embryos. Have you made your decision? Do you want a singleton or twins? Since they were genetically engineered, they won't be identical twins." Dr. Brewer said.

"Can you tell me, do they all have the same biological parents?" Olga asked.

"We suspect that they have the same biological father, and two or perhaps three of them may have the same biological mother, but given Mr. White's egg retrieval practices, most likely not all of them."

"What do you mean?" she asked, confused.

"Usually, in the clinic we retrieve up to a dozen eggs at a time from one donor by preparing them first with fertility drugs. Mr. White didn't do that so his *method* of retrieval yielded only one or two eggs at a time. I don't want to frighten you, Mrs. Smith, but we suspect Max White used his own sperm to inseminate all of the eggs he implanted."

"So he's their father?"

"Yes."

"And the mother?"

"As I said, there are different biological mothers. In fact, given the genetic manipulation involved in creating your embryos, each one could have more than one biological mother. It's possible to use genetic material from two eggs to create one embryo."

"What? How many biological parents do my babies have?" Olga was stunned.

"It takes a village, Mrs. Smith." She patted Olga on the shoulder. "Dr. Manly will be in shortly to perform the selective reduction procedure. He will decide which embryos are the most viable and go from there. Please remove your clothes and put on that gown so the ties are in the front. You may sit on the table or wait in a chair. We'll be back soon."

Olga stared at the shiny tile floor, listening to the tapping of Dr. Brewer's heels. "Wait, can I ask you something, Dr. Brewer?"

"Of course. Don't worry, Mrs. Smith. You are in good hands with Dr. Manly." Dr. Brewer stood in the threshold, her hand on the doorknob.

"Who is, are, the mothers of my babies?" Olga asked tentatively.

"Why you are the mother of your babies, Mrs. Smith, in every way that matters."

"Please, who is the biological mother? Please tell me." Olga heard herself pleading.

"Standard procedure dictates anonymity, Mrs. Smith. To protect you and the donors." Dr. Brewer closed the door, came over, and sat in the chair next to her. "But nothing about your case is standard."

"So you'll tell me?" Olga asked, her eyes full of hope. "I need to know. I think of nothing else. It is important to me to know the identity of the biological mother of my child, children. That information will help me cope with this whole situation, especially today's *procedure*."

"I'll tell you in the strictest confidence. But you must promise not to mention our conversation to Dr. Manly or anyone else at the clinic." Dr. Brewer's brown eyes flashed and pinkish clouds were visible on her mahogany cheeks. "As I said, the biological father of all five is Max White. We know that for sure."

"Dr. Manly's assistant?"

"Yes, him."

"He used his own sperm?"

"That's correct."

"And the mother?" she asked, then held her breath.

"We believe there were two egg donors, Mrs. Davis." Dr. Brewer paused.

"Do you know who they are?" she asked, and then it dawned on her. Dr. Brewer had called her by name.

"You know who I am?" she asked.

"Olga Davis, wife of Ronald Davis," Dr. Brewer said.

"And the two women, the biological mothers?"

"One of them is dead. Died the night of the egg retrieval. The other one is Jessica James, a philosophy graduate student at Northwestern."

"One is Dead?" Olga gasped.

"Yes. She died from complications from the extraction." Dr. Brewer's lips tightened.

"Oh my God. It's my fault then," Olga said, clutching her purse to her chest.

"No, it's not your fault, Mrs. Smith. You just relax and prepare for the procedure. I'm sorry I've worried you. I shouldn't have…"

"Tell me more about the other one, Jessica James," Olga interrupted.

CHAPTER TWENTY-EIGHT

HER FIRST CLASS of the quarter had been a disaster. Jessica couldn't wait to get back to her apartment, crawl back into bed, and hide under her duvet. She and a bottle of whiskey had pulled an all-nighter trying to prepare a proper lecture, but with Jackass and Max still missing, she'd been too distraught to concentrate.

Now, on her way home, the rattling and swaying of the train lulled her into a delirious semi-sleep. When the train squealed to a stop, her head jerked and she awoke with a start.

Jessica sat up, pulled out her phone, and reread Jack's strange messages. He'd been texting her every day since the nightmare at the clinic to say he was still studying for an important exam. Jackass had been known to hibernate. But she was worried about him. It was weird that he'd just disappeared and refused even a coffee break. She vowed that after a good long nap, she'd go looking for him. The train pulled into Morse stop and she staggered off before the doors closed. Fighting the wind, she stomped into the packed snow to keep her footing and counted the steps to her building to stay awake.

When she opened her apartment door, the toe of her boot kicked an envelope and sent it sliding across the wooden floor where it skidded to a stop when it hit a pile of dirty clothes. She picked up the envelope and turned it over, staring at the gold script on the back of the thick ivory envelope: *Mrs. Ronald Davis.* Why was Olga Davis writing to her?

Maybe she'd realized Jessica had stolen the ransom note from her handbag. Jessica sniffed the thick paper and a floral perfume filled her nostrils. Fetching a knife from her closet kitchen, she sawed open the letter and extracted a gilded invitation. *You are cordially invited to join Olga Davis for tea at her home, 1336 North State Parkway, 2:00pm today. No RSVP needed.* Pink ink bled into the thirsty paper with a personal message written in loopy cursive handwriting, *I hope you can come. I have something very important to discuss with you. Love, Olga.*

Jessica flopped onto her bed, coat and all, sniffed the note again, and reread it. *"Love Olga," what does that mean?* Officially, they'd never even met. Would a woman angry at the thief who stole a letter from her purse sign an invitation with "love"? Jessica was too tired to figure it out now. She set her phone alarm for noon, curled into a fetal position, and fell asleep.

Jessica was back home riding Mayhem through the meadow, racing towards the Whitefish Mountains. The fire was licking at his hooves, threatening to light his tail. She gave him the spurs and together, one sweaty mass of flesh— not girl, not horse, but a hybrid creature with long blonde mane, round blue eyes, and strong muscular flanks, left the earth and soared through the smoke, up into the icy blue ether, where horse and rider dissolved altogether into the pure energy of life's force. A buzzing disturbed her flying, and she fell back to the ground with a thud. She swatted around her head, but the buzzing wouldn't stop.

Opening one eye, Jessica awoke to find herself still in her parka and snow boots, her face stuck to her pillow in a tacky combination of sweat and drool, her cellphone alarm determined to ruin her day. She groaned, rolled over, and pulled the duvet up over her head. A sharp corner poked her neck. She reached for the offending critter, but instead pulled out the embossed envelope, rolled her eyes at it, then tossed it across the room. She had just under two hours to clean herself up and get her butt downtown if she was going to accept the invitation to tea. *What does a poor cowgirl wear to a fancy tea in Chicago's ritziest neighborhood?*

She dragged herself out of bed, tore off her sticky clothes, threw herself into the shower, and leaned her head against the cool tile, hoping the hot water pelting her back would revive her.

She decided on a black woolen vintage dress from her great-grandmother's collection, a wide patent leather belt from the Goodwill collection, and her bright red cowboy boots, her own couture creation. She restrained her unruly locks into French braids, one running around each side of her head, and even applied a dab of tinted sunscreen to the purple plums under her eyes. She scooted to her closet kitchen, opened her miniature refrigerator, and downed her last Coke, a boost of caffeine and sugar to face the wind chill and the white witch. She hoisted her parka over her dress, wrapped a fleece scarf around her neck, tugged her Trapper down around her ears, stuffed her hands into furry mittens, and headed out for her first up-close encounter with the alien world of wealthy Chicago socialites.

Jessica stood in front of the dark wooden doors examining her reflection in a tiny window's one-way glass. Bedraggled from lack of sleep and an hour on the "L," she nearly fell off the stoop when she looked up and saw Nanook of the North staring back at her in the mirrored glass. She ripped off her Trapper and stuffed it into her parka pocket. She pressed the doorbell and glanced around. She smoothed her hair, pinched her cheeks then waited at attention. The handsome brownstone building on North State Parkway was edged with perfect boxy green hedgerows and black iron fences. The entrance was framed with matching ironwork and large black lanterns.

A small woman with dark hair and an accent opened the large door, gestured her in, took her coat and scarf, and led her to a sitting room. Inside the house was surprisingly light given how dark it was outside. The carpet and furniture were white, and the floor to ceiling drapes were baby blue. Fresh white flowers stood in crystal vases on every table throughout the room. An ornate brass chandelier with white candlelights hung low from the ceiling. Jessica took off her boots, left them at the threshold, and tiptoed into the room in her stockinged feet.

"Please have a seat, Miss Jessica," the maid said. "Mrs. Davis will be right down."

The thick wool rug was plush beneath her feet as she

padded around the room admiring Chinese lamps, crystal bowls, blue satin ottomans, a marble fireplace, and finally the arched twelve-foot windows looking out onto a back courtyard. She felt like she was in a museum house, a place to look at but not to live in.

"Jessica, so nice of you to come, and on such short notice!" Olga Davis appeared in the doorway, all smiles. "I was hoping to meet you. I know you must wonder what this is all about. Or maybe you can guess."

Jessica froze in place and stared at the wealthy woman, exuding privilege and grace, in her baby blue dress, bleached blonde bun, and sheer nude stockings revealing shapely legs, toned but not muscular.

Beaming, Olga strode across the room, coming straight at her. "Oh my. You are very pretty," she said, her green eyes sparkling, offset by the baby blue drapery.

"Thank you," Jessica said, wondering what was up.

When Olga moved in for a hug, Jessica felt a distinctive bump in her midsection. The telltale "baby bump."

"You look familiar," Olga said, holding her at arms-length. "Have we met before?"

Jessica's face was hot, and she took a step backwards, almost stumbling over her own feet. "Actually…"

Olga interrupted. "The Holly Ball. You were the nice girl in the bathroom. Oh my gosh, you'll never know how much you helped me that night."

"I did?" Jessica asked, embarrassed that she'd been so excited to steal the letter.

"So tell me about yourself, Jessica," Olga said.

Jessica wrinkled her brows, wondering what this rich

lady wanted from her. "No much to tell. I'm getting a Ph.D. in philosophy at Northwestern."

"Philosophy. How interesting." When Olga sat next to her on one of the sofas and gazed into her eyes, it gave her the creeps. "What is your philosophy?"

"My philosophy?" She clasped her hands together in her lap to keep them from trembling. Must be PTSD; she was having a flashback to her oral exam when one crotchety old phenomenologist grilled her on the meaning of "the world." Whiskey on his breath, he'd pointed his knobby finger straight at her and asked in a gravelly voice, "What is the world, Miss James?"

"At this point, having my own philosophy is beyond my pay grade." She troubled the velvet tie on her dress between her thumb and forefinger.

"Where are you from? Where did you grow up? Who are your parents? I want to know everything about you," Olga said, rosy cheeked and smiling broadly.

Jessica's eye twitched involuntarily, and she brushed her bangs into her face to conceal her body's betrayal. She wondered why this rich lady wanted to know about her trailer trash family, and would play along until she found out what Olga Davis really wanted from her. "I'm from Montana. I grew up in the mountains. My father worked in a lumber mill. He died in an accident when I was a kid. My mom worked as a noon goon…"

"A what?"

"At the grade school, patrolling recess."

"And were you always a good student? You must have been to be getting a Ph.D. in psychology."

"Philosophy. I guess I've always preferred the world of my imagination to the real one. Less heartache."

"So your father died in an accident? Not from a disease, I hope."

Jessica slipped her phone out of the pocket of her dress and peeked at the time. "I probably should be going soon," she said, reading another message from Jack. *Where the hell was he?*

"But we haven't had tea yet." Olga rang a little bell and the small dark woman reappeared.

"Yes, Mrs. Davis?" the maid asked.

"Please bring us some tea, Maria," she said to the maid, then turned back to Jessica, "unless you prefer coffee?"

"I really can't stay long, Mrs. Davis."

"Oh, please call me Olga." She turned back to Maria. "Tea and some cookies."

"Mrs. Davis…uhm, Olga, why did you invite me to tea?" Jessica asked. "Was it because I took your letter?"

"Letter? What letter?"

"The night of the Holly Ball when I took the letter from your handbag. But, I don't have it anymore. I gave it to a friend." Jessica stared at her scarlet wool sock, a bloody gash against the nubby ivory carpet. "I'm sorry."

"Aha! So you gave it to Vanya. I thought he'd stolen it on his own. Did my husband hire you to follow me, too?"

"No, I just went along for fun." Her face was burning. "Apologies for following you into the bathroom and taking that letter from your…"

"I don't blame you," Olga interrupted. She straightened her skirt and glanced around the room. "And, please don't mention blackmail," she whispered. "Or my husband. I invited you to tea to discuss more pleasant topics." Maria entered with a silver tray and poured two cups of tea and offered Jessica a cookie. She took one to be polite.

"Remember the night of the Holly Ball and I told you I'm pregnant?" Olga asked.

"Yes," Jessica said. "Congratulations again."

"Thank you. Can you keep a secret?"

Jessica's face caught fire again. "I guess so. What kind of secret?"

"Ronald and I have been trying to get pregnant for some time. But it wasn't working. Truth be told, I was afraid of getting pregnant because my sister had a terrible disease that I could be carrying, too. So, I have been treated at a fertility clinic at Northwestern Hospital. And, that's how I got pregnant."

Jessica picked at the scar that the dumpster had left on her palm. She stopped when she noticed a tiny spot of red threatening the white sofa. She had an uneasy feeling about Mrs. Davis.

"So, I'm going to have twins, a girl and a boy. Dr. Manly and his assistant both told me that she is a very special girl, very special." Olga sipped her tea and peered up over the edge of the cup, her green eyes welling with tears. "My baby girl is special because she has a very special mother."

Jessica tried to take a sip of her tea but she couldn't swallow, afraid of what Olga was trying to tell her.

"That very special mother is you, Jessica James."

"Holy crap." Jessica's hands were shaking so badly that the tea flew out of her cup and splatted all down the front of Olga Davis's baby blue baby bump.

CHAPTER TWENTY-NINE

THANK HEAVENS FOR Witches Brew tea. Pre-occupied by being a bio-mom, corpses in freezers, dumpster girls, and Jackass gone AWOL, Jessica needed something to help her exorcise her demons. She had been drinking teapot after teapot of the strong elixir all afternoon. She was sitting in a booth at Blind Faith Café trying to focus on grading a stack of boring student papers that began with epic phrases like "Since the beginning of time…" and "The world's greatest philosopher once said…"

Like the ice cream cone she'd get after a painful trip to the dentist, she was rewarding herself with sweet apricot crepes. The flambé of apricots and caramelized bananas topped with crème fraiche made up for a multitude of sins.

Whatever else life had to offer, there were always pancakes. She licked the cream off her upper lip and let herself be carried away by the orgy of burnt sweetness exploding in her mouth. "Ahhhh." She sighed in contentment, grateful for a few precious seconds of joy after weeks of worry and strife.

When Lolita slid into the booth across from her, Jessica was holding her plate in both hands, licking it clean.

"That the way they do it in Montana, like animals?" Lolita asked.

Jessica flushed. "What are tongues for if not licking cream?"

"Yes, my little *Kotyonok*," Lolita purred. She waved down the waitress and ordered a double espresso. "Speaking of animals, any sign of Jack?" she asked, removing her leather gloves and motorcycle jacket.

"He answers my texts with cryptic messages but won't say where he is." Jessica poured the last drop of tea into her cup and drained it. "The whole world is upside down. Jack is missing. I'm going to be a bio-mom. Dr. Frankenstein has vanished into thin air. And to top it off, I have to teach at eight in the frickin' morning."

"Well, we solved the mystery of the dumpster girls," Lolita said. "We're the lucky ones who survived. We'll find that freaky fucker. And when we do, I'll harvest his gonads through his nose with a sharp metal straw."

"Well, he won't get the chance to implant your eggs and mess with your head by making you a bio-mom." Jessica held up the lid to her teapot, waved to the waitress, then slouched in the booth. "In the last week, I've found out that I'm a genetic mutant and a biological mother. It's messed up."

"Messed up is an understatement, kitten," Lolita said.

"What does mother even mean when you can have three women contributing genetic material to the embryo, another woman carrying it to term, and as many more raising the baby?" Jessica asked. "Before paternity tests, fatherhood was as uncertain as life on Mars, but motherhood was for sure. Now, maternity is becoming just as uncertain."

"Mothers and fathers are the people who take care of

you and raise you. All this gene splicing is irrelevant." Lolita sipped her espresso. "Olga Davis is going to be a mother, not you. She's rich and the kid will be fine. Don't worry."

"I'm not worried about the kid. It's just so weird. It gives me the creeps. Max White stole part of my body and used it to make another human being without my consent." Jessica's hands were trembling from over caffeinating. "And where is Jack? Why won't he see me?" She stared up at the ceiling to keep the tears pooling in her eyes from running down her cheeks.

Lolita narrowed her eyes and nodded towards the restaurant entrance. "Expecting company?"

Jessica turned to see Detective Cormier weaving through the crowd coming towards their table.

"Oh crap!" She turned back around, face hot. "What does he want?"

"Maybe he wants to buy you breakfast again." Lolita smiled. "I think he has a crush on you."

"That's not funny."

"A cop in love with Jesse James. Yes, that's funny." Lolita laughed. "Breaking news. Law and order rides off into the sunset with chaos outlaw."

"Shhhhh…" Jessica whispered, leaning across the table, "he'll hear you."

"Good evening, Ms. James, Ms. Durchenko," the detective said in his buzzing baritone. Smiling, he tipped his brown wool fedora. "May I join you?"

"Of course, Detective." Lolita smiled sweetly.

"What are you doing in Evanston?" Jessica asked. "Did you come all the way to Blind Faith for dinner?"

"I've been looking for you all afternoon," he said, removing his gloves and overcoat and sliding into the booth next to her. "I went to Brentano Hall, and Mrs. Bush said if I didn't find you at your apartment, I'd probably find you here."

"Me?" Jessica asked, a lump in her throat. "Why?"

"Actually, I'm looking for your friend Jack Grove. Have you seen him or heard from him since the night at the clinic?" the detective asked, unwinding the cashmere scarf from around his neck.

"No. That was the last time I saw him. Any leads on Max?" Jessica asked.

"Nothing. But Jack seems to be busy," the detective said.

"Sometimes Jack goes into hibernation when he's studying for an exam. I guess with the new quarter just starting, he's pretty busy." Jessica poured another cup of witch's brew and took a sip. "He's not in trouble, is he?" she asked, peeking over her cup at the handsome detective. She inhaled his spicy aftershave and flushed, playing out Lolita's romantic scenario in her imagination.

"Jack Grove couldn't be working with Max White could he?" the detective asked.

Jessica glanced at Lolita then back at the detective. "Jack hates Max White. Why?"

"In the last week, the Northwestern campus police have had two reports of a young man wearing a Greek fisherman's cap approaching women, initiating conversation, identifying himself as Jack Grove, and then drugging them. They later woke up outside the biology building. Slightly different pattern, but similar enough to the so-called 'dumpster girl' cases."

"What?" Jessica asked.

"Where?" Lolita asked at the same time.

"These cases follow the same pattern as the other dumpster girls. Our perpetrator is a clever fellow, disrupted the surveillance cameras both times."

"Emily," Lolita said, glancing at Jessica. "That's what happened to Emily."

"Who's Emily?" the detective asked.

"My roommate. A guy calling himself Jack Grove drugged her."

"Did your roommate report it to the campus police?"

"No. She wasn't sure what happened, and…" Jessica said.

"If we're going to stop sexual assault on campus," he interrupted, "it's important that you college women start reporting criminal incidents like this one." The grim-faced detective took out a small notepad and pen. "What is her full name and contact information?"

"I'll send it to your phone," Lolita said.

"You have my cell number?" the detective asked.

"You gave it to me last year when we were collaborating to bust those frat rapists." Lolita tapped her phone. The detective's phone responded with a ping.

"773-330-2929," he read off his phone, then turned to Jessica, and said, "Show me the texts you've received from Jack in the last week. He's been racking up quite a credit card bill."

"Jack? Are you sure? He's the most miserly person I've ever met. He invites me to take *him* out to dinner." Jessica scrolled through her text messages. "Here's the latest, from yesterday. I asked him where he was and if he was okay, and he sent this weird message." She read the text aloud. "Hey Sweetie. I'm fine. MJ & abnormal psychology. Yours always,

Stoner Jack. Then a winking smiley face. See." She held her phone out to Detective Cormier and his lips moved as he reread the text.

"MJ and abnormal psychology," he repeated.

"Marijuana," Lolita said. "Jack's a total pot head."

"And he studies abnormal psychology. Weird text, huh? I'm not his Sweetie, and he never calls himself Stoner Jack." Jessica said.

"Has he been acting strange lately?" Detective Cormier asked.

"He always acts strange," Lolita said. "You're his best friend, what do you think?"

"One thing has been kinda strange," she said, staring down at the table.

"Go on," the detective said.

When she glanced up at him, she noticed amber flecks of light in his brown eyes and wondered if he had the genetic mutation heterochromia iridum, too. "Jack has been joking around a lot lately about his eternal love for me. It makes me feel weird."

"Weird good or weird bad?" Lolita asked. "It's obvious to anyone with eyes that Jack's in love with you."

"Jack? That's nuts." Using her index finger, Jessica wiped up a dab of whipped cream she'd missed from her plate and popped her finger into her mouth.

"If he keeps using his phone and his credit cards, we should be able to pinpoint his location soon enough," the detective said.

"He's not at his apartment or his cubicle?" Jessica asked.

"Maybe he's with my little rat cousin, Vanya," Lolita said. "They've been together a lot lately."

"Jack is not attending class. No one's seen him in the last week, not even Vanya." The detective's phone buzzed.

"He's not going to class? Okay, now I'm really worried. Jack may be a stoner, but he never misses class," Jessica said. "Something's wrong, very wrong."

Detective Cormier answered his phone. "Cormier here. Yes. Guest House. Motel Row, Bryn Mawr off Lincoln. Got it. I'm on my way." He tucked his phone back into his interior blazer pocket.

Jessica kicked Lolita under the table, and her friend scowled at her. "You'll have to excuse me, girls. I've got a lead on the last place Jack used his credit card." The detective slipped his arms into his overcoat, tapped his fedora onto his head, and pulled leather gloves from his pocket. "Thank you for your help, and sorry to interrupt your dinner."

"Where did Jack last use his credit card?" Lolita asked.

"I know he's your friend. But this is police business now. You girls stay out of it. Don't worry. We'll find Jack, and if he's innocent, I'll deliver him back to you myself, safe and sound."

"Safe, maybe," Jessica snorted. She watched in admiration as the well-built detective sauntered towards the exit.

"Come on. Let's follow him," Lolita said. "My bike's outside."

"I'll look up the address for the Guest House on Lincoln. The way you drive, we can beat the detective." Jessica checked her phone. "Hey, I have another message from Jack," she said, tapping the screen. It says, "Meet me at my cubicle in an hour. Bring Lolita." She narrowed her brows. "Detective Cormier's on the wrong track. Jack isn't at The Guest House. He's at Feinberg and he needs our help."

CHAPTER THIRTY

OLGA STARED DOWN at her Cle de Cartier watch. Only four hours left before the deadline to deliver the ransom money. She had no clue how to get into Ronald's safe since he'd changed the combination, and she hadn't been able to get his wallet away from him to see the new one. She sat at her dressing table brushing her hair and gazing at her reflection in the gilt-framed mirror. The woman gaping back at her looked old and haggard.

She put her head in her hands and tears ran down her cheeks, pooled onto the glass tabletop then soaked into the elbows of her dressing gown. If she couldn't get the money by midnight, the blackmailer would expose her unnatural pregnancy to the media. Then the old man would learn Ronald wasn't the biological father of his grandson, and he would cut them out of his will. Ronald's political career would be over. The old man would pass everything on to Daniel, and Ronald would be ruined. Ronald would blame her, promptly divorce her, and throw her back out onto the street.

Olga had come from poverty and she wasn't going

back. Grabbing a handful of tissues, she wiped her eyes, blew her nose, and steeled her nerves. She rummaged through her purse until she found her phone then reread the blackmailer's text: "$100,000 by midnight, locker 423, Fienberg Medical School. Expect locker key via UPS." She checked the ID details; the text came from a Chicago area code, 773-330-2929. Fingers shaking, she typed, "I need an extension until tomorrow. Please." "No deal" came the immediate response.

She distractedly ran her index finger over the pink and gold diamond face of her watch. The sharp stones were like braille under her fingertips, sending her a message. She jumped up from her chair, dashed into her closet, took a tiny key from a hidden hook behind her gowns, and quickly opened her jewelry safe. She removed a red leather box as round as a large dinner plate. She snapped it open and stared down at the glittering Trinity Ruban necklace Ronald had given her for her last birthday.

He'd give her expensive gifts, but ask him for money and he'd blow his top. She slid the necklace out of its box and into her robe pocket. She ripped the silk cushion from the bottom of the box and threw it onto the floor. Opening several more oversized jewelry cases, she slipped two diamond bracelets, a pair of emerald earrings, and a ruby necklace into the stripped down Trinity case. She lifted the Trinity Ruban from her pocket and dropped it back into its leather box and carried the bulging box to her dressing table. That was easily two or three hundred thousand dollars worth of jewels, hopefully enough to pawn for the ransom money. Trouble was, she had no idea how or where to pawn anything, especially at this time of night.

Olga went back to her closet to chose an appropriate outfit for a pawnshop, something understated but serious, needy but not desperate. She went with the "London Bump Kit" black dress and black leggings then added simple diamond stud earrings and a sweetheart gold necklace just in case she needed extra cash. She pulled on her thick woolen socks and Florentini rabbit fur boots. She removed an oversized herringbone coat from its satin hanger. *Now what?*

She trusted José, but this wasn't a job for her lovable and honest chauffer. She draped the coat over a silk divan then, perching on the edge, she placed the jewelry box on her knees, and rubbed her temples. Careful not to disturb the jewelry box, she leaned back against the divan and buried her face in the wool coat. *Herring under a coat.* Yes, *Selyodka pod Shouboy*, the answer came to her. She set the box aside on the divan, rushed across the room to her dressing table, picked up her phone and tapped it awake then scrolled through her contacts until she came to "V."

"Vanya, it's me, Olga," she said breathlessly. "Olga Davis. I need your help."

Vanya had been all too happy to help "the daughter of Sergei Yudkovich, meanest *blyad* in all of *Bratva*." Bundled up against the cold, arms folded over her bump, she rode in silence trying not to inhale clouds of secondhand smoke and listened to Vanya boasting about her father's criminal activities. Her Russian was rusty, but she still knew all the curse words. Rounding the corner from respectable to seedy, Uptown City Pawn and Jewelry's big green dollars sign neon lights flashed with the dangerous promise of the ransom cash. Olga clutched the jewelry box on her lap and glanced over at Vanya.

"I called Boris and he's opening up special for you, Miss Yudkovich. Still, I'd better come in wit you," he said, and she winced at her maiden name. Even though it was dark, she put on her sunglasses.

"This ain't no place for a lady." Cigarette dangling from his lips, Vanya reached up and patted something under his jacket. "Don't worry. Me and my trusty *vul* is right behind you."

A group of homeless men huddled around a fire in a trash bin under the "L" tracks across the street from Uptown City Pawn. Olga pulled the collar of her coat up around her ears, adjusted her sunglasses, and headed for the entrance. The metal bars on the glass door were rusted and bent, and the ripped plastic awning hung low over the doorway. Olga tried the door but it was locked. Vanya pressed the doorbell, and the man inside waved and buzzed them in.

"Hey Boris. How's tricks, *chuvak*?" Vanya asked.

"Good, good."

"Boris owns this joint," Vanya said, turning back to her.

"Pleased to meet you, Boris," Olga extended her gloved hand. The longhaired proprietor chuckled, stopped rearranging Rolexes, and grasped her hand with enthusiasm. Surrounded by glass cases pregnant with merchandise, Olga could have been back in Kiev. Flat screen TVs, DVD players, guitars, electronic keyboards, and computers lined shelves above cases filled with jewelry, watches, necklaces, and rings. Rows of felt-lined boxes filled with emeralds, diamonds, and amethysts, with Uptown City Jewelers etched on their lids sat on the countertops.

"Those diamonds are out of pawn," Boris said. The muscular jagged-faced Russian spoke with an accent as he pointed to one of the boxes. "There are pieces from all over the world, only the real thing. Those Rolexes are out of pawn, too."

Olga clutched her leather box to her chest. "I would like to…"

"We don't deal on the floor. We have booths in back for more privacy. This is a first-class place." Boris gestured towards a steel door. "I'll buzz you in."

Vanya held the door open, she scooted inside, and the proprietor followed. He led them to a booth with two chairs on either side of bulletproof glass. "Security is our priority," Boris said, holding out a chair for Olga. "I understand you need a loan on some jewels."

"That's right." Olga sat down on the edge of a chair; she was still gripping the jewelry box with both hands.

"At Uptown City Jewelry, we're here to help. Ninety percent of our merchandise is jewelry. I have a jewel lab in back and a degree from the Gemological Institute of America, but I don't even need a loupe. I can look at a diamond with my bare eyes and tell you what it's worth." Boris patted a felt topped table with his big paw. "Let's see what you've got."

"Alright." Olga opened the box and dumped the jewels out onto the cloth then spread them out and arranged them to their best advantage, the white gold and diamond Trinity Ruban necklace in the center. The bejeweled ribbon of platinum paved with diamonds coiled around a large solitaire entwined by a swirl of "love" as Ronald called it when he presented the elegant gift, "the infinite circle of an eternal bond." The necklace effervesced under the harsh lights, reproaching her for disposing of Ronald's love, one piece at a time. "I need $100,000," she said, snapping the box shut. This was most definitely not what Ronald had meant by *bond*.

Boris whistled. "You've got some nice pieces. But $100,000 is a lot of money."

Vanya pulled a cigarette from the pack in his shirt pocket and clamped it between his teeth. "Mind if I smoke?"

Boris pointed to a No Smoking sign above the door. Knee bouncing, unlit cigarette dangling, Vanya crossed his arms over his chest, leaned back in his chair, and shrugged.

Boris picked up one of the diamond bracelets, weighed it in his palm then examined it under a light attached to the table. "Hmmmm." He placed it back on the felt and picked up one of the earrings and rolled it between his large fingers. "Uh huh." He dropped it back onto the table. He carefully cradled the Trinity Ruban necklace in his left hand then plucked up its catch between his thumb and forefinger and let the Trinity dangle under the light. "My, my," he said, grabbing the bobble and bringing closer to his eyeball.

Olga looked at her watch. Less than one hour left. "I hate to rush you, Mr. Boris, but I'm in a bit of a hurry."

"Yes, most of my clients are in a hurry," he smiled, brushing his long hair back over one shoulder. He took a small calculator from his shirt pocket and punched its tiny keys with his large finger. "I can loan you seventy-five thousand for the lot."

"But I need one hundred," Olga cried.

"I'm sorry, Ma'am, business is business."

"What about this?" Olga removed her Cartier watch and placed it on the table.

"Hmmmm…. Very nice," Boris said, examining it. "Yes, very nice. I'll add another ten grand, brings us up to eighty-five."

Olga desperately took off her diamond stud earrings and her sweetheart necklace. "And these?"

"Well, I shouldn't because they're not really worth it for me, but I'll go up to ninety-five, just to help you out," Boris said, fondling the necklace.

"But I'm still five thousand short. That won't do." Olga glanced at Vanya, tears welling in her eyes.

Vanya sat up in his chair and spit out the unlit cigarette. "What about this?" he asked, pulling the gold grill off his front teeth. The mouthpiece glistened with spittle and stood out amongst the luxury jewelry like a prostitute in a ballroom.

Boris moved the light to examine the grill without touching it. "Another thousand."

"What?" Vanya asked. "Them cost me three."

"Business is business."

Vanya scowled and pulled a gun from under his jacket. "How about this business?" he asked, pointing the pistol at the pockmarked proprietor.

"Hey, Vanya, dude. Chill." Boris chuckled nervously.

Vanya laughed. "Just messin' with ya, *chuvak*." He sat the gun on the table. "Genuine Russian *Vul*. How much for it?"

Boris whistled again and picked up the pistol. "Wow. A PSS silent wool. Don't see many of these. That's what we call Hollywood quiet," he said, turning the gun over and weighing it in his hand. "I love this pistol." He smiled at Vanya. "Okay. One hundred thousand for the lot." He turned back to Olga. "I'll have you sign our standard terms." He retrieved a form from a drawer under the table. "Here, you can read at your leisure. Main thing is you have one month to repay the loan or your goods go out of pawn and become our merchandise."

Olga took the paper and pen. "Yes, I understand. Thank you," she said as she signed the contract.

"I'll just need to see your ID, Ma'am."

"Identification?" she asked. "I didn't bring any."

"For security, you understand. We have to make sure the goods aren't stolen. We aren't a fence."

"You think I stole them?" Olga asked, the blood draining from her face.

"I'll vouch for her," Vanya said. "This here's Olga Davis, Mrs. Ronald Davis. Heard of him?"

"Ronald Davis," the proprietor repeated. "The name sounds familiar. Who is he?"

"He's a rich *súka* whose family owns half this city."

"Yes, well unfortunately we have a lot of wealthy clients down on their luck. But the city still requires us to check ID. We have to file reports on anything over five hundred dollars."

"What about Sergei Yudkovich? Does that name ring a bell?" Vanya smiled, tapped another cigarette from his pack, flipped it into his mouth, and lit it with his titanium lighter.

The proprietor scowled and flexed his biceps. "Sly's dead. The Oxford Don had him killed for double-crossing him. That was twenty years ago. What's Sly got to do with this?"

"This here's Sly's daughter. And she says he's alive, hiding out in Kiev. You wouldn't want to upset Sly's daughter, would you?" Vanya asked. "*Bratva* has eyes and ears everywhere. You heard what happened to The Pope for stealing from the Yudkovich family." Vanya ran his finger across his neck to make a slashing gesture.

"Okay. I get the point. Your word is good enough for me. I just need to go to the safe and get the cash. I'll be right back."

Olga waited for the proprietor to leave the booth then said, "I wish you wouldn't mention my father. No one here knows about him, and I'd like to keep it that way. For all I know, he *is* dead. If word gets out, he might come looking for me and that would be disastrous. I have a nice life here now, and I won't let him or anyone else ruin it. And don't use my real name either. From now on, call me Mrs. Smith."

"Don't worry. My lips are sealed. And my pal *Vul* and I will make sure Boris can keep a secret." Exhaling a ring of smoke, Vanya snatched his grill up off the table, stuffed it into his pocket then picked up the gun and checked its magazine. "Don't think I can part with these after all."

"You're not going to kill him?" Olga asked, her head spinning. She was getting nauseous again.

"Nah. I never kills nobody unless absolutely necessary." Vanya leaned back in his chair and puffed on his cigarette.

A buzzing sound signaled Boris's return. He entered the booth holding a large manila envelope in one hand. "It's all there. Look inside." He held out the packet to Olga. She took the bulky envelope, licked its flap to glue it shut, then stood up.

"I'd count it, if I was you, Mrs. D…Mrs. Smith," Vanya said.

"We really must be going now." Olga tucked the envelope under her arm and pointed towards the door.

"Pleasure doing business with you, Miss Yudkovich."

"Mrs. Smith, if you please."

"Any time you need a loan, please stop by. Any time of the night or day. I can't believe the daughter of Sly Yudkovich was in my shop. Wait until I tell the boys."

Vanya stood up and raised the pistol to the proprietor's face.

"You won't tell nobody or else me and my *Vul* will be back to shut your mouth forever."

"Hey, that gun belongs to me," Boris said. "You pawned it."

"I changed my mind." Vanya waved the gun at him.

Olga shuddered. The affable Russian had transformed into a tough gangster. Her palms were sweating inside her kid gloves, and she was eager to leave.

"Of course, Vanya. Mums the word." Boris buzzed them out. "I won't say anything to anyone. It's like you were never even here. Nobody will be the wiser. It's our little secret." The proprietor chattered on and led them to the front entrance. Vanya kept the gun pointed at him until he'd led Olga outside.

He took her by the elbow and led her to the car then opened the passenger door and she climbed up into the Escalade. He ran around to the driver's side, hopped in, and used the last ember of one cigarette to light another.

"No grill, no gun. I was naked back there." Vanya's

gray-toothed smile was sorrowful compared to the golden glow of his missing grill.

"I'm grateful for your help, but we're running out of time." Olga looked at the bare spot on her wrist where her favorite watch once was.

"Oh, I've got a present for you, Mrs. D…Smith," Vanya said, reaching into his pocket and pulling out his grill along with her watch. He held his palm out to her, and she took her watch. He popped his grill back into his mouth and pushed it up over his front teeth.

"That's so sweet," she smiled at him, as she wrapped the familiar watch around her wrist and fastened the band. "We need to hurry. It's almost midnight."

CHAPTER THIRTY-ONE

JACK HAD LOST track of time. Holed up in this rancid motel, it must have been at least a week since that wanker White had drugged him and locked him up here, wherever *here* was. The night he'd been kidnapped from the clinic, he vaguely remembered looking up from the floor of Max White's van to see a tunnel opening in the front façade of a boxy windowless brick motel and feeble neon arrows flickering, pointing the way to a secluded parking lot in the rear.

Doped up on whatever Max had injected into his neck, the ugly building swallowed him like a giant whale. Now he lay on a pockmarked bedspread, handcuffed to a brass spindle on a cheap headboard, staring up at the water stained ceiling, and listening to Max White drone on about his precious genetic research and his genius insights into the humane genome.

"What are you doing in there, White?" Jack asked, out of boredom as much as curiosity. His arms ached from holding them overhead for days. "I have to take a piss." White had set up the grimy bathroom as a make-shift laboratory. Jack couldn't imagine it was sanitary let alone the proper environment for sensitive embryos, even with the fancy equipment White had "borrowed" from the lab.

"Now, now, Jackoff, where are your manners. I have to take a piss, *please*. Didn't they teach you anything last summer at Oxford or at the Sorbonne? Why you got that fellowship and I didn't is beyond me. You merely want to study the criminal mind. I can eliminate it."

"You can start by looking in the mirror. You embody the most dangerous sort of criminal mind. Classic grandiose delusions, accompanied by the manic phase of bipolar disorder, possibly even the early signs of schizophrenia."

"Fools are far more dangerous than criminals. You dear Jack, are a fool." White shouted over the sounds of water running in the bathroom. "You and your arm chair psychology."

"You're right. You're not pathological. You're just a run of the mill arrogant asshole and control freak all too prevalent in the halls of academia. Narcissistic psychopath, all ego and no empathy."

Max White appeared by his bedside holding a petri dish. Towering overhead, his face contorted into a sly grimace, he said, "Lolita Durchenko's eggs should fetch a pretty price on the black market. I'd better get these babies back into the freezer."

"So you're selling on the black market now. And Manly, is he part of this scheme?"

"You don't think I can go back to Dr. Manly's clinic after you and your insane Russian friend interrupted my work, do you? You've forced me underground, but you can't stop me, and neither can he. The future of the human race is at stake, and it's up to me to save it." White returned to the bathroom. Jack heard him bustling about, petri dishes snapping together, a scalpel clattering to the floor, the toilet flushing. White reappeared carrying a temperature controlled sample case. He stopped and stared down at Jack then lifted his cashmere coat from the back of a chair.

"Lolita's eggs may fetch me a pretty penny, but Jessica's are a genetic needle in a haystack. Our daughter will be magnificent." Max White's incisors gleamed under the flickering fluorescent overhead light.

"Your daughter?" Jack asked. "What do you mean your daughter?" His limbs stiffened.

"Yes, Jackoff. I made an embryo using Ms. James's splendid eggs and my genius sperm. Golden blood. And the rare variations on her X chromosomes. I've never seen anything like it. Those mutations at OR5A1 *and* OPN1MW, absolutely amazing."

"What are you talking about? What mutations? Jessica's blood has no Rh factors? She has universal blood?"

He put his coat down and strolled to the bedside to gloat. "More than that, she has olfactory enhancements to rival a bloodhound." Max White smiled down at him. "Our daughter will share those genetic gifts along with my own."

"What did you do to Jesse, you bloody bastard?" Jack yanked on the cuffs, his eyes filling with tears of rage.

"I'm tempted to make a trip out to Missouri. I'd love to meet the genetic pair who created Jessica James."

"It's Montana and good luck with that. Her father has been dead for years. Probably turning in his grave right about now." Jack dug his desert boot into the mattress.

"Now, now, Jack. Calm down or I'll have to give you another sedative." Max patted him on the head and Jack flinched.

"You're insane," Jack said.

"To the contrary." Max smiled down at him. "Black market eggs are big business. Better than any research grant. Desperate wealthy women want designer babies and they're willing to pay top dollar. They don't care how they're harvested as long as they are from the best stock, attractive Ivy League girls. The money I earn selling these eggs will fund my research and allow me to move into better accommodations that you could afford, Jackoff."

Max White put on his coat and gloves then picked up Jack's Greek Fisherman's cap. "What do you think?" he asked, clapping it onto his head. "How do I look? Like stoner Jack Grove?"

"Where are you going, White?"

"To meet someone, get some cash, and finish what I started with Ms. Durchenko. Her DNA is worth fighting for." He chuckled. "I'll leave this filthy hellhole to you. Your own private room, for as long as you last, which won't be long. That's one good thing about this flea bag. They respect privacy and don't ask any questions. Scream all you want. They're used to it here. Oh, and I hope you don't mind, but I maxed out your credit card. If you'd had a higher limit, we might have been able to afford nicer accommodations." White tipped his cap and headed back to the bathroom.

"Wait a minute, old boy," Jack said. "You aren't going to just leave me here to rot!"

"That, *old boy*, is exactly what I'm going to do. And by the smell of you, it won't be much longer now." White packed up the rest of his equipment and samples from the bathroom and stacked them neatly into a suitcase on the luggage rack then shut and locked it.

"Ta, ta, Jackoff. The room is paid up for a month, but someone will smell your body before then," White said as he picked up the suitcase in one hand and the sample case in the other.

"Max, be reasonable. Come on, dude, don't leave me here," Jack yelled. "Please, Max…come on…"

Max White sat the cases in the hallway, made a show of hanging the Do Not Disturb sign on the doorknob, and then turned back and saluted him. "The guest quarters leave something to be desired, huh Jackoff. Probably not even up to your subterranean standards of cleanliness."

"Don't leave me here to die," Jack shouted. "Whatever else you are, you're not a murderer…." He stopped himself. Maybe White *was* a murderer. "You killed Professor Granowski, didn't you?" he blurted out.

"I must admit, oversight at the clinic got a lot easier to deal with once she was out of the way. I'd love to stay and chat, Jackoff, *old boy*, but I've got an appointment. Enjoy the rest of your stay." White chuckled as he shut the door.

"Fuuuuuuuu!" Jack strained at the handcuffs until his wrists were raw. "Somebody bloody help me! Help!" He screamed at the top of his lungs. He kicked his desert boots into the lumpy mattress. "Bollocks! Let me out! Max White, you asshole, wanker, deranged psychopath!"

Jack wilted into the saggy mattress. "Shit," he said under his breath. He closed his eyes and inhaled a lungful of piss smell, stale cigarettes, and cheap motel sweat. Struggling to prop himself up against the headboard, he surveyed the dingy room: scratched wood paneling, stained carpet pocked with burn holes, boxy old television set, puke yellow lamp sitting on a chipped fake wood night stand, and an old-fashioned beige push-button telephone.

Hands still manacled to the headboard, Jack twisted sideways on the bed and clamped his feet around the hefty phone. Tightening his abdomen, he slowly moved his legs back over to the bed. The phone slipped from his feet and bounced onto the bed, the receiver dangling over the edge. He hooked the phone with his heel and inched it closer to his torso. But without the use of his hands, he couldn't punch the buttons. Frustrated, he kicked at them with his boot until the phone flew off onto the floor. "Come on," he yelled thrashing around on the soiled bed, handcuffs gouging his wrists.

As he writhed in anger, a rickety metal spindle popped off the headboard and liberated one of his wrists. Encouraged, he scooted as far up on the bed as he could with one arm still fastened to the head rail, leveraged his feet against the flaccid mattress and yanked with all his might. The bedpost groaned and creaked, rattled and shook, but wouldn't release its stranglehold on his wrist.

Arms stretched wide, he tried to reach the phone on the floor but couldn't. He gasped and fell back on the bed exhausted. He'd hardly eaten in days; and Max kept shooting him up with shit that knocked him out. He closed his eyes and thought of Jesse. He didn't need a geneticist to tell him she was special, and the idea of that wanker invading her body, stealing her eggs, and inseminating them, made him sick. Most likely, he'd die chained to this bed and never see her again. He wanted to bawl.

Noises from the hallway brought him to attention. He leaned on his elbows and shouted, "Help! Someone help me!!" The rattling of a cart approaching stopped right in front of the door. "Help me!" he yelled.

"You alright in there, Mister," an accented voice said from the other side of the door.

"I'm handcuffed to the bed," Jack replied.

"Sorry to bother you. Remember to use your safe word. I'm not allowed to open doors when guests are in the room." The creaking of the wheels started up again, moving down the hall.

"No. Come back! Help me!" Jack screamed at the top of his lungs. He listened. Nothing but silence. He fell back on the bed and wept. He was a dead man and he'd never see Jesse again.

CHAPTER THIRTY-TWO

EVERY TIME THE Escalade swerved around another corner, Olga grasped the handhold and white-knuckled the armrest. Smoking like a Cossack, Vanya seemed to be enjoying the chase. She glanced at the clock in the dashboard, five minutes before the ransom deadline. The Cadillac skidded to a stop in front of the Medical School.

Olga said, "I have to go in alone. Could you wait here for me?" Clutching the bulging manila under her arm, she glided out of the car and walked briskly toward the entrance. She pulled on the heavy door handle, but it wouldn't budge. It was locked. *Now what?* She knocked on the door hoping someone would hear her. Hand shielding her eyes, she peered inside the glass door.

No one in sight. She rummaged in her purse for her phone to see if she'd misread the instructions. She considered texting the blackmailer to tell him to come let her in but she was already running late and he'd warned her not to contact him.

"Door's locked at midnight," Vanya said, coming up behind her. He pulled a key from a jangling set attached to his belt loop and stretched its retractable cord towards the lock. "I work here."

"You work here?" she repeated, stepping out of the way so he could unlock the door. "You can't be a doctor," she said in horror.

"Nah, I'm a security guard. Campus cop." Vanya smiled and opened the door.

"You're a policeman?" she asked, even more incredulous than before. "You work undercover?"

"It's good to see things from both sides," Vanya said, holding the door open and motioning her inside.

"Do you know where to find the lockers?" Olga asked. "I need to locate locker 423."

"Follow me." Vanya led her by the arm towards the elevator. "The lockers are on the fourth floor across from the lounge. Some kids sleep up there. They've got showers and everything."

Olga pushed the button to call the elevator. She looked at her watch, ten minutes late. She paced back and forth in front of the lift and pressed the button again. She was heading for the stairs when Vanya called out, "It's here." She turned around and walked briskly back to the elevator. His tattooed hand stuck out across the door, and she stepped inside and pressed the button to the fourth floor. Her heart was racing as she watched the numbers light up above the door, 2…3…4. She followed him out of the elevator and glanced around the expansive foyer wondering which way to go.

"This way," Vanya said. He took off and she rushed to catch up. He turned down a deserted hallway. She heard voices up ahead. Gathered in a vending machine area in an alcove at the end of the hall, a few students were drinking sodas and eating granola bars, a midnight snack. The young people just watched as she and her gangster escort bustled past and rounded another corner.

Hurrying down the next hall, she glanced into a large room with cubicles where a few students sat hunched over their computers. Across the corridor and along the opposite wall were rows of lockers. She counted the numbers, 334, 335, 336, as they blurred past. Number 423 was at the very end of the row. Out of breath, she stood in front of the locker staring at a note attached to it. Vanya grabbed the folded paper, and read it, "You are late." He looked at her and crumpled the note. "That's all it says."

"Hopefully not too late," Olga said, removing a small key from her purse. Hands shaking, she had trouble inserting the key into the lock. Tiny beads of sweat moistened her forehead as she turned the key and slowly opened the locker door for fear of what might be inside. She peeked in. The locker was empty. She slid the manila envelope inside and shut the locker door. "There. It's done. Let's go."

"With blackmail, it's never done," Vanya said. "Believe me. I knows. He'll just keep axing for more money. The more you gives, the more he wants." He glanced around the hall. "Come on," he said. "There's a janitor's closet." He took her arm, led her across the hall to a wooden door then took out his massive set of keys and used one to open it. "Cops got universal keys. Cool, eh? I don't even need to break in or nothin'." He opened the door and pulled her in behind him. "We'll just watch and see who comes to pick up the package."

"The blackmailer is already here and probably watching us," Olga said, trembling.

Vanya patted his right shoulder where he kept his gun holstered under his jacket. "We'll get the drop on him."

"I don't like this. If he's here now, he already knows I didn't come alone and maybe he'll take the money and go to the media anyway." Olga reached for the doorknob.

Vanya touched her wrist. "That's why we're staying put. We've got to stop him blackmailing you once and for all." Vanya pulled her further into the janitor's closet. "Get back in the shadow, and I'll watch out." He cracked opened the door and a slice of light cut through the closet. Olga spotted a five-gallon plastic drum in the corner, sat down on it, and put her head in her hands as another wave of nausea crashed over her. "Don't worry, barking dogs seldom bite," he said, smiling at her, an unlit cigarette dangling from his mouth.

"Olga Yudkovich," he said. The cigarette bounced up and down as he spoke. "I can't believe I'm in a closet with Sly's daughter. Blows my brain."

"Do we have to talk about my father?" Olga asked. "I hardly know him. And from what my mom told me, I don't want to."

"Sly was a cool customer." Vanya clicked his lighter open and shut, click, click, click. "His old man, the Oxford Don, sent his own brother to kill him."

"So blood isn't necessarily thicker than water." Olga pointed to his noisy lighter.

"Sorry," he said, and slipped the lighter into his pocket. "Your dad's a legend in *Bratva*. Sly 'bezelled his own father and the Oxford Don don't tolerate no one stealing from him, not even his own son." Vanya sighed, and took his lighter from his pocket and started playing with it again.

Olga nodded at the lighter. "Better stop or he'll hear you."

"Oh, sorry," Vanya said, putting it away again. "Habit." He smiled, but his bearing suggested melancholy lingering beneath the surface.

"Do you miss Russia?" she asked. "Will you ever go back?"

"I dunno. I left coz the Oxford Don put a contract out on me, too. But now that's he's dead, maybe." He flipped a cigarette into his mouth. "How about you? Will you ever go back to Kiev?" he whispered, still vigilantly peering out the crack into the hallway.

"Me?" she smiled wistfully. "No. I'll never go back. This is my home and…" Footsteps in the corridor stopped her in midsentence. She stared up at Vanya, eyes wide, heart pounding in her ears. He turned back to her and put his finger to his lips, then slowly pulled his pistol out of its holster, and peeked back out into the hallway. Muscles taut, an Amur leopard on high alert, Vanya's body froze focusing on his prey.

She heard the door to the locker squeak then Vanya sprang out of the closet and leapt on the blackmailer. The door to the closet flung open, and Olga watched as the two men wrestled and writhed on the floor, first one on top then the other.

"Doctor?" she asked. Vanya was locked in combat with Dr. Manly's assistant, the handsome young doctor who had implanted her embryos. "What are you doing, Dr. White?"

The doctor was sitting astride the Russian. He had him

pinned to the ground under the lockers. Both hands around Vanya's right arm, the doctor banged it into the floor over and over again trying to loosen the pistol from the gangster's grip. Vanya punched the doctor in the face with his left fist and sent him flying backwards onto the floor. The doctor knelt on the tile next to Vanya, holding his bloody nose with both palms, his white shirt turning red.

In one graceful move, the Russian rolled over, popped up onto all fours, and leapt on top of the young doctor. Vanya raised the pistol into the air and brought it down hard, aiming for the back of the doctor's head. The doctor ducked just in time. But the momentum from the swing pitched Vanya forward face first onto the tile, splitting his lip, and sending the pistol clattering down the hall.

The men struggled, rolling back and forth on the floor, as blood splattered onto the lockers. During the fight, the doctor grabbed Vanya's leather jacket and when the Russian wriggled out of it, red fangs on his shoulder appeared from under his shirt sleeve.

The streaks of fresh blood against the clean tile made Olga lightheaded. She retreated into the closet and took some deep breaths. Listening to the grunting, groaning, and clanking of keys hitting tile coming from the hall, she knew she had to act.

She searched the closet for something to use as a weapon. She grabbed a broom and a quart of bleach. She stepped out into the hallway and threw the bleach bottle at the doctor. The cap flew off as the bottle hit the tile. Swirls of red joined the clear liquid as it pooled on the floor. The color slowly drained from the fighting men's clothing as it soaked up the bleach. The pungent smell made Olga's head spin. Despite her dizziness, she raised the heavy broom over her head and aimed for the young doctor, but she couldn't land a blow because Vanya kept getting in the way.

"Mrs. Smith, no," the doctor said, kicking Vanya in the jaw. "Please, you could harm the babies."

Vanya lunged for the pistol, giving her a clear shot at the doctor. When Olga lifted the broom again, the nausea overcame her and her knees gave out. The doctor jumped up in time to catch her before she collapsed to the floor. "Mrs. Smith, you need to be careful. We worked hard to make those babies," he said, holding her upright.

"But Doctor," she asked. "Why are you blackmailing me? I don't understand."

"I need funds to continue my research, and you have money. It was the only way." The doctor held her tight and pulled her back towards the locker.

"Get away from her or I'll shoot," Vanya said, marching pistol first down the hall.

"You won't shoot," the doctor said. "It's too risky. You might hit Mrs. Smith or harm our babies."

"I don't think so, *súka*. I can hit a black-beaked Capercaillie between the eyes at thirty yards in the dark." Vanya cocked the pistol and aimed.

"No. Don't shoot, Vanya," Olga cried. A shot echoed down the corridor, and she lost consciousness.

CHAPTER THIRTY-THREE

JESSICA JUMPED UP from the desk chair and burst out of the cubicle. "That sounded like a gun shot. Come on," she said, tugging at the sleeve of Lolita's leather jacket. "This way." She hightailed it through the maze of partitions, passed a few hardcore med students pulling all-nighters, and hoofed it in the direction of the shot.

From the study carrel doorway, she could hear voices coming from around the corner. She skated down the hall, the soles of her cowboy boots slick against the polished tile, and slid around the corner, skidding to a stop when she saw bright blood splattered across the bleached tile. Two forms were struggling near a body on the floor.

"Holy crap," she said under her breath. She glanced back as Lolita slid past her and rushed headlong into the chaos. When Jessica caught up to her friend, she saw Olga Davis sprawled out on her back in a pool of bleached blood, with Max White kneeling next to her and Vanya standing behind him, gun in hand. "Oh my God. Is she dead? What happened?"

Max bolted up, knocked the gun from Vanya's hand, grabbed it off the floor, snatched up a manila envelope lying nearby, then headed for the emergency exit. Lolita took off after him. A lightning bolt, she threw her body into the air and pinwheeled her legs. One black boot after another struck the fugitive's head and sent him hurtling into a brick wall. Staggering forward, he clutched the envelope and waved the pistol as he stumbled towards the emergency exit.

"Watch out, Lolita," Jessica yelled, running full on towards the geneticist. "He's got a gun." She lunged at Max's feet trying to grab him by the ankle. He pointed the gun straight down at her and pulled the trigger, but she'd rolled out of the way just in time. The crack of the bullet hitting the tile next to Jessica was deafening.

"You won't get away with this!" Lolita shouted as she landed an axe kick to his arm, sending the pistol skittering to the floor. Jessica scrambled on hands and knees and grabbed it, tripping Lolita in the process. Her friend landed on top of her.

"He's getting away." Jessica wriggled out from under her friend and fired the pistol at the exit Max had just lurched through.

"I'll get him," Lolita said. She righted herself and ran after Max.

Jessica followed her friend through the exit into the stairwell. From the fourth-floor landing, she saw her friend fly down the stairs in pursuit. Lolita caught up to Max on the second-floor landing. His back to the wall, Max pointed the gun at Lolita. Jessica saw a black booted butterfly kick knock the gun from his hand and send his head slamming into the wall behind him. Lolita followed with her signature Kin Geri kick to the nuts. "You won't be inseminating any unsuspecting ova in the near future, asshole," Lolita said. Max lay in a fetal position on the second-floor landing gasping and holding his groin with both hands as Lolita pinned him to the floor with a lethal boot across his throat.

"Good work, Coz." Vanya appeared on the fourth-floor landing next to her, and flashed his golden smile. "Mind if I cuff him?" he asked, taking the stairs down two at a time.

"Be my guest," Lolita said, her boot still pressed against Max's neck.

Jessica watched from above as Vanya danced down the stairs and knelt next to the moaning geneticist. He removed handcuffs from his back pocket and snapped them around Max's wrists. "Maybe I'll like being a cop," he said, hauling Max to his feet and grabbing the bloodstained envelope out of his hand. Jessica supervised from above as Lolita and her cousin dragged the mad scientist back up two flights of stairs. Struggling like a cat in a sack, Max kicked, clawed, and bit at his captors.

When Lolita gave him a quick elbow to the jaw, he became more cooperative.

"Jessica, dear," Max said, glancing up in her direction. "Would you mind checking on our babies?" He was bleeding from his mouth and one eye was swollen shut. "I'm worried that their gestational carrier may have been damaged in the fight."

"Olga, oh my God," she said. She ran back up the stairs, through the exit door, and down the hallway towards the motionless body. Winded, she leaned on the lockers and stared down at the unconscious woman lying in a pinkish pool. Her platinum bun had unspooled, and her cashmere coat was marinating in bloody bleach. Jessica bent down and put her fingers on Olga's wrist to feel her pulse. White as a rabbit, the socialite opened her eyes and stared up at her.

"What happened?" she asked weakly.

"Are you hurt? You're bleeding." Jessica lifted Olga's tie-dyed herringbone coat to find the source of the blood and check her body for injuries. "I'm going to pass out if we don't get out of this hallway," Jessica said. "The smell of bleach is wicked strong. Can you stand?" she asked as she helped Olga to her feet.

"Are you bleeding?" Jessica asked.

Olga pointed to the stairwell. Vanya had just emerged restraining Dr. Frankenstein. "It's their blood. I'm okay. I just fainted. The bleach is my fault. I don't know what I was thinking." Her coat was dripping with the stinky stuff, and some of the velvet on her black leggings had dissolved into the puddle.

"At least their wounds won't get infected," Jessica said, leading Olga down the hall to the foyer. "Let's get rid of that reeking coat before I puke." She helped Olga out of her coat and threw the offending article at a trashcan. Putting her arm around Olga's waist, she guided her to an easy chair in the lounge in front of the elevators.

"Rest while I call for help." Jessica knelt down beside the chair and looked into Olga's weary eyes. "Do you want some water or something? I can get some tea from the kitchen."

Olga nodded her head and pouted like a sick child. As Jessica rushed off towards the carrels, she saw Lolita and Vanya dragging their prisoner down the hall towards the elevators. Jessica waved as she ducked into the room then weaved her way through the cubicles to the kitchen in the back. She filled the electric teapot with water, depressed the lever on its side, then took out her phone. As she waited for the water to hiss to a boil, she called Detective Cormier. No answer.

She rinsed out a dirty mug then grabbed an herbal tea bag, stuffed it in the cup, and filled it with boiling water. She tried the detective again. Damn. Still no answer. Walking as quickly as she could without spilling, she carried the steaming cup back out into the foyer.

Olga was still sitting in the lounge area with her head between her knees, panting.

"Are you okay?" Jessica sat on the armrest and rubbed the pregnant woman's back. She held the cup in front of her face. "Here, try some tea. It will make you feel better."

Jessica glanced down the hall and saw Vanya pinning the cuffed geneticist up against a locker and Lolita talking on her phone, hopefully with the police.

Olga sat up and took the mug. "Thank you. I think I'm just in shock." She sipped from the steaming cup. "That's the doctor who did the implants...the biological father of my...our...babies." She glanced up at Jessica with sorrowful eyes.

"The babies may be real, but Max White is no doctor," Jessica said. "He's nothing but a double-dealing, no good thief, and crazy to boot."

"What if my children are as unhinged as their biological father?" Olga asked.

"Nurture is as important as nature. Anyway, aren't maternal genes the dominant ones? My bootcut genes may be scrappy and rough around the edges, but they could beat out Max White's wimpy genes any day of the week." Jessica smiled and tucked a lock of Olga's hair back into her soggy sorry-assed bun.

Lolita and her cousin dragged Dr. Frankenstein toward the lounge, pushing him across the carpet, then shoved him into a chair. He looked as crazed as he was with his wild eyes, broken nose, and bloodstained shirt. Snakes of black hair slithered off his head in all directions. Slouched in the overstuffed chair, hands cuffed in front of his torso, jeans torn and soiled, long legs flopping off to one side, Max was anything but the hot intern who'd seduced her at O'Tooles. Now he looked wrung out and wrecked. Jessica almost felt sorry for him.

Lolita must have read her mind. She sauntered over to his chair and spit in his face. "No one violates me and gets away with it."

Max contorted his swollen lips into a sly smile. "At this very moment your feisty genes are multiplying. Whatever you do to me, you can't stop our genetic codes from performing the dance of life. We are forever linked, and our progeny will shape the future of the human race."

Lolita grabbed a fistful of his wavy hair and jerked him upright in the chair. "Listen to me, asshole, you're going to return to me what you've taken or I'll bash your head in." He shook his head free of her grasp, leaving her holding a wad of his hair in her hand.

"I'll gladly return the embryos to you, if you'll take off the cuffs. I'll even implant them for you."

Lolita scoffed.

"What do you want? A ring?" Max asked. "How about you, Jessica? Together we could create your precious Übermensch*en*. I'm a better match for you than Stoner Jack."

"You're the one who's been texting me from Jack's phone," Jessica said. "What have you done with Jack?" she demanded, pounding her first on the arm of the chair so hard the impact made Olga bounce.

"Order that goon to take off the cuffs and I might tell you," Max smirked.

"Vanya, take this psychopath to the police station," Lolita said, "then take Mrs. Davis home." Lolita zipped up her leather jacket and headed for the elevator. "Come on, Jessica, let's go find Jack."

"Me go to the police station?" Vanya asked. "That's like axing me to strip naked and jump into a shark tank."

Lolita pushed the elevator button. "Suit yourself. We're going to The Guest House Motel on Bryn Mawr. Unless you need help handling Dr. Frankenstein, we'll meet you there." She stepped into the elevator and barked, "Come on, Jessica. Let's go."

"Hold your horses," Jessica said. "Are you sure you're okay, Olga? Do you need Vanya to take you to the hospital, or would you rather go home? Maybe he can drop you off on the way to the Guest House."

"Yes, I'd like to go home," she said. Jessica put her arm around her and squeezed. She stood up and marched over to the chair Max was sprawled out in. "Where is Jack?" she demanded.

"Sit down next to me." Max nodded toward the arm of the easy chair, and she obliged. "I'm a geneticist, not a murderer. I've had to use extreme measures because these are desperate times. If the human race is going to survive, we need to evolve and fast."

"Where's Jack?" Jessica asked, staring straight into his endless blue eyes.

"You know I can't resist your considerable charms. He's handcuffed to a bed in room 28 of the Guest House on Bryn Mawr. The key to the room is in my pants pocket. I'd give it to you, but as you can see my hands are incapacitated. But you can retrieve it yourself. Be my guest." He stretched his legs out further and nodded towards the right front pocket of his jeans.

Jessica leaned in, glanced up at him, and then slipped her hand into his pocket. As she fished out the key, he sat up and kissed her on the cheek. She spat at him, but he just laughed.

"You are a marvel," he whispered as she wrangled the key out his pocket.

"And you're the dumbest smart person I've ever met," she said. "You'll have plenty of time to write up the results of your creepy research in prison."

"I'm leaving without you if you don't get your ass in this elevator," Lolita said. "We may still be able to get to Jack before the detective hauls him off."

"Operation Rescue Jack," Jessica said as she jumped into the elevator just before the doors closed. In her skintight leathers, helmet liner, and sheath gloves, all Lolita needed was cat ears to top off her avenging panther outfit. "I hope you know what you're doing," Jessica said, waving the motel room key.

Lolita's Harley was still parked on the sidewalk out front of the Med School where she'd left it. Straddling the beast, she handed a helmet to Jessica then revved the engine. Jessica zipped her parka up to her ears, tugged on her Trapper, and perched the helmet on top of her head, the straps barely reaching around her chin. She wrapped her arms around her friend's waist and held on tight.

The frigid early morning breeze bit at her cheeks and made her eyes water. She squeezed her eyes shut and buried her face into the back of Lolita's leather jacket.

When they reached Motel Row, the sun was breaking over Lincoln Street, and block after block of seedy dives. Over the years, the once respectable family destinations had deteriorated into rent-by-the-hour joints serving prostitutes and drug dealers.

Lolita decelerated and cruised up and down the sleazy motorway looking for the Bryn Mawr. Jessica spotted the street sign, tapped her friend on the shoulder, and pointed. When they coasted around the corner, Jessica saw lights in front of a squat building set back from the road. The motel blended into its seedy surrounding so well, it was hard to pick out. No doubt about it. With its dark cavernous opening, the rundown joint was a viper's den.

"That's it!" she shouted over the bike's rumbling and pointed to the boxy brick fortress. Two police cars sat on the street in front, lights flashing. Lolita pulled up behind them, and Jessica jumped off the bike. The cops were sitting in their cars drinking coffee and eating Pierogies. She walked over and tapped on the window of one of the patrol cars. The cop scowled and rolled down the window.

"Can I help you, Miss?" he asked with his mouth full.

"Is Detective Cormier around?"

"He's waiting round back. Can I be of help?" he asked,

staring at Lolita as she took off her helmet and cap and liberated her long ebony hair. The cop swallowed hard.

"You already have been." Jessica hightailed it back to the bike. "The detective's behind the motel," she said to her friend and hopped back on the motorcycle. Lolita put it in gear and drove through the dark tunnel to the back parking lot.

Detective Cormier was leaning against his unmarked car drinking from a steaming paper cup. He narrowed his thick brows as Jessica approached. "I thought I told you girls to stay out of this. What are you doing here?" His black Lincoln was the only car in the lot. The flickering neon arrow in the tunnel created an eerie strobe effect in the empty back lot. Beyond the asphalt was brush strewn with trash, a good place to hide a body.

"Where's Jack? Isn't he here?" Jessica asked in alarm.

"The door to room 28 is locked. We're waiting for a search warrant. The crazy old lady at the desk wouldn't let us in without one. She insisted they respect the privacy of their clients. Once the warrant arrives, we'll go in. One of the maids told me she heard a man yelling for help and called the police. But we were already on our way. As soon as we get the warrant, we'll find Jack."

Vanya's black Escalade appeared out of the mouth of the cavern and into the back lot. The detective pointed at the SUV. "What's he doing here?"

"He brought you a gift," Jessica said. "Max White has been using Jack's phone and credit cards. He's the one responsible for the dumpster girls and assaulting Lolita and me. He stole our eggs. He's been drugging college girls and extorting money from rich women who want designer babies. Vanya's got him handcuffed over there in his rig."

"You should put us on the payroll, Detective," Lolita said, ambling over to join them.

"Perhaps you're right, Ms. Durchenko. Excuse me a minute." Detective Cormier opened the driver's side door of his Lincoln, sat down, and reached for the mic. "Frizzel and O'Brien, get around back. I've apprehended Max White," he said into the police radio.

"Okay, the boys will take him down to the station," he said, getting out of his car. "I'll wait for the search warrant. We still have to find Jack Grove. He's still a suspect...."

"Jack's innocent," Jessica interrupted. "I know it." She turned to Lolita. "We don't have to wait for no stinkin' warrant. Let's go get Jackass."

"The door's locked. We've already tried."

"But I have the key," she said as she waved the key and trotted across the parking lot. "Operation Rescue Jack."

Before the detective could stop her, Jessica dashed towards a dark corridor, read the rusty placard pointing the way to 28, then glanced over her shoulder at Lolita. "This way," she said, pointing straight ahead. Her friend sped by and was already pounding on the door when she reached room 28. Jessica inserted the key and popped the door open. When she burst into the room, she was assaulted by a rancid odor, a mixture of sordid afternoon trysts, stale cigar smoke, and rubbing alcohol. When she flipped on the lights, she saw the stained carpet, peeling wallpaper, and broken headboard.

"Jack!" she shouted. Panting, she ran into the bathroom and then back out into the bedroom. "Jack," she gasped.

The stained bedspread was shoved to one side of the bed, the flimsy metal headboard was broken and missing two rails, and an old-fashioned phone was splayed across the floor. No sign of Jack. *Where was he? What had Max done to him?* Her heart ached with the need to see him safe. "Jack," she whispered, a tear sprouting in the corner of her eye.

CHAPTER THIRTY-FOUR

D
AWN WAS BREAKING as Jack staggered through Rosehill Cemetery. No weed, no phone, no money, no coat, he wasn't sure where he was heading, just away from the Guest House Motel. After a week chained to a bed with only enough food to survive and nothing else, not even hope, he wasn't just running away from death. He was running away from something worse, his own demons.

He was so desperate for food, shelter, and warmth, so driven by the basic necessities of life, he'd do anything, even kill someone. He'd studied the so-called *criminal mind* long enough to know desperation could lead almost anywhere. Hopelessness, hunger, and despair could lead a man to steal, murder, even torture. His fingers were numb and his urine-soaked pants frozen stiff. Still cuffed, his wrists were cut and bleeding from beating them against the bedrails to free himself. His distended stomach rivaled only his soul for its emptiness.

Floating amongst the long dead, he realized that something inside him had died after a week's captivity. He couldn't even imagine what it must be like to endure months even years of solitary confinement. Might as well be interned in one of those graves.

Seduced by a ray of golden light, he followed it to an alabaster gazebo. The monument was at the center of a hub of headstone spokes radiating out in five directions. In a daze, he stepped up onto the shelter's marble floor and gazed down at a life-sized sculpture of a supine beauty, hair parted in the center, one arm draped over her sleeping head, and the other cradling a sleeping child.

The stone woman's head rested on two alabaster pillows, her fingers resting against the ivory cord and tassel and her flowing stone robe now dappled with moss and mildew. Jack reached down to touch her peaceful lips, but their cold hard rebuke sent him reeling. He felt the dead cold lips of Sara Shaner and stumbled forwards, fell onto the grass, and listened to the sound of his breathing.

He could feel his heart pounding against the frozen ground. He rolled onto his back and gazed up at the pink clouds, the living flesh of the sky, pulsating and bleeding into another day. He held his arms overhead and stared up at them against the sky. The shiny cuffs blinded him, and the raw skin reminded him he wasn't made of stone or marble.

Surrounded by death, and nearly dead himself, for the first time he saw what he wanted, not the transitory pleasures he'd bartered as compensation for a life of disappointment and loss, but something deeper and more permanent. The aching in his chest grew with an urgent yearning, its force bending to the breaking point until it snapped into a primal need for love. He loved Jessica with all his heart, and he'd give anything just to see her again. Stirred by the clarity of his revelation, he resolved to find a way to survive for her sake.

He sat up, shook the frost from his hair, and watched an icy cloud of breath escape his mouth. He had to think. Rosehill Cemetery. On the other side of the cemetery, Bryn Mawr continued all the way to the lake. The Bryn Mawr "L" stop must be about a mile away. He had no wallet, so he'd have to panhandle. Maybe someone would give him the fare. *But then what?*

He had no keys to his car or apartment, no phone to call a friend, not even two quarters for a payphone. Recalling Jesse's small hand on his arm and their tight embrace the night he'd clung to her behind the dumpster, he stood up and headed out of the cemetery in the direction of the train.

Still early, the street was deserted as he stepped out onto the sidewalk. He wrapped his arms around his torso and pushed onward headfirst. His face burned, and he could barely see through the frost forming on his lashes. Up ahead he saw a sign for Neumann Family Services, and a light bulb went off in his head.

He picked up his pace, took Ravenswood to Gregory Street, and searched the row of neat brick houses until he found Ashley Horton's address. After training as a psychiatric nurse, she'd gone to work with mentally disabled adults at Neumann; that was right after he'd broken up with her and before he'd left for Oxford. He rang the doorbell, trying to hide the handcuffs under his shirt.

A tall man in a terry robe answered the door. "Can I help you?" he asked in a sleepy voice.

"Is Ashley at home?" Jack asked.

The man squinted and gave him a sour look. "Why? Who are you?"

"My name is Jack Grove. I'm an old friend. I'm in trouble. I need your help. Please get Ashley. Please let me talk to her," Jack begged.

"Who is it, honey?" a familiar voice came from inside the house.

Without a word, the man shut the door in Jack's face, and with it his last best hope. Jack crumbled into a heap on the front porch. Tears streaming down his face, too weak to move, he lay there, staring up into the barren branches.

When the door reopened, Ashley stood blinking down at him, Jack was only semiconscious and the world was a blur. He'd forgotten where he was and how he got there.

"Oh my God," the voice came from above. He looked up and recognized the beautiful red hair. "Jack. Are you alright? Jack?" He moaned and heard the screen door click shut again. "Honey, help me. Jack needs medical attention. Help me get him inside."

Strong hands gripped him under the armpits and hauled him to his feet. "Get him to the sofa. But wait until I get a sheet to cover it. Hold him there a minute." When Ashley returned with the sheet, the strong arms lowered him down. Unable to steady himself with cuffed hands, Jack fell back onto the soft cushions.

"Jack, what happened to you?" Ashley asked. "Why the handcuffs?"

"Who is he?" the tall man asked, wrinkling his nose.

"His name is Jack Grove. He's an old friend. Honey, go get him a glass of water. And bring some warm washrags. I've got to clean those wounds on his wrists."

"Thanks," Jack whispered, barely able to speak. After a glass of water and a cup of coffee, he was more coherent. "I've been held hostage for the last week by an insane geneticist."

"What? Why?" Ashley asked as she bandaged his wrists, her long red curls falling into her face.

"I don't have the strength to tell the tale. I haven't eaten in days."

"I'll get you something to eat," Ashley said. "Then you can tell us what's going on."

Her partner sat staring at him in silence from across the room, then he got up and turned on the radio to a classical station. Jack closed his eyes and let the sounds wash over him until he heard Ashley padding back into the living room.

"We need to call the police," Jack said. "There is a mad geneticist on the loose."

"Honey, call the police while I feed Jack," Ashley said, setting a plate of cheese, crackers, and sliced apples on the coffee table. She sat down on the couch next to Jack. He reached out with cuffed hands and took a piece of cheese. When Ashley handed him a cracker, he noticed how thin and pale she was. She wasn't the fleshy redhead he'd bedded last summer.

"Are you okay?" he asked her. "You look ill."

"Thanks, Jack. You always were a flatterer."

"Really, you don't look well. Remember, I'm a med student."

"Yes, I remember all too well. Anyway, it's your fault, Jack Grove," she said with a weak smile.

"My fault?"

"You showed me that ad in the Daily Northwestern and suggested I could make some easy money donating eggs?"

"I was just joking," he interrupted.

"Well, I donated and ended up with severe internal bleeding. In fact, I almost died. The irony is that now I might not be able to have my own kids." She glanced over at her partner.

"I'm sorry to hear that Ashley. I really am," Jack said, distracted by the radio news in the background. "Can you turn that up?"

"The radio?" the man asked as he reached over and turned a dial on the stereo.

"What is it?" Ashley asked.

"Listen," he said.

"After weeks of investigation, a Northwestern University post-doctoral fellow, Dr. Samantha Brewer, has been taken into police custody for the Thanksgiving Day vandalism at Feinberg Medical School. Cook County is reopening the inquiry into the death of Dr. Janet Granowski who was found dead in a laboratory freezer over Thanksgiving weekend under suspicious circumstances." The music started playing again.

"*Merde.*" Jack tried to run his hands through his matted hair but the cuffs got in the way. "Can I use your phone?"

"What's going on, Jack?" Ashley asked. "Thanksgiving Eve, I was at the emergency room that night. Your precious cowgirl friend Jessica James was there, too. Didn't she tell you?"

"Jesse? Look, Ashley. I'll tell you everything later. We can have a coffee or a drink and I'll describe the whole sordid affair in every gory detail. But right now, I need to use your phone. They've got the wrong person in jail. Where are those cops?"

Without a word, Ashley removed her cellphone from her robe pocket and tapped her password and handed him the phone then crossed her arms over her chest and pouted.

"Are you sure that's a good idea?" her boyfriend asked. Ashley just shrugged.

Jack balanced the phone between his knees and entered the number. Since hers was the only number he knew by heart, he called Jesse. She didn't answer. He fumbled with the phone and glanced up at Ashley.

"I can't type with these cuffs on. Can you type a text to the number I just called?" he asked, handing the phone back to Ashley.

She rolled her eyes. "What do you want me to type?"

"It's Jack. Need V's number ASAP." No sooner had Ashley pressed send than the phone started buzzing. "Must be your cowgirl calling back." She handed him the phone and smirked.

"Hi Jesse," he said, holding the phone in both hands.

"Yes, it's really me. Yes, I'm okay. Detective Cormier? Stall him. I need to reach Vanya right away. He's there, too? Even better. Tell him to pick me up at 1717 Gregory, near Rosehill Cemetery, off Ravenswood." He glanced up at Ashley again. "I can't talk now. See you soon. I promise. I'll call you later."

The sound of Jesse's sweet voice revived him. Just knowing he'd see her again gave him the courage to do the right thing. While he waited for Vanya to show up, he polished off the plate of cheese and crackers, and was working on the apples when a wailing horn outside signaled Vanya's arrival. For the last fifteen minutes, he'd managed to keep his mouth too full to answer Ashley's barrage of annoying questions. Now he remembered why they'd broken up.

Jack hopped up and said goodbye. Ashley moved away from his attempt at a hug and clung to her boyfriend. "What should we do when the police arrive?" she asked as he scooted out the door. "Send them to The Guest House Motel off Lincoln," he said, bolting across the yard toward Vanya's Caddy.

Jack opened the passenger door and climbed in.

"That detective is looking for you. You told Jessica to stall, so that's what she's doing. She's a real *lapochka*." Vanya grinned.

"What's a lapochka?" Jack adjusted the heat vent and held his cuffed hands in front of it.

"A Sweetie pie. Wheweeee. The opposite of you, *chuvak*. What sewer did you crawl out of? You must stink pretty bad if I can smell ya." He held up a cigarette. "Self-defense." He took a drag then blew out a wall of smoke. "What's with the bracelet?"

"That bastard White cuffed me to a bedrail. Any idea of how to get these things off?"

"Open the glove apartment. There's a black leather case inside."

"Glove apartment?"

"Yeah, that apartment in the dash." Vanya pointed at the glove box.

Jack opened it, removed the case, and handed it to the Russian. Vanya unzipped it and removed a slender tool. "Hold your hands out." He inserted the metal shaft into the lock. "Hold still. Here, press your hands into this."

He tapped on the center console with the lock pick. Jack obliged, and within a few seconds the gangster cop had popped the lock and he was free.

"Thanks, dude," he said, rubbing his wrists. "Have you heard about Sam?"

"Sam? What about her?" Vanya asked, his smile disappearing.

"She's in jail, accused of vandalism at the lab, and maybe more." Jack braced himself for the Russian's reaction.

"No way. She would have called me," Vanya said. "How do you know?"

"That phone call stuff in the movies is crap," Jack said. "First thing they'd do is take away her phone and lock her up. I heard it on the radio."

"They don't have nothin' on her," Vanya said, clicking his titanium lighter. "She's innocent."

"You think that matters? You have more faith in the criminal justice system than I do."

"We've gotta go get her out. Poor little *myshka*." Vanya's clicking was picking up speed, a metronome gone wild.

"Do you have the money for bail?" Jack asked. "That's the only way to get her out, unless you're planning a jailbreak."

Vanya put the Caddy into gear and peeled out into the street.

"Where are we going?"

"I know where to get the bail money."

"Where?"

"Ronald Davis. He owes me." Vanya pointed to a fat envelope laying on the backseat.

"What's in there?" Jack asked.

"I've been a busy little ant." He smiled. "I knows a guy does the best print work in town."

"Print work?"

"You know, birth 'tificates, bloodlines, stuff like that." He took a drag off his cigarette.

"I'm not following."

"Forgeries, *chuvak*." He shook his head. "You gots lots to learn 'bout the biz. This stuff's worth fifty grand."

"I'm not in the business, remember?" Jack rubbed his sore wrists.

"Let's go collect from Mr. Bigshot and I'll show ya how it's done."

"Good plan. But can we stop by my place first so I can change my clothes? I don't think I'm presentable to subway rats, let alone Chicago's royalty."

"No time. *Myshka*'s rotting in some stinkin' cell. We'll get the fifty grand and go get her." Vanya swerved around the corner and headed for the Gold Coast.

"Look, Vanya. My place is on the way. It will only take me five minutes max. More importantly, do you have that surveillance tape?"

Vanya veered onto US 41 North then slammed his foot down on the accelerator.

"Calm down, dude," Jack said. "Sam will be fine. Don't worry. I won't let her take the rap for something I did. But I didn't kill Professor Granowski and neither did Sam."

"That popsicle lady doctor?" Vanya glanced over at him.

"Yeah. The cops maybe have decided the vandalism and her death are connected. They've reopened the case. This is much bigger than a little spray paint and freeing some rodents. We're talking about a murder charge. That's why we need that tape. Where is it?

"It's hidden under the spare tire." Vanya nodded towards the back of the Caddy.

"We need to watch that tape before we go to the cops," Jack said. "I have a hunch."

CHAPTER THIRTY-FIVE

OLGA SHIFTED THE phone to her other hand. "Please come to my appointment with me," Olga begged. "After everything that's happened, I'm afraid to go alone, and I can't tell my husband, or anyone else."

"It's too weird," replied the sleepy voice on the other end. "I didn't choose to have a baby, you did."

"I'm not asking you to accept this baby as yours, Jessica, or even to be part of its life. I'm just asking you to help me, as a friend." Olga had locked herself into her dressing room and had avoided seeing Ronald since she'd arrived home from last night's disastrous ransom delivery. At least she had the money and could get her jewelry out of hock before he noticed it was missing.

"Look Olga, I haven't slept all night and I'm exhausted. How about I come with you to your next appointment. I promise."

"My appointment isn't until this afternoon, so you could take a nap first. My driver and I can pick you up. Then I'll take you for high tea at the Drake. Have you ever been to the Palm Court for tea?" Olga hoped the bribe would work. No girl would be able to resist high tea at the Palm Court.

"High tea at the Palm Court? Can I invite my friend, Jack?"

"Of course. They have everything, dear Jessica. It's marvelous. You'll love it. All the tea is from France, and the pastry chef is a friend of mine. He can do vegan, gluten free, you name it. We deserve a treat. What do you say? Pick you up at 2:30, and we'll go to the clinic then tea." A knock at her dressing room door startled her. "Can you hang on a minute, Jessica, someone's at my door?"

Olga slipped the phone into her pocket, tightened the sash on her satin robe, and went to the door. "Who is it?" she asked, hoping it wasn't Ronald. She couldn't face him until she retrieved her jewels.

"It's Maria, ma'am. Miss Olga, I thought you'd want to know, two men are waiting downstairs for Mr. Ronald. One is a Russian with lots of tattoos. I put them in the parlor and opened the chimney flue in there just in case."

"Russian? Okay. Thanks Maria. Good thinking to open the flue." Olga winked. She headed for the divan next to the hearth, took the phone from her pocket, and sat down. "I've got to go. Vanya's here at the house to see Ronald," she said into the phone, her heart racing. "Please Jessica. I need you," she begged. "Now, I've got to go. See you at 2:30." She hung up, slipped her phone back into her robe pocket, then knelt next to the fireplace and moved the screen. She opened the flue to the fireplace and listened. She could hear voices coming up from the parlor. She hurried across her dressing room and scooted her vanity chair over to the hearth. Very clever of Maria. Now she could eavesdrop on Ronald and Vanya's conversation; she'd learned this trick with the flue from Maria and was glad to have the maid on her side. She shuddered to think of Ronald's reaction when he found out her father was a Russian gangster, and even worse, she'd been knocked up by a mad scientist.

The toes of her slippers sticking inside the fireplace, elbows on her knees, Olga leaned her chin on her palms and listened. She heard Vanya's distinctive Russian accent. "Delicious," he said. "Sure, I'll take coffee, thanks." Maria must be serving them her fresh blueberry coffeecake, her soft voice background music as plates clanked and cups jittered on saucers. Olga heard the clicking of heels on the marble floor. Maria must be going back to the kitchen.

"These rich wankers live in a pretty swanky place. You should ask Mr. Davis for a raise." She didn't recognize the voice. Maybe it was the strange sullen psychiatry student with Vanya the first time they'd met at Pavlov's Banquet.

Olga sighed. They must be waiting for Ronald. Maybe she should run downstairs and stop Vanya before he gave her husband the sordid report. Maybe she could bribe the Russian with the ransom money she'd gotten from pawning her jewelry. She wondered how much Ronald was paying him.

She'd hidden the manila envelope full of cash in her underwear drawer, waiting for a chance to get back to Uptown Pawn and get her jewels out of hock. She could run down the stairs and offer Vanya the money to keep quiet and get him out of the house before Ronald showed up. $100,000 was nothing to sneeze at.

She strained to hear what was going on in the parlor. The silence below emboldened her desperate plan. She dashed to her dresser, opened the drawer, clutched the envelope, and was on her way out the door when she heard her husband's booming voice drifting up through the fireplace.

She stopped short, hand still on the knob, and listened as a door slammed shut downstairs. It was too late. Shoulders sagging, envelope hanging from the end of a slack arm, Olga shuffled back to the hearth to hear the verdict and prepare for her punishment. She sat down on the vanity chair, fat envelope in her lap, and pricked up her ears.

"Why are you here?" Ronald asked. "I told you never to come to my house or even to contact me. Did anyone see you? And your friend here looks like shit. Are you in trouble?"

"Relax, Mr. Davis. We're cool," Vanya said. "Once we conclude our business, we'll be on our way, real discrete."

"Well, what do you have? Did you find out about her parents? And where she goes every month?" Her husband's irritation was obvious. She wouldn't be surprised if he called his bodyguards to throw the Russian out.

"How about you pay first, then we talk," Vanya said.

"You'll tell me what you know, and then you'll receive the second payment, and not before." Ronald sounded angry.

"Okay. Okay. Calm down, Mr. Davis. No problem... Delicious cake," Vanya said.

"You've had enough cake. Let's get this business over with now."

Olga shifted in her chair, anticipating the worst. She heard dishes clink and a chair scrape along the floor.

"Bottom of the barrel, Mr. Davis, your wife is not havin' no affair. She goes to a clinic for mommies coz she's gonna have a little one..."

"Yes, yes. I know that," Ronald interrupted.

"Dr. Manly is the leading researcher in the country," the sullen voice said. "He's developing new maternal serum markers and fluorescent in situ hybridization probes for X chromosomes, especially as applied to polar bodies and single blastomeres."

Olga held her breath. Had that damned medical student just told her husband that she'd used IVF and genetic engineering to have a baby?

"I don't want any mumbo jumbo, just the facts," her husband said gruffly.

"What my associate means is this: Dr. Manly's the best doctor in town and your wife's in good hands." Vanya chuckled.

"Dr. Manly is a specialist in…" the medical student started up again, but Vanya interrupted. "The doctor is the best. That's all you needs to know. You're a very lucky man, Mr. Davis. You got a beautiful, *faithful* wife, and she's gonna have your pup. What more could a man want?"

"True, true. And what about that baby picture from Kiev? What did you find out about her parents?" Ronald asked impatiently.

Every muscle in her body tensed. Olga squeezed her eyes shut and gritted her teeth. When she covered her face with her hands, the envelope fell from her lap and hit the fireplace screen, sending it crashing to the floor.

"What was that?" Vanya asked. "You got ghosts?"

Olga grimaced as she carefully righted the brass screen. She heard the bell ringing, and then Maria's heels clicking across the marble floor.

"Maria, check on that noise upstairs. Go see if Mrs. Davis is okay." The maid's footfall receded again.

"The parents," Ronald said. "Tell me about them."

"Well, it's a long story, Mr. Davis," Vanya said.

"Give me the abridged version. You have five minutes before I call my bodyguards to throw you out."

"And the second payment?" Vanya asked.

"Don't worry. You'll get your precious money. Now, tell me what you found out about the damned parents."

There was a light knock on the door. "Miss Olga? Is everything okay?" Maria asked.

Olga took a deep breath and held it. The moment of truth had arrived. She might as well start packing. Ronald would send her back to the streets of Kiev when he found about her questionable genealogy. Her past would ruin his future career as Senator.

"Both parents long dead," Vanya said. "Died in a car accident. Baby Olga went to the state-run orphanage, very strict. As a teenager she left and became a ballet dancer."

"A ballet dancer? When I met her she was dancing in Skybar, not exactly ballet." Ronald laughed.

"In Ukraine and Russia, ballet has different meaning."

"Look, Mr. Ivanov, I may be running for political office soon, and I don't want any skeletons coming out of the closet. What did you get on the parents?"

"No worries. No skeletons. Mrs. Davis has royal blood going back to the Rurik Dynasty. Ever heard of Prince Oleg of Ryazan, called Oleg the fair?"

Olga took her hands from her face and stared down into the fireplace. *Where was Vanya getting this royalty stuff?*

"No. And I don't want a damned history lesson. Get to the point," her husband bellowed.

"Point is, she's royalty. Olga's named after Prince Oleg, see…"

"I didn't ask for ancient history," Ronald interrupted. "Just her goddamned parents. Who were they? What did her father do?"

"Okay. Okay. Keep your shirt on, *chuvak*," Vanya said. "Her parents…they was artists. Yes, artists. And very religious, super religious. They died on the way home from church. Yes…after the party when Pope John Paul met Gorbachev. End of Soviet Union and start of freedom in Ukraine."

Olga opened her mouth and gaped into the hearth. Ronald would never fall for this preposterous story.

"Gorbachev," Ronald repeated. "I thought her mother was a prostitute and her father unknown."

"No, no, not at all." Vanya said. "Your wife's people was very religious, good people, fighting against communism. That's good, right?"

"Hmmm…Yes, I guess that *is* good. Can you prove any of this? Did you find any records?"

"Of course," Vanya said. "But first, my money."

Olga heard shuffling and chairs scraping again. She imagined Vanya patting his concealed gun, flashing his golden grin, and threatening her husband. In this house, the wiry Russian was definitely outgunned. No doubt Ronald had his armed guards right outside the parlor door.

"I'll have to go to my safe to get cash. You produce the proof, and I'll hand you the cash."

She heard Ronald's heavy footsteps and then the door to the parlor slam shut. She rushed across her dressing room to make sure her door was locked and listened at the door to her husband's footfalls in the corridor. There was no way Vanya could have proof of his ludicrous story. The game was up. Ronald's bodyguards would beat the truth out of him.

"What in the hell was that all about?" the med student asked.

"Good story, huh?" Vanya replied. "You didn't know Vanya was such a history buff. Ask me anything 'bout Russian royalty, go ahead."

"Who is Prince Myshkin?"

"Who? Never heard of him. You sure he's Russian?"

"He's Russian."

"You's lyin' to me, Clyde. I knows all the Russian princes and princesses. All of them. There's…"

"Forget Myshkin," the med student interrupted. "You're not going to get Sam's bail money unless you produce some evidence. Do you really have proof for your fairytale? You don't want to mess with this guy, Vanya."

"You worry too much, *chuvak*. Have some cake. It's…"

"Delicious. I know. How can you eat? I'm a nervous wreck. We've got to get the bail money and show that tape to the cops."

Olga heard Ronald's footfalls coming back down the corridor from his study. There was a familiar knock on her dressing room door. She froze and clutched the envelope on her lap.

"Are you in there, darling?" Ronald asked through the door. She bit her tongue. "Are you napping?" She held her breath until she heard him leave. When she heard the parlor door creak and bang shut, she exhaled.

Why couldn't Vanya have made up a more plausible

story? How was he going to produce these princely ances-
tors and religious parents? With the backs of both hands,
she wiped the tears from her eyes, careful not to smudge
her mascara.

"Here's the cash. Now where's the proof?" her husband
rumbled.

"Proof's in this here envelope. Pictures, passports, birth
'tificates, you name it. All here," Vanya said.

Olga's hands flew to her chest and she started crying
and laughing at the same time. *Could it be true?* Had Vanya
just saved her neck? She didn't know what he'd done or how
he'd done it, but she hoped it worked. She heard papers
ruffling and put her head back into the fireplace to listen.

"Hmmmm... hard to believe. My Olga from
royal blood."

"Your children will have wealth, beauty, *and* nobility," the
medical student said, in what sounded to her like sarcasm.

"I suppose you're right. Wonderful."

"Where is the princess now?" the smart mouthed student asked.

"She's out. Probably seeing her doctor, best in the country as you pointed out. It's been a pleasure doing business
with you gentlemen. Now please leave my house and never
come back," Ronald boomed.

Olga strolled to her vanity, wiped the tears from her
eyes with a tissue, and then went to her closet to select her
cheeriest maternity dress.

CHAPTER THIRTY-SIX

JACK CLIMBED INTO the passenger's seat of the Caddy. "I can't believe you pulled off that prevarication. Royal blood, pious parents, you're quite a storyteller. You should write novels," he said laughing.

Vanya grinned, lit up a cigarette, and then revved the engine. "Pretty good, eh?" He blew out smoke rings and patted the fat envelope of cash in his jacket pocket. "Now we spring Sam," he said, backing up into the street.

"I'm telling you, we have to look at that surveillance tape first. And, I'd really like to change my clothes. Did you see the way that maid looked at me? I'm surprised she let me in." He wiped at the stain on his jeans. "Seriously, dude. Samantha isn't just being held for vandalism. I heard on the radio; they've reopened the inquiry into Professor Granowski's death. We need to see that video then show it to the cops to prove that Samantha didn't kill Granowski."

"What? Sam wouldn't hurt a fly."

"We know that, but the cops don't."

"Yeah, and we knows you's the one what vandalled the lab. If we turn over that tape, them cops'll lock you up."

"Well, I can't let Samantha take the rap for something

I did. Let's go to my place. Let me get cleaned up, and we can watch the tape. Then we'll go to the cop shop and I'll turn myself in. How much money do you have in that envelope? I hope enough to bail out Samantha *and* me." Jack ran his hands through his hair. His wrists wore reddish purple bracelets from the cuffs, and a leprosy of white, brown, and green stains spread across the front of his tan turtleneck. "Do you have anything stronger than tobacco?" he asked the Russian smokestack.

Vanya tapped out a cigarette from his pack and held it out to Jack. "I don't go for anything what dulls my senses. Nicotine keeps me sharp."

Jack took the smoke. "Can I borrow your lighter?"

"No one touches my lighter." Vanya stroked his shiny designer lighter. "There's a plastic one in the glove apartment." He pointed at the glove box.

Jack lit the cigarette and took a long drag. It tasted bitter and harsh compared to the sweet weed he was used to smoking. He'd gone a whole week without a joint, breaking a decade's record. Another reason to get back to his flat before going to the cops. He wasn't about to turn himself in sober. He needed to get higher than the Sears Tower to face jail time.

Vanya parked in front of Worcester House, an unsightly postmodern combination of stone, brick, glass, and steel. Since he didn't have his keys, Jack had to ask at the manager's office to get into his apartment. Vanya paid the $25 fee so the jerk could spend five bloody minutes taking the elevator up and opening the door to his studio. Too busy at school and the hospital, he didn't spend much time there, and the place was a mess. His unrepentant slovenliness and the paper-thin walls were only two of the reasons he never brought girls over. He didn't like people in his private space. Showing girls his apartment revealed a grungy little corner of his mind that he'd rather keep to himself.

"Whoa. What a pigsty," Vanya said, waving his hand in front of his nose as he entered the room.

"Yeah, well other than Jesse, you're the only person who's seen it." Jack kicked a path through the dirty clothes until he cleared the way to a saggy couch. "Did you bring the recording?"

Vanya held out a small black box on the palm of his hand.

Jack took the box and turned it over in his hands. "How does it work?"

"I dunno. Don't you, college boy?"

Jack examined the box. He saw several ports of different sizes, and climbed over the back of the sofa to reach the desk and his computer. "I guess you have to plug it into a monitor. I hope I have the right cord." He rummaged through a tangle of cables in the bottom desk drawer. "Bloody computers. I hate them. So insulting when neurologists compare the brain to hardwiring." He unwound cord after cord and, one by one, tried to plug them into the storage unit. "I give up. See if you can figure out how to hook this to my computer while I get cleaned up." Jack opened the top desk drawer and took out a baggie of weed and some rolling papers, then concentrated on rolling the perfect joint.

After years of practice, he had it down to an art. Just handling his favorite fragrant flora, crumbling it between his fingers, lifted his spirits. He licked the edge of the

paper then admired the plump cylinder before putting one
end between his lips and lighting the other. He took a big
drag and held the smoke in his lungs as long as he could.
"Ahhhh...." He sighed out a cloud of smoke.

"Can I borrow your phone, Vanya? I promised I'd call
Jesse."

Vanya reached into his pocket and removed the envelope of cash and then his cellphone. He handed Jack the
phone then opened the envelope and started counting hundred-dollar bills. With every toke Jack took, Vanya's golden
grill seemed to grow more brilliant.

"Hmm... It keeps going directly to voicemail." Jack
held out the phone, but Vanya was too busy shuffling Ben
Franklins to notice. "Guess I'll call her later." Jack put the
phone down on top of a stack of psychiatry journals. "When
you're done fondling those bills, how about you set up this
thing so we can watch the surveillance video and then go
bail out Beagle Girl. Remember her? Your girlfriend?"

Vanya glanced up, smiled, and stuffed the bills back
into the envelope. He slid it into his jacket pocket, and
pulled out his gun. He lifted it into the air and was about
to bring it down on the black box when Jack caught his
arm. "What in the bloody hell are you doing, dude?" he
asked, taking another toke off his joint. The sweet spicy
burn melted away layers of the last horrid week.

"Using the tools I knows best, *chuvak*. I'm no hacker."

"Just keep trying those cables until you find the right
male to plug into that female," he said, holding smoke in
his lungs.

"I ain't no robot matchmaker either."

Sending buttons flying, Jack ripped off his dirty shirt,

threw it across the room, then unzipped his fly, tugged off his jeans and boxers, and headed for the bathroom. He turned on the shower and, waiting for the water to get hot, puffed until the last embers glowed. Nothing as soothing as a hot shower and a good buzz.

He stubbed out the roach on the sink and stepped into the stream of water. The soap stung his raw wrists and encouraged him to hurry. He dried off with his only towel, put on a clean pair of jeans, the Spock T-shirt Jesse had given him, and a flannel shirt. Rubbing his head with the stiff towel, he wandered back into the living room a new man. He stopped short when he saw the wanker building manager messing with his computer.

"What's going on?" Jack asked, stubbing his toe on a stack of books in his rush.

Vanya smiled. "Mr. Patel got the right *struchok* for our female." The Russian patted the manager on the back. "Thanks, *chuvak*." He handed Mr. Patel a crisp hundred-dollar bill.

"Any time," the wanker said on his way out the door waving the bill. "Any time."

"Okay, male and female hooked up, so how do we get this *súka* to work?" Vanya asked.

Jack threw the wet towel over the sofa, knelt on a dirty sweatshirt lying next to the desk, and then probed the black box for an on-off switch. He pressed a button near its base, but nothing happened.

"Did you plug it into the electricity?" Vanya asked.

"Right, thank you Captain Obvious," Jack said, crawling under the desk to plug the cord into a power strip. He emerged and tapped his computer to life. "Bloody technology," he said as he tried to access the storage unit now connected to his computer. "I hope they're compatible."

"Maybe you shoulda tried dinner and a movie first." Vanya chuckled.

Jack jiggled the cable and a purple icon labeled DS411 NAS appeared on his screen. "Aha!" When he clicked on it, a rainbow wheel started spinning in the corner of his screen. Vanya lit a cigarette and stared over his shoulder as Jack knelt with his finger hovering over the keyboard. "Come on," he said to the stupid machine, "damned computer."

Vanya hammered the box with his fist and the obnoxious spinning rainbow gave way to the pot of gold. Finally, the screen was populated with files arranged by date. Jack clicked on November 24, Thanksgiving, and a black and white image of the door to Feinberg Animal Research Lab flickered onto the screen. He clicked the arrow at its center and started the video. The time appeared in yellow letters at the bottom of the image and ticked along with the video.

A hooded figure appeared at the lab door, dropped a duffle bag, and waved a piece of paper in front of the security system.

"Bloody hell, is that me? I look like an idiot," Jack said.

"Pretty goofy, you and your homemade mask, Clyde."

Jack cringed as he watched the video playback of his bungled entrance and his struggle with the spoof fingerprint. A few seconds after the lab door closed, the video jumped forward in time by twelve minutes, and Samantha Brewer stood in front of the lab door, pressing her thumb onto the security screen, then entering the lab.

"Hmmm... must be motion activated," Jack said. The yellow numbers on the screen jumped forward again. The door opened and Samantha walked by the camera and entered the lab. "There must be another file for the cameras inside the lab. We can search those next if we don't find him on this one."

"Him?" Vanya asked.

"Granowski's murderer."

The next image was of Jack leaving the lab, makeshift mask over his face, duffle bag in his gloved hands, glancing around at the camera, looking like a cartoon thief. "Okay. Let's see who goes in next," Jack said. As the yellow numbers changed to 1:34 P.M., Jack leaned closer to the computer screen and saw his own mug again, sans mask, with Jesse following close behind. She was so cute in that crazy hat. The video made him ache to see her in person.

"Something's wrong," Jack said. "This can't be right." The recording skipped ahead again, and so did the time. Samantha was reentering the lab. "We went into the lab. That's when we found Granowski's body in the freezer. So Granowski had to enter the lab between my break in and this moment here."

"Unless she was already an ice cube when yous went in the first time," Vanya said, snapping his lighter open and shut.

Jack closed the file and clicked on the one from the day before, Wednesday, November 23. "Good point," he said, then double clicked on the playback arrow. Never taking his eyes from the screen, he rolled another perfect joint. Sitting back on his heels, he puffed away as he watched various graduate students, post-docs, and research assistants, come and go from the animal lab. Vanya sat next to him, pinched the spent end of his smoke, and pulled another pack of cigarettes from his pocket. He tore it open, tapped out another, and lit up.

"There!" Jack spotted her through the cloud of smoke encircling the computer screen. He paused the recording. "Look. That's Professor Granowski."

"Looks like she's fighting with that man," Vanya said, pointing at a shadowy figure pushing her through the lab doors. The recording and time skipped forward again, and this time they watched the murderer walk back out through the lab door alone.

"I knew it," Jack said, disconnecting the black box from his computer. "Let's go spring Sam."

CHAPTER THIRTY-SEVEN

JESSICA RUMMAGED THROUGH her closet until she found her favorite wool dress bunched up in a wad where she'd thrown it after the Holly Ball. She shook it out, stretched it onto a hanger, and hung it on the back of her bathroom door to steam out the wrinkles while she showered, then moved the dirty dishes from the tub and into the sink. Crusty pots, caked plates, and slimy spoons spilled over the tiny sink, and half a wedge of veggie pizza splatted onto the tile floor, moldy cheese side down.

She wiped her grimy hands on a stiff towel then wriggled out of her underwear and kicked them into the corner. She turned on the shower and watched as debris whirled down the drain, and when the water was steaming, she stepped into the bathtub.

"Ahhh...." She inhaled the calming mist and let rivulets of water massage her scalp. She thought of Jack, at least he was safe. She wished she could continue enjoying the warmth and comfort of a hot shower, but Olga Davis and her driver would be arriving any minute. Jessica had slept through her phone alarm and had to get a move on.

She turned off the water, stepped out of the tub, and

rubbed herself dry with a garlic scented towel, then she gave her gnarled hair a pass with the blow dryer. Her heavy leggings stuck to her damp legs as she wriggled them over her butt, and the wool dress clung to her ribs when she tugged it over her head. She scrambled to find a pair of warm wool socks, stuffed her feet into her boots, threw on her parka, hat, and gloves, then dashed out the door, down the three flights of stairs, and outside into the courtyard.

Standing on the sidewalk in front of her apartment building, she yanked the earflaps of her Trapper over her wet hair and zipped her parka up to her neck to brace herself against the frigid lake effect. She stared down at her scarlet cowboy boots shining in the brilliant winter sunshine, hopping from foot to foot to keep her toes from freezing and slapping her gloves together to ward off frostbite.

The tip of her nose was stinging and her eyes watering by the time the limo pulled up to the curb. Before she could open the door to the backseat to join Mrs. Davis, the chauffer had jumped out and opened it for her. Jessica crawled in next to Olga Davis.

"Thanks for coming with me," Mrs. Davis said. "Just one stop on the way. I hope you don't mind." There was no refusing Mrs. Olga Davis. God knows she'd tried. At least she'd get a fancy meal out of it, High Tea at the Drake.

"Not if you don't mind that my friend Lolita is meeting us at the clinic," Jessica said.

Mrs. Davis's eyelid twitched and she turned away. "I'd hoped to keep this our secret," she said.

"Lolita is silent as a grave. If anyone can keep a secret, it's her." Jessica removed her hat and gloves and buried her bare hands inside the Trapper's fake fur. "Anyway, she's not after your secret. She's got her own bone to pick with the clinic."

Mrs. Davis didn't reply. She just stared out at the sleet pelting the window. Jessica followed suit and watched the wind blow trees into a macabre frenzy of barren branches. As her body relaxed into the comfy warmth of the sedan, a violin concerto playing on the car stereo soothed her nerves. The city blurred past in slushy browns and grays, and to her surprise, she longed for the evergreen world she'd left behind in Montana. Already January, and she still hadn't told her mom what happened or why she hadn't come home for Christmas, for the first time ever. She felt a pang in her chest.

When the limo turned off the street and into a parking lot in a dubious neighborhood, Jessica glanced over at Olga Davis with a questioning look.

"I'll be right back," Mrs. Davis said, tugging on her leather gloves. She picked up her handbag off the seat, and got out of the car. The chauffer met her with an umbrella, walked her to the entrance of the dumpy joint then waited next to the door as Mrs. Davis went inside.

Jessica leaned over the front seat and peered through the windshield at a bright neon sign, Uptown City Pawn and Jewelry. She stared out the window at the bums warming their hands over fires in barrels under the "L" tracks. She'd never been in this part of Chicago, and she'd only seen stuff like this in movies.

A few minutes later, Mrs. Davis came out of the pawn-shop with a red box under her arm, and the driver escorted her back to the car. He opened the door for her, shook off the wet umbrella, and climbed back into the driver's seat. "To the clinic, Mrs. D?"

"Yes. Thanks José."

"What were you doing in there, Mrs. Davis?" Jessica asked.

"Getting my life back," Olga replied. "And please call me Olga." She opened the case, took out a pair of diamond studs, and put them in her ears. "Ah, better. Now let's go to my appointment and see how our babies are doing."

"Not our babies, your babies." Jessica knitted her brow. Riding in silence with her baby mama, Jessica sunk into a gloomy haze.

When the limo pulled in behind the clinic, she saw Lolita's red Harley Superlow parked near the back entrance. Her fearless friend was standing just inside the glass door, arms akimbo, a full metal jacket glint in her eyes.

"Hello, ladies," Lolita said when she opened the door. Before Olga Davis could catch up, Lolita took Jessica aside to one of the potted ferns in the corner of the foyer and whispered, "Have you talked to Jack? He's been trying to reach you."

"He has?" Jessica reached into her parka pocket, but her phone wasn't there. In her rush, she hadn't even checked for messages; she'd slept through her alarm; she'd left her cell on her nightstand. "Why? Is he okay?"

"What's the matter, girls?" Olga Davis asked, coming up behind them.

"It's our friend. Go on in without us, we'll be along in

a minute," Lolita said, handing her phone to Jessica. "Read Jack's text."

"What the hell!" Jessica reread the message.

"Shhhh…." Lolita put her finger to her lips. "We can't alert the creep," she whispered. "We have to act normal until they get here."

"But I thought it was an accident." Jessica lowered her voice. "Isn't that what the police finally determined? That the freezer door was broken and she locked herself in?"

"Apparently not."

"Did you mention an accident?" Olga Davis asked, lingering a few feet away in the foyer. "What's going on?"

"Not. A. Thing," Lolita said.

"Odd that no one's here to meet us. Usually someone meets me here at the door. Maybe I should go check in at the desk."

"Good idea," Lolita said.

As Olga Davis headed towards the reception desk at the end of a short hallway, a young pretty nurse intercepted her. "Mrs. Smith, so nice to see you again," the nurse said.

Jessica rolled her eyes at her friend. Lolita just shrugged. "Rich people," she said under her breath.

"Please follow me to the waiting room. Would any of you ladies like something to drink? Tea or coffee? There's fruit and cookies. Help yourselves. The doctor will be with you shortly, Mrs. Smith. Your friends can wait with you until we come get you." The nurse smiled and gestured them into a posh lounge.

Jessica made a beeline for a plate of cookies and stacked three golden brown chocolate-chip cookies onto a napkin. She pumped coffee into a ceramic mug, then glanced around and, spotting the half-n-half inside the glass refrigerator door, trotted over to fetch it. She poured a good two inches of cream into her coffee, dumped in two packets of sugar, stirred it with a silver spoon, then took a seat on the leather sofa. She sat her plunder on the glass coffee table. Sugar and caffeine would prepare her for whatever was next. She was munching on the third cookie and considering going back for another stack when the nurse returned.

"Mrs. Smith," she said, a clipboard in her hands, "Dr. Manly will see you now. I'm afraid your friends will have to wait here."

Jessica glanced at Lolita and grimaced.

"Jessica is the biological mother of my babies," Olga Davis said. "And I'd like to have her come with me for the ultrasound."

Jessica's stomach did a flip, and she wished she hadn't just scarfed three cookies. "We're okay waiting here," she said.

"Actually," Lolita said. "Since she's the biological mother and I'm her girlfriend, we'd like to see the ultrasound."

"This is highly irregular," the nurse said, scowling. "Biological mothers are anonymous. It's a strict policy designed to protect all concerned. We never give out those records. How did…"

"Anonymous or not," Lolita interrupted, "the buns in her oven belong to us. My girlfriend provided the eggs to make them against her will I'll have you know."

The nurse looked confused.

"Max White stole my eggs," Jessica said.

"And the least we're going to do is see the ultrasound of the little beasties he created," Lolita said, towering over the petite nurse.

"Please, nurse," Olga Davis said, "I would like to have them with me if it's okay."

"I'll have to ask Dr. Manly," the nurse said, turning to leave.

"Mrs. Davis requests our presence, and she's the paying customer. I know your clinic prides itself on service." Lolita purred, then put her hand on the nurse's elbow. "Why don't you lead the way to the examination room, and we'll all wait there together for Dr. Manly."

The flustered nurse sputtered and gasped but took them down the hallway to an exam room. "If you'll wait here, I'll get the doctor."

"Oh no, you won't," Lolita said as she took the clipboard from the nurse's hand, shoved it into the plastic holder on the wall, then shut the door. "We'll all wait together."

"What is this?" the nurse asked. "What's going on?"

"Really," Olga Davis said. "Why are you being so rude? I don't mind if you see the ultrasound, but there's no reason to be mean to this nice nurse. She's not responsible for what that unethical doctor did to you."

"He's not a doctor," Jessica said.

"My apologies," Lolita said, turning back to the nurse. "Didn't mean to be so rough."

"Thank you," Olga Davis said. "I think we will all feel calmer after we get this over with. Then we can go enjoy our tea at the Palm Court."

"I'm not coming to your tea party," Lolita said. "I'm here to get back what's mine, whatever it takes, including hijacking my eggs from someone's gold-plated womb."

When Olga Davis gasped, Jessica gave her friend a dirty look.

Lolita put her finger to her lips. "Be quiet everyone," she ordered, glancing around. "The cops are on their way, and we don't want to alert Manly."

"What?" Olga Davis asked.

"We need to stay calm until the police arrive," Jessica said.

The cute nurse stared, open mouthed, then bolted for the door. Lolita intercepted her and held her by the shoulders.

"Police?" Olga Davis repeated.

"They're on their way right now to arrest Dr. Manly," Jessica said. "For murder."

"Murder?" Olga Davis shuddered and slumped into an oversized chair.

"Bernard isn't a murderer," the nurse said. "We're getting married in June." She held out her left hand to show off a diamond engagement ring.

"Surely there's been some mistake," Olga said. "Who did he kill?"

"Dr. Janet Granowski, his ex-wife and lab partner. Jack has proof that he murdered her. Her death was no accident. Manly went into the animal lab with her and left by himself. And the door to the freezer was intentionally jammed."

Olga Davis looked stunned. "Janet told me she wanted to leave the clinic," she said thoughtfully. "I knew it wasn't just because of the divorce."

"Maybe Janet Granowski learned about the illegal *harvesting* at the lab," Jessica said.

"Bernard isn't involved in anything illegal. And he's not a murderer. We're getting married." The nurse's face turned blotchy and tears sprouted from her round eyes.

As the sound of sirens blared into the parking lot, the nurse squeaked and grabbed the doorknob. Jessica tried to stop her, but she slipped past and was almost out the door when Lolita stuck out a long leg and tripped her. The nurse did a face plant then sat whimpering on the floor.

"Was that really necessary?" Jessica asked.

"She was going to warn Manly."

"As if the sirens weren't warning enough." Jessica rolled her eyes. "Sometimes, my Russian friend, you scare me."

CHAPTER THIRTY-EIGHT

GLAD TO BE leaving the fertility clinic far behind, Jessica inhaled deeply and closed her eyes to enjoy the invigorating frosty air. She released her arms from Lolita's waist and stretched them towards the azure eternity overhead. Even the exhaust from four lanes of traffic in each direction couldn't mar the glorious afternoon. In the distance, the Lake Michigan was dancing in the sunshine of a brilliant winter's day. She was looking forward to pork fat and frozen vodka shots at Pavlov's Banquet. Money could buy a lot of things, even genetically engineered babies, but it couldn't give meaning to the accidents of life

Lolita exited the expressway at Hollywood Avenue and skidded to a stop at a red light. She turned back to Jessica. "Reach inside my jacket pocket and check my phone. It's been vibrating. Might be Jack."

"Four messages from Jack. Holy crap! He says he's turning himself in at Central Police Station on State Street. Hurry Lolita! Turn around. Jack's going to jail if we don't help him."

"Calm down, my Montana friend. I know a short cut." Lolita ran the red light, did a U-turn, and swerved between the oncoming cars until she got to Sheridan Road, then skidded around the corner. Jamming the bike into high gear, she sped towards downtown, at one intersection nearly hitting an old lady crossing the street.

"You're going to kill us!" Jessica shouted.

"You're the one who wanted to hurry. Hold on!"

Jessica wound her arms around Lolita's waist and burrowed her head into her leather jacket. She couldn't watch as the bike wove in and out of traffic and ran red lights. Her friend was enjoying the excuse to drive like a maniac. She squeezed her eyes tight and hoped they hadn't already locked Jack up. She'd never gone a week without seeing him, and if he went to prison, she might not see him again for years. She bit her lip and willed the bike to go faster.

Fifteen minutes later, the Harley jumped the curb in front of Central Police Station, and Lolita parked her bike on the sidewalk. "Come on," Lolita said as she removed her helmet, "Operation Rescue Jack." She shook out her long black hair, stowed her headgear in the storage compartment on the back of the bike, and strode toward the entrance. Jessica took the bowl off her head and followed her friend. When she reached the double glass doors, she slid inside behind Lolita before they could close in her face.

The police station waiting room was packed with a throng of sorry humanity. A familiar voice came from a bench along one wall.

"Coz, what are you going here?" Vanya asked, smiling.

"I could ask you the same thing," Lolita replied.

"I'm bailing out Sam," Vanya said, patting a space next to him on the wooden bench. "Come sit down."

Next to the Russian, a bedraggled Jack was slouched

on the bench, leaning back against the wall. "Jackass, you look like crap," Jessica said. He'd gotten even thinner, and his sunken eyes looked like pitted plums gnawed around the edges. His slicked back wavy brown hair revealed cuts across his forehead, and his lip was swollen and gashed. Jessica sat down next to him and put her arm around him.

"Are you okay?" she asked, taking his hand. "Holy crap!" She examined his wounded wrists. "What happened to you?" She felt tears welling in her eyes and stared up at the ceiling to keep them from falling down her face.

"That psychopath Max White had me handcuffed to a bed for the last week. Not a pretty sight." He turned his face away from her, and she thought she glimpsed his eyes glistening, too. "I thought I was a gonner."

"What's this about turning yourself in?" Jessica wrapped her fingers into his. "I don't want you to go to jail, Jack."

"Believe me, I don't want to go to jail. But, I can't let Samantha take the rap for vandalizing the lab. If there were any other way…" His voice trailed off.

"Mr. Grove, Mr. Ivanov," a policewoman called their names. "Sargent Prescott will take your statements now. Please follow me."

Vanya jumped up carrying a small black box in his hand.

"What's with the NAS device, Vanya?" Lolita asked.

"The pictures in this box's gonna 'xonerate Sam." He patted his jacket pocket. "That and a butt load of cash." He grinned. "Come on, *chuvak*, let's show 'em what we've got."

Hands still intertwined with hers, Jack stood up and lifted Jessica to her feet. He put his arm around her waist, and drew her close into the warmth of his familiar fried onion and spicy marijuana scent. He gently pushed a lock of hair out of her eyes then, lips brushing against her ear, whispered, "When I was chained to that bed, all I could think about was you. I thought I'd never see you again." His voice cracked, and she looked up into his moist eyes. "I needed to see you, Jesse. Because facing death, I realized I had only one regret. More than freedom, more than life, I needed to see you again. More than anything, I needed...."

Jessica felt the pull of his sleepy brown eyes. His bruised full lips were magnets drawing her in. Overpowered by an uncanny desire, she brushed a wavy curl from his face and, to her surprise, her mouth followed her hand. She kissed his cheek and then his lips. Desperate with longing, she wrapped her arms around him and held him with all her might. "I love you, Jesse," he whispered into her ear.

"Ditto," she replied with tears running down her cheeks.

"Mr. Grove, the Sargent is waiting," the officer said.

Jessica wiped her face with her palms. "When will I see you again?"

"Maybe they'll let me off for good behavior."

"Be good, Jack." Jessica put her hand on his cheek and kissed him again. "And if you can't be good, be careful," she whispered.

"Ouch," he said.

"Sorry." She stroked his unshaven chin.

"Here, a souvenir to remember me by." He pulled a faded plastic tag from his back pocket and handed it to her.

"What is it?" she asked.

"It's the Do Not Disturb sign from The Guest House." He smiled. "Something to look forward to..."

"Why don't you wait a week to turn yourself in and we can use it now." Jessica said, nuzzling his ear.

"Mr. Grove? Are you coming?" the policewoman asked impatiently.

"Oh Jack. Why didn't you tell me before?" Jessica held onto the tips of his fingers as he moved away.

"I did, Jesse," he said. "But you never heard me."

"I'm listening now," she said.

"Too bad I had to risk death and prison to get your attention."

"I'm sorry, Jack. I didn't realize...I'm sorry...I wish..." she sputtered.

When he smiled, his eyes danced. "As Nietzsche says, Everything decisive in life comes against the greatest obstacles. You, Jesse James, are the beautiful answer to life's riddles. Without you, nothing makes sense."

"I'll bake you a vegan cake with a file in it," she said, a smitten smile on her beaming face. "No seitan, I promise. Jack, do you really need to do this?"

"Think of it as field research on the effects of incarceration on the criminal mind," Jack said as he fell in behind Vanya and the officer. Jessica waved goodbye and he waved back. He blew her a kiss as he disappeared around a corner. Once he was out of sight, she broke down sobbing.

Lolita wrapped her in an embrace. "Don't cry, Sweetie. It'll be okay. Come on, let's go get those vodka shots."

"How could I not know?" Jessica said through her sobs.

"To quote my best friend, you're the dumbest smart person I know." Lolita removed a tissue from her pocket and handed it to her. "It was pretty obvious to everyone else."

"It was?" Jessica blew her nose.

Lolita rolled her eyes. "You two, always quoting Nietzsche, poking and prodding each other every chance you get; you can't keep your hands off each other. Both sci-fi and philosophy geeks, both brainy party animals. As my grandmother says, *Dva sapoga para*, two boots make a pair."

Lolita pulled out another tissue and dabbed at Jessica's cheeks. "Don't worry. He's not going anywhere. He's yours if you want him, although I don't understand why you would." She drew her closer. "Don't cry. What do you say we go to Pavlov's and celebrate?"

"What do we have to celebrate?" Jessica asked.

"Max White is behind bars and bound to stay there for a long time. Manly the murderer didn't get away with it. My missing eggs are most likely on their last legs, languishing in some petri dish. And yours are growing into at least one very special mutant girl, a cowgirl philosopher like her mother."

"Don't call me that," Jessica sniffed.

"But you are a mutant. White only proved what I always knew. You're a very special girl, Jessica James."

"Just don't call me a mother. I'm not a mother. I refuse to be a mother."

"Refuse all you want. Your genetic material seems to have cooperated."

Jessica frowned and pulled away from her friend.

"I'm sorry, Sweetie," Lolita said, brushing wet hair from Jessica's face. "I was only joking." She squeezed Jessica's shoulders.

Jessica smiled weakly. "Thanks Lolita. I don't know what I'd do without you."

"Get your ass kicked from here to Montana, that's what. Now let's go to Pavlov's Banquet and get hammered."

"I just wanna go home and drool into my pillow," she said, sniffling.

"Okay, how about we get your favorite poison and drink to geeks in love?" Her friend wiped a tear from her cheek.

CHAPTER THIRTY-NINE

THE NEXT MORNING, a wave of nausea hit Jessica so hard her eyes flew open. She stared at the empty bottle of Jack Daniels lying on the pillow next to her gazing back at her. *Damn. Wrong Jack.* She threw off the duvet and sat up. Head spinning, she gripped the nightstand for support then hauled herself to her feet. The damp outline on the sheet where her drunken body had landed the night before filled her with gratitude for her own private pigsty. She staggered to the bathroom. Squinting against the harsh daylight streaming in from the tiny window, she smacked her parched lips and wiped her cottony tongue on the sleeve of her shirt. Relieved when she made it to the sink, she leaned against the cool porcelain and splashed cold water onto her swollen eyes and into her mouth. Staring at her sorry reflection in the mirror, she swore she'd never drink again. She used her fingers to tame her wild hair, then padded back into her nest, and rifled through the pile of clothes until she found some cleanish underwear, a matching pair of wool socks, and her flannel-lined jeans. Steadying herself against the wall, she put one foot into the underwear, then the other, but when she bent down to pull up the panties, she was so light-headed she slid to the floor, landed on the pile of dirty clothes, and sat there, hands over her eyes.

The thick scar where the dumpster had torn the flesh of her right palm was smooth and cool against her forehead. She wondered if her skin was getting any thicker. Her dad had always warned her, "You're too sensitive, Jesse. You need thicker hide. It's a man's world." Of course, he meant the world of professional rodeo, but the same was true in the world of professional philosophy. She ran her finger across the scar, but the heart of her hand was as vacant as the empty lot she'd found herself in that terrifying night ninety-two days ago. Maybe her dad had been wrong. Better thin skin than a hard heart.

Struggling into her underwear and jeans again, Jessica spotted the culprits sprawled sideways under the bed. She crawled on hands and knees and reached under the futon to drag out her boots. She'd just jammed her feet inside when her phone skittered across the nightstand. She jumped up and immediately regretted it. The room was spinning faster than a Montana twister, and its momentum threw her backwards onto the bed. "Ugggg…" she moaned as she reached for her cell.

"Hello," she croaked into the phone.

"Why haven't you called me back? I've been worried sick," her mom scolded.

"I've been busy with school," Jessica lied. "But I was just about to call you." She lied again. "I'm helping a friend with some research on genetics and he needs some information about my parents. Do you or dad have golden blood?"

"What? Your dad, bless his soul, was as red-blooded as

the next man. What the hell is golden blood?" her mom asked. Jessica heard the tinkling of ice cubes in a glass, liquid chugging from a bottle, followed by the sound of her mother taking a drag off her cigarette. Nothing ever changed at Alpine Vista Trailer Park. She could imagine her mom playing online poker for hours, sitting in the ripped-up lazy boy, Stoli the orange cat curled up in her lap, a Vodka Collins in her hand, and a cigarette dangling from her lips.

"It's like universal blood. What about a really strong sense of smell? Do you or did dad have like an overdeveloped sense of smell? Like an animal's?"

"Why are you asking all these questions, Jesse? Is everything okay? You're not in trouble again, are you? What's this all about, Jesse?" her mom asked. The cat yowled in the background. Her mom must have thrown him on off her lap and started pacing around the trailer like she did whenever she was anxious.

"It's a long story, Mom." Jessica sat up and leaned into her pillows. "Have you heard of egg donation?"

"Like to a food bank?"

"No, human eggs as in ova, fallopian tubes…The kind that's fertilized with sperm and grows into a fetus." Jessica was on a roll.

"You mean a baby! Are you pregnant? Who's the father? I hope you're getting married. Am I finally going to be a grandma?"

"Mom, I'm not pregnant and I'm not getting married…." She was enjoying tormenting her mom. "But you are going to be a grandmother, sort of."

"What do you mean, *sort of*? Jessica, what's going on?

KELLY OLIVER

You sound like you're not playing with a full deck, and you're scaring me." Her mom's voice raised an octave.

"My eggs were fertilized and implanted in another woman's womb. Olga Davis is her name, a Chicago socialite. She's actually pretty nice. Anyway, you could say I'm the biological mother and she's the birth mother." She tucked her feet up on the futon and sat crossed legged against her pillows.

"I don't understand. Someone else is having your baby? Why?" She could hear the familiar frustration in her mother's voice. "What have you done now, Jessica? Am I going to be a grandmother or not? Are you having a baby or not?"

"Well, yes and no," she said in a singsong voice, relishing every minute. "The baby was created using my genetic material but the baby is really Olga's. See, it's possible to have two biological mothers if a geneticist splits the eggs. Then there's a birth mother, the one who carries the fetus in her uterus, and sometimes a different social mother. That makes four mothers for one baby." She was enjoying taunting her mother with genetic science.

"You're talking nonsense. Four queens is a damned good poker hand, but I've never heard of four mothers... Uterus mothers, social mothers, biological mothers. What nonsense. A mother is a mother."

"If you had a lesbian mother and her partner adopted, that would make five mothers," Jessica said gleefully.

"So, am I a grandmother or not?" her mother demanded.

"Well, technically yes." She giggled. "But actually no."

Her phone buzzed. A message from Lolita: "I'm outside." As she texted back, she heard the mournful sound of her friend's air horn howling from the street. Jessica was supposed to have been downstairs ten minutes ago. A Fauvism exhibit just opened at the Art Institute, and last night in their drunken state, she'd convinced Lolita to go.

"Gotta go, mom," she said. "Lolita's here. Love you." She heard her mom still ranting as she hung up the phone.

Riding on the back of Lolita's bike rejuvenated her, and by the time they arrived at the Art Institute Jessica felt herself again. She was looking forward to drowning herself in the choppy blue *Barges on the Seine* painted in the style of the "Wild Beasts."

"Jessica, is that you?" A familiar voice came from behind her, and she turned to see Olga Davis wearing a smart black maternity dress, elegant little boots, and a matching emerald necklace and earrings that set off her green eyes.

"Olga, what are you doing here?"

"I was at a fundraising luncheon. Are you here to see the show? It's magnificent." Olga gave her a baby-bump-hug.

Lolita appeared with the museum entrance stickers and nodded to Olga. She stuck one on Jessica's flannel shirt, then with a curious look, peeled it off again, staring at the offending sticker.

"What's wrong?" Jessica asked.

"This sticker," Lolita said, attaching it to her index finger and holding it in front of Jessica's face. "Remind you of anyone?"

"Max," Jessica said. "Also known as Dr. Frankenstein."

"Max White, the unethical doctor who fathered my babies?" Olga asked.

"Max White isn't a doctor," Jessica said emphatically.

"And he's more than unethical; he's a criminal," Lolita added.

"I need to sit down," Olga said, taking Jessica's arm. "Would you two join me for tea in the café? I never got to treat you to high tea at the Drake." Olga smiled weakly.

On either side of the pregnant woman, Jessica and Lolita led her through the museum to the airy café in the back. Remarking on Olga's distress, a waitress let them jump the line and seated them at a table near the window overlooking the courtyard fountain and gardens.

"Do you think a glass of champagne would hurt the babies?" Olga asked.

"Nah. If they have Jessica's genes, a glass of bubbly will go down like mother's milk," Lolita said.

"Doctors used to prescribe wine for pregnant women," Jessica added.

After a glass of Prosecco, Olga was calm and cheerful. "I want to show you something," she said, rummaging around in her purse then pulling out her phone. "The first baby pictures." She handed the cell to Jessica.

"Looks like two slugs inside a tomato." Jessica passed the phone to Lolita.

"It's my last ultrasound," Olga said, pouting.

"The finest babies money can buy," Lolita said. "Genetically engineered to perfection."

Olga stared, blinking like a deer in the headlights. Jessica kicked her friend under the table. "There's no such thing as perfection. Everything is cracked and broken. That's how the sunshine gets in," Jessica said.

"Every parent would do the same if they could," Olga said. "Who wouldn't do what's best for their child?"

"The moneyed elite," Lolita said under her breath. "Designer babies," she scoffed.

"Nurture is at least as important as nature. And Olga will be the perfect mom." Jessica scowled at her friend. She thought of her own mother, slumped in an easy chair, sloshed on Vodka Collins, chain-smoking cigarettes, and playing on-line poker as little Jesse played with matches in the kitchen, lighting her dollies' skirts on fire then stuffing them down the garbage disposal to hide the evidence. Her mom eventually found out and locked her in a dark closet for an hour; but when she came to liberate the unrepentant arsonist, Jesse asked if she could play in the closet for the rest of the afternoon just to spite her.

"You've been such a good friend to me, Jessica," Olga said. "I hope someday I can repay you. You've given me more than I can ever say." She moved her chair close to Jessica's and tapped the camera button on her phone. "You, too, Lolita. I want to take a picture of us together."

Jessica put her arms around her two friends and smiled as Olga held the phone overhead to take a selfie. After the fourth attempt, her smiling was fading. She raised her champagne flute and her friends followed suit. "To friendship," she said, clinking their glasses. "As Nietzsche says, 'love is blind, but friendship closes its eyes.'" Her friends laughed and sipped their Prosecco. She thought of Jack and drained her glass.

"Let's see the pictures," she said as she picked up Olga's phone then swiped through the selfies. "A toast." Jessica raised her glass again. "To three peas in a pod and two slugs in a tomato."

PLEASE REVIEW

FOX on Amazon.

Book Club Discussion Questions

What did you learn about the I.V.F. and new reproductive technologies? Did anything surprise you?

How did you feel about Jessica and Jack's relationship? Were you glad they got together in the end?

Is Max a good villain?

Did you learn anything about genetic engineering? What do you think about negative (getting rid of all diseases and disability) and positive (improving the human race) eugenics? Are they ethical?

Do parents have an obligation to make the "best" babies possible? Should genetics do away with disabilities if possible?

What did you think about Olga's relationship to her husband, Ronald? Should she stay with him? What are her options?

What do you think about the animal rights subplot? How do you feel about animal experimentation and glow-in-the-dark mice and cats?

What do you think about the possibility of multiple biological mothers?

How do you feel about sperm and egg donation? How do you feel about college men and women making money by donating their sperm or eggs?

About Kelly Oliver

 **Kelly Oliver** is the award-winning (and best-selling in Oklahoma), author of *The Jessica James Mystery Series*, including **WOLF, COYOTE, FOX,** and **JACKAL**. Her debut novel, **WOLF: A Jessica James Mystery,** won the *Independent Publisher's Gold Medal* for best Thriller/Mystery, was a finalist for the Forward Magazine award for best mystery, and was voted number one Women's Mysteries on Goodreads. Her second novel, **COYOTE** won a *Silver Falchion Award* for Best Mystery. And, the third, **FOX** was a finalist for both the *Claymore Award* and is a finalist for a *Silver Falchion Award*. The latest in the series, **JACKAL**, came out in September.

When she's not writing novels, Kelly is a Distinguished Professor of Philosophy at Vanderbilt University, and the author of fifteen nonfiction books, and over 100 articles, on issues such as the refugee crisis, campus rape, women and the media, animals and the environment. Her latest nonfiction book, **Hunting Girls: Sexual Violence from The Hunger**

Games to Campus Rape won a Choice Magazine Award for Outstanding title. She has published in *The New York Times* and *The Los Angeles Review of Books*, and has been featured on ABC news, CSPAN books, the Canadian Broadcasting Network, and various radio programs. To learn more about Kelly and her books, go to www.kellyoliverbooks.com.